CW00376918

***To my Mother,**
*whose unerring zest for life
is an eternal inspiration*

Ellerker
The Journey from Packwood

Melissa Mailer-Yates

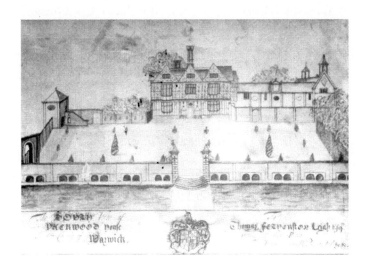

Finders Publishing

Published in Great Britain by
Finders Publishing
Revised edition

© Melissa Mailer-Yates

This book is copyright under the Berne Convention
No reproduction without permission
All rights reserved

Finders
Keeper's Cottage
Haselor
www.finderspublishing.co.uk

ISBN 978-0-9570004-4-5

Typeset in Times New Roman
Printed by Lightning Source

Index

Introduction

One late, warm, August afternoon, I was walking slowly down the worn footpath through the trees towards the Elizabethan house called Packwood. It is in the Warwickshire countryside, about 15 miles from Stratford-Upon-Avon. It is a very beautiful house, much visited by the public, and the centre of many childhood memories. As I slowed before opening the small, iron, gate and descending the fan of steep brick steps leading to the formal grounds I could sense a scene around me. There were a young couple holding hands, standing on the same spot. Looking at each other through sad, but loving eyes. The striking figure of the man was holding the reins of a horse in his free hand, and there was a sense of resignation about the two of them.

All but two miles from Packwood is another, older historical building called Baddesley Clinton. On the walls of the great hall hangs a portrait of an elderly gentleman by the name of Ralph Ellerker, painted when he was 73 years old in 1632. He is my Mother's great, great.., etc grandfather. At the moment of sensing the scene I felt that here was Ralph as a young man, saying goodbye to his childhood sweetheart. She was due to marry Ralph's cousin William Ferrers the next day, and their secret love affair was to end.

I knew Ralph was related to the Ferrers, indeed it is the Ferrers who inhabited Baddesley. I just enjoyed the creation of the moment, feeling the need to write the scene down with no respect for historical accuracy, neither for the real histories of the people, nor the chronological coincidence of their existence. I named the young girl Eleanor Maine and penned the opening passage.

Once the story started to unfold I felt I had to go and look at the portrait of Ralph and perhaps learn a little more about him. I went across to Baddesley and took note of his kind greenish-grey eyes, a few other physical details, and checked the dates to ascertain the exact year of the story, in the painting he is portrayed as a noble, old man, curiously with a small, tooled ring on the little finger of his right hand. I made him 23 in 1582 at the onset of his tale. Moving across the hall the various Ferrers are recorded in stained glass as coats of arms and simple details in all of the windows. There are a number of William Ferrers starting from as early as 1270. One of the windows contained the inscription "William Ferrers, Lord Ferrers of Groby, married Elenor, daughter of Mathew, Lord Lovaine of Staines."

It was quite a shock to find my Eleanor Maine was Elenor Lovaine. I altered her name in the story accordingly. I would be lying if I where to tell you that there haven't been other coincidences since then. Jane Mainwareing was indeed on the passenger list of John White's ship to Virginia. The character of Catalina Menendez de Aviles was formed long before I discovered her, and the fact that only *she* would be able to fulfil the qualities of the woman I needed to exact that role was truly amazing.

So it is that all of the characters have a solid foundation in historic fact. My initial intent to disregard historical accuracy soon disappeared, and this novel is the result of many hours of researching, reading and discovery. Out of necessity I worked my way through documents written in the language of the day, and used a magnifier to track routes over old maps which still retained the township names of the age, and thereby related to those papers.

My love of both Packwood House and Baddesley Clinton meant I had some knowledge of them from childhood, but this research brought with it a whole new understanding. I travelled to St Augustine in Florida, and was fortunate enough to correspond with some of the scholars there who led me to further discovery. In fact, this was as much a journey for me as it is for Ralph.

Despite this infusion of historical fact and detail, the innocence of the original working has not changed in essence. I sat and watched, and wrote my story as I saw the pictures unfold before me, each person there at the right time, in the right place.

**

WILLIAM FERRERS, LORD
FERRERS OF GROBY MARRIED
ELENOR DAWGHTER OF WATER
LORD LOVAINE OF STANES

The walled Garden

Stepping between those old brick walls
Their hearts met with the joys we ourselves once
                                                    beheld.
The laughter and games of centuries through
                                    were played out again
As did we,
As did our parents, and more before them.

The gardens, sown with wonderment,
Welcomed them in,
Leading them from one treasure to the next.
Circling the great yews they ran
Until their hearts might burst.
Their shouts and cries of delight
Mingling with history's multitude of echoes.

The shadows long,
Another page is writ,
Their childish happiness is planted
To flower forever in God's special garden
That is Packwood.

                                    1999

Risby■ *Hull*

Packwood■*Baddesley*
Coughton Court *Stratford-upon-Avon*

London■

Prologue

A shady, straight path lined with trees leads between the two small ponds that lie in the parkland opposite Packwood. Timbered gables and groups of twisted chimneys define the beautiful Elizabethan house. The year is 1582 and Ralph Ellerker of Risby in Yorkshire, walks that familiar path with Elenor Lovaine, daughter of Mathew, Lord Lovaine, on his arm.

Beside them walks Ralph's horse, a large nine year-old grey, with an intelligence that portrays the understanding of a lifelong friendship. The girl is young with long, straight hair and a fragility that disguises her strong character. The broad, handsome figure of the twenty-three year-old Ralph by contrast is powerful, but with an elegance born of fine breeding.

Their steps are slow and faltering. There is no joy in their pace, nor yet a desire to progress further than the footpath's end. Instead, they cling to each other, aware only of the futility of their wishes.

S at silently in a grand chair in the sombre dark of the great hall within the chill interior of the moated house at Baddesley Clinton is an old man. His hair is white with the passing of many years, but the youthful light deep within his eyes tells more than this simple picture. His memories are warm and sincere, the feelings which filled his heart with the passion of that day, so long ago, still stir within him, and give him comfort.

He speaks gently of his mind, not to any person who stands to listen, not for any audience, but for his own ears, his own reflection. This day marked the start of his greatest adventure. This scene he plays out not for the sorrow that lives in that brief moment, not for the loss, or the wish to relive that farewell, but for the years which followed, the people encountered, the lands loved and lived.

It is a memory to which he returns most days, and most hours. It is a memory that intensifies through its re-telling, but most, it is a memory which can never die, not for him, not for those whose faces come to him in his mind, not for the lands which still bear the mark upon them for his having played his part.

Book 1

Ralph Ellerker

Baddesley Clinton, Warwickshire, 1632

It is said that age dulls the wit and slows the mind as it does the quickness of the spirit and limbs alike. In truth, those who look upon my lined face, my thin grey hair, see only the fading embers of my life. They do not know that each line is a well-trod road to far off lands, they cannot revel as I do in the images which dance wildly in my mind, carrying me still through the years of my life. Brilliant, joyous paintings of my youth, a tableau of seasons, places and people, memories more real, more keen than the still days which now mark my winter in this quiet place.

I sit, and watch the rainbow glass paint stories on the dark, polished oak at my feet. On a warm, autumn breeze, carried through the open window, trickle the sounds of childhood, beginning where I once began, their spirits free, their minds not tethered by experience. The shouts and laughter mingle with the golden shapes, steadily creeping across the floor as I watch time sliding inexorably into the late afternoon. Blue summer skies, green lands, the vermillion of passion and love, all fading into the dark which marks the passing day.

There was a blackness once, more lost for light, which held my mind more lost for understanding, and heightened yet by pain which ran throughout my body, coursing through every limb and dulling my sensibility. A moment of such total incomprehension, it was as the hour of my birth, and yet, perhaps it was so. Try as I might I could not focus my eye to any discernment through the black before me, my senses reeled and my body shook without control. A loathsome sickness welled within me causing me to lay my aching body onto the hard, uncaring, damp wood floor. Strange smells invaded my head causing my blindness to weep through its bite. The world around me seemed unstill, unsteady, and disturbingly unfamiliar. In a conscious effort to escape this discomfort I pushed my mind through the incessant hurt to a place far beyond. While the metal that cut into my shackled feet held my body imprisoned, my mind took flight and flew to a sun-soaked, August day. To a pathway, grassed and familiar, guarded by great oaks along its length, and raised before the welcome sight of a house were I had known truth, and I but 23 years, just a grain of existence amongst the sands of my lifeglass. Thus I found myself stood before her, captured only by the beauty that shone forth, and there, nested gently in mine was the softness of a delicate hand.

Packwood House, Warwickshire, 1582

A hand created with such perfection, as though it were designed by the craftsman-ship of a master painter. Deft flecks of burnt sienna set on fine ivory defining the inno-cence of pure femininity. The slender fingers curled gently, held like a pearl safe in its setting.

I gazed at the sunlight as it caressed her long hair, the golden fingers running deep within the folds of her flowing robe. Her mellow, green eyes longing for something, all-giving, all-trusting, needing to know if the moment was real. Our conversation passed in silence as words could only serve to spoil the sincerity of the moment.

My other hand was tugged by impatience; the worn leather distinctly the antithesis of my fairer ward, my noble horse knew nothing of our care. The danger of the heights of my relationship with Elenor was something that the stability of the bond with this creature could never have. I wondered if perhaps it was the fragility of our love which had created that all encompassing thrill, or the inner knowledge we possessed that dared not speak out loud, yet shouted within our minds, and set our hearts to beat with such abandon. Surely our hopes and beliefs had to be that it would exist forever, just as in that golden moment, but we knew it would not, nor could not.

Whilst we both knew that our subterfuge was a crime against our families, I was less of a mind to worry. For Elenor though it was a sin against her father, indeed, against God, and something she did not bear lightly. She bore the pain of breaking her bond, racked by the deceit that kept the truth from all sides involved in her betrothal to William, my cousin. She carried the dread of her guilt with her every day, and the fear that we might one day be discovered. If we were it would bring shame and dishonour both to her and her family, her life would be worthless. Any such discovery of my part in the secret tryst would be lightly treated, even lauded by some, not a belief I held, but it was just so. This precious jewel would have to remain our secret, a prize to be kept until both our days' end.

And so it was, that hot, late summer noon. Our footsteps gently pushing the tall grass flat to each side of us until that familiar, wooded path came to its end. There we stood. Wrapped in our embrace like the folded petals of a rose, carefully layered, holding tight to each other. Now in front of us rose the proud walls of Packwood. High gables demarcated by dark timbers, the sandy face of the walls glowing in the low sun while the many tall chimneys, some twisted, some straight, proud sentinels, watched over the formal gardens below. Here was our full stop. This treasure box of a house which I had called home was our end this day, until now it had been our haven.

Each time my gaze falls upon the dramatic facade of that house a multitude of memories surface, bubbling up in a frenzy of delightful thoughts. My earliest visits to Packwood were at a time when that happiness was provided by the simple pleasures of intriguing games formulated through the innocence of childhood. The many quarters of the gardens were inter-linked by little gates, passages and narrow paths. The fascination of the maze-like layout was enhanced by statues, urns and all manner of popular garden accessory. The excitement was heightened all the more by the occasional fits of bravado that took us all off to the forbidden reaches. These craven fruits were headed by the vast expanse of the lake. The dangers inherent do not exist at that age to any child. We were no exception. Its small inlets and outlets provided us with opportunities to try our hand at great engineering feats in the guise of very poor dams.

Never in all the years did any of us succeed in stopping the incessant flow of the water. More often than not the results were all too familiar. Wet sleeves, wet feet, muddy apparel in general. The excuses for the dishevelled state grew ever expansive, and ingenious, yet, despite great contrivances between William and myself, not once must we have succeeded in our subterfuge. The joy of it was that the adults were never so mean as to let on that our deceit was plastered over our every person. The short-lived guilt at coining the lie was sufficient to keep us away from that dangerous territory for a short time at least.

The interiors of the house did not afford the same freedom, nor the same opportunity to disobey. The many passages and little rooms off were a fascinating world nonetheless. It was still possible to appear lost at the most inopportune moments for the rest of the household. This was the usual attempt to avoid meals and leaving times.

Leaving time, I believe, must be the one emotion most associated with the house. I would stay for most of the summer months each year since Risby was no longer the home it had been in past times. As such, Packwood provided the family life I so yearned for. In those childhood days, to leave was to abandon a whole world, a universe. Here we were different people, different beings, and different rules applied. Just so was it even now.

The loathsome dictate of our separate lives loomed before us. This visit had been shorter than most, and shorter than one would have wished. We knew the day was to arrive, and so it had. The speed with which it despatched us to our different quarters was a cruelty that the disparities of time took advantage of. This quirk that the measure of our lives has of quickening and slowing never seems to play in our favour. Faced with the boredom of a tedious task the hours lengthen to interminable extremes, but present the master with a precious minute and it will turn a day into a glimpse.

The end of the path was the end of our day. Yet another force was in play. Elenor's destiny was laid out before her, pre-defined by her family. Her choices were not the consideration, my own were determined as a consequence.

How many times does one rehearse the final moments of a farewell? I knew my lines to perfection. The stage was set, the players all in their respective places and moods. Even the weather was on my side. I knew my lines. Would Elly know hers, would they be the response I expected, would I have thought of every contingency?

The thunderous sound of hooves on the gravel was on us in a second.
" Ralph! Elly!"
The scene was lost.
"Will!" I replied. For a second Elenor was stunned. Torn from a suspended moment she reached for a breath denied her. She gave nothing away. William Ferrers' bride of the morrow was the image of perfection she always portrayed. Contentment, assurity and, above all, beauty. I threw off the mantle of disappointment as best I could. That bitter pain would be with me for a long time, now was the moment to assure all that I was party to the celebration. The festivities surrounding the marriage of my cousin were foremost in the minds of all, and so it had to be for me, both for his sake and for Elly's.

What lay beneath was to be buried at this point. Both Elenor and I had agreed that there could never be another intimate time like this. To chance the slightest exchange was to court disaster. William had absolutely no knowledge that there had ever been anything between us other than the friendship we had all shared since childhood. The progression to William's arms had been set in stone virtually since Elenor's birth. Lord Lovaine was well aware of the advance that would be gained by the allegiance with the Ferrer's name. Elenor's dowry was a small price to pay for such a social furtherance, and the joining of two loyal Catholic families represented much about our time and our beneficent Monarch. Although our love had overtaken us, we had always been prevented from pursuing it as we should have liked and as our hearts dictated. We knew our destinies were divergent and to some extent we had revelled in the excitement of the subterfuge. The inevitable end gave our romance a depth only achieved by the sadness that one day it would not continue. While we were immersed in this tragedy there was a comfort in the playing of it. Only recently had the emotion turned to one of fear at the approaching loss.

"I trust I shall bear the full weight of your eloquent wit tomorrow, Cuz?"
" I hope you do not view tomorrow as anything but a serious matter, Will?" I rejoindered.
"I am in no doubt that my future in-laws will take anything you say seriously Ralph, that's what worries me. I'm counting on your usual dry humour being transparent enough to assay such laughter as will leave them assured of the insincerity of your slanderous tales. I knew I should have kept this day from you. More fool me that I should let you anywhere near the haven of my future. Let me tell you, I worked hard on my wholesome character the last few months. I feel sure I have just got them to a point of, of......"
"Incredulity?" I offered.
"Trust", he rebuffed. "Trust and belief in me as a gentleman."
"Ah! Then they *do* have a good sense of humour!"
I was in the saddle before he had finished laughing. I floated a glance into Elly's eyes as my head

turned, taking her soul with me a few strides before the pace of a blistering gallop fought back the tearing pain in my gut.

"Tomorrow!" Will's voice echoed into the trees. I lifted my hand without glancing back. I could feel the tenuous link of her gaze snap as they turned to walk to the house. I slewed to a halt some distance off with a cloud of dust and a clattering of loose stones. I watched the two figures disappear, her arm resting on his, her life in his destiny. The blowing dirt hanging in the air obliterated their detail for an instance. By the time it had cleared they were gone from sight.

For all William's wish to have me present on his great day, I knew it to be an impossibility. I could not give an excuse and neither would I. It had not entered any of our conversations, but I had never imparted my intentions to Elenor either. She would be aware of the disappointment that would be Will's on hearing of my absence, and I could not let her endure more anguish than the common ground we already had. For myself I never could have thought that I would find myself in this position. We had done so much together in our lives, my cousin and I. We had always been there for each other, through good and bad times, so to think that such an important day as his marriage would be a time for us to go our separate ways was too extraordinary to comprehend. And yet, here I was, on the road to a different life in a vain attempt to avoid experiencing the knowledge of his union with Elenor Lovaine.

I had no doubt that the ceremony would continue unhindered. To all else I had no part to play in the day. I knew William would shrug it off. He would be curious as to what might have delayed me, and he would curse my absence in a genuine way, but his day would happen just the same. Elly would understand. Her role in life had changed, she knew her duty, she knew her place. Personal feelings count for very little. As a woman her allegiance, respect and fidelity to her new husband were foremost in her mind. She would not be able to allow herself the comfort of a thought for how she felt. It was entirely her duty to portray the perfect bride. I could only wish that somewhere, in the depths of her heart, there would be a corner reserved for a hint of the feelings we had for each other. I could never hope that would endure for long, but a selfishness within me could not let go of a need to still own something of her aspect on this day when she was to give her all to another.

My own plans had been mapped out well in advance.

The journey home was uneventful. The usual two days meandered into three. I was not diligent in my progress, nor did I care. My senses ranged from reproach at myself for allowing my emotions to goad me into playing the love-sick fool, through to *playing* the love-sick fool. I was angry at the situation as it had evolved, in turn I was equally angry at the flies that tediously played around us if I slowed too much. Rational thought was distinctly absent until I touched on the rolling hills of the Park. My sensibility returned completely as I entered Risby and preparation for my leaving had to be attended to.

There was nothing particularly inviting about the sombre face of Risby. It had its place in my life as my home, but it lacked a heart. It exemplified the stiff severity of an old nurse whose kindness was only apparent in her discipline. The shadows of the day were running long which magnified the austere appearance, emphasising its monstrous, grotesque shapes and angles. I had always imagined some architect who had failed to impress with his individual efforts, putting together some vast plan to involve all the facets of his learned knowledge. Crashing them together in one final effort, only to breathe a cold existence into this fantastical beast of incoherence. However, I knew that it was to be a long time before I could call this 'home' again, and that, at least, lent it an air of sympathy.

The boy rushed out to take my horse from me as I entered the courtyard. His my only reception. The house smelled stale, there was no sense that anyone had been resident for a while. I threw myself up the broad stairway without attempting to investigate further. I felt no urgency to seek out those who would not wait or look for me. My few belongings were packed and stood as they had done, where I left them some weeks before. I lifted them onto my shoulder and went to start for the door. On turning I glanced through the far window and caught sight of a figure below. A small circular, grey stone fountain centred the courtyard. Although it had remained without function for years, its boundary afforded a comfortable seat which caught the sun through a gap in the high walls. I bowed to the weight of my conscience and went to the west garden, leaving my bag in the hallway.

The small hunched figure responded little to my approach. Mary had been the single source of constancy in my life. She had nursed my Mother through her illness, and taken on the responsibilities that were hers from that time, thus I was more a product of her beliefs and values than anyone's. Her attention had taken a natural turn toward my Father in time. I had been slow to see this in the innocence of my youth, but when I did it was the sense that it provided a source of much idle gossip for the surrounding society that left me uneasy. My objections I had directed, perhaps unfairly, at my father. While this did not appear to have any marked effect upon him, it only went to emphasise and widen the gaping chasm that existed between us. As for Mary, it did not alter her care for me nor yet my affection for her. It had always seemed natural to respond to her attentions. There had been a Fludyer attending the Ellerker's as far back as people remembered, yet Mary was never so much attending, as, in truth, she represented my only real family.

27

I suddenly found myself embarrassed by the towering figure I represented as I stood over this frail body. Her head craned to look up at me. I dropped to my knees instantly to spare her the discomfort. Her age was carved into the pale skin like tooled leather, and yet her blue eyes stole the sunlight's dying rays and shone a pure stream of kindness and gentility. She shared my pain. She was the one person with whom I had discussed every jewelled moment of my stolen love affair. She was party to every exchange, every hopeless promise, the soaring heights we had gained as covert lovers. There was nothing I wouldn't tell her except for my imminent departure. I had tried to think little about the moment, even to avoid it completely, but now I had to bid farewell when I knew her years were numbered and due to fall within my journey's span.

"Take care Ralph, I will watch for you." she spoke at last.

"What are you saying Mary?" I began, but the futility of the pleas of innocence fell about me as her gentle smile portrayed a knowledge that forbade me to deny anything. Perhaps she knew it was an inevitability of my loss, or perhaps she was astutely aware of my movements by my simple preparations. Either way we embraced as I imagine a mother must do a son who is away to war. The sense was one of impending loss, a loss beyond mortal control and quite unkind. This episode of sadness was complete as I watched a salty tear make its way down her still smiling face, touching at her slightly trembling lip before dashing to the ground. I wiped my thumb across her damp eye, kissed her forehead through the grey hair as I stood, and walked quietly from that place.

The morning broke across the horizon before even it seemed the previous day had left us. The dew lay heavily along the little-trod pathways, and the damp coldness around my feet contrasted oddly with the heat of the brisk pace I had maintained through the night. Whilst the myriad stars were company the sensation seemed only natural and provided a freshness to the progress, but with the herald of a new day the sense of weariness was added to by the weight of the sodden boots and thus became a burden. There was not even the comfort of an imminent rest as it would be a few hours yet before the heat of the day would allow me any chance of a dry bed. I strode on propelled by the knowledge that a long sea voyage would avail me of sufficient time to recuperate my strength and my spirit. I contented myself with feasting upon the wonders set out before me as the daylight made clear the surrounding countryside. The land sloped gently away to my right affording a magnificent vista of rolling hills beset with clumps of trees all the way into a distance that appeared to go on for ever. On my left was a tall ridge that marked the general route, strewn with bracken and ragged bushes. The remarkable thing of the dense foliage was the city of networked cobwebs picked out by the low sun, all beset with a thousand jewels, consisting of the most intricate and innovative patterns designed to sustain their purposeful construction. I couldn't help but muse on how many spiders there must be in that one spot, and just how long it would have taken each to build this labyrinth of lace. Do the webs last more than one day, or is it that their lives consist of this daily chore, calling on their ingenuity and dextrous expertise to cannily weave this splendour at the turn of every morn? How lucky then are we that, although our existence relies on a readiness to do what is necessary in order to survive, we at least have something of a choice should we decide that the day is fit only for something else. Perhaps of all that number of eight-legged beasts there are those who do, on occasion, decide to lay-a-bed first thing, and worry not about the ensuing hunger that is consequent to that action.

The path was becoming more defined now as various other tributaries joined at every turn. Each contributing to the competition of footsteps, forming a great library of passage. Signs of other life as yet were confined to the occasional chimney stack liberating gently rising smoke from freshly laid fires. The air took on a new scent, in no small way enhanced by the burning wood, but the warmth of the day has a smell different from the night hours. In it hangs a sense of impending good, a promise of new opportunities. It is the sense of safety that greets one on walking through the door when returning home, the sensibility that everything is where one left it and the world is still turning as God designed. A new strength rushed to my limbs as the heat of the Sun's rays drove under my cold skin.

Within a couple of hours the sun had dried the undergrowth sufficiently, and I took a well-needed rest. Stepping off the road some way I trod some heavily brackened ground, making sufficient noise to remove any stubborn, unwanted reptile, and lay down on a slight slope. This afforded me less vulnerability by virtue of the fact that I was able to rise from the position rather more quickly should I have to. The idea of lying flat, gazing up at the heavens held a certain appeal, but I would be certain not to actually sleep. I had always believed when a child that manhood brought with it an inherent sense of security and well-being. Presumably afforded by virtue of gaining greater stature, having more knowledge and having the natural ability to deal with any importunity that might befall one with a mature reaction. The realisation that the insecurity experienced as a child is not something that ever really goes away is a very sobering experience. If anything, knowledge is the single thing that one could probably do best without. To bask in the serenity of childish ignorance is, like so many things, something to look back on and only wish for. There is no doubting there is an advantage in acquiring the knowledge that a vixen's scream in the light of a misty moon is as such and not the fervent cry of a wild banshee. Nevertheless, I was all too aware of the many tales I had heard around various courts and inns of the treacherous, villainous occasions that had beset many a traveller in these parts. Thus I set myself on this incline with my sword to hand, but secreted in a respectable fashion. I pulled my hat over my eyes and settled in no time to a deep sleep.

There are times when it is easy to make a fool of oneself, and this was one of those moments. My thoughts where roughly wrenched from the depths of a many faceted dream. Its content was of little significance as in a moment I started to my feet, remembering in an instant my predicament and possible danger. My hat lingered momentarily in front of me obscuring my view for what seemed like an eternity. My careful preparation only managed to present my sword an inch from its proper grip. As such, my grasp fell short, succeeding in knocking it forward from the hilt, projecting the trailing end at my feet. The consequence was a noisy and undignified stumble that cast me forward, at least obscuring me for that instance from the source of my concern. I peered nervously from the spot, parting a large clump of ferns that had somewhat cushioned my fall. The fearsome sight was all of a wooden cart pulled by an old horse. Various metal artefacts were fastened loosely about it, their ceaseless clanking no doubt the source of the noise that had made me start so. At the reins sat an elderly man bundled up in a grubby, oversized blanket. The vehicle was now stationary, the face of the man visibly grinning in my direction. I ridiculously glanced behind me as if some other sight of greater mirth might present itself. At that moment I became conscious of half-stifled giggles from the same direction. I refocused and could make out two young, female faces peering out from under a single, large tarpaulin that covered the whole wagon contents. I was immediately aware of the acute embarrassment I had afforded myself. I regained my feet, acknowledged them, and set about straightening my attire and my self-esteem. When I looked back to the road the cart was setting off again with the three faces plainly set to me still. The elderly man beckoned to me. His intention, undoubtedly, was that I should ride with them, neither by question nor invite, but by plain fact of my being there and the road leading but one way. I did not take much convincing, despite my ignominious introduction. I put on a quick pace and launched myself onto the rear board, which was set open. The main cover was thrown back during my ascent and my appreciative audience sat up before me.

That they were sisters there could be no doubt. They were adorned with copious amounts of rolling, black hair that lay about them like great storm clouds falling and cascading in curls and waves. Their skin, by contrast, was pale, but shot with a healthy country glow at their cheeks. Without some acquaintance of a few years it would have been nigh on impossible to have ever told them apart. They leaned against each other, all the while their gaze fixed on me. They were, however, only able to laugh to each other as I greeted them, turning in with embarrassment and false modesty. I say false because any notion of modesty would have had them dress with a little more care than that which was presently displayed before me. Each had about their shoulders a loose shirt with no apparent means of fastening its entire length. Indeed I was aware that they felt no need to contain their ample size of which the majority was in front of me at any one moment.

"Don't mind 'em", croaked the old chap from the front. The cart had seen better days and creaked and groaned under our steady progress, but it seemed decidedly well-oiled in comparison to this cracked, rusty voice.

"Ned's the name, and thams Rose and Lilac. We calls 'em that 'cause we'm like flowers as those, see." "They won't say much, but they's gooduns, I can tell 'ee." "What they call thee, eh?"

"Ralph, Ralph Ellerker." I ventured. "Thank you for the ride."

"Ain't no extra to me, old nag'll pull just as slow with thee on't as without. She were good in her day, but that were a while back now." " Ralph you say, that's good. I s'pose your set for Hull then, eh? Don't go nowhere else so's you'll have to, eh?"

"Yes."

I felt the need to strike up some meaningful conversation, and yet every indication was that Ned was the only person I would get any sense out of, the two girls preferring to remain consistent at least with their only contribution a timely giggle.

"I have a ship to catch. I'm heading for Holland. There are some people I know there." Each sentence seemed to fall short of its mark, eliciting no reaction from our driver. I felt as clumsy in conversation as I had just been in the undergrowth. I turned my back on the party and settled to the wooden board. As I gazed at the gently passing scenery overhead Ned continued to hold his soliloquy.

"I've been telling myself now nigh on three year to replace her, but while she's still standing and moving forward seems not right to do so, eh?"

The patchwork canopy above us filtered the flickering sunlight, set in a deep blue sky. Ned's drone continued unabated, echoed sympathetically, yet more sonorously, by the sound of bees about their business. As I listened less to the content of what was being said my mind drifted back to Elenor. Each jolting yard took me from the reality of our divergent paths. The warm air blew the sweet smells of the countryside over me, and with it the sweeter memories of our years together. Pictures of places, feelings and sounds ran as a breeze through the corners of my mind, lifting autumn leaves that had lain for a while, moving snowdrifts frozen to a spot for so long, and trailing the flowing strands of her hair, so long and fine.

A sharp jolt from a large pothole in the road caused my head to bang audibly which set the girls off again. I soon realised that Ned's creaky, lullaby had soothed me back to slumber and we were in fact a good deal further on than I had expected. I started as a single horseman shot past the rig at a great speed. Indeed, there were a number of travellers about us, and the path was now properly a road. The distant horizon had spawned a sea, and a great deal of activity and buildings could be spied at its margin. I decided the sad pace of Ned's cart was too tedious to contain the impending expectation I had of what lay in store. Besides, my bones were stiff and aching, somewhat from staying still for so long, and not unduly due to the discomfort of the crude vehicle. I leapt from the back and strode level with my companion travellers. I thanked Ned for his kindness and bade farewell to the sisters who returned a smile that they were unable to contain from becoming yet another trickle of laughter. As I walked on apace I was sure I could still hear Ned continuing his ceaseless conversation.

The outskirts of the town brought a general growing bustle of people about their lives. As the crowds increased the preceding days took on an air of non-existence, and a certain purpose seemed to take hold of me. I reflected, as I walked, on the chance meeting that had led me to this destination.

I had sat in a local inn as had become more of a custom than one would have thought sensible over the past few months. Drinking alone is never a right thing to do in times of despair. History dictates that it can only lead to further despondency and compounds the misery rather than dulling it, as is the intention. This particular night a group of rowdy fellows had entered late. The landlord, rather than rebuke their custom at such an hour, welcomed their petitions as the night had been quiet. In fact, besides myself, I had only seen a gamekeeper's dog that I knew to be the most regular customer. His usual dish of water was not going to afford our host much of a livelihood. The arrival of this band of revellers was manna from heaven for the poor chap, and he set about supplying copious amounts of ale and some food. It wasn't long before I was spotted trying to keep to myself in the corner of the room. In no time I was a part of their revelry. Though I knew not what was the reason for their good cheer I abandoned myself to their hospitality and for the duration became one of them. As the night subsided the landlord resigned himself to his bed, having entrusted to the good nature of his guests what little remained of his stock. The level of conversation had fallen to a hushed tone, with individual conversation dominating rather than the chorus of voices battling to be heard that constituted the greater part of the night.

We had regaled each other with tales of all sorts through the hours, such that we were no longer strangers. They knew of my pitiful sadness and had gone to great lengths to ensure that it would be furthest from my mind before very long. This they had succeeded in.

The inequalities of life always dictate that every group such as this will inevitably have a member who must be considered to be a leader. And so it was that I fell listening to the tale of the commanding figure that was George Mainwareing. His stature and appearance demanded instant respect and attention. He was virtually as wide as he was tall, his attire marked him as a man of wealth, yet it sat ill upon his frame, his bearing decidedly that of a man unafraid of hard work, enforced all the more by his mass of unkempt black hair oiling the fine fabric on his shoulders. His face was as geographic as the list of places wherein he had made his mark. As the deep resonant tones fell on the eager ears of those around him I was of the impression this was a tale that perhaps had not been told before. On reflection I believe I was the only newcomer to the oft-spoke lines, and that the feigned interest on the other faces was probably more a trance brought on by an excess of alcohol. Nonetheless, I was enthralled by his words.

"Take my word for it", he spoke,

"You have never seen the like before. The top end of the ship was above my head like it had been planted in the ground. My grip held steadfast despite the incredible angle I found myself standing at. The sea water poured from the deck above me all the while in an attempt to pluck me to its murky depths, but I was having nothing of it. In an instance the front end dropped like a stone and I was flung as high as I had previously been straining to see. All around me I could hear the cries of others who were failing to keep their hold. I seemed to swallow more salt water than my stomach could ever possibly hold. This lasted for what felt like an eternity, the sea unceasing in its efforts to take all life to itself. My hands were so numbed I could not remove them from the rails if I tried. The pain was only superseded by the need to live, to survive. A large object flew through the air, some piece of jetsam that should have been more securely lashed to the deck had found its destination in the back of my head."

At this he revelled in pulling his head forward to display an ugly scar of some four inches to the base of his skull where hair no longer grew.

"The next I knew, the daylight was burning my salty skin. I looked around for signs of life, but there were none, at least not immediately so. Just the call of a few sea-birds. The significance of that sound was slow to dawn, but I remembered the bird call being remarked upon by an old sea-hand on a previous voyage. The fact being that a bird must signify we were in sight of land. That being the case I worried little about the state of the vessel and the others on board, content to allow the gentle drifting sensation to comfort me until such time as I felt a little strength return to my tortured body. When eventually I did rise it was to notice a shoreline with much life and a great many other ships sat at its ports. I looked for those that might convey my sorry self to the safety of that land, but as I searched about me I was not aware of another soul. The fear of my singularity gave way to a dread as I realised the ship's drift was somewhat lateral to the shore, in no way was I heading in the direction I wished. Despite my many travels I am not versed in the ways of seamanship. The vessel seemed to be in an extremely sorry state of repair by any crude judgement. I glanced nervously at the calm waters not knowing what dangers may be lurking there. My alternatives were fast receding as the harbour

slipped away. I threw off my heavy boots and anything else that might encumber me, I gripped the
rail and threw myself to the mercy of the depths that
had only a few hours previously claimed the lives of
so many others. The icy cold water was a shock for
which I had not prepared myself. For a moment I
felt I too would join the other unfortunate victims of
the storm. However, I managed to claw my way to
the surface, regain a sense of my situation, and
headed as best I could in the direction of the shore.
Horizons viewed from the sea have a habit of pre-
tending to be close at hand. I dragged at the sea for
all I was worth exasperated at the slow rate at which
I appeared to be making ground. As the waves began to break over me the closer in I got my strength
was all but gone, and again I feared I would not see
another day. Eventually the flow bore me to a
rough, pebbly beach whereon I lost consciousness
again.

This time my awakening found me in very comfortable circumstances. I was surrounded by crisp,
clean linen. I felt dry, and the sound of the sea was
nothing but a distant murmur. As I turned my head
I felt the pain from the blow I had incurred on the
ship. Raising my hand it was apparent that it had
been attended to with a dressing of some fashion. I
became aware of voices. I was at pains to listen to
what was being said, but found I was unable to
grasp the content. It was a while before the realisation that they were not speaking English dawned on
my numbed mind. My regaining consciousness was
noticed by one of those present and a number of
people came over to me. They lavished attention on
me, supposedly asking after my well-being, showing great care in their approach. They soon realised

I was not able to comprehend a word of their conversation. After a little discussion amongst themselves one ventured a few words in different languages. I caught a French sentence and decided that I could do little more than gesticulate and repeat 'Anglaise' as often as might have some effect. Indeed there was a certain amount of satisfaction in the ensuing exchange between them. This resulted in one of the group being despatched from the room. The other faces settled to some contentment and sat silently around me, smiling. Whilst I felt in no immediate danger, I did feel particularly uneasy. After a short, uncomfortable time the door opened and the large figure of a very noble man stood before me. Behind him was the errand boy, obviously happy with the success of his task. The gentleman spoke to me in impeccable English. At once I mumbled an apology for my lack of expertise in foreign tongues. The importance of the figure was of little doubt. His clothes were of a very fine nature, bedecked with jewels and gold trim. He announced that he was happy to welcome me to the Netherlands. He was a merchant and ship owner of some repute. One of his men had found me washed up on the beach, he had ordered them to bring me to his house to repair me as best they could, and he was eager to hear my tale.

After going through the circumstances that had led me to my sorry state, he offered me a chance to reorder my life. He furnished me with new clothes, boots to replace those I had discarded, and a little money. To repay him he asked that I work for him for a month. This I gladly accepted, in truth I had not any plans prior to my shipwreck and would have been seeking some form of employment in the course of time. So I set to a number of menial tasks for the period, content to work off the debt in whatever manner proved the simplest. Some days later, whilst attending his office, I was party to a conversation of which I was an unnoticed participant. My newly acquired Dutch, while enabling me to achieve a few essential necessities, was still far from able to comprehend the complexities of the negotiation I was now witness to. Indeed, my interest in it was no more than an effort to see how much I could understand and to possibly improve upon it by connecting those parts that I could understand. After a time I became aware that all was not right in the conversation. They were discussing books and documents that I believed to be personal to Hans Zeigler, my new Master, and his business, and should not be out of his personal possession. I became acutely aware that should my presence be detected I might, perhaps, be in fear of my life. I crouched slowly in my position, trying as best I could to secrete my person. Had I stayed as I had previously been I feel sure that I would have remained of no consequence. However, my frightened movement set a large stand to move behind me. I became aware of it and lunged to save it from falling. The commotion, although minor, was enough to cause the exchange to stop. An eerie silence ensued. I hung in the balance between a need to fly and a knowledge that to remain was more sensible. As the faces looked about them I could plainly see them and felt as though I was standing naked in the centre of the room. The reality was that they did not catch sight of me. Hurriedly they finished what they were saying and departed. For my part I remained in that position for what seemed to be the best part of an hour unable to hear anything more than the enormous thud of my racing heart.

Days later I was accompanying Zeigler on a business of some importance. He led the way to a large house in the town belonging to a man of some note by the name of Van der Gelt. Immediately upon entering his office I recognised him as one of the men I had overheard. I felt some discomfort at being in his presence, but was at some pain to disguise the fact. We made light conversation, exchanging pleasantries. The two gentlemen talked of nothing more than the delights of their daughters. At this point another group entered and was introduced. To double my discomfort I noted two more of the same set I had hidden from. My inner embarrassment was soon overtaken by the perplexity of this second group being introduced by Zeigler to Van der Gelt. Upon doing so they greeted each other as perfect strangers would. I managed to check myself, as my natural inclination was to volunteer the information that they had already met, as though to remind them. The realisation of the stupidity of such a move fixed me to the spot. I felt as insecure as the previous time. The ensuing hours were interminable. It was very soon obvious to me that we were in the final negotiations of a very important contract that involved a great deal of money. I did not need to know the detail of it, nor was I making any attempt to understand it. I was too concerned with how and when to tell Zeigler of the knowledge I had. I conjectured it might not be of any significance, in which case I could make a fool of myself and jeopardise my comfortable life, or it could be of such importance that were I to ignore it the consequences to my employer and rescuer could be terrible. I kept quiet and watched carefully. I was filled with dread and tension, watching for anything that might commit the child of innocence this huge man was now portraying. I remained ready to pounce should there be any suggestion of signatures being set to documents.

At the outcome we all departed with nothing more than an exchange of papers. I felt a sense of relief, but I was still tense at the prospect of imparting the knowledge to my benefactor. So embroiled was I in the turmoil which beset my mind Hans eventually enquired after my silence. I am not known for staying quiet for long. I assured him that all was fine, all the same chastising myself in my mind for not using the opportunity. Eventually I could contain myself no longer and began to tell him a brief outline of what befell me. He said nothing. We strode on forcefully to his house, all the while any previous concerns dissipating and a sense of foolishness taking their place. As we stepped inside he beckoned me immediately into his library. The room was ill-lit and airless. I suddenly realised his concern and knew this to be a place where none but we could be present. He asked me to go over my experience in every detail, stopping me occasionally to ensure I missed nothing out. His anxious and adamant tones left me feeling like a child interrogated by his father after being discovered at some mischief. Once I had finished I was still in great doubt as to the validity of my tenancy in this man's household. He sat back consumed with a deep pensive air. Eventually he shot forward, grabbed my hand with both of his, smiled a great smile and told me I had done him a great service. I was not to worry, but was to carry on about my business as normal.

Most importantly I was to say nothing of this to anyone. I swore to this final, emphatic demand, and left his presence.
I became aware of activity over the following two days during which time a great deal of whispering was to be heard. All the while the master smiled at me as we passed, his demeanour returning immediately to the seriousness of the matter in hand. The details of the subterfuge were never divulged to me, but I found myself the proud owner of my own house in a very fine part of Amsterdam and a handsomely paid position in the employ of Hans Zeigler."

The conclusion of this ludicrously fantastic tale came with such an abruptness I was quite taken aback. The story had lacked sincerity to an extent through George's desire to embellish each aspect to gain the most impact. In fact the entire history was short of a certain credibility through its obviously coined construction. Yet the telling of it was compelling. Taking me to the edge of my seat, making me live every moment as his robust character brought it to life. The silence that ensued gave me to think that his entire audience where given to a stunned expectancy. However, on looking about me I became immediately aware that I was the only one in attendance to this mastery of words. The table around was heaped with the cradled heads of soundly snoring bodies. My spellbound attention had allowed George to indulge himself. The fact that the rest of the band had lost him in the process had no effect on his moment of triumph. He was content that a new soul had allowed him to plough great fields of wonderment within which the seeds of intrigue, plot and excitement had been sown. His

44

harvest was my obvious display of incredulity and exasperation at the story's end.

"Tell me", I said, "You must tell me what became of the conspirators?"

"That I cannot. I was never aware of them again, and I was never given to ask after them. My master is a very private man and would not easily give up information of that nature. All I do know is that I had it on very good authority that my actions saved Zeigler from certain financial ruin. That was five years ago now, and my life has just got better since."

"So what gives you to be travelling back in this country, so far from your adopted nation and with such fine company?"

"My business for Hans Zeigler takes me to many corners of the world, and yet this is my first such visit here. Naturally I have taken the opportunity to re-acquaint myself with those who I have known. I have travelled hereabouts for the better part of three months now, and my journey back to the Hollands is due. I am no longer travelling alone as these good friends are coming with me. Part of my task has been to recruit good and honest folk as I know in order that I might direct them in the business. Such is my position now, I have mastery over a number of positions within Zeigler's firm, these I have to make grow and secure further income for the betterment of the Company. It seems to me as your life is no longer running on quite the course you once intended. If you were to travel with me I could see you into good employ and a much happier life than is presented before me now."

My natural instinct was to politely decline the invitation. I reflected for a while on the habitual reaction to such an offer realising just how reactive it was, unsubstantiated by any constructive thought. The opportunity had been presented to me to start a life away from my present turmoil in a completely different country. I would be unknown and would be required to take on a profession. Were I to find the position untenable I could simply return to my dull existence here, none the worse for my venture. Adventure indeed was the sense I was feeling. There was a distinct thrill in the notion that I might simply turn my back on all I knew and follow such a flimsy whim. My mind ran to the possibilities fuelled by the energy of what I had just been listening to. A fantastical story, but an adventure nonetheless, the truth of it was of no import. Until that moment I had contented myself with the sense that all I ever wanted in life was contained within our beautiful island. To stray far from England's shores was not a notion I had ever seriously entertained. The thought that just such events may come my way made me hesitate enough for George to note my muted interest.

"There's no need to join me immediately." he jumped in quickly "I can furnish you with all the details of travel and how to find me upon your arrival. I make no time limits. If you wish to come to a new future, you come when you are ready. I shall expect you only when you turn up."

I appreciated his openness. I was still unsure of making such a decision, yet I was most intrigued by the thought. Despite my enthusiasm I was still very aware that I was perhaps not as clear-headed as I might like to be after such a heavy night. Indeed, it was only a very short time before we too joined the rest of the throng in a slumber that took me through to the late morning, and a rude awakening by the landlord. Our late night had left him to oversleep and now his haste caused him to create a very unwelcome noise in his preparation for the day. As his cacophony brought me to my senses I realised I was now the only other person in his establishment the others having left me to my heavy sleep and gone on their way. I was much troubled by their departure as I had not acquired the necessary information from my host in order to take up his kind offer. I swung to ask after them as the landlord busied himself nearby, but his toil took him from the room at the same instant as I felt the inside of my head follow him of its own volition. I cradled my sorry face in my hands in an effort to steady the progression. My brains swished about in an unchecked manner that forced me to hold still for a time. Regaining some composure I took stock of the hellish night and immediately threw the wild notions of voyage based on the inane stories of a passing traveller out of the open door in front of me. My life was my life, and it was unlikely that it would ever amount to very much more than it had done already. The world felt heavy about me, but I resigned to drag it into the daylight and off to greet what remained of the day ahead of me. The bright light of the day burned deep into my eyes causing me to reel somewhat. I imagine I described a sorry sight to any that might spy my dishevelled state at that instant. I wheeled aimlessly turning on my heel as a shout rent the air behind me.

"Good Sir! Sir!" It was the Innkeeper.

"Hold hard my kind Sir." He was much short of breath as his portly stature was not given to chasing as an errand boy, "I should have taken it upon myself to hand this to you earlier, but I was mindful of your tender state. The gentleman from last night left it with me before he went this morning. He said I was to make sure I gave it to you."

I took from him a small scrap of paper whereon I discovered a scrawled message stating the details of Master Mainwareing in a poor hand. I thanked the Innkeeper and bade him farewell whilst pressing a coin into his hand for his trouble. I felt something of a spring in my step as a consequence of the note, but was quick to return to an aimless amble that eventually took me to the corner of some remote room where I slept the greater part of that day.

Now, as I made my way through the narrow streets, the bustle of the crowds created an offensive din. The noise seemed to hammer inside my head in a most disagreeable manner. Courtesy had no place within the walls of this town. They were only intent on their own business, any who should bar their progress even for an instance were barged out of the way without the merest attempt at an apology. I felt distinctly ill at ease in this place, a stranger. Eventually the clutter of the buildings laid back and I was greeted by the expanse of the wide, open sea. There was as much business here, but the backdrop of the blue horizon lent the scene an air of tranquillity, certainly so in comparison to the Hadean maze of the streets.

There were ships and boats of all sizes, gently lifting and sinking at their berths as the waves breathed life into the earth. People ferried great carts back and forth, narrowly avoiding huge loads swaying in the air as creaking cranes heaved their great weight on board a vessel, or on to the dockside. There was still a great deal of shouting as orders flew about the place, apparently without direction and yet prompting actions here and there. I was amazed to watch so much order arising out of so much confusion. I felt sure I would never be able to exist in such a place for long without losing my sanity. I was even more at a loss now to explain to myself what on God's earth I was doing here as there really seemed no place for such as I. Still, I headed into what appeared to be something of a fashionable hostelry in order that I might find some sustenance, and perhaps make some progress in enquiring after the destination of some of the various vessels in the port.

The inn was a far cry from the usual quiet drinking holes I was acquainted with at home. People were everywhere. Drinking, shouting, singing, arguing. There was no obvious corner to retreat to so I took some time working my way through the rooms before I eventually found a spot to rest my weary self. Aside from the discomfort of squeezing in amongst this rabble, accepting the constant noise and crude, dirty, spittle-dabbed creatures that inhabited the place, there was an over-riding aspect that was particularly difficult to endure, - that was the stink. Whilst one can accept that a place where a great many fish are landed and traded would have something of an odour, this went beyond. Everything and everyone reeked of old fish. I took comfort in the pleasure of a heaped tankard of ale, much needed after the long journey. I cannot begin to describe the dismay and the loathsome feeling deep in the pit of my guts at discerning it too had a distinctive flavour of yesterday's catch. This putrid mal-odour lodged itself deep in the crevices of my being to leave me with an extraordinary dislike of any form of seafood to this day. I retched as the foul liquid slipped down my gullet causing me to grope my way through the morass of bodies to reach the much welcome fresh air outside. I staggered into the gloom of the descending evening and a clammy cool that spelled the progression of nightfall. I was unsure of where I was to take rest for the night, the fact was I knew little of exactly where I was. I certainly did not feel I was frequenting the most convivial neighbourhood of the town. Everywhere I looked there seemed to be shabbily-dressed, pitiful old women or children, stashed away in corners. The pallid eyes stared out of thin rags that clung to their faces, following in silence my every move.

These were not human creatures surely. They fared no better than an animal cast out, or an age-ridden pet no longer wanted in a clean house, left to feed off the scraps discarded by their fellow man. I had seen poverty before, plenty of it. There were always families in our parish who were in need, often as a result of warfare when menfolk had gone away and not returned, or illnesses that had beset whole communities and left the remaining members of households without the means of survival. As a parish we always had something of a contingency for these folk, and oft-times they would soon find themselves in some useful employ or such like. That surely is the duty of every neighbour or kinsman, but who was here for these dark, sorry beings?

I was still reeling from the sickly slops I had partaken of at the inn, this sight which I was so unprepared for simply added to my affected state. Was this part of the world I inhabited or had I stepped into another? One that is constructed to hold all the horrors of our own and thus keep it free of misery for ourselves. In an instant I felt pathetic that I had indulged myself for so long in my own personal sorrow. The content of which put beside the suffering I was now witness to was as insignificant as a finger pricked by a thorn at the edge of some cataclysmic battlefield.

My eyes fell on one small child who was clutching a bundled object to him or her. It was an impossibility to discern the gender of this poor soul. The face was masked by years of dirt layered upon it, probably as many years as it had been in existence. The only vaguely clean parts were small rivulets that descended down the cheeks where countless tears had washed away the grime on a regular basis. There was something unusual about this one child. Through the dirt glowed two enormous eyes that beckoned to something within me. I sensed deep pain, hopelessness and utter abandon. I was gripped by a need to sweep this child from its hell-hole, to take it and show that the world is a happier, brighter place. I bent down in order that I might talk to the little, lost soul, for what reason I know not, perhaps out of guilt for the comfort of my own carefree life. As I levelled to the pitiful sight of the wretch I was suddenly aware of another, more disturbing aspect, a meaningful look in the eyes that over rode those sorrowful tears of before, there was a surety I did not understand. I felt uneasy as the countenance took on a malevolence that shook me rigid. At that moment I became aware that the small bundle held so tightly was the partly decomposed body of a tiny infant, which must have died a good while ago. The shock of this discovery stopped me in my tracks, locking me solid without the physical possibility of movement one way or another. In this state of immobility I was aware of scuffling behind me. A number of individuals were on me in an instant, and for that moment I was still unable to regain any kind of sensibility. My head felt very heavy and I was aware of an acute pain upon it, but my circumstances were changed. I was alone and situated in total darkness.

From the shock of my dreadful encounter and this new cognisance that all had changed, it took me what seemed an eternity before I was able to make sense of things. Slowly it dawned on me that some time had passed during which I had been taken in an unconscious state from my previous situation to a new and entirely unfamiliar confinement. The pain I was experiencing I could surmise came from the blow or blows that had led to my loss of coherence. I was altogether preoccupied by it to pay any note as to where I might find myself.

My first reaction had been to gaze into the blackness that I might discern something of the child and his ghoulish charge. The sudden start and swing of my head announced the injury I had sustained and I clasped my hands upon it. My fingers, far from slipping through the familiar strands of my thick hair, met with a hard, crusted mass that lay caked to my skull. This abstract sensation coupled with the events that had led me to this point caused my whole body to convulse in an uncontrollable tremor that kept me suspended in fear for a great length of time. Eventually I started to make sense of some of the sensations beyond my sorry state. There was a sound that had a certain regularity to it, whose very presence slowly calmed my shaking limbs. It is strange that to be in such a position with no point of reference nor understanding of what has befallen oneself presents a Herculean task to make sense of the merest thing. I fought to put my mind to work on the dissemination of the rhythmical noise that was, for a moment, the only sensation outside of me.

There was a feeling of enormity in the sound. It was certainly not the product of human endeavour, but moreso of the wind or the sea. The reality of it came like a lightening bolt as the source of its making rang in my aching head. The sound was that of a ship's timbers creaking with the roll of the open ocean. No wonder the unfamiliarity had left me devoid of understanding for so long.

As I started to my feet my head smote the low roof above causing me to cry out in pain. As I made a stride forward to recover my balance my foot suddenly and sharply came to an abrupt halt causing me to fall to the hard deck. I paused momentarily to take stock of my situation without inflicting any more injury upon myself. Reaching above me I was dismayed to discover my confinement was bounded above by a ceiling no higher than four feet at any point. Coupled with the darkness and the fetters I felt an unnerving need to break free into a space that would accommodate me fully. Where I could breathe a breath of fresh air and feel the warmth of the sun on my face.

I took an inventory of everything, re-ordered my thinking and tried as much as possible to make sensible what had befallen me. I was in no doubt that my confinement had already been of some duration. The dried blood in my hair lay testament to that. I had undoubtedly been subjected to such a blow as had split my head and caused me to unconsciousness for sufficient time to have had me transported to my present predicament. I had a raging thirst made all the worse by the sound of the water crashing around me. Whilst my head still pained me greatly I was stabilised somewhat with the knowledge that the movement of the ship was the cause of what I had previously attributed to a severe dizziness. To know as much did not lessen the nausea however. I felt decidedly unwell, and was still at a complete loss to explain how or why I should find myself a prisoner. I decided that I should do no more than lie back and think of little until such time as something might happen to remedy my dilemma.

Although I had a need for water that I felt could never be satisfied, I found it peculiarly easy to relax and let my mind wander again. I lay my back against the curved wooden wall and my thoughts moved quickly from the situation I was in sliding with ease into the memories of my familiar home that was Packwood. A myriad of pictures flew through my mind bringing comfort with each moment. Through the rush a light shone brightly and warmly, taking me into its arms and dragging me from the place just as the gentle touch of a mother lifting her child from its crib. Elenor's familiar face smiled a joy into my heart that removed any sensibility of discomfort.

It was an evening in early autumn. The earth still retained the warmth of the passing day. We had both been attendant at a festivity to celebrate the fortune of the harvest. Many people from all around had been openly invited to enjoy the benefits of a great feast laid out at the House. It was not yet an annual event. This was, in fact, the first of many years that did follow. There was a time long before when the occupants of the house had done this on a regular basis, but there had been a change of ownership and the practice had fallen into misuse. It was a long time after the present family had taken on the estate that they decided to resurrect the fete. An uncaring succession of owners had seen it decay and fall into a sorry state. When Elenor's father had inherited the property from his uncle he was initially unprepared to take on such an onerous task. The inordinate amount of repair it necessitated was a lifetime's work in itself. Eventually though it was decided to generally re-build within the structure, incorporating the very best materials and construction of the day, and the family moved to it. There followed years of improvement and further building before it became the magnificent home it now represented.

The original celebratory festivities were brought to the attention of Lord Lovaine sometime later. The house had always been a focal point for the local villagers. Somewhere to approach for representation in times of trouble, even in the lean times. As such the Lovaines, as the new occupants, rapidly became aware of their lordly role. A paternal occupation that was as much a part of the inheritance as the fabric of the building. Thus, after a little investigation the detail of the event was learned and the practice re-instigated.

This then had been such a day. Now the shadows were reaching further into the corners of the gardens, the roasted ox was nothing more than a picking for the lurchers, and the few remaining revellers were either the worse for the free ale or were busying themselves with helping disassemble the day's business. I had happened by about noon that day and had only glimpsed Elly from time to time. Tradition held that the family made themselves available to act in a sense of servitude. This enabled the employed staff to enjoy themselves without the responsibilities that would have normally taken them away from such pleasures. The Lovaines found this particularly satisfying and set about their tasks with a zeal. They were ably attended by many of the village, but no one was engaged in any practice they did not willingly undertake. Thus it was that a great sense of freedom, fun and enjoyment infused every aspect of the day.

For me it kept Elenor busy and away from where I would have preferred her. But to see the happiness that reigned in every face I would not have had it any other way. In fact my heart took great pleasure in the glimpses of her delicately flushed face as she moved around to each task that befell her. Despite her fragility she ably lifted great pitchers of drink and carried all manner of things in her enthusiasm to keep all happy. There was a magic about her that lent an air of complete tranquillity and sublime beauty no matter how busy she was kept. Like a rare flower in a wild meadow that catches the eye she would appear in a moment only to be lost from sight a second later. In this way I was content to simply admire her, not willing to pluck her from the spot for fear of spoiling the picture. In truth I would have feign pulled an oak from its root. Elenor Lovaine's sense of duty would have denied any who might try to deflect her aim. I knew all too well the deft way she would reduce those who might attempt such foolery. She could leave one standing like a naughty infant, severely chastised, with a sense that it would take immeasurable time to regain the now forsaken respect, when in fact her forgiveness was as sweet as her tongue had been sharp.

This is sometimes the way of women, the tricky ways with which they can get their own way with a man. But Elly had it off to a particularly fine art. Always retaining her composure, elegance and assurity. There was never an opportunity to create a definitive argument. Given the tools of a constructive argument most men will embattle until such point as they can finally feel they have achieved some redress. That is not to say that they will have in any way won, just that they will simply have taken part and had the opportunity to introduce logical dissemination into the situation, but a woman skilled as Elenor would never leave that gate open. Any time I had tried in the years we had grown up together she had always left me stranded like a beached whale.

Thus I had learned to watch and wait and read the signs. Oft times do we say how fickle are the ways of a woman, but in reality the notion is more that we men are just slow to translate the intricate codes and ciphers that constitute a woman's communication. I had judged for myself at this point in the day that about now was clearly the right time to go in search of my dearest friend.

I caught sight of her appearing from the corner of a small tent wherein some form of refreshment had been served throughout the day. She was virtually dragging an enormous vessel that was too large to be successfully manhandled by her small frame, and apparently too heavy to really get off the ground.
"It seems I came just in time, Sparrow!"
Elenor reached her hand into the wide neck cupping a quantity of liquid and proceeded to cast it in my direction. Whenever I felt brave enough to poke fun at her I called her "Sparrow". It referred to a time many years previous when the thinness of her childish ankles became the object of some insult. What provoked this unfortunate jape eludes me, sufficient perhaps that we had been of an age when trading of insults was a common pastime. For this one time I had paid dearly, but the allusion had grown comically affectionate and was now no more an insult.
"I thought I had noticed you around today, Ralph."
she said as if the glances thrown in my direction since I arrived had been unintentional.
"Make yourself useful instead of making fun of me, and take this back to the house."
"What is it?"
I asked.
"Oh, nothing but water."
I assessed the situation very quickly. I could take the opportunity to have some sport at her expense making her feel decidedly foolish, and risk the consequences, or ignore it and chance looking fairly stupid myself, incurring more effort than necessary. In the outcome I decided upon the middle ground.

She was too tired and deserved better than to be ridiculed. I silently stepped forward and without ado emptied the contents of the stoneware onto the dry grass at our feet. With a gentle smile I lifted the now greatly reduced burden onto my shoulder and held my other hand out to take Elly's. Her face displayed a realisation of the absurdity that she might have tried to haul the great weight back to the house to empty it there. Quickly her expression returned the same smile that was set before her, and we steadily sloped back to the cool interior of Packwood.

Despite Elenor's enthusiasm to return the house and grounds to normal it appeared that no one else currently shared that need. Even the lurchers were strewn about the stone floors like so many loose woven rugs. They had run amongst the crowds with all the excitement and abandon of young children, and were now feeling the consequence of that overt exertion. Slow voices could be heard from one or two of the far rooms as members of the household picked lazily over the success of the festival. All unwilling to do another jot of work for some hours yet. Content instead to luxuriate in the satisfaction of their work completed and well-done. For our part, although the coolness of the house was welcoming, something bade us leave these recumbents to their self-congratulations. Our minds ran together for an instance and we headed out the other side to a place that had always been special to us.

No words passed between us despite our separation throughout the day. The air was still and there was a wonderful calm that pervaded every step. In the corner of the estate was what remained of an old chapel. Most of the walls remained and some few interesting architectural aspects that were probably functional in some way when the chapel was used. Now there was no roof and the interior floor was indistinguishable from the outside. The grass grew up deeply to the structure which was made of stones set in a kind of grey cement. Great clumps of small flowers marked the summits of miniature promontories. A long stream of sunlight measured the late hour as a natural aisle, formed from a single remaining arched window high up in the end wall. The rest lay in shadow and was as cool as the interior of Packwood had been moments before.

We carelessly flung ourselves to the floor, sitting on a particularly raised piece of the earth. It was thick with a deep, dark green moss which had withstood the punishment of being used as a cushion for years. From when we were children this knoll had always been called the pew as it demarcated that part of the church where it was possible to sit comfortably as though one were at a service. I leaned against the un-level, cold stones set in the wall and Elly, in turn, leaned her fatigued self against me. Eventually I ventured a futile sentence to initiate some fake interest in the proceedings of the day. A delicate touch of a sweet finger reached to my lips to halt the intrusion. The surprise at the intimate touch sent my heart reeling. I was suddenly full of a racing sense within that I was at pains to control. I remained silent and motionless, and yet I felt the heavy beat of my heart must be discernible several yards hence, thus I was fearful of some secondary reproach. The cool of the chapel was lost to me as a huge inferno welled up from inside. What was I thinking? This was little Elly. Sure she was heaven to me. I knew her every aspect as though it were a part of myself. I had always held her preciously within my heart, but our youthful friendship, whilst deep, had never been intimate. So why at this moment did a simple touch feel like a thousand kisses? I shuffled gently to accommodate her gentile frame more comfortably against me. As I did so I felt her turn her face toward me. Expecting to see a reproachful stare, irritated by my movement, I turned slowly to apologise. My eyes met a look I had never experienced before in my life. Those soft, green eyes took hold of my very soul and held it transfixed. For an instance I thought my heart had ceased beating altogether. Then a storm of emotions rained down, soaking my senses with a passion that washed over my entirety. With a barely sensible motion we moved toward each other and our lips met for the very first time. No passionate force or wild entanglement, but a whisper of touch that sent me trembling throughout. We hung, floating in mid-air, our lips hardly touching, but providing a bridge whereon crossed the enormity of a lifetime's desires in a moment. I reached up to the side of her face, slowly cradling its softness in my hand. As I did so it was met directly by her own. As her delicate fingers became entwined with mine I sensed a slight tremble. We were on the edge of some vast precipice where off we were about to leap with abandon and complete conviction. There was a fear, almost a terror associated with the action, and yet a surety that was not going to allow us to falter.

We stopped, only to face each other for a brief moment. Almost to assure each other that this was reality, and this was us. The drapes of uncertainty fell away from us unveiling a truth that was a gateway to the stars. Our lips met fully and we melted into a oneness. Our desires enveloped each other, unable to distinguish one from the other. The feelings surpassed anything physically I had known before. I could only conjecture that we had entered a new kingdom, unknown to ordinary mortals. A world of supreme passion and joy. Whereas my movements would have been calculated and clumsy at other times, now I did not even have to think of such things. We were guided by angels, supported on clouds. The air was full of her scent, which seeped into my consciousness as a garden of sweet herbs beyond the imagination, dulling my mind to anything outside of us two, an opiate to our dream.

Effortlessly we sank supine to the embracing earth. Pillowed by the lush green we continued to kiss for an eternity. My hands ran over her smooth shoulder, slipping off the soft material. With ease she slid from me and moved to one side. Standing she gazed unfaltering at my questioning face. Reaching to her sash, in one movement her robes fell with a rush to her feet. She paused awhile, remaining standing before me. The golden sunlight from the old window lighting her from behind, creating around her something of a halo. Her silhouette presented me with a portrayal of perfection. My eyes followed the route of her outline. That long, beautiful, familiar hair lay over one side cascading like a waterfall, taking on every curve, caressing her body, flowing down to roll off various jewelled facets and slopes. She was turned slightly to one side and as such the wonder of her small, perfectly formed, naked body lit in this heavenly manner took me further still into my ethereal realm. I reached up a hand, whilst fervently hoping that I had not fallen to sleep and was just party to some flight of my unconscious mind. But she reached for mine and we met in reverence in a kneeling position. Thus we fell to the consecration of our love. That moment could only be described as a prayer. I wondered if devotion of such magnitude and such sincerity had ever passed from that spot before. As my fingers and my lips ran over every inch of her silken body I felt in such communication with God as I could have died and entered the eternal gates of heaven already.

As we finally subsided and came to rest the songs of the birds and other natural things slowly became tangible again. We knew we were alive. Their myriad voices sounded as the final hymn to our celebratory service and yet we were unwilling to abandon our pew. Instead we lay, both, gazing at the clouds moving with indiscernible speed against the celestial blue. For that moment we had joined Heaven and Earth by an invisible thread. A thread fabricated from a love so pure and so powerful that whatever befell us in our futures it could never be parted. It would connect our souls for eternity, even though our physical paths would undoubtedly lead in different directions.

Still no spoken word had passed between us. In time we aided each in re-assembling the others attire. As we walked from that holy place we hesitated. Turning back to its peace we silently made a sign of reverence, both aware that the history of those broken walls had afforded us a private service at which only the Almighty and ourselves were present. Thus in a state of sublime happiness we me-

andered hand in hand back to the house and inevitable reality.

Book 2

Elenor Lovaine
Packwood House, Warwickshire, 1582

Our Farewell was complete before we reached the end of the path. I had read his eyes, felt his pain, and knew we were at our cruel crossroads. We had re-lived the years of a lifetime, and stood, helpless, as fate led us to our different journeys.

Whilst I knew he wished to speak the poetry of a thousand goodbyes, no sound came from his lips, save a close breath as he gently kissed my brow. He could not know how much I felt the loss. He could not feel the ache that tore my every sinew. But he could sense it as I could his. My gaze fell from his beautiful, kind, misty-grey eyes, no longer able to contain the salty flow that stung my own. His strong hands could not disguise a tremble that echoed through my weakness. I looked back to his face, the late sun picking out the strong lines that carved his beauty as a sculptor hews a likeness in ancient marble. The changing colour of the air lent his features a warm glow that served only to portray the fading embers that would be extinguished for evermore.

I felt him move to speak, but was grateful for the intervention of my new life. All had been said, and more had been spoken in the silence between our two hearts, now I turned to William in my new role and cast off the robes of my childhood in that second. The spell was broken.

I stood smiling on the outside as Ralph and William exchanged a few japes and pleasantries. I watched as Ralph struggled to regain his composure, never truly reaching a state of normality. I recall not what was said, I just remember Ralph's promise that he would be with us for the next day's celebrations. I knew he would not. I knew he could not. I knew this was our final farewell as he sped from us on Chester. That noble horse had been the only witness to our secret tryst, and provided the final curtain as they disappeared in a cloud of dust kicked up from the dry road. I heard a falter in the sound of their departure, but did not dare look back as I was lead into the house on the arm of my husband of the morrow.

As was his manner William immediately launched into a myriad of conversations, running from one subject to the next with hardly a breath between. Ralph and he were not so different amongst the company of their kinsmen, but I knew of a contrast that set them in different countries, different worlds. The covert love I had shared with Ralph had a tenderness no one could dream of matching.

Our childhood friendship had been precious, but then so many aspects of that happy time echoed a similar sentiment within us all. William too had played a part and had been a part of that joy, but we two had stepped aside, out into a forbidden corner of the garden, wherein we walked a path beset with dangers, but strewn with feelings beyond that of any mortal existence. We were both aware that the forbidden fruit was an initial source that heightened our every moment together, but soon enough we transcended our stolen state, and escaped to our land, our heaven. No one knew we were there, no one shared our secrets, no one but we two.

I do not remember the day that the joy began to get heavy, but slowly, as the inevitability of our departure approached, the weight of sorrow began to rest upon both our shoulders. Our words grew fewer, our childish laughter melted away until our final path had led us to this moment and out of our garden of delights.

The loss was more than I could bear, and the sounds of those who greeted us now flew around me and past me without sensibility. I was there before them, the young bride to be, but I was hollow, and my mind rested in the caring arms that had held me so tightly only moments before. William was filled with the excitement of the moment. He was always liked wherever he placed a foot, but for this day and in this household, he was king.

A firm rather than strong hand broke the trance as I was yanked to one side, out of the grip of William who seemed to notice little of my departure. He was quick to replace his hold on me with that of a large tankard of ale, undoubtedly the first of many as the evening of celebration began. The stern presence of Nanny Walker was enough to bring anyone to their senses. Throughout my life I had loved her as much as anything or anyone, yet it seemed she had spent her life chastising me. However, I knew that behind her steadfast grip lay a golden heart that beat full of kindness. My reprobate childhood had always given her cause to constantly reprimand. For me though it was a game without which life would have been very dull for most of the time. I had always believed that Nanny Walker viewed it in the same way, but disguised it well, a notion that truly had not served her well whilst she tried to keep me in check. Her portly figure and ruddy cheeks could never portray her as anything other than kind and gentle, no matter how much she tried to act harsh. My wicked grin in this instance caused her to deepen her frown still more, dragging me through to the staircase that led to my room.

"You wicked girl." she started.
"Where have you been? Everyone has been frantic looking for you to ready you in time for Master William."
Already she was disrobing me as she had done since I could remember. It seemed odd that it was a function that would no longer be a part of her duties within a few short hours. And yet she had no thoughts of savouring the moment. No precious memory, just a need to prepare me as she had planned to much earlier in the day.

"I don't know what you were thinking of. Just look at you. How you could think Master William would even look at you dressed so is beyond me."
And so she continued to scold me whilst I continued to look out over the courtyard through my open window, drifting on the warm breeze which carried the rich scent of the countryside. What she thought

I had been up to I dursen't have thought, but a slight tremor went through me as she brushed a small leaf from my hair. Ignoring it she continued.

"I made up a bath for you so long ago, but that's not my fault."

In all honesty I don't know why she bothered making the boy carry heated water upstairs for me. Nanny's idea of bath time and mine just never coincided. I felt it was her one chance to inflict something of a punishment upon me without actually admitting to it.

As I stepped into the shallow water I was almost grateful for the soothing sensation of the cold. Slowly and deliberately I poured the water around and over me, watching it remove the remnants of the day. The dying sun just lit the falling crystal running off my body, carrying away our love and finally dissolving it. The evidence of our secret mingled with the dust of the day, hidden forever and gone from me.

Stepping out I was grateful of the warmth as Nanny Walker enfolded me in cloths to dry me. Gone was her bluster. I felt she sensed something of my serenity as I had reached my point of completion. My little ceremony had brought me to a fresh start, a clean Elenor was embarking on a new life, a new role, and all was prepared for me. With great pride Nanny displayed tomorrow's garment and the finely crafted headdress of flowers picked by her that afternoon. She had chosen my favourite robe of red damask. It had an intricate edging of needlepoint that trailed over my feet and flowed elegantly behind as I walked. The bodice was thick velvet, embroidered with real gold thread. The sleeves

74

comprised of layers that hung wonderfully low, displaying the differing materials enfolded within each other. Many pearls and other adornments added to the weightiness. There was a degree of discomfort in its wearing, added to in no small way by the most cleverly devised rufflette at the neck. However, the pride I felt when dressed with it was quite sufficient to dispel any thought other than the grandeur it displayed. My Father had it made for me shortly after my Mother died. It had come all the way from Italy and was designed to try and lift my mood through that sad time. Now I felt that she could at least be a part of the celebration, albeit only in spirit, in memory.

I felt a new fervour returning to my limbs. Helped by Nanny I slipped on this night's apparel, a lighter, more plain affair. I smiled reassuringly to her and she, relieved, returned the same. Why my eyes glanced back to the now still water I do not know. I think I expected to find some comfort in the knowledge that I was separated in every sense from my lover, safe perhaps. Instead something stirred. Something deep and completely unknown to me, a sense, a feeling. Something remained, something I could not simply wash away nor forget. As I turned away and made to leave I knew it was something that would stay with me forever.

The evening was full of laughter. Most of the guests had arrived, and all were keen to be a part of the excitement. Too much wine was drunk, and the excess would be bound to take its toll on one or two poor souls. William was inseparable from his cousin, Charles Townsend. They each took turns in telling of adventures that grew more unbelievable as the hours progressed.

For myself, I could not profess to spending a quiet evening. William's sister Caroline and his cousin Sophia, of whom I was very fond, had caught me deficient in my duties. The measure of mead I was supposed to have supped in the preceding month was anything but consumed [1]. By way of just punishment they decided that it was only fit that I should drink the entirety of what remained. As I had, in fact, only remembered to sip from the vessel three times in the four-week, which left a considerable amount. Lucky for me that in the eventuality I was enthusiastically helped out by my little group. However, the dilution as such did not stop us from matching the noise and revelry coming from the other end of the hall.

Our susceptible bodies were less practised at consuming such playful liquids of course. Thus, light-headed, we ran about the rooms and corridors just as we were children again. Full of carefree thought, discourtesy and abandon. The freedom from the fetters of responsibility and propriety lifted my spirit to a happiness that had been sadly lacking of late. We fell about in noisy games with no sense, and no aim nor end.

Only once was my laughter stifled by a returning thought of Ralph. My mind had drifted momentarily to such a game played before, but at a very early age, before the innocence of a childish spirit had been thieved by the promises of first loves. The excitement was the same, so also the place, everything as though it were then. I chastised myself and cursed Ellerker for his intrusion. He had stolen my love, he was stolen from me, and he was not about to steal this light hour. I turned in defiance and headed swiftly from the moment.

The day had broken almost before the previous one was ended it seemed. Sleep had not been my companion through the night. What, with thinking about Ralph, about the wedding and William. I suddenly felt most unprepared for what was supposed to be the biggest event of my life. It saddened me somewhat when I realised that I had been so consumed by my illicit romance that I had paid scant regard to that which all considered my first concern. I was sad because it suddenly seemed unfair to have such little concern for William. He was, after all, to be my husband. We were to live together for the rest of our lives. We would raise children, and be a part of those who lived with us and worked for us. Not as separate individuals, but as a family. These were not small concerns. They were not the musings of a planned party or a visit.

I felt foolish and childish, and the irritation, almost anger, I had fleetingly felt the previous night returned. Only this time it was more lasting and was a sober thought. Indeed, a sobering thought. Was I at all prepared for this? I had no choice in truth, but I could at least have readied myself for it. Instead I had drifted like a cloud in the vain hope that the rain would not actually fall. I had ignorantly believed I could continue to float up there forever if I simply ignored the changing of life's seasons.

My realisation started to manifest itself in a fear of my future. After I had been dressed in my blood red dress, the laces pulled tight to hold me to my task, I stood alone. I picked nervously at the tracery on the hem of my sleeve, and gazed at the image in the glass before me. Slowly a warmth from within rose to my pale cheeks, a gentle smile painted itself to portray the returning confidence I was feeling. I had thought of my Mother. I sensed her love upon me. Her gentle voice rang a comfort through my mind. I took solace in the knowledge that she would always be looking over me, and rejoiced in the safety of that belief. I slid my hands over the rich bodice, up to where I should meet hers. Entwining our fingers I tugged at the twilight memories of her care. With my eyes closed I could still discern an image. Unclear, uncertain, indistinct, but something of her face. Full of the confidence and surety that would help me step from that small room to the waiting ceremony. Eyes still closed I let my hands drop from that dreamy clasp and held them tight to my breast, discerning my now more quiet heartbeat.

His ring! There was his ring. My eyes shot wide as my clasped hands touched on something other than my body's rhythm. Not daring to look, I touched the facets of the small ring on my finger. All my strength, all my resolve was lost, blown like the seeds from a dandelion, scattered by the icy blast that had just chilled me through.

No one had ever questioned its presence, nor yet sought to ask from where it came. But today I was to receive a ring of significance. A symbol to all of my allegiance to my new husband. I sank to a small seat placed beside the open window, and gazed at the air. I had not thought that I would find it so difficult to divest myself of this little trinket, and yet now I was lost again inside of my emotions. Far from having the strength to take on the day, I found myself unable to perform the merest physical act.

All I had to do was take the ring off. But he had put it there, and there it had remained since.

By contrast to this day it had been a cold one. The gaunt plants where dressed in a fine, silvery frost, and sparkled in the winter's light. I had to walk far longer in the garden than I expected. As such I was beginning to get a little uncomfortable. I had lost all sensation in my toes, and I was irritated by the possibility that Ralph might have been persuaded away to some other duty.

Just as the warmth of the house seemed to be winning favour I heard a movement behind me and turned at the moment he rounded the corner. Offering absolutely no word of apology for his tardiness, he took my arm and we set off across the small bridge that spanned the river at the bottom end of the lake. We walked far enough to know we were safe from any who might happen by. Stopping he turned and looked into my eyes. Our warm breaths joined together in great clouds before our lips met to kiss. I sensed something of a determination in his manner, and looked at him somewhat quizzically.
We were stood by the foot of a large ash tree. He threw off his cloak and bade me sit on it, the roots of the old tree affording us a comfortable seat. Reaching into his purse he retrieved an object to which I was not yet privy. As his smiling eyes flashed mischief my curiosity got the better of me.
        "What are you about Ralph?"
I lunged for his clasped hand as I spoke in an effort to find out for myself what secret he was holding so tight. Had my patience lasted that little bit longer I might have saved myself from much of the taunting that followed. I was no match for his huge hands

and his beguiling smile, both of which were not about to betray this prize. I was not to give up that easily.

I pushed at him, quite catching him by surprise. He swung backwards off his perch and fell flat in the leaves behind, yet still keeping his grip, and still the teasing smile, unspoken, unchanging. I leapt at him as he rolled to his feet and was around to the other side of the tree in a second. I crept to it, holding my breath, slowly making my way around to catch him from behind. My confusion at his disappearance was short lived as he took hold of my waist. Our voices echoed through the trees as we chased, cracking twigs beneath our feet and kicking great piles of brown, dry leaves in our paths. Crows cawed in disapproval as their peace was broken, and they flew off cursing noisily.

Eventually I could run no more, and in disappointment I sank into a heap of autumn's tears. Ralph threw himself onto the ground beside me with a great sense of triumph, laughing unkindly at my indignant face. At last he softened and took my hands in his. Our exertions had now increased the volume of our billowy breath that puffed and panted from us as we regained our composure. Kneeling, he breathed warm air onto my still cold fingers, kissing each one in turn.

"Close your eyes." His voice was as soft as the fluffy white that drifted around us. Obediently I did so without question. The cold of the metal as it slid on was a strange but exciting sensation, and my eyes fell open at the first hint of it. A band of gold with a blue stone in a finely tooled setting now adorned my trembling hand.

"Ralph … ", his fingertip rested on my lips halting my protestation.

"I had it especially crafted. There are letters cut inside of it." he said.

"A.W.Y."

"What do they mean?"

Holding me closer than ever, his beautiful grey eyes gazing deeply into mine he whispered,

"Always With You."

My eyes filled with tears made even keener by the cold, and we kissed until I felt I should burst.

"I love you Elly."

The words were just too much for me. I ventured to return the same, but found myself unable to make a sound.   My happiness filled every part of me. Eventually I sobbed something indiscernible, and we remained on that spot for what seemed hours. Just held in an eternal embrace, neither one willing to let go of the other.

And now here I was about to remove that very token. 'Always with you', but not now. Gone and forever. The ring was off. I wrapped it in a lace kerchief and pushed it to the back of a small drawer.

The honeyed nectar had not been kind to me in its memory, and the imprint of its merriment now hung like a dead weight in my head. This feeling held no measure to the notion I had grown up with when imagining this special day. The menfolk had, it seemed, their own way of dealing with the turgid consequence of imbibing too much the previous night. Their answer was simplicity itself, carry on drinking without pause. While they had cause for celebration they would celebrate. And thus it fell to the women of the house to take charge and keep order.

It was tradition to wed within the house at Packwood, but this morning was to be different. I was embracing not just a new life, but also the inherent intrigue and possible danger of a papist family. Whilst both families were known to be sympathetic to the Catholic cause, the Ferrers in particular were uncommonly active in support for the highly suppressed minority that trod the fearful path of their religious zeal.

The family was well respected however. They had always displayed loyalty to the monarch. Indeed, at an early age William had been received at Elizabeth's court, presented by his cousin the Viscount Charles Townsend, a close friend of Robert Dudley, Earl of Leicester. William had proved to be a great favourite amongst those in the capital. His ready wit always capable of winning him favour one way or another. His features then, though still flushed with the ruddiness of youth, betrayed the foundations of a most handsome visage, combined with a solid body and crowned by the golden locks of a Greek God. He graced any group, and his company very quickly became sought by many. In some respect through this time he acquired a wisdom beyond his years. He learned when to speak on a subject, but more importantly when not to. This had both served him well and kept him safe.

We had left the uncertainty of our early history and we now lived in a so much more enlightened age. There were still the dangers associated with power and religion, but all knew how that was. Our lives had been spared the whims of a monarch that would turn our faith this way and that. We had the stability of a Queen who knew what she wanted, but cared for and loved her people. We had enjoyed years of good fortune and plenty due entirely to her astute stewardship. Most were keen to retain that status.

The Protestant religion was the demand of the realm, and forsure, many of the old Catholic families oftimes found themselves in uncomfortable circumstances, but the air seemed to stay fresh with certainty for all that. Religion was not spoken of openly within the family, but a traditional reverence and adherence to the beliefs and the history of Baddesley snuggled deep in the heart of the building, enwrapped by the flowing waters that stood to guard its every face. No stronghold or fortress of stone, but a home of safety through care and love.

Within the building at an upper level was a particular room set aside for devotion. It had long since been decided that the service to join our two souls should be held within this small place. The accommodation thus suited only a minimum congregation. The usual space in front of a church allowed for as many as wished to attend, but this fanciful arrangement led to a most uncommon ceremony.

That August morning in 1582 began with the most picturesque of events as the entire party walked the two miles from Packwood to Baddesley. I was set on a carriage bestrewn with flowers and wonderful garlands that towered overhead in great colourful hoops. On each hand sat Caroline and Sophia. The trembling of the vehicle as we traversed the uneven land let gentle showers of loose petals fall as we progressed. The sun lit the day from a perfect blue sky, catching the colours of those few leaves that had already succumbed to autumn's taunt, and the air smelt clean and crisp. Behind us rode William and his fellows. Charles directly at his side, the immediate successor to our absent guest. The bridles of the train rattled and clinked in contrast to the solid thump of hooves in the soft earth. The air rang with an excited conversation that rolled and ran from one and to the other, accompanied by occasional tunes on the lute, viol and pipe from the musicians who were to play us through the day.

I did wonder if some of those to the rear of the procession would make the distance, and wished at one time that some provision had been made for the less able walkers. However, the journey soon ended, and as we entered the house the guests were encouraged to amuse themselves wheresoever they wished as the families congregated for the wedding inside.

Thus it was that we came to find ourselves a party to the blessing of our marriage in the solemnity of the little chapel, and in the solitude of our small group, whilst around us could be heard the continuing merriment of those in attendance, but quite divorced from the proceedings. For my part I found it refreshingly satisfying to sense their joy so apparently, but for some of the older members of the families this was not so. They viewed it in a far less sympathetic manner. Various attempts were made to issue forth great 'shushes' in a futile effort to quell the hubbub. The result, unfortunately, rather more added an almost farcical nature to the proceedings. Certainly I could not contain a small giggle, particularly when I saw how hard William was biting on the inside of his lip in order to control what could only possibly become an unforgivable breach of propriety. My weakness earned me some of the most severe stares from those stone-faced devotees present. William's elder brother, Henry, commanded instant respect with a glance, and brought a faint glow to my face as I stood like a child caught red-handed in the midst of some impish ill-deed. There was not an instant's doubt that I should return my demeanour once more to one of total respect.

In all, I felt more than a little sigh of relief as we were dismissed, now one. Instead of the great surge of joy I was expecting, I fair ran from the place.

Within seconds that expected joy flooded over us in great waves of excitement as we returned to the waiting throng. Still we were not in control of our destiny as a tide of enthusiasm swept us through the rooms and out into the bright sunlight. The music struck up with a new fervour and the party, no longer divided, spilled into the garden where long trestles were set, laden with a great feast. There were meats of every possible variety arranged with great artistic as well as culinary skill. A true feast fit for a king and queen. The biggest spectacle though had been provided by the guests. Left to their own amusements whilst we were secreted within the house, they had ample opportunity to indulge in the cake building. As was usual each had brought cakes of various sizes with them to pile as high as possible, but having been given the space to take some care, various guests had taken it upon themselves to organise the layers with great skill. The result was the most enormous tower set high in the centre [2]. Our immediate task as husband and wife was to conceive of how we could possibly even attempt to kiss across this monument. A great cheer went up as we were momentarily stunned by that which lay before us. The building party stood proud by their achievement, sure that they had achieved the ultimate, and certain of a glorious catastrophe.

I saw the challenge light a spark in William's eye. A plan was hatched in an instance. Charles led me with much ceremony to the far side of the assemblage followed closely by the young James Bassett. James carried a wooden board with him and laid it before me. I grew most nervous as their intent became clear. With a great deal of objection on my behalf I was coaxed onto the board and took a hold of each shoulder with a grip that elicited a wince from both of my supports. Slowly I rose into the air, my insecurity contrasting directly with the broad, confident smiles each side of me. A chant from the guests grew to a crescendo of expectation as I cleared the peak and leaned, shaking, toward my husbands waiting lips. A brief touch was achieved before I made my retreat with a great deal more haste than I had made my ascent. In a moment I was back to the arms of William in an embrace that drew yet further cries of joy from all.

And so the festivities continued. Those elderly guests who would admonish such outrageous behaviour discussed the dangers amongst themselves, whilst inwardly remembering the same fire that lit their younger lives. The group of builders showed a momentary face of disappointment as they were thwarted in their plans to court disaster, but they soon busied themselves with the task of dismantling and distributing the edifice, basking in the enthusiastic praise and backslapping that resulted from their prowess and skills. The trees echoed with the shouts of excited children running at speed amongst the more sedate guests, and music sparkled without cease it seemed throughout the remainder of the day.

While William and his friends continued to plunder the depths of the ale barrels, I began my solitary role of maintaining a care for our guests, young and old, but especially old. I was aware of the etiquette required of me as the new lady of the house. It was my duty to ensure their every need was attended to, a duty I relished. It was not so far removed from the role I had played in the stead of my mother on behalf of my father, for which in return I enjoyed many years of gratitude and a kindly friendship.

I must confess to fussing rather moreso over him and his guests, maintaining my previous position for every last moment I should be allowed. A well-concealed sadness in his eyes betrayed not an inconvenience, but a loss at the realisation of my new station. There was a finality to the celebration that signalled a change. Though blessed by him and welcomed for its success, nonetheless a bouquet of roses beset with thorns. We had learned a certain reliance on each other that had earned me respect at many levels. My gratitude for the surety I had gained sat on the other side of the scales to my father's little hostess, but the latter side would now stand empty.

As the long shadows rose to meet the horizon and there knit to form the blanket of the eve, most had settled into more quiet discourse, the day having taken its full toll. By way of a message sent out by Lord Lovaine I came to my father's side. He stood, full noble, resplendent in his still pristine attire, lit with drama by the large fire behind him in the main hall. I formally lowered myself before him. He reached and took my hand with great care, and we sat to one side. I felt led back to a much younger age when he was my absolute hero. The age when a father's foibles are unnoticed, when he could do no wrong. I felt safe and yet I felt the insecurity of the impending farewell. He reached into his heavily embroidered doublet and pulled something from within. He moved closer and revealed a silver clasp on a chain. I recognised it immediately. It was delicately engraved with the Lovaine coat of arms and decorated front and back with the most wonderful tooling. I knew it to be in my mother's possession until the moment she died, until now I had been unaware of its whereabouts. Holding it up my father pressed on some secreted spot and caused the front to fly open. Within the device was a deep blue velvet lining and a small, light strand of hair held captive by a wire about it.

"We cut this from your pretty head when you were but two months old Elly."

Father's voice, so deep and resonant, echoed back down the ages to my beginning.

"Your mother and I were so happy. We had no doubt you would grow up to be the jewel you are today. She wore this about her every day she graced God's earth. While I see her light in your eyes I could wish nothing more of the Almighty than to keep you for myself. But the longings of an old man play no further part in your progress. I have more than enough fond memories to see me through my winter. Carry her light for me and find full happiness in your future."

His beautiful, large, soft hand held my face as he leaned and kissed my forehead, and as he leant back I could detect a moist rim where I had never seen one before.

"We have served each other well my daughter. Take my blessing and live in truth as the same pure gem in a different setting."

I threw my arms around his neck quite forgetting myself. I felt small and vulnerable, and the soft grey whiskers of his beard afforded me the childhood comfort I had grown to rely on. My sobs subsided quickly for it was not seemly to profess such emotion in the present company. But the beauty of his old face never left me. His love endured for me through each and every day in the memory of that gesture.

I wandered off lost in a mist of my childhood up to my chamber leaving the grand old knight to his thoughts. I knew how much he missed my mother. There were many tales of their great love and this day had borne them to the surface, perhaps more than any mortal frame could bear, but to me this man was greater than any.

As I turned the corner to my doorway I was startled by the sudden appearance of Rosie, my new maidservant. She was flushed as she shot past me and horrified at treating my presence with such little decorum. She flashed a look at me and cried a swift apology before crossing the landing and descending the stairs at a rate.

I made to check and enquire after her haste, but she was gone from sight before I could quite recover myself. I turned back to my room confounded by the occurrence. My heart fair leapt from my mouth as I found myself faced by a darkly dressed gentleman standing directly in my path. His visage was not pleasant, adding to the discomfort I felt. His skin had an uncommon pallor, and his large hooked nose was accentuated by a single, bushy brow. For his part there displayed no surprise, just a weak insincere smile. My shock led me to enquire:

"What, Sir, are you?"

Immediately the words left my lips their dramatic nonsense filled me with a sense of lacking either control or safety. He seemed to find amusement in my question, and did nothing more than slide past me to the passage whilst maintaining his stale grin, yet fixing those heavy set eyes all the while to my own. His ill-mannered boldness was floored in an instant as Nanny Walker flew in, her arms laden. She turned immediately to the stranger.

"To what purpose do we find you here Master Francis?" she said firmly.

Without shifting his gaze he deepened his brow.

"What notice is it of yours, good mistress maid?"

"Well, if you wish to remain you can be mindful of my task." At which she laid the contents of her arms in his, being bed linens and the like.

"I shall be minded to inform Master William of your usefulness." She threatened in her sarcasm. At this the unwanted party dropped the neatly folded linens to the floor and made good his exit with no further word.

Rather than the calm, dismissive woman she had just displayed, Nana shook some as she retrieved her bundle from where it now lay. She apologised to me as I seated her, now visibly shaken.

"Who was that Nana?" I enquired, still at a loss to make any sense of the odd situation. My happy day had been dented, and I was already beginning to feel the irritation of the intrusion.

"You pay no mind to him m'lady. He's a harmless fool."

"But who is he?" I insisted, "Poor Rosie seemed quite distressed."

She was up and busying herself with her original intention as she spoke some more.

"You have met him before, a long time ago. He was just as much a weasel then. You were invited across to the great Court at Coughton for an evening when once you was staying here. The family was to visit and, as a guest of Master William's, you joined the party. As I remembers you couldn't have been more'n nine. Sir Francis Throckmorton, for it was he just now, took a fancy to you. William, although a great deal shorter at that time, took to bloodying his nose. Much reprimanded and chastised for his behaviour, he explained that he did not much like the idea of sharing his friends as it spoiled his games. But in truth, it seemed, he had proved himself a worthy champion."

I confess I did feel some pity for the miscreant despite the circumstances, but Nana assured me he really was nothing but a weasel again, and I warrant the description suited him well.

For some minutes more we discussed the various arrangements of my belongings in their new place. Once Nana had placed everything and smoothed the linens with her strong mottled hands, she made something of a furtive move to the landing then retreated back inside, closing the door tight behind her. She appeared to need assurance that we were quite alone. She sat beside me as she had done for many years.   This was usually a sign of an impending scolding for my various misdeeds, or else would herald some knowledge that had befallen to her to impart to me in order to aid my passage to womanhood.   Taking my hands in hers I felt the warm consequence of her travail, and felt sure I was not to be reprimanded.   Her manner was unsure as she struggled to phrase what she had to say.

"My dear Elenor." she began with the least formality.   I snuggled in close putting her more at ease.

"There's many a custom as plays a part in the nuptials as you are aware already."   I was lost as to her direction.

"Well, there is one aspect as you might not have met before, you not having sisters and the like. There is a practice that will affect you on the morrow of which you may not be aware.   Tonight is your wedding night and there are certain duties that will be expected of you which in turn will leave their mark."

I was starting to feel uncomfortable at this point, as I was not sure where she was going with her words. It was some years since she had broached the subject of what befell between a man and a woman, so there was no new subject there, surely.

"The morrow will bring a further ceremony. The linen from your wedding bed will be taken to sight proof of the fulfilment of the marriage between you and William."

For all Nanny Walker's attempts to make clear what she intended me to understand I returned nothing but a blank look as I was non the wiser by her statement. Frustrated, she returned further:

"My precious child. Your Nana kept many secrets for you, but she has also been party to some of those you thought belonged only to you."

I stiffened somewhat, but she reassured me with her gentle tone.

"I am not sitting in judgement for that is the place of the Almighty and him alone, have no fear of that. Just know that the secret tryst between you and young master Ralph was a thing of joy and danger I was privileged to observe."

My hands shot to my mouth. How much of this was known? Had we been so careless in our subterfuge?

" You cannot shield the eyes of someone who knows you as I do. In truth, there were occasions when my being aware so afforded me the opportunity to give the lie as to your whereabouts or activity. And thus it is now that I speak to you in haste."

"Nana!" I said still shocked, "You knew all along?"

She just smiled. I didn't know whether to feel more vulnerable or whether to bask in the comfort her protection had afforded me through the years.

"I had my suspicions." she continued. "Your happiness spilled over in such excess at times I felt there must be a source. It didn't take me long to catch sight of the brightly-lit glances that danced between you both. You had always been thick as thieves, but I sensed the care change to something deeper and not of this world. From then on I could make my observances from a discreet distance. Whilst I cannot say I was pleased with the young man's dalliance, I could not help but enjoy the radiant happiness that shone from you. In the same way, I have felt and shared the growing sorrow that has been the consequence within recent memory. And I can't say as I think much of his absence today. His thoughts should have been only of his duty."

I was too taken aback to disagree with her when admonishing Ralph for his inability to face the day. In some sense I felt a comfort in finally sharing my tortuous secret. It was, after all, something I had a want to shout to every corner of the land. The emotion therein had been of such a pitch that it truly was too much to retain alone.

"To what end do you tell me of this now?" I asked. She reached into her purse, a permanent feature of her large, white apron that spanned her ample waist. She held aloft a little glass phial. Within it was contained a small amount of a red liquid. I could only guess that it was blood of some sort, as that is what it resembled.

"I am returning to you your maidenhead." said Nanny. "For this is what will be expected of you in the morn. Take it and hide it for now, and we shall speak no more of this."

Indeed I did speak no more of it. I felt shame. For all the honesty of the love I had for Ralph I felt mortified that it should be necessary to exact this artifice. That night I had no difficulty in executing the plan. William's excesses had led him to reach a world of slumber the instant his body met our bed.

I had no doubt the same would engender a surfeit of forgetfulness the next day also. I reflected on the irony that if I had not loved Ralph as I had, there still would have been no prize for the morning guests without Nanny Walker's preparedness. Regardless, I despatched the anonymous contents of the glass, and watched the slow progress of the lie creep across the woven threads, embroidering prowess for William and false honour for myself.

My mind slipped from the grip of ignominy to the remembrance of my maiden's release. I envisaged the dark trickle soaking gently into the deep green grass, imbuing the sacred earth with the richness of a truth, my true marriage, consecrated in that holy place. The honest stain apparent to God's angels who wished only to witness a love blessed under heaven's skies.

I turned to the figure of William, kissed his sleeping face, and whispered a promise. This would be the last lie. Ralph was gone, and beside me lay my husband, my liege. I would hold sacred the promises I had made that day, and bury forever my secret past.

How short a time the reality of that promise held true. October was drawing to a close and yet I felt a need to sit out of doors in the damp, morning air. Looking to the milky sky I wished for the sun to reach through and warm my place, just enough. Just enough to linger more in that spot and bring a hint of warmth before our winter set in. Within my heart it was that winter already. Cold and lifeless, and warmed not, yet within my belly a Spring had begun. New life was engendered there, and had set to grow that many months since my nuptials. But there was the lie. The stain that marked my bed was taken to mark the start. Yet the start was already begun one full march of the sun prior. For myself I was torn betwixt what should have been and what was.

This lie hurt *me* though, not him. Whilst around me was the joy professed by all at the prospect of a new Ferrers, I hurt deep inside. I hurt because of the deceit I bore. This Ferrers was an Ellerker and none but I knew it. I hurt because I needed to profess my joy so badly, but could find no soul on Earth with whom I could impart that yearning. Mostly I hurt because the one person, the progenitor of my child, my Ralph, was not there to share in our creation.

I knew I should have but one thought: the allegiance to my husband and the safe carrying of his first born. I knew it, and fought to hold true to that notion. I felt sure I could resist the impetuous invasion of the memories that stole my mind at every quiet corner, but my body too was taken. The thought of our child within me tore me from the grasp of my true responsibilities. I reached to the now perceptible mound that had started to form. The cold air reached in to chill me, but I was insensitive to its touch. Where was he? Where did he go, and how long would his absence keep me in this tortuous state?

As I lay my head back against the hard, uncaring wall and stared to the sky, I noticed the passing of the year had reached that stage when I could detect my breath. I watched it float heavenward and let my mind wander to the improbable notion it might drift and so happen upon that which was undoubtedly leaving Ralph the same moment. Anything. Just the smallest encounter. Just some hint in the ether that surrounds us which might possibly convey to his far-flung self this knowledge, the truth of our love.

Again I chastised myself for making this pain still greater, but where was my husband? Where was the love that though professed was never honoured? I had no distraction from my thoughts. The promise of the new marriage had proved to be hollow, and lacked anything of the relationship that had filled my every minute whilst Ralph and I were together. Occasional minutes were all I had with William. His business took him away at every chance. I was not even party to his comings and goings. Indeed, I had never felt so alone in my life. I longed for the familiar comfort of Packwood, the caring stricture of Nanny Walker's dictates, and more, the illicit ventures which my Ralph and I stole at every chance. How I needed to hear his voice, to feel his caring touch upon my body, and to gaze into those beautiful grey eyes.

What of this child? If it were a boy, would it bear the self same strengths and beauty of his father? What a joy that would be for me to behold, watching those features grow to shape a copy of that love. Yet, what pain would it bring, a constant reminder of my loss forever. A gain, a loss? What madness I felt.

I wanted to scream out-loud, to profess what I knew not, but I felt trapped, imprisoned in my own doing. I had always known the folly of our joining. I had carried the inevitable end to our happiness just in my being. It could never have been different. No one could change that which had been set down virtually since my birth. So why had I allowed it to happen? This was no one's fault but mine. Now it was no one's pain but mine.

I rose from my seat and wandered indoors still lost in my thoughts. The large fire in the hall blazed and afforded me a little physical comfort in its restorative heat. The sickness I had been experiencing that heralded my little visitor's settling was beginning to subside these last weeks. I was keenly aware that the cold air had been an aid in suppressing the flux, this warmth was not so welcome as it might have been otherwise. I moved from the hearth across to the windows overlooking the court. I was often sat in this place. On fine days sunlight would stream through the stained glass sending colours across the seats and floor, marking the time in an imperceptible movement of rainbow pastiche. This day showed only a sluggish shadow.

My timing was well, as a group of horses pulled to with a scattering of stones. I moved to greet my husband as he strode in without ceasing a heavy conversation. Just as I was about to protest my being trampled so, William swung and swept me to him and kissed me full. Before I could recover he was introducing me to those who accompanied him. Each bowed before I could make a coherent attachment of the name, except one. He stepped forward and made to kiss my hand. I reacted without thought as I recoiled from his grasp. Those dark set eyes, that constant cold smile were instantly recognisable. William glared at me for an instant and turned back.

"It seems, Sir Francis, you are not in favour. Childbearing does so affect civility. Perhaps my good wife will make good by attending us with refreshment."

With that the party repaired to the reading room on the upper floor. Whether through his own volition or not it seemed this man was always going to cause me displeasure in some form or other.

I could not believe how I had demeaned myself in the eyes of William and his friends. Now I had been relegated to nothing more than a serving maid. I stormed about the kitchen venting my discomfort on the staff. The jug of wine and attendant vessels together with small victuals was far in excess of what I was able to carry, but I was not about to succumb to the burden. I proved myself capable of its management and entered the room fully laden. The discussion halted immediately. The discomfort from my earlier impropriety, as such, was not lessened. Indeed, I was fully aware that my duty done I was no longer required. William smiled and turned to the attendance of his guests. I made swift my exit, hastily took my way downstairs, and back out of the house, all the while suppressing my rising anger at the humility I had felt.

I strode over the bridge and headed down the bank, across the stream to the little glade at the back of the carp pool. I flung myself to the floor at the foot of a tall pine and finally wept. Those were the first tears since our departure. I had determined that my relinquish of Ralph would never result in shedding another tear past my wedding day, and yet here I was, a-flood.

After an eternity, with all the pain spent, and the hurt washed down my cheeks, I slowed to a heavy, steadying breath. I turned and leant against the gnarled trunk and, tipping my head back, gulped in mouthfuls of the fresh air. Just then a break in the clouds passed overhead, the sun's warmth bathed my face and set to drying the wetness upon it. Its gentle caress returned my sensibility, and I felt a stilling within me. My mind drifted to a day some six years since, in that very glade a group of us sat. A dry, early summer's day, not this dank, late time.

A rug lay on the grass scattered with pillows and bolsters scavenged from various rooms around the house. I sat picking at a small sampler, started in earnest some months back, but now lacking the enthusiasm that spurred its initial working. At my side Sophia Onslow and Caroline Ferrers played childish hand-games, and talked of petty things. William Ferrers and Charles Townsend preferred the rugged comfort of the grass. They were falling about with laughter, much to the annoyance of James Bassett who was about to prove that it was possible to catch one of the carp by simply reaching in and taking it so. At his tender age the span of his hand was hardly sufficient to take proficient grasp of any but the smallest fish.

"The smaller they are the swifter they swim." reproached Charles. "You'll never do it."

"Of course you can." countered William between gales of laughter. He was intent on watching James prove himself foolish rather than make himself worthy of the company which was his only wish. Both he and Charles rolled about, holding their sides as James grew wetter and more frustrated due to both his failed endeavours and the raucous laughter at his expense.

A movement caught my eye as through the bushes appeared Ralph, leading his horse down the small path toward us. My heart leapt, and I took small pleasure from his tethering the great steed next to my sweet pony, Maude. It was evident from the sweat foaming on the horse that he had ridden hard and fast. Indeed, there was a glow about himself, and he too glistened across his broad chest. William and Charles hailed him readily, and controlled their merriment enough to explain the fun at hand. The addition to the audience drove the young James to further exertion, all the more keen to elicit praise.

Caroline stopped playing with Sophia and took up a more genteel pose. She was perfection in her white summer attire. Her hair hung in golden curls about her shoulders, and her skin was as pale as a swan's wing. She had such a natural elegance about her, she never failed to attract young men. Ralph made a general obeisance to our three, but I felt sure his gaze fell upon Caroline, and I knew I didn't like it. Ralph was my friend, it had always been so. Now his presence caused deeper stirrings. Feelings I was unsure of, and worse, jealousy. No matter how I arranged myself I felt at a complete loss to match the beauty of William's sister, yet I so wanted him to look at me. Why on this Earth should he? I was but twelve years of age, he a manly eighteen. This Goddess that took his eye was three years my senior. Three years that took her into womanhood and left me the foolish child who could only yearn in abject silence. Sophia simply took her delight from continuing with the daisy chains they had started earlier.

Ralph strolled forward and stood with his back to the enthusiastic fisherman whilst engaging in light conversation with William and Charles. There was an air of expectation which arose between the trio, a sense of mischief. Without looking around, nor faltering in his words, a gentle backward movement of his boot made contact with the crouching boy's behind. With no chance of regaining his balance from such a precarious position, James tipped headlong into the water.

Hardly able to spit the words out William asked,

"Did you catch one? Did you?"

The laughter continued unabated as Ralph quietly bent to proffer a hand to the sad figure, splashing about and coughing up great volumes of the foul water.

"Take my hand, little carp."

Instead, the drenched boy kicked out, succeeding in sending a deluge in the direction of the perpetrator of this ill deed. Stepping from the pool, with no further words, he dragged his much maligned and soaked body off into the house, with discernible sobs and a very heavy heart.

"Oh Ralph, you are funny. Come sit by us and we shall dry what wet is upon you."

Caroline made a space between herself and Sophia ensuring that I was not to be allowed to lessen her effect.

"Ellerker, we have a bow strung for you and a wager at hand, all speed to the lawn."

Ralph lifted his shoulders by way of mute apology and headed off after the two. In no way thwarted, Caroline sprang to her feet and was hooked into his arm talking fair nonsense before he had gone but two paces. I was certain of his discomfort, but surely he would hold from expressing it for courtesy. Much aggrieved at Caroline's forthright manner I hurried to gather Sophia. She protested at the interruption of her chain-making, and was at pains to ensure the survival of at least the larger of them all. As such, much to my annoyance, I found them all gone from me before we were able to follow on.

"My legs don't stretch that far!" Poor Sophia adamantly pulled back against the hand that led her at a speed beyond her years. I had determined that Caroline would not be allowed any more time alone with Ralph than I could help. I had not counted on shepherding my little ward though. Indeed, she was cousin to all four of the rest of the party, so why was I confined to this duty? I turned to the sorry little figure trying with all her might to hold onto her daisies. Unable to grasp her hem, encumbered as she was, she tripped at every step as her feet caught in the layers of her petticoats. I halted, took pity, and carefully wound the interlocked flowers into a more manageable fashion, taking their care upon myself. Thus we strolled at a more sensible pace up through the large box hedges to the big lawn on the other side of the house.

"Hurry on Sparrow!" cried a familiar voice.

"We are paired up for fair competition."

"Fair is it?" grunted an unhappy looking William.

I loosed Sophia's hand, returned her garland and skipped over to the group.

"Who is paired to whom?" I enquired tentatively.

Charles broke in; " I have our little fish. Methinks there is much for him to prove this day."

In changed clothes and happier demeanour James was once more party to the fun. Standing together they portrayed a formidable team.

I looked to William and managed to suppress a laugh as he agitatedly tried to explain the finer points of the art of the bow to Caroline. She in turn was struggling to make sense of the timing and complexity necessary to exact a good shot, passing the instrument from one hand to the other in a portrayal of complete ignorance as to its workings. I looked to Ralph who had that same mischievous grin upon his face from earlier, aware of William's frustration and his own good fortune.

"Shall we show them how it's done Sparrow?"

I smiled back to him, and a warm glow rose from within me. I became aware, however, that if I could not control my feelings, my light head and trembling hands would prove our downfall.

The sun shone in a clear blue sky directly overhead. On two opposite corners of the neat lawn stood large wicker constructions. They were rather reminiscent of a monk's cowl in shape. Within the body of each was placed packed straws, and onto them was painted brightly coloured circles within circles, ending in a single red spot. There was little wind, and the waterfowl in the moat beside the house were, for the most, sat patiently on the grassy bank, some safe distance hence. With Sophia sat safely behind us, still protesting at not being allowed to take a part, and William and Caroline still sniping at each other, we set to.

Each pair was allowed one sighter shot from their best archer. Both Ralph and Charles overshot the target, but William lodged an arrow directly upon the outermost ring. He was aware of his advantage this being his usual practice place. His prowess had assured him first in the order. He took up a stance as we all held our breath for the release of the first arrow. His long golden hair and the fullness of his strong arms lent him a very dramatic air. The first went wide of the mark, but the following two made good, setting a high score to beat. Charles matched Will', and it fell to Ralph's turn. I could not help but shiver as his proud figure stood tensed and ready. The earlier sweat had not entirely left his skin and it seemed to highlight the flawless structure of his perfection. The bow seemed as a toy in his grasp, bending to his whim, and tensed to breaking point with his powerful arms at full stretch. With hardly a flicker the arrow was released and flew to its destiny. For all my awe at this wonder, the scoring stayed even across all three.

The party moved to the centre of the lawn in order that we secondary players might have some chance of success. Caroline took her position, her brother behind, encouraging her all the while. The more he moved to give instruction, the more irritated she became. She would not let this game better her, not in the sight of Ralph Ellerker. Confidently she stood with a somewhat awkward stance and achieved a very reasonable draw, empowered, no doubt, by her pride. With apparent alacrity, no care for sensible aim, she released both hands at the same instance. Much to everyone's surprise the arrow took flight, and further, made the mark. William was ecstatic. Caroline remained calm with a face that simply conveyed she had expected nothing less. Both myself and Ralph stood mouths agape. Sadly for her, she was not to repeat this initial success. Much to her chagrin, the next arrow dropped to the floor at her feet. The following made greater progress, but failed to clear more than six paces. In addition, Caroline managed to snag herself on the snapping bow causing her to tears for more reasons than one. Nursing her pain she sat by Sophia as James took up his place.

All three of his arrows found the target, but only two fell within a score. He was rightly proud of his self, and certainly had gained something of his much sought status. By now I shook with fear. I was all too aware of the possibility that I might demean myself as had Caroline. I could not let such a thing occur. I breathed deeply, and placed the notched end of the shaft to the twine. As I prepared to draw it back I felt Ralph close behind me. I was not about to shrug off his aid as had William's sister. Instead, I wished for him to move in. My hesitancy was enough to prompt him forward. He gently took my shoulders, turning them to a squarer position.

"Concentrate."

His voice so close in my ear took my mind away, but its instruction pulled me to the task, and I determined to make it count. I released the arrow with the song of the bow making it fly. I clipped the outer edge of the scoring and closed the gap in the summing up. Left to my own business the second shot fell short. My head dropped as I felt the disappointment, not just for myself. Once more Ralph stepped forward and squared me off. This time his hands slid down my arms to guide my aim more fully. I could feel the warmth of his body, and my head reeled from his natural scent. I don't even remember opening my eyes.

"You can do it." echoed through my dreamlike state. The arrow whisked away, and a cheer went up.

Before I had a chance to even check what might have been the outcome, I was swung through the air and found myself perched upon Ralph's shoulder. As we danced across the grass, spinning around and around, I managed to get a sight of my shot. There, lodged right in the middle of the blood red centre spot, was my arrow. What angel had ferried it there I could not tell, but the God who had guided it now bore me aloft.

I shot my arms to the sky, and whooped together with Ralph as we span and span in our victory dance. I was dizzy for more than a single reason, but I still caught a glimpse of the dejected Caroline storming off to the seclusion of the house, no doubt to sit and lick her wounds. It was a victory in truth, and the dance went on and on.

Thus I bore the growing burden through those grey months. My ease coming with my constant return to those days when happiness had seemed eternal. I drifted oftimes to the corners of my memories, uncovering such delights as brought peace to my unsettled heart.

On the seventeenth day of May, 1583, a new soul fought its way into this world. In contrast to the silent drop of the myriad blossom drifting past my window, this child's coming was anything but gentle, and was wont to signal my mortal departure. I knew I must garner what strengths I could to not allow it so. I was not about to forgo the gaze of those all too familiar eyes to any but myself.

Henry William Ferrers was a Ferrers to all but me. William had a son and an heir to follow him. As such his manner turned more fully to his family. I, consumed by love for this child, and now enjoying a caring from my husband, slowly shook off the haunting dreams of my childhood. New life came to the house and to me. I regained my strength all the more quickly as I now revelled in the foundation of a true family. William became the most loving father, and his affection for me was apparent to all, but especially to myself. Our days were spent enjoying the antics of our son and talking of what he would grow to become. We planned his future much as ours had been set before us when we were children, bringing us each to this happy estate. I thanked the Lord each and every day for the good fortune which was bestowed upon me, and I prayed forgiveness for my selfish and foolish ways that led me to such sorrow before.

A full half year passed with our little family playing and growing within the safe walls of Baddesley. Each day brought us new joys and wonder, and a happiness that pervaded all. As the Summer's light faded and the fogs of November began to envelop our world, a bleakness returned somewhat to the carefree demeanour of my William. I enquired once or twice as to his worry, but met with little response that served to satisfy my concern. He continued to play with little Henry, talking of the games they would play as he grew older, and the adventures they would entertain together, but I would watch his gaze become more distant as his mind settled to other matters.

It was December. The household was in turmoil with the advent of Christmas but two weeks off. Henry was sensing the growing excitement, and was trying the more to make use of his strengthening legs. His mobility on all fours already caused us some distress, as he was apt to find his way into much trouble. His antics, however, served to lighten the sombre air, and added to the festive preparation. William's brother Henry was still the master of the house, but his business kept him from us for the most time. He cared little for partying, and was apt to be absent at these times of the year. As such, I was somewhat surprised when he arrived at the house and repaired to his chamber as if for a long stay. It did little to settle William. Indeed it seemed he was concerned far more by his brother's return than any.

There was some serious matter to hand to which I was not party, as much as this I could surmise. Soon enough Henry summoned William to his study with all the formality of a father. I moved to reassure William, but was dismissed with scant care. I took little Henry to my chamber to nurse him and whiled the time away, dispelling the worry with the soothing suck at my breast.

At last I heard footsteps about the house and was aware that the matter had been dealt with. I wondered how long it would be, or if at all, before I was privy to the matter in hand. To my surprise the door opened and William stepped inside closing it gently behind him. I was taken aback to find him here as it was not usual for him to be with me at these times. I hurriedly attired myself, pulling the infant from me and placing him on my shoulder for comfort and relief from the feed. My husband seemed not to be aware of my fluster, but moved slowly to the edge of a large chest besides me upon which he sat. He was pale, and his closeness betrayed a weakness in his breathing that was uncommon in him. I made to speak, concerned at his situation, but he gestured silence to me in a kindly manner.

At length he spoke. A little unsure, but conveying a seriousness that caused a hollow in the pit of my stomach as I knew that no good words could be forthcoming.

"My sweet Elenor", he began. "These past months have taught me much of love and the importance of our union. Through your pain you bore to me a son whose delight has led me to understand that all I hold important in life is right here with me now, in this room."

My stomach tightened further. I had oft wished to hear such loving words, and yet they now were proving to portend something else, something I did not wish to hear.

"I have grown to love you and Henry in a way that I never thought capable of. But further, I have, as a consequence, learned of my shortcomings when first we were joined. There were too many times when I put others before your well-being, and indeed that legacy has now come to haunt me."

I felt I needed to reply, to add comfort to his now apparent pain, but I grew dry and unable to make a sound. I sat quiet, Henry asleep in my arms, he oblivious to his father's plight.

"You know of my association with Sir Francis Throckmorton."

I barely moved my head to signal acknowledgement of the fact, the mention of his name adding further to my discomfort.

"I learned some weeks ago of his arrest by the Queen's men under the direction of Lord Walsingham. In brief, it seems he was working on behalf of a gentleman by the name of Don Bernadino Mendoza, the Spanish Ambassador, who has since been sent back to Spain. There is some consideration that Sir Francis has been charged with plotting against our Queen and is to face death as a consequence."

He turned his head away from me, unable to look into my eyes as he continued, gazing instead out through the window and beyond, distant and lost.

"When the arrest was made at Coughton a thorough search of the rooms was made and a document was recovered. It stated therein the names of ten, so-called, fellow conspirators. I can tell you now that the truth of that claim is hollow, but my name was amongst them."

I felt my head go light as the words reached me. He saw me and moved to hold me and Henry before I dropped further. I turned to his sad face as he held us both, and espied tears falling, wetting the golden hair that lay across his cheeks. I still uttered nothing, but lay secured by his strong arms and his reassuring calm in the face of such dread news.

"All is not lost my dear, dear Elenor, my Henry." His grip felt safe, and I listened without sensibility, our little family held together by some tenuous hope.

"My brother has informed me of all this. The news came to him through my cousin Charles. Yet with it comes a remedy of sorts. You are aware that Charles is a close neighbour of Robert Dudley, Earl of Leicester, and as such they enjoy each other's company on numerous occasions. Leicester has suggested, by way of a favour, that if I were to agree to a posting within his army, he would be able to secure receipt of my name from Walsingham's hand without it becoming apparent to the courts. Naturally, without recourse to me, Henry has accepted the offer on my behalf already. As such a messenger was despatched to effect the arrangement immediately."

I recovered somewhat and restored myself to my previous seat, placating the now wakened child. I had not been immediate in my response as I had felt so distraught by the initial blow. Now I was clearer I grew quickly to a differing viewpoint.

"You could have saved me much pain had you imparted to me that you are now safe before telling me of the circumstances that had me losing you to the hangman!" I suddenly retorted. William was shocked and sat back. I felt much aggrieved at having been subject to the horror of the disclosure when in actuality the outcome was quite different. I stood and turned sharply, presenting my back to William, thus shielding his gaze from my face and the tears that were falling fast. I hugged Henry tighter and fell to sobbing, unable to contain the emotion within. William stepped to me and wrapped his arms full around me. His apology draped over me returning my mind to one of gratitude. We had been spared the nightmare that had become the reality of those others not so fortunate who were implicated in the same misdeed.

I turned back to him and we kissed, a warmth flowing through and around us. Our beautiful little family, safe within the moated walls of that fine house.

It was not until the February that William left us to take up his post. He was given a position as a Captain, responsible for a company of men numbering about eighty. He was answerable to the father of our dear James, Sir Arthur Bassett, whose company it was, under the direct command of Lord Leicester.

His leaving bore nothing of the tragedy that had been the original mark. The Christmas festivities had been levelled as a consequence of the revelation, but we had now moved to a sense of nervous excitement. Indeed the intervening months had taught us much of what lay in store for William, and now the exchange seemed almost unfair. Forsure, we were much increased in our gratitude for having been offered the arrangement. It seemed that the position was one that brought with it certain esteem and a privileged standing within the court of Leicester.

Much had been spoken of the closeness that existed between our Queen and Sir Robert, much of it, no doubt, doubled by lazy gossip amongst those with little else to do. There was no doubting that his influence and general regard amongst the courtiers ensured a goodly following. There were those who held jealousies that might mark him as a man with enemies, but with his reputation of office, his friends seemed to be well in excess of those who might wish him harm.

To command within his army was a great honour. While there was much in the world that might cause a soldier concern, Elizabeth appeared to have no taste for war, and we held steadfast to a faith in her ability to keep our country out of the affairs of others. This happy state, however, brought with it a maddening aside which I had not anticipated. No sooner had William fallen to his new role, advised us of the importance of his rank, and the responsibilities which befell him, but he was off away to pay service to that undertaking.

His enthusiasm did elicit from me certain support in the first days, and yet I found myself widowed to the absence of my husband through a new-found allegiance. His men, no doubt all fine husbands too, took him away from Henry and I again. Their well-being became William's single focus, his true family falling to one side to make way for the new pretender. I found myself somewhat renewed in my vexations of before, and most reluctant to succumb to a subverted situation once more

William D'Aurange was not a name that had been spoken of within our circle. The news that an obscure Dutch Prince had been assassinated elicited from me no more than a maternal response of concern for the family that were so affected. I had learned little of the politics of the day, although William's position had caused me to an interest in the noble Leicester. The stories that ran from the court of this handsome young knight, whose stature had stolen something of our virgin Queen's heart, conjured up such imaginings, and fed our women's discourse with sighs and dreams.

.•

I sat on a low chair beside the intricately carved crib that now barely managed to contain my child of fourteen months. The firelight glowed from behind me, and coloured his perfection with a warmth that echoed his peaceful slumber. As my hand nudged a gentle constancy to his sleep, I reflected on another mother who may have, at that very moment, been comforting her own. What might be their lot now that this child's father had been taken from them?

•

The shadows around us held unanswered questions, but none of the disquiet that must now creep around those members of the Prince's family. I shuddered at such dark thoughts. The face before me, as it so often did, gave me a glimpse of my own lost love. His beauty pervading any darkness, and yet bearing with it the greatest question of all. Henry's father was lost to him before he knew him, and I, bound by my silence, knew that nothing of this truth would ever find its way to his legacy. My lie, my deceit, would die with me, buried with the loss I bore with so much pain.

I could at least lead my enquiring little man to the retreats secreted among the various houses that bore witness to the many joyous days that had constructed my childhood. Through yew hedges we stole, down little trod paths, behind walls, beside lakes flashed with silvery fish, on shores visited only by faeries. We played our games and laughed, and I related tales of excitement and adventure to a mind too young yet to conceive of their meaning. His happiness though was apparent in our joy as we shared those magical moments, some re-lived, some anew. I had not ever believed that the love I lost at Ralph's departure could ever be regained, yet my love for Henry filled every open wound, healed every scar, and slowly melted the frost that had once settled over my heart.

As the months passed I saw less of William, but my cares ran only to the well-being of my child. My world became small, and my triumphs were confined to the achievements of a growing boy. Henry knew little of his father. As his speech grew it saddened me to find that 'papa' was not amongst his early words. Moreso, the man in whose footsteps he should learn to follow, was so absent that on the occasions he chose to enter his household, the clamour and bustle of his coming drew little but apprehension and fear from the ignored child.

For my part I viewed those brief visits as nothing more than an intrusion into our happy life, and paid little heed. I played my part as was my duty, but I had a single mind and was not distracted from care for my little Hen'.

In the mid August of 1585 we were taking a meal out of doors with a small party of wooden soldiers. The summer had seemed to meet its end already despite September not yet gained. The skies lay heavy with a grey cloud that sailed across a weak sun, allowing us only a fleeting glow from its over-played peep-po. The trees swished overhead as a chill wind drew our arms in to hug what little warmth we could find. As the unkind air bade me move to recall us to the comfort of the house, I spied a figure close by.

I looked to Henry who was sat astride a small straw horse, which was barely discernible as such having been ridden too hard through countless adventures. I rose from the spot eliciting a cry of disapproval from the horseman who leapt to the rescue of the few soldiers I caused to fall as I brushed by them. As he tended to the wounded and remonstrated with those who refused to return to a standing position, I stood silent as William's gaze brought an unspoken news. His arms enfolded me a short time, then he led me with a gentle hold to the playing boy. He paused to look at me once more, kindly and with assuredness, then stooped to set the little general on his knee.

Though curious and rather more keen to attend to his painted troops, the grey eyes fixed on the figure of a man he knew so little, but recognised as his father. As such he was aware he commanded respect and attention, thus he remonstrated not. The kindness and the care of the voice caused no reaction in Henry, his tender age refused him neither the understanding nor the sensitivity to the sentence. Despite our separate lives the words caused in me my blood to freeze like a stream in the depths of Winter.

"I have to go to war, my Son. I place a charge on you to guard and care for your dear Mother whom I love deeply. I shall think of you constantly my little man, and shall write to tell you what occurs and when I shall be coming home."

He gently kissed his forehead and placed him back on the worn, cloth saddle. Standing, he held me once more. Tenderly lifting the hair away from my face he kissed me, smiled, and walked from that spot with no further word.

Book 3

William Ferrers
Amsterdam, Holland, 1585

29th December, 1585.

To my dear Wife, Elenor, and my good Son, Henry, may these words find you blessed with health and well in spirit. I send you greetings from a foreign state, and earnest love to you both.

First may I impart what good fortune has been bestowed upon me. In the greater part for that I was not asked to fight at sea, for truth be told I was never meant to be a mariner.

We finally bade farewell to our sweet land at Harwich the 18th day of this month. All were of a high spirit. To be part of such a spectacle as were we, perhaps as many as 100 vessels in all, sails full with the sea wind, and flags, and great cries of joy on every side, lent us each an air of such import. Sad to say, the monotony of the rolling waves soon took many of us to an ague from which we had no escape.

I was one of those whose motion was confined to a fixed spot at the side of the craft, from which I had no wish to remove myself, nor yet be removed.

Such wretchedness I felt. My incapacity was not how I suspected the outset of such an adventure would pass.

For two whole days we lurched toward the Dutch shores, eventually landing not at Brill, as had been expected, but instead at another place, Vlissingen. My cognisance of it was limited with my brain numbed so through this sailing plague. The ground itself felt odd for some while once the earth had been regained at last beneath my feet.

My dear Henry, heed me now. Do not consider any life with those who would venture on the sea. Our place is surely on a land that has no will to move of its own accord.

And now; if this is war then long may it continue! Such feasting and ceremony I have never before seen nor experienced. We were met at once by Sir Philip Sydney, Nephew to the Lord Leicester. He is presently sited here as Governor of this place, and commands much respect as a result. We departed the ship in a grand retinue numbering amongst us: Sir Robert Dudley The Lord Leicester, The Earle of Essex, The Lords Audley and North, Sir William Russell, Sir Thomas Sherley, Sir Philip Sydney, Sir Arthur Bassett (alongside of whom I was set), Sir Walter Waller, Sir Gervase Clifton, Charles Count Mansard, Sir John Norris, Sir Roger Williams, The Lord Willoughby, Sir William Pelham, together with many other officers and Colonel Morgan. As we passed between the tall, Dutch buildings the people thronged about us in a great press, cheering and waving and making a great show of their delight at our coming. Ofttimes the cry of "God Save the Queen" rang about us, well-learned by the population, their own tongue being much of a mystery to our ears. The further into the town we rode the larger still the crowd grew and the clamour and excitement doubled until our conversation was no longer discernible between us. Lord Leicester, at the head, held his arm aloft in salute, acknowledging the adoration of the people who undoubtedly beheld their saviour. Indeed, his figure represented no less than Her Majesty, Queen Elizabeth, as if she herself were present.

Once acquainted with the local gentry, I was quickly dispossessed of my comfort as we returned to our vessels which took us on to our first stop, a large island, the town of Middleburg.

Again the people pressed about us and shouted yet more, proclaiming our arrival as nought less than a gift from God. There was no mistaking their affiliation, as our entrance through the gate was marked by a sizeable English cross adorning its great mantle. I followed quietly, somewhat bemused by the noise, but proud to be a part of this honoured procession. I watched as Leicester was introduced to a party of finely dressed fellows by Sir Philip Sydney, gunfire sounding all around us, at first disconcerting, but then exhilarating as we learned of its signal to mark our presence. The people of this country take great pride in their artistry as, indeed, there was erected a glorious crystal castle, set on pearls, with silver castings all around it with all manner of wonderful beasts set therein. I was not sure of its significance, but I was assured its semblance was meant to depict the beneficence of our great Queen.

From thence we travelled to Dort, where again homage was paid through a magnificent inscription laid atop the gate, its Latin script enabling all to fully enjoy its content. And more ceremony was prepared.

We passed Brill, our original landing place, and took our fleet down a wide river to a small town called Delft. We were all much agreed that this pretty place afforded us some sense of familiarity, as it strikingly resembled a little London. One or two of our company were minded of their homes, and I too fell to thoughts of you both, my Elenor and my Henry. Although the excitement around us soon dispelled thoughts of sadness and had us once more celebrating our victory before yet we had even begun our task.

And so we came into the great port of Amsterdam. Much had we already heard of this town, but little could prepare us for the spectacle. How wondrous these people that they can yet tame the mighty beasts of the sea, for our very ships were towed by lines attached to great whales and others to progress us to the landing stage in the market place.

This is a world beyond anything I could have imagined. Never once did I ever believe I would live to see such things. God save the souls of those poor unfortunates who were not so lucky as I to take this course. For it is surely by their misfortune I have come to gain so much. The strangeness of this turn of events I cannot begin to comprehend. Is this the strength of our prayers? What task must I undertake to balance out the burden of my guilt?

If we had thought the sounds of the people before had made great noise then they were but whispering in comparison to what we heard here. Great fireworks and bonfires lit our way as our advance took us to greater luxury and adulation. Our time spent amongst these peoples makes us feel like princes, and Sir Robert Dudley is marked as a King.

We have been feasted and honoured thus for all these days now, but at last we have gained more permanent lodging at the Capital, The Hague. It was good to be assured that any return to the boats would be unlikely before our return to England. We took comfort in this and set to making the most of this time.

And thus I return to my first remark that if this be war then long may it continue. We drink and make merry most nights, and celebrate some more through the day. Leicester dispenses his hegemony from as noble a position as any man in Christendom. Those worthy fellows amongst us who are not entitled by right are suitably ennobled as each in turn wins favour in the Lord's eye. Thus you find me surfeited in good spirit at least, and I cannot pretend that it is not solely so, as the other spirit too does inhabit my body as much. Forgive my exuberance at this time, for I would wish you no less happiness, and hope to bring home this feeling with me on my return. I am assured such a date shall not be long in its coming. It seems that Parma will soon be despatched simpering back to Philip in Spain. The sooner the better my love, as I miss you both.

God's blessings to you and the safe watching of the Saints afforded to you both in your solitude.

Your most affectionate,

William.

*

January 2nd, 1586

To my wife Elenor, and my son Henry, great joy and felicitations I send to you, and God's benediction that you enjoy happiness and health in this year of Our Lord, 1586.

Already within such a short time you find my pen at paper to tell you of yet more news.

The most wondrous event has befallen us in this Holland. Some good few of us became aware of a wild rumour on the noon of yesterday, and forsure its truth has been borne out this very day.

We witnessed something of an official procession into our accommodation in the early hours of yester noon, with a party of Dutch notables entering announced by a shocking flourish of trumpets. They bore an air of some import, and strode with purpose toward where they knew they would be received, there they stood whilst having summoned Sir Robert to their midst.

They, in all their finery of fur and silver ornament, stood purposefully, but with some sense of agitation. When the Lord Leicester appeared before them, he came in no ceremonial state, but was attired much as he had come direct from his bed chamber.

They saluted him and calling him Excellency, a term he now acknowledges little, it suiting his position within the environs of this people, bade them adjourn to his private rooms wherein they might discuss the matter in hand.

We fell to conjecturing on the likely content of the conversation, all of us unsure as to what the outcome might be. The rattle of voices echoed from the walls. Some were of the opinion that already our time to encounter Parma was nigh, the thought of which caused some concern.

Soon enough the party left in good cheer and Leicester returned to his rooms with something of a serious countenance, but a lithe step nonetheless. We were bemused and none the wiser until the afternoon.

We were advised of more commotion and came too late to witness directly, but moreso were informed, that the English Ambassador, William Davison, was now in audience with Sir Robert, and also Henry Killigrew, and Bartholomew Clerk. Of the latter two I only learned that they were English resident members of the Dutch Council, I knew them not myself. Yet with William Davison, however, I already had an acquaintance.

I was some time once at Elizabeth's court, having been introduced by my cousin Charles. Then I felt very young and embarrassed at my shortcomings, as

I am sure most are at such an age. I was fortunate though in befriending another in similar circumstances. We were drawn to the same opportunities to partake in sport when we could, and found much comfort betwixt us. He was slighter than myself and perhaps even more shy, he was as able as I to wrestle when called on to so do during our gaming evenings, but his intellect and ability to debate with skill the politic of the day I had no match for. We corresponded for a short while, but until this day I had not seen him for nigh on six year.

The word went around during the day with various conjectures about Lord Leicester, but all now pointing to some form of honour. Certainly we were not party to any detail, nor could we ascertain for sure that we were indeed correct in our assumptions.

So it was not until the next day, this day, that I espied William Davison again. I hastened to him catching him quite off guard and startling him somewhat. Once we had remade our acquaintance I pressed him for the detail of what had passed. Fearing for his position he foreswore me to secrecy on the matter, as he considers his position to be one of trustworthiness, a virtue he holds in great esteem. I urged him still with vague promises that were of little necessity as I quickly became aware that there were more than I who already knew of the affair.

Not content with the greeting we have received of great feasts, votive tables, grand archways, and multitudes of cheering Hollanders, the Dutch Government have elected to offer Sir Robert Dudley the absolute government of all the Provinces. As Elizabeth's Governor General he has power over all their armies, Governments, revenue etceteras. He will become their ruler as much, at least, as William D'Aurange had been just maintaining, the same title too, that of Stadholder.

Naturally our minds fly to thoughts of our own positions now. We shall be in the direct service of a new royal figure. What grand titles shall we inherit then, and bring home with us?

All these things have us quite drunk with excitement. Although Sir Robert is not so much. He seems out of sorts with the prospect, although for what reason we cannot conceive. He conferred with those three on the subject and they have convinced him subsequently that it is very necessary, for all our sakes, that he accepts forthwith.

We most certainly will serve him well, and have no doubts that he is most suited to the title. I shall write more of this when I have a moment to do so, for I feel sure you will want to know what estate this will bring to our family. I must close now and join the merriment, we have much to celebrate.

Blessings, care and love to you both.

William

*

January 24th, 1586

My Wife Elenor, my Son Henry, blessings to you both in this auspicious time, God's care, and the health and happiness of the home that is the Country provided us by our Gracious Queen, Elizabeth.

It would seem that my enthusiasm has led me along a path of celebration in my letters, and yet all is not quite the happy estate I previously set out before. My excitement at Lord Leicester's good fortune has been dampened by subsequent events.

I took a visitor to my room late last night. None other than William Davison came, without my call this time. I proffered him a comfy seat and a flagon of ale, and yet his general demeanour forestalled this favour. I detected an agitation that caused him to move around the room uneasily, whilst he tried to find the words to convey what he would have me learn.

After some starting which faltered each time, I was finally able to command his attention with my original offer of hospitality. He seated quite close and leaned back as he quaffed his much needed draught. Refreshed he took in the air deeply and settled to his business.

At length it transpired that the great Lord was not so eager to claim his prize of these people. His hesitancy was sourced from a direction of the Queen of England Herself. It seems Elizabeth has already forbade him of taking any such title or name, if it be proffered on her behalf or no. Lord Leicester bore this acutely as his friendship as well as his honour avows him to a loyalty that sways him not from absolute obedience. Yet those around him, both Dutch and English, have convinced him to forsake his Royal oath and take on the mantle of this care for those in his keeping. He has not taken on this task easily, and has written a full account that his Queen might understand the reason for his departure from her express wish. With this justification he has notified the Estates General of his acceptance, and is due to be sworn into office on the morrow.

For sure I felt some sadness that Sir Robert should be so troubled, we know of his close allegiance to the Queen, yet equally I was heartened by the news at the conclusion that he is to continue with the role offered him. However, it transpired that we had not in fact reached the denouement.

No, William Davison has been secured for the task of delivering the letter from Dudley to our Queen directly, yet he is not at ease with the task. He is affeared of the Queen's wrath and has delayed his departure. He is set out for Brill now, but has informed me of his plans to rest there a while until the inclement weather betters. In truth, the weather is not so intolerant of sailing just now. It would seem that the reason is an excuse still for avoiding his task at hand. I fear that his conduct may have a damning effect on the situation. I ventured as much to the nervous Davison, but could not sway him from his worry, nor could I convince him to follow any path but the one he now treads. His fear of the Queen stays his position and delays his departure.

Other letters have been despatched to Burghley and Walsingham that they might intercede on the Lord's behalf, but unless the Queen is in receipt of Leicester's own words on the matter before she learns of his enoblement elsewhere, then I fear Davison's worries shall be rightly founded.

I have heard nothing further of his departure this day and as such have taken it upon myself to lay my concerns before Sir Arthur Bassett in order that the delay might be learned of in time. I know that I was spoken to in trust, and my ways have always been founded on an honourable premise, yet I cannot stand to and remain unspoken on the matter. In truth, I consider it my duty to protect the interests of my Commander and of my fellows.

I was comforted somewhat by a commendation by Sir Arthur for my astuteness. I am sworn to silence on the detail until such time as Sir Arthur might take control. I will wait and hope that this matter shall be resolved without further consequence. I pray so and shall inform you as it occurs.

With love and care, may God preserve you both in happiness and health.

William

*

February 15th, 1586

My dearest wife Elenor and my treasured son Henry, I send you love and blessings from this country, and hope that you are both well in spirit and body. I remain resolved to rejoin you with more news and information of what befalls us on this adventure, and thankful that I am in good health accordingly.

What light your letter to me has brought in this darkening space. The joy of its sight was my first impression, but since its reading, the imaginings that have been afforded me through your words has both fed and starved me. I am full with a happiness to hear your news, and yet I now hunger for that life I have left behind. Oh for my leafy Warwickshire now. Your sweetness and Henry's little noises would stand as rich as any gold or sundry treasures that could be offered in exchange. In truth it would be no exchange, I would forbear the wealth of all Christendom to be with you now.

I did so love the report of our Hen's time in the snows about the house. I could picture his pink cheeks and broad smile, and the true amazement that such play affords. We here do not have the pretty sight of snow, yet the cold is evident in ice on the waters. I venture that both he and you have not suffered any ill as a consequence of the cold and wet from this dalliance, apart from the numb toes and fingers that you undoubtedly warmed by the hall fireplace.

I was much pleased that Caroline had treated you so kindly. The Lady vexes me ofttimes, yet I feel sure that your visit with her to Leicester House was not done for any insincere reason. I understand from your muted expressions that perhaps the day was not all it might have been though. Certes, she will have wished to gain something by way of her standing, and perhaps you were, as you suggest, "a very nice piece of jewellery".

The news you impart on Lettice, however, does add wood to the hearth. It would appear that her intention to venture to the Low Countries is not without its consequence. I cannot help but remark on a marked similarity between her and dear Caroline. I can only guess that my sister will be joining the retinue of gentlewomen should this expedition pass as you have described. No doubt Lettice has seized on the reports of her husband's new found status, and her wish to come abroad as such with so great a court is her languishing in the role of a new Royal with all the ceremony of that station.

In itself, I might be so bold as to suggest, it has drawn some humour out of those who perceive it so. However, the circumstances could not be less propitious. There is no doubting that the report of her intention has vexed the Queen immeasurably. The rumour is that our Sovereign is displeased beyond redress that another Lady of her realm should have placed herself in such esteem as to overshadow that which is rightly and solely hers. Lord knows we have met such displeasure before betwixt the cousins, Lettice seems bent on redoubling the soreness that marked her life with Essex as much as with Leicester, as if that hurt has not been felt already[3]. On its own this would be a trivial matter but for the tragedy unfolding in this house.

In my previous letter I wrote of William Davison's delay in delivering the personal entreaty to the Queen from Sir Robert. My words to Sir Arthur on the matter actioned an immediate instruction from Lord Leicester to Davison at the port. I am glad to say he then made haste to depart upon his task. In that time he has since returned, and I have spent some hours in his company listening to what tragedy has befallen our great commander. For sure, the Queen, as Davison rightly feared, was furious at what had passed.

Although I had betrayed the trust of Will Davison, it seems he has sought some refuge in our friendship. He has not earned favour in Leicester's court by his earlier selfish notions. For my part I have sympathy with his actions as I am sure, under the same circumstances, I might have done similarly.

On arriving in England he had made haste directly to Walsingham, his colleague for whom he is principal secretary[4]. Immediately he was warned that it was unlikely that the Queen would grant him audience as she was so displeased toward Leicester. Walsingham entreated with the Queen and she allowed Davison to come before her. He shook still as he recounted his futile attempts to speak and present his cause. All the while she raged, not allowing him the space to make a true speech. Furthermore, despite his several entreaties that she might take to her the letter in his possession, she refused it flat, and dismissed him without ceremony. He was desolate in his failure and had resolved himself never to go before her again, but Walsingham took him aside.

144

He explained how she had writ a letter to Leicester and one other to the Estates General of the Netherlands, together with instructions therein. The letter to Sir Robert berated him most severely for having contemptuously defied her express commands. He was commanded to comply with the instructions sent with the letter without excuse at risk of losing more, most likely his very title. That letter to the Estates made clear their actions flew in the face of that which she had declared publicly before the world. She had expressed no wish of sovereignty nor allegiance, her actions were intended to be a simple act of assistance in their time of desperate need. They were instructed to remove the office bestowed on Leicester in order that he might remain loyal to his Sovereign. She insisted that she believed their cause to be a true and worthy one, yet her honour she held in greater esteem.

Walsingham, in full knowledge of the letters' contents, had pleaded with her not to send them until such time as she had listened with Davison, as their content could have dire consequence. Despite not allowing Davison to represent in full she felt satisfied that she had fulfilled the request, and so dispatched the letters with Sir Thomas Heneage the following day.

Forgive me if the detail of this intrigue should lead to a tedious script my dear, but its content could be of more than a passing interest to you. If Caroline were to hear the import of this affair then perhaps she might influence the intentions of Lettice, and thereby lessen the Queen's much vexed temperament. I have heard that Sir Philip Sydney has written to his Father-in-Law on the matter hoping that he might dissuade Lettice from her visit. However, I am too aware that Walsingham is much busied with the meat of the matter to concern himself with tempering the excesses of Lady Leicester.

Sadly, Sir Philip's letter lost us great entertainment as his messenger, Will' S.[5], has kept us merry for many nights with his wit and great eloquence in story-telling.

As Heneage set sail with the said letters, Walsingham calmed William Davison somewhat and convinced him of the absolute necessity that he must not give in to his desolation. A sleepless night followed as he strode about his chamber, coining new phrases and arguments that might sway her to be more gentle and understanding of his submission.

When he represented himself on that day he was weak with exhaustion and found himself unable to recall the mastery of his dissertation so carefully planned through the night. Instead, as he struggled under her continued tirade of railing against Leicester, he fell to tears. Through salty eyes he pleaded that she might at least take the missive in his hand from Sir Robert. The pathetic sight before her melted her heart for a moment, enough for her to take the letter, break the seal and note something of its opening. She faltered in her mood and thrust the paper into her pocket. Calling on Burghley she sent word to Heneage that the letter to the Estates be withheld, but Sir Robert was to learn the full extent of her displeasure. The trouble that had been sparked by William's tardiness he does at least appear to have assuaged somewhat by his resolve.

There is much discord about the place due to these events. What shall occur as a result is still unclear. Leicester has still fulfilled his role in the meanwhile as Governor of these Provinces and that too has had consequence. Taxes have been raised, and some martial law instigated restricting certain occupation of the inhabitants. As such we find the people about us to be less than content. It would seem their jubilation at our coming has fast evaporated, and in its stead there now resides a general dislike for their formerly perceived saviours. We are now much an invader of sort. We have lost the kindness of the general population which causes us some discomfort. We are now much more minded to our own business, which in turn has focused our minds on the preparedness that should be our concern. Planning is afoot to move on various towns about us that are consequent to Parma's movements. Let us hope that the confidence of the united provincial government remains with us in order that we can at least be wholly successful in our military objective.

Heed my earlier words, my dear Elenor, in that conversation with Caroline might play some part in this resolve.

I remain your loving and caring husband, and father.
William

*

February 18th, 1586

Dearest Elenor, dearest Henry, may the blessings of heaven rain upon you, may all the days bring happiness and joy, may this letter bring some comfort in our parting, and may the hour come soon when we are again together under God's sun.

A most unhappy time has settled upon us. Daily it seems I find William Davison seeking solace in my company. Much as I am heartened by his holding my comfort in such esteem, it is yet tedious to listen to the repetition of his folly. Truth told I have little sympathy for I am very much aware of the hurt caused by his slackness in taking to heart his master's task. Yet I learn more of the comings and goings surrounding this upset through his daily discourse.

It is plain for all to see the sorry and disturbed demeanour of our great General. He is late taken to hanging his head as does a young child caught out in some wrong doing, at pain to redress the wrong, and yet unable to carry the burden of the hurt caused by his action. It would seem he has to hand the letter some days brought to him by Thomas Heneage, direct from our Queen. The content is passed on and somewhat diluted in its exactness, but the tenor is one of extreme displeasure.

Despite Davison's earlier indications, Heneage informed Leicester of his obligation to deliver the Queen's letter to the Estates. We are still somewhat bemused by Heneage's zeal as there can be no doubting of the damage a letter writ to the Dutch

Authority which might bear a semblance to Leicester's own.

That moment has been saved a while whilst Sir Thomas Sherley is sent with a further pleading missive from Sir Robert. His path crossed that of the returning Davison, and we await his return in that we might learn of the success or otherwise of his presentation. Sherley's manner is altogether much differing from the arguments and constructive rhetoric that was the content of William Davison's approach. Indeed, he has a mastery of the flatterer's art. A course perhaps more suited to the court than the field. I have entrusted Davison to interrogate him directly on his return.

I must presume that you and my dear sister are amongst those councillors who proved successful in deterring the Lady Leicester from her proposed sojourn. There has been no further talk of her coming nor preparation that would indicate anything to welcome the grand retinue that was to mark her visit. This at least we are grateful for. Inasmuch as you played a part I send you many thanks and to Caroline also.

Forgive my impetuous need to write so often with detail of this sorry matter, but I feel an absolute necessity to maintain a watchful eye. I do not profess that I can determine an outcome by my actions, yet I am at least empowered to make some attempt to carry on in the way that my first report of Davison's inaction has effected something of this.

I am reminded somewhat of Caroline's inquisitive nature in my demeanour, and hope that I shall not be labelled as such, like some interfering snipe-cheek. I trust that the enquiries I make relate to a greater good than does the colour and fashion of Lady Butterworth's new attire.

I shall write soon as I become aware of further intrigue. Please make your prayer heard at church and beg that God in his greatness will resolve this upset in order that my time here may be short and successful.

Love as ever to you both,

William

*

28th February, 1586

Dearest Elenor & Henry,

How the tides of time and fortune wash upon our shores leaving the flotsam and jetsam of our wrecked lives.

Already Sherley has returned and spoken of his news. In turn Davison has related the fullness of it to me. The Queen gave him shrift, as she had with her previous messenger. A new letter was still not a temptation to her sweeter nature. Sherley soft spoke to her, yet her heart remained hardened. Some days he remained till he should chance upon her again at leisure in her garden. Quickly he spoke of Leicester's need for a physician. He has previously suffered an illness that had been attended to by Goodrowse, Elizabeth's own physician. Intimating there could be a possibility that Sir Robert might just fall to the malady again due to his woeful state, he asked of her that she might once more send the physician to his aid. Through this deceit he found yet the soft spot that still resides within the Queen's heart.

Sir Thomas then, with the help of Hatton, a sweet of Elizabeth's, induced her to accept the letter. As before, once taken it was secreted with all haste, to be perused in solitude. Sherley is much pleased by his success, and yet William and I rank it indifferent from his own notable success. Truth, his was the first and rightly the more fraught.

We have news that Sir Walter Raleigh has since writ. Wherein he states that the Queen is much moved to endear Dudley once more. He is again her 'Sweet Robin'. The difference is plain for all to see. An excitement has returned once more. There is talk again rather more military than domestic. Still more correspondence is winged toward our sovereign, but the release in temperament that is apparent in Leicester has lent us all that same fortunate gate.
Something rather more sinister and unsavoury though has tainted the lightened air. I have news through a different source that a letter arrived in London of a much more formal nature than the fawnings of our sad General. Elizabeth has received an apology detailing the misapprehension that led to this unfortunate incident. The letter is a

state reply from the Estates General of the Netherlands. The absolute content of the letter I am not privy to, yet by its very nature it has to be a reply to the letter Heneage was carrying. I am not aware that the arrangement to hold off delivery to the Dutch Authority was ever revoked. All were of the opinion that it should be kept from them by whatever means, as the content therein could only serve to entirely undermine our position and understanding in this land.

No one seems to have made question of Heneage, his intentions or his actions. While we can be assured that the Queen will restore her faith in the campaign, we have no such assurance that any such undertaking will be forthcoming from the Dutch. On this score I have much concern. There is little doubt, as I mentioned in another letter, that the people here are much less accepting of us in general. There must be a worry that the Authority will be somewhat disillusioned by this unseemly show of discontent. They have contracted to support our endeavours with sums that are intended to match those coming likewise from our Sovereign's coffers. It would seem to me that perhaps their inclination might be to hold off those promises as their confidence is so weakened. I have not spoke of these things other than in long exchange in private quarters. The official tenor is so much in relief of seeing the balance to home being restored that little thought is given to such other matters. Time will be our teacher. Perhaps when these peoples see our uplifted spirits, and when we begin on the field to rid them of this Spanish plague, then surely all thoughts of discord will vanish to the ghosts of yesterday.

As for myself, the cold is still intense here and does not cause invitation to venture far from the hearth I am fortunate to share. I feel at a loss for recreation, my thoughts are turning to our mission more. This space has led my mind to grasp something of the actuality of the scenes we played out before we left. The practice in the safety of our homeland is so un-like the prospect before us. Then we moved models around maps scratched in the earth, we talked of strategy, sent men hither and thither with no real aim. Our weapons were tried, but in their shortcom-ings we found humour. There can be little laughter in facing those who would cause us harm. When real lives come face to a stranger who can wield his weapon with accuracy and devastating effect, what then?

These thoughts have me long without sleep. My mind is tortured by images of you and Henry safe where I should be. I blame none but myself. My zealous actions were prompted only by a belief that F.T. was full of excitement and energy. I know that you tried to sway me otherwise many a time, and I heard those words, true, yet I listened not. Your young wisdom would have served me well. I was spared the hangman's noose, that I felt fair, I had no vehement belief that should have borne me there, but this punishment, rightly so, must be for not heeding your caring words. The icy cold winds that blow across the flat land have cut through my flesh and torn the arrogance from my heart. All that is left is a soft corner reserved for you both. In its gentility it yet holds strong against all elements that might set hard against it. It is fenced in by my re-solve, and warmed by your love. At its centre is the essence of a son of whom I shall no doubt be most proud. I am planning much for my return. Not a day shall pass without my tending to him. We two shall share in our little creation, nurturing him and watching him grow, undoubtedly to greatness. We shall make sure he does not visit the follies of his father.

I shall write soon, and perhaps by then we shall have made some progress to ending this unholy thing. May God in his goodness defend you from all bad that may pass, and may he bring you sweet joys through the musings and growing of our fine Henry.

Much love

William

*

10th March, 1586

To my dear wife, Elenor, and my most precious son, Henry, God's blessings and the care of all the saints I send to you this day.

The news is, in the general, good, which tempers somewhat the vehemence of the discordant Dutch, and enlivens the stagnancy of spirit that has o'er taken our group.
Long have we sat through exchanges which are winged with all speed back and forth betwixt these two places. Yet the tedium of their faltering delivery and nervous reply has led us to depths of de-

spondency. Every letter occasions a short-lived respite as the air lightens with each. Still we sit and wait, and talk little of our duty.

We remain, for the most, amongst ourselves, having little wish to venture forth to inhabit foreign streets. All supplies are met by courier and despatch, their complaining at the ill-treatment afforded them in their task continues to grow apace.

There is little doubt that the fare with which they return comes at a greater price with each journey they make. While the Dutch merchants grow fat at our expense, our own resources dwindle daily. There is little sign yet of the monies promised us to replenish our increasing shortfall. If this were to continue we should be hard pushed to feed those in our charge, a constant worry.

We are at pains to avoid our oft-spoke requests becoming mere bleatings, such a thing would lose us much respect and lessen our status. Such shortcomings could prove most dangerous in these volatile times. We must preserve our roles if we are to be successful in our overall objective.

But now Leicester is in receipt of a formal letter of instruction issuing him with the entitlement, Lieutenant-General of the Queen of England's Forces, in place of Absolute Governor. He retains the same office and stature, the Queen no longer expecting him to relinquish that which has already been bestowed by the Dutch authority.

Yet, by my reckoning, if I am right about Heneage, it is come too late. The Dutch are suspicious and do worry, they have lost a great consideration for their new Governor-General. The discord that has run through the veins of these past months has already set the malady into this broken body.

Forsure, Sir Robert is a new man. Tempered in his excesses, but keen to return to the matter at hand. He has directives that concern our finances, and has a need for a summing up of what expenditure has been passed and where. This has caused us to act as though we are clerks in order that a coherence might be made. I know not of a single man who has managed to present a matching tally for any item or occasion. There is not, nor has there ever been, a record keeping of this nature. It would seem we simply cannot comply with this request, even though the Queen herself is in need of these figurings. I believe that we should find ourselves in a grave position if the consequences of our inability cause her to address the matter of finance contrary to our needs. But what then are we to do? We are meant to come here as an army, not as a school.

I see little contentment amongst the ranks at foraging for what little sustenance is availed them, and I can find no relief in our failing to quantify what has already been spent here. Our expedition was originally affirmed with One hundred and twenty six thousand pounds for each year from England's coffers, which was then to be matched by a doubling from the Dutch. Naught but a trickle has been forthcoming from either side as yet, and a wage has not been paid to a single man this year.

We are now added to in number, a swelling in part due to the attachment of Sir John Norris who is late come from Antwerp with his contingent of men. Also we have now amongst us those Dutch soldiers who would wish to stand beside our force. This at least might afford us some sympathy with those who provision us, without extorting what little remains of our reserve. Yet Dudley is apt to turn his buoyant nature in churlish argument against these good men, perhaps in sport or just through ill-judgement, I cannot tell.

The good news I speak of is thus much quieted. With the Lord's regained position is growing his arrogance daily. There can be little good to be had from berating the burghers and lawyers about us, as he does.

I grow more unhappy with each passing hour. I curse those whose actions took me from you to this dark place. I have no wish other than to return to the family that is rightly mine. I lack a care for those in my charge, which serves me not well. I can enthuse little for the cause. Perhaps the rumours amongst the Dutch have a truth, in that our Queen may consider a treaty with Parma and Spain, perhaps then the Dutch shall need us no longer and we should be spared the bleakness of this moment.

How I pray for my return to you. May God hear my penitent prayer, and grant me that favour. Keep me true in your heart, Elenor, and hasten my return with your own supplications. The hours are long and empty without you.

Your loving Husband,

William

*

23rd April, 1586

My dear Elenor, my dear Henry, may good fortune prevail for you as it has us this day, and may the light of God's face continue to shine upon us all. Forgive my tardy hand, it is not for want of writing to you, the time for doing so has not been allowed this past month, and the itch to do so has driven me to madness at times.

At last we have news this day that is most welcome. Our military might has been proven, and the course has been set and marked by the success of which I must now tell you. I am privy to news concerning our first real encounter in these parts. Although the making of it is not at the hand of mine own Company, but it is to be celebrated and enjoyed by all. These past months since our arrival a detachment of men have been engaged in a business at a place, by name, Grave. The town is some distance east of here and lies on the banks of the river Meuse. What with all that has passed these recent weeks we have been little concerned with the news, coming infrequently with its regard until now.

By and by the rule of our engagement has been closely adhered to, and the party have been entirely busy with the intricate planning necessary to attempt to supply the people of Grave. But all the time Parma's men have held fast and have besieged those within the town walls.

Now to make quite clear I must re-emphasise that rule of which I speak. It is a term of our Queen's fair-minded and gracious consideration that we are not to be driven to make war upon those invaders. Indeed, it is our very objective that ensures we do nought but defend the good Dutch peoples, giving what assistance we can to aid them in their struggle. This does not mean we do not make use of the martial training we have undertaken, e'en so, from the talk and preparation I witness around me it is clear that the interpretation of the letter will be fairly flexed.

Parma's long held siege of Grave had caused some disquiet amongst the Dutch, and his ability to contain the eight hundred or so valiant defenders of the town had held some four months already. Sir John Norris and Count Hohenlo had been despatched with three thousand men, no less, to breach the containment. No sooner had they begun to esconce themselves nearby than the Spanish hurled themselves at the newly arrived troops. The surprise was such that they had no choice but to retrench further off. Only a short time after Sir John re-assembled his foot regiment and returned the consideration. A savage battle ensued on the river bank. It seems the English pike is not something the Spanish soldier is meet to encounter. The prowess of the troop under this honoured command broke through Parma's lines. No less than seven of the Spanish officers were killed in the run of things. Sir John Norris himself received a hurt, but it is reported to be of little consequence, thank the Lord. This land is cursed with waterways and is met with the sea often it seems. To contain it great walls of earth are constructed to break the flow and conserve the earth. It was by clever use of this that the day was won. Count Hohenlo saw the benefit and cut a swathe through the largest bank causing the waters to rush in apace. This caused some distraction to the Spanish and allowed Hohenlo to send boats straight to the town laden with victuals and men. By this means the town has indeed been provisioned for at least a nine month.

The success has fired great excitement, and it is sure we shall march some more and put Spain's great force to shame. News of the victory has spread throughout, and the fear amongst the Spanish soldiers is apparent as I shall tell you.

We are moving east to bring relief and stability to the central part of this country. It is dominated by a network of rivers, most notably the Rhein, the Waal and the Meuse. Once we have control of these waterways there can be little space left for the Spanish to control, and their forces will be dismantled and despatched back to Philip with puppy-tails between their legs.

It is now St. George's Day. How fitting then that Sir Robert has dictate that this be the day set aside to celebrate this great victory. The air is sweet with merriment and high spirit. We can feel again the headiness that marked our arrival. It was just a matter of time, and that time is come. Confidence has returned and with it a strength to our limbs to spur us on.

We are in Viroche for this glad time, and already we are leaving the feasting tables for our maps and strategy. We are to travel down through the area between the rivers. Due to its land being surrounded by these watercourses it is properly called an island, although it is of some great size to be named so. We hear that the celebrations have reached London, and all expect many more great victories to follow. What a joy will it be for young Henry to espy his father in our victory parade when we are returned. Forsure, I will regale him with my tales through his ages until he will come to know them all by rote, and will be driven to distraction by their over-telling.

My letters to you recounting these great times will remain constant my love, and yet I feel that the times will be rarer when I can write what has occurred. Therefore do not linger for the messenger to bring that word, but go about your business without concern. Regard it instead a pleasant surprise when my letters do arrive, and fix in your mind the day when it shall be myself that is winged to your hand, and not just the scrapings of a quill on paper.

Much love and care to you both in these good times for the day is at hand.

William

*

14th May, 1586

My dear Elenor and dear Henry, love and light remain with you this day as it eludes me in this dark hour.

The blackest of days. Such a sorrow has turned the aspect of my last letter to the content of this.

We did indeed make a steady progress through the Betow, the river island of which I spoke. The Spanish soldiers were quick to disperse before us offering very little by way of resistance or battle. Our spirits were high and our demeanour as such was not to be reckoned with. The area was quickly turned over to us and rid of the invading army. It seemed that the victory at Grave had paved our way so that progress was a simple continuation of that time.

We eventually built a great sconce near the Toll House, thus ensuring that the land remained in our control and free from any of Parma's troops. Certes, it was clear that we should progress with the same ease throughout the land and thus return it to the rightful heirs.

The news has come to us of which I now write. It seems that Parma was not for giving up Grave. He has re-built his beaten army and set to the town once more. The beleaguered garrison left in the place to preserve the free status of the townspeople was a very little match for the enormity of the Spanish General and his troops. The Governor of the town, a man called Van Hemart, perhaps tired by all the previous assault, prepared not for a defence. Instead he gave up the town almost immediately into Parma's hands. For, in truth, he was reported a formidable adversary, and the terms were such that the garrison was allowed to leave without encounter or reprisal.

The thunder of Lord Leicester's vehemence was a match for that of Parma's great re-entry into Grave. I have yet to see such fury again in any other. He could not conceive of how Van Hemart could have so easily given up the poor townsfolk into the hands of the Prince of Parma. With it went not just the town of Grave but the whole belief in Leicester that had previously been so strong, so admired and had served us so well. Those who were responsible for this turn around have argued strong to explain the terrible force that they were faced with. The Spanish ordinance has long been feared by the Dutch, but to try and present true argument to Sir Robert was to try and extinguish the sun's fiery heart. He would have none of it. He is still not to be reckoned with, and all avoid his gaze as it were the plague itself. We are in accordance with his ire and feel the despondency that is come with the capitulation. However, none are of the opinion that his action this day is right in any sense.

For example to those who might do likewise, at noon he ordered and despatched Hemart by hanging. We none of us can contemplate the reason for this without fearing a mistake of our own might allow us the same fate now.

There can be none who think that this was the just thing to do. Nor that the intention was prompted by anything other than a vengeful want rather than necessity. Living under his command we do not see the blame as his, and yet his premise is that indeed this is how it will be perceived. In each instance it is surely never right to direct blame in such a demonstrative and unfair act.

What then for the future now? Our enthusiasm is blown to the winds, and our once joyous march forward is now a faltering penury. We shall follow orders to the letter and forsure we will not give in lightly, but then neither would we have done so before. Not through fear, but rather through pride and belief in our endeavours. How much this changes our lives we cannot know. The worst for me is that I had grown to see all around me through the coloured glass of the window that was our just cause. Now that window is shattered, and the sight before me is yet again a dismal scene.

The sea seems wide at this moment presenting a gap so vast between us that there can be little to keep myself from giving in to it all. I cannot tell you of the sadness that dwells within me, and the deep yearning to be home this minute. I pray you keep my memory well and have as much as a half of the love I have for you.

Yours in truth,

William

*

2nd June, 1586

Dearest Elenor and Henry my son, better times I wish to you both, heartfelt love is conveyed to you along with this message.

My business with this war is much increased since last I wrote. The elderly frame of Sir Arthur Bassett was not designed much for activity on the field, and thus I am re-assigned to ride beside my Lord Willoughby.

I find in his countenance a pleasing air, and his courage is undoubted. There is a strength to be had from his words and his actions are much recounted in the camps. I feel most fortunate to be in his command, and have ranged across much of the land hereabouts as we progress his strategies. He is made Governor of Bergen-up-Zome, a pretty town near the sea. It being close by Vlissingen I am heartened by a sense of closeness to my return, it being our point of entry those months ago. I would actually be so bold as to state that there is much relief to be enjoyed from no longer being in the company of our Great General. Although I would hope that this word should not fall into the hands of any who might convey such sentiment thus as I fear it would do me much ill.

I am also honoured to be numbered amongst those who now frequent the company of Sir Philip Sydney. Such a gentle soul as he seems most displaced in these warring places, and yet his ingenuity in strategy is well spoken of, and his fervour for battle unmistakable. I am somewhat at peace here with these folk, and am settled to the task more so. Evening time is oft lightened by entertainment of a gentle nature. We have even had Sir Philip read to us from his own writing, which is most pleasant.

By contrast we have moved around this country with stealth and cunning. The Lord Willoughby is much skilled at device and trickery by way of his planning. This very day we were laid in hiding, as we were party to some intelligence of the enemy's movements. There was no sight of a single man as a column of carts came into our midst. They were attended by a sizeable contingent of Spanish footmen, all of whom where ignorant of our presence. Not until the party was near past did the alarm go up. The shock to the enemy was such that there was scarcely a battle. Instead, their disorder quickly subdued them to our command. The wagons were contained full of corn, this being the provision for the various Spanish garrisons hereabouts.

Not only does this serve us well by way of our notable success in the eye of our Lord Leicester, but we are also provisioned well by the proceeds. The corn will certainly be most gratefully received by all as still we find ourselves much in need of a steady food supply. This at least will lessen the number of men who leave the ranks daily. The growing number of runagates is fast making it difficult to plan with any accuracy as the count of soldiers diminish. While it is punishable by death, who yet can blame them for their desertion. They themselves must feel deserted by those whose duty it is to look to their needs. Whilst we are still not furnished with the means to feed them there is little we can do to right the problem, their pay is meagre when it is forthcoming, and for those whose employment is by way of release from the jails then there can be little difference in their lives. The very clothes about them hang as rags from their malnourished bodies, and fall in tatters from them. Thank God we at least are come to warmer times, else these conditions would be apt to kill a greater number than the marauding

Spanish. Amongst ourselves our victory today will feed our tales, imagination and fervour as well as our bodies for some time yet.

The news from Leicester's camp also holds great promise, and yet not so much achievement. The Prince of Parma, now emboldened by his success at Grave, went into Gelderland, a little further east of Grave. There he encamped before the city of Venlo. A notable pair of Leicester's men, Sir Roger Williams and one Skenk, a Frislander, decided to attempt an entry into the city. They broke through the enemy's camp choosing the cover of midnight to aid their secrecy. Their presence was noticed and some fierce fighting ensued. A number of the Spanish soldiers fell to their courageous hands, and they were said to have reached as far as the Prince's own tent. However, their brave efforts were not enough to effect the breach and they were driven back.

Their exceptional valour has gained them notice and commendation, but unfortunately, shortly after, Parma took the city for himself. Much though is swinging in our favour these days, and we have hope yet of securing peace and returning to our shores and loved ones.

With love and care for you both,

William
8th July, 1586

The days have passed by in number too many, but by my noticing, very few. Our involvement in so much is led to our every waking hour taken up with one thing or yet another. Believe it that no day passes without thought of you and Henry, but truth the calendar moves with such pace that it scarce feels like a week since last I wrote, though I know from the marks that it has yet been a whole month.

As I write my body aches and I am inclined to sleep more than any other thing. We have just left the west to range with Sir William Pelham, General of the English Horse, on our way back to the east, and Leicester.

We carry with us smiles upon our faces, for victory has been ours again. We were led to an assault on a town, Axel, near Ternous in Flandria. What a sight we were to behold. At the lead of it was Sir Philip Sydney himself, and by his side none other than the Count Maurice, rightful son of the Prince D'Aurange, a man of great stature. I will admit to a pride as we rode along, my place, now usual, beside the Lord Willoughby. The attack was planned with much secrecy, surprise was our companion.

Thirty eight men were charged with the first part. They were all chosen for their prowess in the water as it was their task to make an entry by swimming the ditch and then scaling the rough walls. No mean feat. Once inside they threw open the gates and we entered in at a great pace. We were about half of our men within the place before the alarm brought the soldiers to arms. Our entry was so great that they were slain most before realising what was upon them. At the count there were some six hundred of the enemy, most of who perished in the onslaught.

Sir Philip, spurred by this triumph, took a considerable force onto a place by name, Graveling. We remained to bring some order to Axel and establish provision, for this town is hard done by for lack of victual. Some days on Sir Philip returned to recount the adventure. It seems not all was as had been expected. There was an indication from spies that had made lie to the fact that the town would fall to him through help from within. The raid was made under cover of night, but the reports were in fact the contrivance of the Governor, a man named La Motte. He had lain in wait and slew some few of the men immediately, but the mistake realised, Sir Philip made his retreat in haste and saved both himself and most of his men.

Meantime now we continue across Brabantia, inclined to sortie by the direction of Sir William Pelham. His wont is to make many and quick incursions into small places to increase the flow of provision, and to disrupt the foothold of small Spanish outposts that interlace the countryside abouts. Ofttimes we spend our time in transit without much objective, and I am almost beginning to look with favour at re-joining the more stable encampments of Leicester's own. However, news still finds its way to us that stalls that good thought again.

Sad to say the air hangs heavy there as we hear he has, by example, hanged a number of deserting men. Some two hundred were returned having made the coasts. The certain unrest will not easily be assuaged without proper provision. There is a worry that they will turn yet on their General. Heaven help us. Are we to fight two enemies then in one land?

The Spanish seem to have an endless supply of men who have seeped into each and every crevice of this waterlogged country. Can there ever be a halt to them? Indeed there must be else we shall never be allowed back to the safety of our hearths. My mind, at least, is there, and my eye lights upon your fair face sat therein that comforting scene. A reality no doubt in the offing as we progress on our course. A day that will bring with it some surprise I am sure as I must believe my son to be quite grown by now, yet in my mind he is still my sweet, little Hen.

Much love,

William

*

14th August, 1586
Dearest Elenor,

Forgive my brevity with which I return yet more news of our movements. The hour is late and much is afoot. I can scarce keep abreast of all the machinations that contrive to have us in one place no longer than a few hours. How I long for Baddesley at these times. I would dearly love to be stretched out in the grass staring into the heavens, besides our little fish pool, lost in the midst of some fanciful conversation. Much as we did when we were younger. Do you recall those times still? Ralph and Charles, Caroline and yourself. Little did we know in those lost days what would be our lot in this age. I often wonder what became of dear Ralph. I am at a loss to know what kept him from us for so long. There was no sign to be found that should cause him so to miss the day we were wed, and no word since. I should surely wish him beside me now, how much easier would this all be if it were shared so. I am of a mind that it would indeed be nought more than the games we used to play, indeed, I am sure we vested more hurt on each other through those times than ever I have experienced here. I shall make it my duty to retrieve his soul from whichever dark corner he has it secreted the moment I return.

Now we are back encamped with Leicester at Duisborg. It was not our intention to be in this place, but we came to it through Sir Robert's ingenuity. After Venlo, Parma directed his course to Berchen. Therein lay Colonel Morgan and twelve hundred English soldiers. The siege was of the greatest imaginable. The intention had been to relieve Morgan and so deny Parma yet again. However, it seems the enemy's camp was deeply entrenched and fortified so, presenting a formidable obstacle. Added to which we were small in number and poorly provisioned too. The land is open and with no place of retreat it would have been foolhardy to attempt any such action. Instead we turned toward Diusborg and besieged it. We had only to use our ordinance, such that it is, to breach the wall, than they came forth to negotiate a peaceful settlement. This then will serve them well. It has meant little by way of injury, and our promptness has achieved the very purpose in that it will draw Parma from Berchen. We have heard word since though that Parma has in fact anticipated a similar move beyond, and is advancing past us, north to Zutphen. It is our contention that the move to Diusborg so caught him unable to leave Berchen in time, that he is not content to risk our moving onto Zutphen.

Thus I can surmise that we shall not be long in this place. Zutphen is some distance hence, and I sense that it will be some time yet again before I am able to recount what befalls us at the next step.

I shall spend my sleeping hours enwrapped in sweet dreams of you and Henry, out amongst the daises beside our pool as I would wish to be. My minds eye shall see him chase the dragonflies and watch you caring for his safety, bathed in the sunlight of an English summer. Play then and watch for my return, as soon I surely shall.

Much love and fond memories,

William

*

23rd September, 1586

The Lady Ferrers, and Henry Ferrers. I greet you not in the manner with which I should wish to, but instead am directed to inform you thus.

I enclose herein a letter in the hand of William Ferrers, Lord Ferrers of Groby. The content I have noted not. Indeed, the enclosure remains intact, and it is hastened here to you as it is found upon his person.

I shall make attempt at a summary of the events that led to this unfortunate place, and beg your attendance upon these words in that you might gain some succour by their intention.

We had made some movement toward the much fortified town of Zutphen. As we happened upon its margins we espied a column of Spaniards who were occupied with conveying supplies sent thither by the Prince of Parma. Having ascertained the extent of their route we contrived to ensnare them on a subsequent journey.

The morning of 22nd September dawned with a thick fog about us, which served our purpose well. William was by my side as was his usual place, and I was much comforted by this knowledge. I instructed him to remain so throughout as it was like to be a bloody skirmish.

The onset of the assault began with two volleys of shot from our well-placed firearms, thus despatching many of the enemy in an instance and causing much confusion too. We strode in side by side as a cornet of horses thundered through to the aid of the faltering convoy. Their lead was George Cressier who had cut behind me and bore down at speed directly. A call from William, who was a pace or two back, gave me right warning, which in turn led to my unseating Cressier, and so took him prisoner.

That shout was the last I heard from young William. The fog continued to shroud so much of the field, and little could be made of it. The action proved decisive, and William's shout undoubtedly led to my safety and the success in all.

Not until this very morning was his pale body brought to me. There was something of a smile upon his face, no sign of pain, and the paper herein was clutched still at his hand.

I trust you find some comfort in my recount as a braver, nor more nobler man I would yet meet. I shall dearly miss his light spirit, and his stories ofttimes kept us late with merriment.

Please accept my deepest sympathies and my most heartfelt sorrow.

The Lord Willoughby

My Dearest, dearest Elenor,

I must speak to you this instant of a pain deep within my heart. My strength eludes me as I scrape these few words, so forgive my childish scrawl. As I rest to write, a strong sunlight falls across my paper, and yet I am at a loss to feel its caressing warmth. A cold courses through my veins that I am unable to cause to cease. I am certain that a simple caress from your sweet hands would dispel its icy grip. And yet I am impelled to fill these pages with a recount of what befell me yester noon. I was, much as I am now, still paining from the wound I have suffered at the hands of the barbarous Spanish. Worse though, I was taken by a terrible thirst that tore at my very being. Just when I felt I could endure it no longer a retinue of Leicester's men came by. I noted their serious demeanour and became aware of a poor soul in their midst bleeding most sorely from a terrible leg wound. As they drew near I recognised the figure to be that of none other than Sir Philip Sidney. I was shocked to see such a noble figure humbled so. As such I found myself embarrassed by my mannerless staring. To add to my uncomfortable state I was also at the heart of a conversation. This great man halted the procession. Then, whilst keeping his eye fixed on me, gave information to one of those in his charge. At this the young soldier dismounted and headed for my place. In his hand he held a water skin which he proffered me and bade me drink. As I did so he spoke further, explaining that the noble Lord had considered my need to be greater than his and so subsequently gave up his life sustaining vital to aid me. I was entirely without speech as they continued solemnly on their way. Indeed, I have a certainty that I

would not be writing this to you now had it not been for his kindness. But for that moment of light my darkness would be unbearable. I count the days and the hours when I am returned to you. To hold my dear Elly and to kiss your sweet lips is all that I crave. To be back in the safety of your warm bosom is the one hope that sustains me. Know then that I love you forever. Share what you can of that love with dear Henry. Keep my love safe within you until my return.
Your ever-loving husband

William.

Book 4

Catalina Menéndez de Aviles
San Agustin, Florida, 1582

D on Diego de Velasco, *Don Diego de Velas-co!* How I hate that name. Now here again it rang loud to taunt and drag the pain of the past about me. Not this time the shame and despair though, not this time. They had seen fit to bestow upon me my father's title, even if my woman's body denied me the power to govern. I was still Adelentado, and this was one order de Velasco was not going to enjoy complying with. But comply he must, and so would I enjoy it the more.

It seems the English and the French are both content to enslave the local population, or the peoples of the Dark Continent, but we are above such God-forsaken barbarism. All, perhaps, except for men like Velasco. His very eyes are mean, and reflect in their design disdain for those he enchants. His mottled skin and untidy beard lend him a wretched-ness that deny him the ability to appear with any sense of presentation. His large, hunched shoulders add to his ill demeanour marking him as particularly unsavoury purely by sight alone.

When I learned of Maria's attachment to him I was shocked beyond any cognisance. It was sometime later as the betrayal melted into acceptance, months after their marriage, that I realised just how ugly he was. By then it was far too late to lend question to my half-sister's choice of husband.

It is known to everyone throughout all of La Florida just how much hatred I have for this man. His name never leaves my lips but through clenched teeth. This day I breezed airily through San Agustin toward the garrison wherein my quarry lay. The rumours of the English Lord had fired the air in one lightning strike so quickly had we learned of Don Diego's prize. Not known for his subtlety in conversational etiquette, his boasting had echoed off every tavern wall.

Now I was determined in my stride, and made my announcement through the sheer presence I thrust upon the sleepy soldier who dozed in the stagnant heat of the ante-room to Velasco's lair. My singular lack of words did not lessen the man's haste to apologise incoherently for his dishevelled state and inattentiveness. He rose quickly and without care, causing a number of items to fall about him. While still muttering and arranging his uniform he left to discover Velasco from within.

An irate voice barked at some distance, no doubt adding to the distraught state of the messenger. I was not to wait long.

"Doña Catalina! How very pleasant to see you. To what do I owe this undoubted pleasure?"

No matter he tried to act pleasant, sincerely or not, I was not inclined to greet him with any form of amiability. His skin glistened with the humid heat, his hair was matted and in disarray. Beads of sweat sat atop his lip, a tempting sup for the wretched insects that buzzed about him. I made no step toward him, nor yet invited any greeting.

"Don Diego de Velasco. I do not come here for any reason other than a specific business. I trust you will attend to a little matter I wish to exact this afternoon?"

"My dear Sister. Surely you will allow me to fetch wine to my table? We can drink a little and talk of family matters."

With feigned gentility he motioned to guide me through into his dark ante-room. His step toward me elicited an equally opposite movement from myself, and the gloom of the office did little to disguise my fleeting grimace.

"Don Diego. You will not refer to me as your sister. I do not consider that bastard to belong to our family, and as a consequence do not begin to believe you can impose yourself as such."

His face darkened a little, and he slunk to a seat without consideration for my presence. He betrayed not any care for my rebuke, and looked to me with an air of nonchalance. Thumbing a few pages that lay before him he asked what I might want of him.

"I understand that you have within your care a certain English Lord."
He stopped his trawl through the papers and leant back in the chair. How I loathed to be in this dirty

room alone with him. My feelings of distaste choked me, making it quite difficult to persuade my sensibility to remain constant. I wanted to fly at him and scratch out his little black eyes that peered so disgustingly at me now. Yet I betrayed nothing of this. I had no wish to allow him the satisfaction of witnessing the feelings I might have as consequence of his treachery and incompetence.

He replied with mocking, feigned innocence, "I'm not sure I know to whom you refer, Señora. There are many English men held at my request, as in fact there are many who die likewise. Yet you think that I might remember one, or know to whom you are referring when it is only rumoured so anyway."

"Give me a guard immediately that I might make my own inspection of your gaols. If you cannot help me then I shall find him myself."

Pausing only momentarily a sickly smile lingered on his lips.

"Rodríguez!"

The shout elicited an immediate return of the soldier who had previously inhabited the seat. He had made some attempt to bring further order to his uniform, and stood stiffly awaiting his instruction. Without turning to look, but maintaining a fixed stare upon my eyes, Velasco addressed the soldier at his side.

"Take Señora Miranda to the cells and allow her to inspect those occupants within."

Thus I left those oppressive quarters, turning my back on the unmoved figure, to follow the poor fellow whose life, no doubt, was not enhanced by being in the service of this tyrannical officer.

If I had thought the little office uncomfortable then these cells were to prove it a luxury. The smell was unbearable, and the consequential insects that filled the humid air added further misery to the unhappy place. It was still hot outside, but within this confinement the air held an uncomfortable, sticky heat all of its own.

I now understood why de Velasco found some wry satisfaction in having me escorted here. The huddled figures were indiscernible from each other. Certainly no clue was to be found that would indicate anything of the proud figure of an English Lord. They were rather more apt to bring to mind captive animals huddled together in wretched fear than any human semblance.

I enquired of the soldier at my side if he was aware of the nobleman's location. His eyes darted nervously about him, despite Velasco being far removed from us now, he had no wish to betray his commander by the slightest inclination towards helping me. He shrugged his shoulders, stared at the ground and said nothing.

Comfort and good pay I knew was not the lot of these men at arms. Their general discomfort admittedly was added to somewhat by the repressive command of de Velasco, and to a degree this went some way to obscuring any personal want, replacing it instead by a purposeful need to obey and avoid.

That is, *obey* every command without err thereby *avoiding* unnecessary and unwarranted punishment. However, I knew this to be something of a chink in the armour of any such as he. The one thing guaranteed to dissuade the soldier from his mute duty was the sight of gold. Albeit that his first reaction was not immediate, I did not hesitate in doubling the offer and instantly secured a change in his demeanour. With more furtive glances about us, a swift movement secreted the bribe in an instant. Still no words were exchanged, nor further gesture, instead his role of accompaniment became, almost imperceptibly, one of leading. We moved apace to a room further within, perhaps an aspect of the gaol I might have missed altogether had it not been for my guide.

The room was small and unlit. I was not aware of any content apart from the layer of dirty straw covering the floor. My eyes peered through the gloom, struggling to adjust. Unable to make out anything I ventured a call into the stillness. A clink of metal on stone from within signalled the soldier with me was true to his direction. Then a voice sounded, gentle but weary and tentative.

When we were young our father had prided himself on our education. As a great explorer he had always considered the versatility of language to be paramount to life. Thus we had spent good hours gaining a knowledge of French, English and Italian as well as the classics of Greece and Rome. I was surprised at the nervous tremble that came to my throat as I ventured to plunder the depths of my childhood learning.

"Hello. Who is there?" I spoke quietly for I felt no need to make a great announcement at this stage. A shuffle accompanied a stronger voice in reply, and something of a shadow rose before me.

"You speak English?"

I was not about to betray any signs of weakness. I took a step backward and stood taller, summoning up a more authoritative manner.

"Indeed I do. I must presume that you are an English prisoner then. Pray, tell me your name Sir."

"Ralph Ellerker of Risby, my Lady. From England, but not intended for this place. What a joy it is to hear again my home tongue. What angel then are you to be found in this God-forsaken place?"

I decided against continuing with my conversation. I was not sure of my strengths in spoken English, and felt that I was stepping past a sensible point of etiquette whilst still in the presence of the soldier called Rodríguez. I turned purposefully away from the captive, and demanded of the guard that he should obtain the immediate release of the prisoner to me. The original fear returned to his eyes. He was unsure that the authority had ever been granted during the exchange within the office, nor that anything should or could induce him to make that decision independently. His hesitation annoyed me.

"Sir, I am Doña Catalina Menéndez de Aviles. I know that you are aware of that, but you are also aware that I am still Adelantado. Don Diego de Velasco may be your commanding officer, but he in

186

turn answers to my dictate. I have full authority over this prisoner and as such I am commanding you to release him this instant."

There was neither room for discussion, nor any doubt in the mind of the poor soldier as he scurried off to return immediately with the confused gaoler.

Confused or not, here was a man in no doubt as to my authority. He did not hesitate to remove the bonds that held the, as yet, unknown face shackled to the rear wall. Just as quickly he shuffled away, uttering not a single word, just glad to be gone from those who might wish to delay him with yet more onerous tasks.

A sense of expectation hung in the air about. Once the scrape of the worn, carelessly dragged gaoler's shoes had faded, a silence pervaded that space, adding further to the tension. Truly, I had no real foundation upon which to build any construct of the man I had just released to my care. I knew not his manner, nor yet his general demeanour. I had learned no report as to his age, his disposition or physical state of health. As such my actions could be conceived as completely foolhardy and rash, which indeed they most likely were. Yet I was driven by a desire fuelled in part by arrogant revenge, and, additionally, by curiosity.

Rodríguez, in turn, stood frozen by that same expectation. His actions could perhaps be judged to be even more lacking in care. Not that I had allowed him much choice in his decision. He may have had some slight advantage in whatever previous knowledge he had of the prisoner, but I was in his charge, and his predicament was to stand by as I awaited whatever would be the consequence of my resolve. In truth my confident air belied the fear that lurked beneath, the fear of that uncertainty.

The silence of the moment seemed to be enjoyed even by the buzzing insects who were themselves silent with anticipation. The humid air sank down heavily on the shoulders of responsibility. Determined to allay the fear and substantiate my claim I ventured another word. Not wishing to opinion anything other than total authority I stole the silence:

"Come hither poor soul."

A sight overstated, but the drama of the compassion in the command would, I felt, lend me an air of beneficence in contrast to the careless and hurtful treatment that had been the lot of the captive to date.

My carefully contrived plans, my confident air, my authoritative manner, all were dispelled in an instant as I unwittingly allowed a small yet audible gasp to utter from my lips as my prize was lit by the day upon his exit from the gloom. He was unaccustomed to the strong light that made him shield his eyes accordingly; I was nonetheless moved by his appearance.

A tall, young man, I would estimate to be in his third decade, stood before me. His shoulders were broad and of good structure. His captivity in the intense heat and humidity of the cell had stained his attire and left him dirty and unkempt. Despite this he carried himself with brave dignity and displayed the confidence of his station. Once I was party to his unshielded eyes I could sense a kindness that reflected instant respect.

"My good Lady. I must apologise for how I appear before you. In truth I have not been able to avail myself of anything with which I might make repair to my poor state and semblage, neither to myself nor my clothes which have suffered greatly in the fray.

"There is much I would ask of you as I have been able to ascertain very little of my situation in this time. Yet forgive me if I ask but one question. Are you come to inform me of my fate or might it be presumptuous of me to hope that a change in my circumstance is in prospect?"

I could sense such a plea in the tone of his request I felt a need to answer to put him at ease. His eloquent speech and gentle manner betrayed little urgency; indeed, he stood tall before me with hardly a falter despite his obvious poor health, no doubt the result of his enforced restriction. I felt great sympathy for him, and yet I was careful not to allow my emotion to distract me from my mission. I could not let slip any impropriety that might either be witnessed by the soldier still at my side, nor lead this young man to note any weakness in me. Were I to make such a foolish mistake at this point it would serve only to deny me a certain control and position that would be essential to the success of my concept.

"Sir, I have a news that may lighten your spirit, but in turn will serve only to subdue that same sensibility. I am indeed come to take you from this dirty hole that has been your home these past days. I am to remove you to my service. If you undertake to come with me to this purpose I can offer you very little more than a meagre ration and a workload that will occupy your every waking hour. We are not possessed of much by way of comfort in this land. The life is hard, and at times fearful. However, after having witnessed your existence here I sense that the choice to remain would be something of a folly, and perhaps an unlikely outcome of our meeting. First I must warn you this."

I had not hesitated in my words, and I further resolved to stamp my authority by way of a strongly spoken and defiant instruction. He had wavered a little as his strength failed him, but not wishing to spare room for discussion that might give chance to any other understanding of the relationship I was about to suggest, I continued.

"If you undertake to accompany me from this place you must give me your word that you will make no attempt to elude my custody. It would serve you badly. If you are hapless enough to think that you might avoid further capture and certain punishment at the hand of your present captor, then I can assure you that there would be an absolute certainty the local population of indigenous peoples would be upon you before the sun reaches the horizon. If the thought of having your skin removed by means of a sea-shell scraped upon it whilst you are tied helpless to a tree does not appeal to you then I suggest you heed my words and submit to my order."

I saw no sign that might indicate my words, strong as they were, had elicited any reaction. No hint of fear, nor yet one of defiance. Indeed, the very qualities that might suggest the stoic nature of an Englishman were portrayed in the elegant display of perception without emotion. Under the circumstances of the exchange I was moved by this ability. Renowned, reported or told of in romantic tales for sure, but to meet it face on, to feel it as I now did, made for a strange and discomforting experience within myself. I felt discomfort for I wished not to be subject to a feeling so personal, and yet the source and the depth at which it penetrated my body took me by surprise and brought me to an awkward silence. Already my wish to maintain a position of authority was in some doubt. Not once had I ever doubted my superiority over such as he. Indeed, I revelled in a reputation that saw my shell as impenetrable and complete. Despite this my thoughtful acts had kept me in the hearts of those who cared for me, and who had consequently benefited by me over the years. A balance I guarded well. Never once had I weakened in my resolve to maintain the position I had so long coveted as the legacy of my wonderful father.

Now here was man, a usurper, a prisoner, a wretch of no means taking something of my sensibility that no other living soul had touched before. Now should I falter? Was my ignoble motivation to be my downfall? In one foul stroke I could hit back at the hated de Velasco, but was I equally denying everything I had staked my life upon?

The questions rained down upon me carrying my insensible mind in every direction. In that lingering moment I stole yet further into the now opened, gentle, grey eyes of this unknown face that had so moved me. The stirrings were not dispelled, I was undoubtedly further from being able to gain a stronger footing, instead I found myself still held in that unmoving, unspoken place. I sought for, and gained, something of my father's strength coming from within, coursing through my head in the certainty that my choice was indeed a bad one. My motivation was wrong, my body spoke as loud in its inexplicable reaction. Now as I made to explain that I had been hasty and perhaps mistaken all along, I felt a twinge of guilt that once more caused me to hesitate. This time a hesitation that could be read. I leaned slightly with a sympathy that could only precurse a retraction of my immediate offer.

"My Lady. Lest you be in any doubt as to my intention, I can but proffer the true word of an English man. A word that has been vouchsafed by many of good birth, and one which would truthfully be considered good by both Kings and Queens from each corner of our world. 'Tis true that these climes are foreign to me, and the sensibilities of your nation are beyond my knowledge, but my assurance will remain true no matter the differences that might exist betwixt us."

Such was his bearing, the tone of his e'er so weary voice, and the manner of his eloquent delivery that I was immediately persuaded against the oft bided advice from within my head. For this brief moment I was guided by a deeper, stronger source. A depth within my soul, beyond even my heart, led me unswerving to the realisation that I could not deny this man now. His home was with me, not in this unholy, filthy hole. Not with the infamous beast who had already stolen so much of my life. If I had felt weakness at all then I was now drawing something new from my ward. Here before me stood the essence of a truth and strength that I had known before. Not through some bed or false flattery, not in the fawning of a fresh-faced youth who might presume to stand guard by me. Instead from the same spring that I held so dearly within me. The unerring, faultless life that was my father.

The father of my sisters, my brother, the father of the land we now hold so dear, the father of the truths on which we base our lives, the father of a new nation, my most dear and wonderful friend. Now again I sensed something of the majesty he held at his fingertips, bound in the simple affirmation from this poor devil before me.

I was unnerved, encouraged, dissuaded, strengthened and filled with fear, but my resolve was complete. I presented my back in one swift turn, denying any expression that might betray something of what I had just felt.

"Follow me then, and heed my every step."

And so we left behind the stink, the heat, and the silent Rodríguez.

I remained sensible of my prize only through the shuffling behind me of the tired feet that dragged through the dry dust. Not the steps of the noble man whose word I had just accepted, but those of a man whose existence had been demoted to that of an animal. A man for whom I now provided the

merest hint of salvation, but the absolute of a continued confinement. The possibilities trickled
through my head like spring water over shingle.
Not complete in their reality, but rather running together to form an ever-changing picture of uncertainty.

The footsteps continued, unspoken and tired, then at
welcome rest for the entirety of the carriage journey
and voyage north to Santa Elena.

The ensuing days remained uneventful for the most. I had no wish to demean my position by acting as a guide to my acquisition, so I left that responsibility to my faithful old friend Juan Ramírez de Contreras. It was Juan who had taken me to his care when I had remained in La Florida at a time when the consequence of my being there was not of my choosing, but that of ill fortune.

Juan had been a friend of the family from when I was very small. In actuality I do not recall a time when his kindly face was not a part of the familiar faces that made up my home life. It was luck that had him reside in Santa Elena before Hernando and I took up residence ourselves. He had travelled with my father for the most part of the early expeditions, his hunting ability and skill at native languages ensuring him a valuable place at the Adelantado's side. While San Agustin was established he played a considerable role in its foundation and also that of the various outposts. When my father first took the land from the French over twenty years ago, the native population had proved an essential tool to enable that quest. Juan had such a way with foreign tongues that the barriers of communication had quickly fallen, and thus the local knowledge became a part of the Spanish armoury. His considerable hunting skills enabled the settlers to be fed reasonably well too, particularly as the women and children and non-fighting men needed to be catered for before any settlement could be properly established. Later, he had married María de Junco in San Agustin, but they decided to move up to Santa Elena shortly after my father's death. Here he built her the house that was to remind her so much of her home in Ribadesella. It was most remarkable for its sun terrace, a feature of the sunny clime she remembered so fondly, and also for the beautiful flower garden with fruit trees each side around which pecked a few chickens, a measure of the love he would express. Life for me then seemed all the more normal for his being there.

He had an ability to turn his hand to any business, and so retained and oversaw all knowledge of every aspect of our settling and sustenance. I never realised just how valuable his kindness and care were until the sad days mourning our father. It was Juan's steadying words and organisation that bore us all through that desperate time, taking upon himself the responsibility of managing the funeral, our affairs, and our broken hearts. I had always expected my brother and sisters to have the responsibility that I as the youngest lacked, and yet it was not so.

It had been some years since we had all been together, only I had remained with my father in the Americas. My belief was that the stable nature of my brother and sisters gave them an air of sensibility. Although my adventurous zest for life that had seemingly borne away anything sensible had been partly redeemed by my marriage to Hernando, to me it was just as reckless. I felt in all honesty that it simply lent me a way of making safe my wish to remain in La Florida. As such I still retained the belief that I was viewed as nothing more than the wild young child I had always been through our early years in Aviles.

My brother, Juan, had something of my need for adventure, but he channelled it through a vocation at sea. His death had been a serious blow to me as I had always found much joy in regaling him with our tales of how each had met with danger and intrigue. In reality my stories paled into insignificance beside his, but I liked to believe both our lives held the same level of intrigue and danger. The years of court life, civility, and social standing had done nothing to enrich the lives of Aña and her husband Pedro de Valdes. María had, in my mind, completely lost all hope of living when she left to join the convent. None of us saw the world through the same eyes, and thus the time was one of constant argument about formal minutiae and ceremony rather than the fond remembrance and graceful farewell that I had wished for more than anything. I was left in no doubt that had it not been for Juan Ramírez very little would have been accomplished at all. I was a party to the greatest incompetence amongst my family, and as a consequence I resolved to remain in my father's land and, with the capable help of Juan, carry on his good work. I certainly had no wish to join the idiot ranks of my sisters.

As time passed my indignation mellowed somewhat, allowing me to integrate within my family's social circles. The pressure to leave the Godforsaken and barbarous coast of the Americas tore me both ways. I still held a strong allegiance to my father's work and life, but family cannot be denied, nor yet the need to secure a wholesome marriage. I knew that no man could ever match up to my father and thus I had spent little time in male company. When eventually Aña had forced me to partner Hernando de Miranda at a dance in Coruña I had been quite taken aback to find myself actually attracted to him. Little did I know that his insatiable pursuit of sport and other things out of court would prove his downfall. I enjoyed his lively spirit and was happy to be matched with someone who at least appeared to enjoy life beyond the boring social confines that my sister and her husband held so sacred. When he gained the post of Governor at Santa Elena I could not believe my good fortune and was more than happy to acquiesce to his request that I become his wife.

When the dark days of Hernando's departure had left me desolate, it was the weathered, craggy face of our kindly old Juan that had brought me consolation. Thus I had come to rely on him more than ever in the running of the estate, a responsibility he relished. Now the years were beginning to show unkindly in his joints. Much as he tried to disguise his lessening ability I could not deny this man the time to slow down which he richly deserved. The timely incidence of winning a score against Diego and fulfilling this need was something that I was very grateful for. I only hoped that my new worker would fit the criteria and not just bring more trouble than he might solve. For now I could carry on with my own business while leaving the task of introduction and instruction in the capable hands of Juan.

It was a fresh January morning when I ventured to meet again with the 'English Lord'. Mornings at that time of the year were often quite bitter, but rarely did the sun fail to shine and bring its caressing warmth to keep us in good spirit and heart. As I walked I recalled the merriment that now seemed so distant which had marked the days of the Christmas that had just passed, and thought on the lack of that joyous time for him. Stuck in the confinement of a San Agustin cell I wondered if he had even been sensible of the feast, or if he was conscious at all what part of the year we were now in. I crossed the courtyard sensing a tension that I was at pains to dispel. No longer could I recall the face of the prisoner I had freed, nor yet any other feature that I had noted those days before. I knew him to be tall. I remembered thinking that he had something of a noble disposition, even his eyes had made their mark in my memory, but I knew not the colour. I could not even hear an echo of the tenor of his voice in my mind. All manner of doubt came crashing to the fore. Perhaps his weakened state had portrayed him in a kindly light, disguising his real manner. Could I salvage anything from the meeting that would give me an insight before I saw him again? I could not even be sure of his name. Certainly not a name I had heard before, nor one that I could ascribe to any other person to aid a remembrance of it. I now was more afraid of the consequence of my action than ever whilst I had been at the fort in San Agustin. This man was entirely my responsibility. There was no guard to ensure my safety, nor any redress should I simply wish to change my mind. Juan had reported well of him though; I felt some security in that. The old man would never let me down, certainly he would not allow me to come into any danger. He had said that the new man's strength and health had returned rapidly after the first day or so, thus he was able to employ him substantially, and there had been no indication that any refusal to work or lack of enthusiasm had so far proved evident.

I hesitated momentarily before entering the small thatched building wherein I expected to find the resting English man at that hour. A deep breath took me through the doorway. For all that I had prepared myself it took me a moment to comprehend the emptiness and to realise that there was nobody presently around. In one sense I was relieved and yet quite vexed too for having reached such a climax of expectation only to have it evaporate so pathetically. At least I felt I could safely pry into the keeping of the room to perhaps ascertain something of the gentleman's nature. I could not spy a thing out of place, indeed the tidiness that was apparent amongst so little still gave an air of someone who cared much about appearance and civility.

My heart shot to my mouth like a child caught at some mischief as someone entered through the door behind me. I swung around portraying nothing but guilt at something I had not done, but I was made sensible by the relief at seeing Juan standing before me.

"Forgive me Catalina, I did not mean to surprise you so, nor intrude without warning. I had no indication of your presence here and made only to recover something for young Ralph."

Ralph, of course. That was his name. With the sheer mention of it so much returned of that first encounter. Now I remembered those grey eyes the worries were all dispelled in an instant.

"Juan, please do not rebuke yourself. You were not to know I was here. I came in search of our young man as I thought it time I met with him again and ask after his well being in this place. I had expected him to be here, but I suppose you have him busy at some endeavour?"

"Indeed Señora. You recall we had want of a new well for the house that was Anton the tailor's. These past days I have employed him in its construction. This morning we are already seating the barrels to line the hole and were not inclined to halt until such time as they were in place and sealed.

"I can't tell you how much I am warmed to him. He is most certainly no stranger to hard work. It was all I could do to rest him when first he arrived. His enthusiasm serves him well both for the favour it gains him and for the health that it has returned to his bones. Rarely have I witnessed such a fine combination of physical ability, ardour, and comprehension. For sure you have made a shrewd choice in attaining him."

With a certain aplomb I acknowledged the success of the decision. As ever, whether through contrivance or fortune, Juan had managed to restore my confidence and had placed me in a position of security from where I could now greet my responsibility with the correct manner and authority.

"Lead on Juan, I am keen to make some acquaintance with young Ralph."

Stepping past me briefly to reach out a light shirt, with a gracious smile Juan bade me exit before leading me to the place where the work was in progress.

As we approached the site of the new well little could be seen of the figure endeavouring to construct the interior of the pit. Because of the sandy nature of the earth there was hardly any permanence in a structure simply dug into the ground. In order to introduce cleanliness and a useful life to our wells, barrels without top or bottom were set atop of each other in order to line the hole once excavated. This was never an easy operation as the barrels were heavy and unwieldy until in place. Their diameter necessitated that they be set by one man only as they were lowered in. Dropping them could lead to damage, and yet their weight coupled with the constriction of their position made it difficult not to do so. Luckily the level at which the water was to be found was very near the surface in this land, as such usually only two or three barrels were needed to accomplish the job. Once in place and sealed they proved to be a very efficient and safe way of maintaining the essential water supply, the importance of such a commodity was never taken for granted.

"Ralph, we have a visitor!"

Juan's cry betrayed something of a camaraderie that existed already between the two. The casual air of his salutation went further still to put me at my ease.

Instantly a figure pushed up athletically from the mouth of the well, depositing himself on the edge from whence he sprang to his feet and stood waiting. I was not sure whether he was wetter from the seepage into the space below or from the earnest endeavour that he was engaged in causing him to perspire profusely. It was clear that Juan had gone for a cleaner, lighter shirt to replace that of the heavier, now soaked jerkin that had been necessary in the cold of the earlier hours. It was proffered to Ralph, who though clearly uncomfortable, was not about to change into it in front of his new mistress.

He was wet, muddy, untidy and somewhat fatigued from working so hard, yet for all that he managed to demonstrate the full grace of his station with an elegant bow.

"My Lady."

Still those kindly eyes glowed out beyond the ignominy of his dishevelled state, causing a thrill to course through my body.

"I am told much good of your work here already. I trust you find your surroundings a little more comfortable than your previous tenure?"

"In truth, my Lady, I have little to complain of. Señor Ramirez here has been nothing short of a friend to me since my arrival. He has already introduced me to much about the place, and has occupied me with tasks and instruction, all of which I find of interest."

I could sense a struggle building within my head, trying to cling on to the safety of some formality whilst watching the honest sweat trickle down his handsome face to trace a line over the beginnings of a broad, bronzed chest before disappearing beneath the confines of his clinging tunic.

"I am sure there is much to be gained from your employ here, and am glad to know that you already have some sense of it. In time I hope you will begin to look upon this place as your home and not a place of servitude. You can have no better teacher than Señor Ramírez to guide you. I trust you will accord him the utmost respect no less for the great man that he is than because I consider him one of my closest friends."

"You can be assured that I wish to do no other thing than to please you. I shall always be grateful to you for the service you afforded me in my release, and saving me from whatever wretched fate awaited me. May I be so bold as to ask that I might be excused as I wish to make some repair to my poor state?"

I looked to the clean shirt that he held in front of him, aware that I had not turned my gaze from him. Immediately I gave him permission to withdraw and change his apparel. In an effort to appear mindful of something other than the retreating figure of Ralph, I made my way to the edge of the excavation and peered into it, all the while needing to return to my own solitude that I might find some space to explore my thoughts and feelings. What good it might do me making an inspection was obviously too perverse, but the pretext at least gave me room to continue a sensible conversation with Juan.

Once back in the house I again returned to a state of chastisement at my weakness. I had not gone to the trouble of taking enslaved help only to create an amusement for myself. I was well known for my ability to organise and to be diligent in my travail. Since Hernando I had not looked at another man let alone been moved to show or experience any kind of emotion. This surely was just the thrill of something exotic. I had enjoyed the command over de Velasco, and also had a very clear understanding of the need to have someone assist Juan in his age, my plans were not about to gain another ingredient as part of their maintenance.

At least I now knew it was 'Ralph', not just some stranger, or my prize Englishman. I was much improved in my demeanour with the knowledge that not only had he proved to be a capable worker, but was enthusiastic too, a rare combination. How often is the excitement tempered by an inability to achieve, or with skill comes an arrogant disregard for motivation or obedience. So at least I could take some pride in my decision, and perhaps those who thought me a little rash or vengeful would now see my action in a differing light. But could I see it that way too? Was I a fool to my own emotion?

My days were kept occupied with much of the general matter that kept Santa Elena on a level. I still played something of an active role in the government of our people by assisting Hernando's brother, Gutierre, in the social aspects of his care. I had never wished to relinquish what was rightfully my place, not for my own sake, but for the memory of my dear husband. For all that I berated my sister in her complete subjection to society, etiquette and formality, this was indeed my responsibility, and few envied the position.

Civilisation could not be discounted for lack of creature comfort, even in this far outpost. I had long counted the native population a lost cause where this was concerned of course. I had, with others, been of the belief that, as rational human beings, they too could share in the civilities that our nation afforded us in this modern age. Whilst some of us were quick to express our contempt at the savage who was not able to grasp nor understand the finer qualities of gracious living, I learnt quickly that they, in fact, possessed an etiquette of their own, equating it to their rational understanding of the rules that enabled them to co-exist with their surroundings, and to cope with limited resources. This was surely often in conflict with our own views, but then who are we to question them as such. They are naturally predisposed to achieve only a limited success with their lives, but through no fault of their own.

When I was not organising events, or providing a guidance for our residents, my hours were oft directed to nursing those who were in need of medical attention. This had grown out of a need to provide care for our injured and sick soldiers when my father was alive. Then I had seen no reason why they should remain in the uncaring confines of the barracks. It was my belief other soldiers should not be subjected to the constant sight of their injured comrades. This not only caused discomfort by acting as a reminder of the possible fate that awaited anyone of them at times of conflict, but also created an unhealthy atmosphere in which the ill stood little chance of recovering.

My answer to this had been to suggest to my father that we give over some part of our own substantial residence to the nursing of these unfortunate individuals. There was little my father would ever object to if I requested it, thus he acquiesced with little argument, and I had set about installing a few necessaries in order to facilitate their care. Upon my return to Santa Elena, I found it easy to continue with my little hospital, particularly as Gutierre had established his larger residence some way out leaving me to my original home. By chance the need had diminished substantially, incursions by unhappy natives were few, and thus the majority of my patients were only those injured through careless misadventure, or some occasional malady. In all honesty, although I had retained the Governor's house, it was of no comparison to that of my father's in San Agustin. There I had room to command all manner of comfort for my patients, now I only had the use of a single room on the upper floor with space enough to house two beds if necessary. Lord knows what would happen if we were to experience something of the earlier plagues that had beset the people when first my father settled here.

Despite my initial fascination for Ralph, I had very little interaction with him over the first few months of his time with us. I would receive favourable reports from Juan as to the competence of his works, these I would inspect from time to time, and so would exchange a few pleasant sentences by way of encouragement and gratitude. I still knew very little about him, but neither did I feel much need to extract any information. I was just grateful that my judgement had been correct, I now had a competent worker Juan could rely on to aid him at his tasks.

There is a distinct similarity between this land and our own Spain, the sun shines most of the time, and the air wraps itself around you in a familiar manner. However, the surrounding reaches are decidedly inhospitable and lend little encouragement to venture much into the land. This I missed. As a child I had wandered for days alone through the countryside of our home, exploring and getting lost just to follow the moon home, or causing my brother Juan to come find me and take me home to the chastisement of my mother. Hereabouts there lurked all manner of strange, unknown and dangerous beasts. The solid earth often gave way to waterlogged land wherein poisonous snakes and more frightening, predatory creatures lay in wait. My father talked often of times when he and his men walked chest deep through such waters, thick with biting insects and unknown terrors below. It was not unusual at these times to witness the loss of a man, dragged to an unmentionable death by some gargantuan monster whose lair had been passed undetected. I was in awe of such bravery as these men showed.

Beyond the Santa Elena boundaries something of these dangers could be found, yet only rarely did the townsfolk fall victim to anything. The occasional encounter with natives was more often a cause of concern or adventurous tale rather than misfortune. They still represented something of a danger, but much had been done to quell the earlier unrest that had caused us so much upset. We now found ourselves in a position whereby the business of our settlement became our single focus. With now four hundred in our population, the food we grew and the seasonal aspects that affected its agriculture were of great import. Attempts were made to grow many things, but for the most it was only corn, squash, melons, barley and grapes. The latter, of course, at the very least afforded us an opportunity to imbibe good home-made wine. Our animal husbandry met with limited success, but we did have stocks of hogs, some cattle, and chickens. In addition we gave our time over to architecture, and good water supply, social structure and other meaningful aspects of a civilised existence. In deference to fighting for survival it was a life more suited to our well-being and growth, all of which we could be sure would go to prove the greatness of our nation.

So it was the report came to me of a new patient destined for my care. The recent heavy rains had caught us much by surprise, but it was also cause for an invasion of reptiles, confused by the abundance of surface water no doubt. A worker had not been aware of his sharing a space with one such as this, and had suffered a venomous bite. We had a few remedies to hand, but for the most it was simply a matter of whether the body was stronger than the poison. Thus all we could do was give rest, water and care during the period.

I prepared the bed apace and awaited his arrival. I cannot even pretend that I was not shaken by the sight of the victim. He was shaking and perspiring profusely, and was mostly incoherent in his discourse. This I had been witness to many times before, but what I was not prepared for was that my patient was Ralph Ellerker.

My immediate personal concern was not out of place to those who were witness; however, my stupefaction as I stood motionless for some moments could so easily have been the cause of some question. I rallied myself and set about taking the patient into my care. My initial shock I was at pains to cover by an unusually brusque manner, this resulted in a hasty exit of those who had escorted him. How I greeted the space that was afforded me upon their exit was quite extraordinary. Once again I found myself humbled by the simple presence of this man. My head was far from filled with the matter at hand which was necessarily of import to his well being. Instead I raced about my sensibility in an attempt to gain a hold on the torrent of emotion that had taken me away so. My nursing had a perfect system that ran on a well-rehearsed route that gave no rise to question, mistake or hesitation. I never questioned the list, just enacted the role and worked through with the utmost efficiency. With his broken body lying prostrate before me, the sweat soaked shirt marking the line of his body, his care solely in my hands, I lost every thread to my coherence. I stole myself from his side, walked to the still open door, breathed in the good air, fastened the latch, turned and made fast beside my patient. Normality was reined back in, and I began my oft-practised regime.

Wet rags were applied to his fevered brow, dry to his shivering body in an attempt to staunch the profusion of sweat. Fresh water was to hand, and I made some effort to raise his head whilst taking the cup to his dry lips. Some portion of the life-giving liquid made its way in, despite a good majority of it running down his neck to the mass of muscle that filled his well worked chest glistening with the dew of his illness, thus serving only to wet more the cloths set there designed to keep him dry. In response to the cool in his mouth he made an attempt to speak. Although I hushed him some, he managed some words of gratitude. He made no resort to our Spanish tongue as had been his practise of recent, but I sensed he had little sense of his whereabouts.

His words trickled out insensibly for some time as I sat beside him, dabbing at his perspiring body. Whilst my English was certainly of a good level, it was difficult to discern anything of which he spoke. A number of times he uttered what I believed must be a name. It gave comfort when my gentle voice soothed his agitation in return. For the most he spent the hours without consciousness. This gave me some room to be about other business, yet I found myself sat beside him still, musing on the truth of this figure. I resolved that this should be a time when I would ask more of him and perhaps ascertain something of his background. Once he regained a good awake state I could comfortably talk to him without fear of appearing interrogative or prying. With this thought I sat in some comfort and pondered on the many questions I would ask of him. How to phrase them correctly though without fear of disgrace, and how not to appear as if I was asking too personal a question whilst still achieving a full grasp of the story he must have.

He came to with a start, but not with any lucidity. Far from a coherent state, his eyes rolled, and he summoned up what strength remained in him to flail his arms about himself. He seemed angry at some-one. I trusted it were not I, and took hold of both his wrists. I had no option but to lay my weight up-on him in order to quell his unordered motion. Were I not to do so I felt he might injure his self, or even deprive himself of the energy he required to survive this ordeal. As I fought his contortions it occurred to me he may not survive the poison. I might not ever know more about him, he could die without my questions having been answered, his life ended here, in obscurity. My determination was all the more spurred on to hold him still. Perhaps I could impart something of my own strength to his weak body in order that I might aid his recovery and save him from oblivion.

In time his body became still again. His breath was shallow and I was still sensible to the beating of his heart. Although he was now motionless I remained lying across him. For the one part I was much fa-tigued after the battle, but for the greater part I took pleasure in my being there. I drank in his heavy odour. Albeit dank from the fever, it still stirred my inner self in a way I felt was beyond my control. Should someone be witness to this unashamed liber-ty I would struggle to explain myself. For now there was but Ralph and I, joined against a common enemy, a foe which stood to part us before even I might know this heavenly creature.

My wits were shaken to reality by a deep, soft-spoken voice. I woke and jerked upright immediately, shocked by the realisation that I had fallen asleep in my prone position, and had remained so until my patient had regained a conscious and well state. What impression of me had this strange English man now? All my careful preparation, introduction and presentation had been levelled by this one careless act. Standing I straightened the folds of my clothes, and brushed my hair back with a sweep of a hand, as much to dismiss my vulnerability and improper situation as to bring order to my dishevelled state. My immediacy was to punctuate the air with words of explanation or apology, but the face that looked to me halted such inadequate expression. His tender eyes, despite the terrors of the previous hours, glowed with a hint of smile, and without the least manner of rebuke.

"My dear Lady. I can recall little of my circumstance, and have scant knowledge as to why I should find myself the better for your care, but be assured I gain much comfort from your presence."

His gentility vanquished any thought I had of guilt or disingenuity at my predicament. With little ado I seated myself back on the chair beside him, albeit with a much improved deportment.

"Señor Ralph. How do you find yourself? Are you well now?"

"Indeed Señora, I sense that I must have been dragged five miles by two wild horses at least. My body is sore abouts, and my head hurts still more. Pray, what became of me?"

"You were the victim of a snake, of sorts, which took a fancy to the flavour of your blood. By measure of the two marks upon your forearm I would estimate it enjoyed your flesh somewhat."

The light exchange removed every last vestige of discomfort that had resided in me. Ralph was obviously unmoved by the event, or not aware enough to consider it much. He looked at his left arm to discern what I had made reference to. I leaned forward and lifted his right arm gently, turning it a little to reveal the wound. He reached out to hold it for himself, as he did so his hand caught on mine. Again a thrill coursed through my body, but my reaction was a swift withdrawal of the grip.

"Your pardon Señora. Indeed, it seems I am not much used to the wildlife in this land. We do not have such creatures in England."

I wished my hand had remained, but could not even consider the purpose.

"The snakes here are generally peaceful Sir, but perhaps the flavour of a true foreigner proved too tasty a temptation. His poison, however, is a much less welcome aspect of his visit. It seems you have done well to overcome its effects, and perhaps will not suffer more. Do they not have snakes in England, Ralph?"

"Indeed they do, Señora. They are but curiosities in the garden and none carry venom in any quantity that might cause distress or injury. Have I been here long?"

I saw something of the boy in the man that lay before me, innocent in his recovery, and harmless in his simple questioning.

"No, Sir. I have no specific knowledge of the hour it is now, but it was just this morn when you were brought here. Although the descending darkness would indicate the hour to be quite late, it is only the better part of the day that you have been made insensible to.

"I have nursed men through days of blackness and fever, and also those whose battle lasted but a few hours yet with a less favourable outcome. I am much relieved at your return to good health.

"Here, take some water that you might sustain this good rally."

I reached the cup at his side, and aided him to a more upright position in order that he should enjoy something substantial of the drink. He returned the offer kindly by emptying the vessel in a single action, and thanking me generously, all the while taking some further hold with his hand upon my supporting arm. Lying back, his eyes closed, he sank down to draw more on the stock of his healing body. Some moments later his eyes opened once more.

"Are you still in attendance, kind lady?"

217

His words moved awkwardly in and out of the Spanish he had learned and that of his native tongue. There was always something of an elegance in the English he spoke, thus I endeavoured to retain much of the conversation in that language. Certainly, in his tired state it seemed only fair to do so.

"My nursing is talked about even back home Ralph. There are few who can say I am ever negligent in my care. If I were to lose a soul to heaven when it is not due then my people would question my ability, but no such charge has ever been levelled."

"I should think it never shall be."

His smile now strengthened, and the colour flooded back into his once deathly pale face.

"Elenor." I said without expression.

"What?" replied a startled Ralph.

"Elenor." I restated.

He appeared uncertain and struggled momentarily to regain his usual composure, "Please excuse my rude manner. I was not brought up to address another with such coarseness, but you surprised me with the name. Why do you say Elenor, my Lady?"

"My apologies are perhaps needed moreso I believe. It was uncalled for to speak so. I was bemused by your calling the name through your delirium. Tell me something of her. Is she your wife?"

Ralph's face turned away from me at that moment. I could not quite tell whether it was purely to hide any cognisant reaction, or whether remembering what used to be was proving too painful to recall. Slowly his face turned back. He now took on a mood of sadness. The spark that lit his soul flickered somewhat. After a thoughtful pause he began.

"Elenor was my childhood friend. She lived in a beautiful house called Packwood, where I grew up. Although I lived with my father at Risby in Yorkshire, each summer I would spend the days in Warwickshire with Elenor and my cousin William, with James, and Sophia, and others.

"She was more of a sister to me, or at least I was more of a brother. Just before I left she married William."

"Come, come. I sense there is more to Elenor than a friend or a sister. We have some hours to talk. Do not spare the detail for modesty's sake Ralph."

He visibly settled to a more comfortable state, and a calm came over him as his mind moved back to his home and his people.

"In truth she was more than a friend, much more than a sister. It had not meant to be, nor yet was supposed to be, but the years were generous in their gifts to her. Day by day her beauty grew, and as her happy spirit danced with mine through those sunlit days, she became more precious to me than any other thing in this world.

219

"The more we hid our love from those around us, the more it grew, until we could not be parted from each other. We thought nothing could ever separate us."

"So what did?" I impatiently interrupted.

"A truth we denied, a course we ignored until it stood proud in front of us and barred our way. Elenor was to marry William, and it was not for us to argue with the dictate, nor yet even give hint to the love we held for each other."

I was horrified. "Could she not object, or refuse to marry William?"

He continued calmly:
"Her love and respect for her father would never have allowed her to question his wishes. It was important that the families should benefit from such an alliance. We were Catholic families, and in a time of repression it was entirely good sense to draw the bonds tightly.

"Previous monarchs had taught us much of the whims that turn one religion to the top to the cost of another. Our strength lay in our unity, and the good names that were entrenched in our families. The union of the Ferrers and the Lovaines had never been in question, and our childish minds had wandered carelessly without heed to the consequence of our mutual feelings.

"So now it is that William is married to Elenor, and I shall never fill the void left by her beautiful, sweet spirit, ... but such is life!"

I had never before heard a love spoken of with such a depth of expression. Even though Ralph had dismissed the passion with which he spoke by his casual final remark, I was moved to feel strongly his loss through its telling, and I felt rise in me something of a challenge. If this English woman had been such a great love then in my mind no man, no family tradition would bar it. When a Spanish woman is in love with a man he is in no doubt as to her strength for him or reliance. I had been unlucky in that I had never found the love I could not deny, and yet my allegiance to my husband surely none could question. The love for my father was the honest love of any child for a great figurehead. It would be unfair to expect any man to live up to that, yet I felt a little jealousy that this man's heart should be wasted on so fickle a love, a childhood love. Perhaps I could show him just what great lovers the Spanish are, show him what it is to love a real woman.

I looked down at the innocence of his cool eyes, wandering through his memories, the pictures real to his mind, as he told of the stolen fruits that were his lost love. Would it be fair to play him so? Perhaps it wouldn't matter, after all, it was only for my own sport. Without another witness to my shallow thoughts no harm could possibly come of it. I resolved to tame this man in a way he could not even imagine. For some hours more he told of the days he spent with Elenor as I sat and watched him, his gaze flickering lights in the gloom of the evening, lost in his memories.

The following day I caused him to remain at his bed in order that his strength might return more. Although I did not tarry much at his side, I was constantly in his sight, keeping at my business with a care, but not indulgence. I asked of his opinion in one or two small matters, not because I had no answer for myself, but because I wished for him to feel important in some small way, significant in my world. Thus it was that his time in my care passed pleasantly, but quickly.

Some weeks went by, it was mid July, and I summoned him to me. Juan introduced him onto my solana and left. It caught the afternoon sun gently, and was my favourite place to sit, when I had time. I thought the informality of a room outside of, but part of my house, suited my means so much better. Seated on a wrought white chair I bade him sit in the adjacent piece yet addressed him, by contrast, with some formality. I had to maintain a sense of propriety, else my proposition could be judged a little forward for a woman, or even questionable from my position.

"Mr Ellerker. I am much in need of an escort to the house of my brother-in-law, the Governor of Santa Elena. It is a small event by comparison to those we are used to at home, yet it is traditional to celebrate the feast of Santiago, and thus we do. It is my request that you accompany me for the evening whereupon you will eat at table beside me, and, if requested, partner me for a dance. Do not think this affords you any favour or improvement of position, it does not. However, I shall be grateful for you doing so."

His expression betrayed very little of the surprise he must have felt, yet I detected a shift in him which he disguised by standing, without a rush, and executing a sweeping bow, his eyes kept cast to the floor giving nothing away.

"I would be only too delighted, Señora."

"Well, do not be too delighted, as you may consider it no more a task than your everyday work."

Still in his lowered position he raised his head a little and set his eyes to mine.
"Were my everyday tasks such as this, then surely I should be a King for my profession."

How had he caught me off guard so? His soft spoke compliment had held my breath for a moment, suspended by the line that hung between our tethered gaze. I turned my head away and sent him off with a sharp directive.

"Go now with Juan who shall take you to the tailor Anton, son of Alonso, in order that I might not be seen arriving with a tramp."

With this he was gone. My heart banged about so heavily I felt sure that anyone passing might hear it and venture to ask after my well being. I was much pleased though with the first stage of my subterfuge.

My most nervous state was not apparent, in truth I could deny anyone the opportunity to read my disposition if I so wished, however, there was no doubting my anxiety as I swept up the pathway to the reception with my English attendant. For certain I was on the arm of the most handsome fellow in all of the Floridas, his eloquent charm complimented so perfectly a stature he supported with such finesse and elegance. I was perfectly aware of the envious glances from every female present, and the singular discomfort from the men, who no doubt found difficulty in allowing a foreigner to offset their own vanities. I was unsure from the outset how I might explain my decision to come, accompanied as such, to my brother-in-law Gutierre. On the surface it could so easily be mistaken for a selfish denial of my husband's memory, but I was not to come alone to the evening, and my choice was my own. If Gutierre, or anyone else, found cause to question me then they would have to accept that in these wild and treacherous lands it is sometimes necessary to make the most of whatever material comes to hand.

It was warm, and much of the heavy, wet air that had oppressed us of recent had now gone leaving in its place a very comfortable evening. The lessened light of the ending day allowed the coloured lanterns that festooned the grounds to lend a happy atmosphere. As we moved into the assembling group the music was already lifting spirits into a festive mood. One or two proffered greeting, but none could shift their eye from the man at my side.

Ralph, for the most, remained silent but attentive. His broad shoulders were accentuated by the cut of

the fine jacket tailored for the occasion. His striking features together with his light skin lent him the
air of a God. I thrilled inside when first he had presented himself at my doorway, and now too I felt
the same again with each soft-spoke, half hid exchange from those who now marvelled at what they
saw. I knew I had won the evening.

The dark glance that shot at me from the far end of
the room took my victorious pride from me in a second, replacing it instead with a fearful grip that had
me falter and hold fast to the spot. Gutierre's face
portrayed so much of the tenor of my poor Hernando that for a brief moment I did feel some guilt. As
he moved forward with a forceful stride, no doubt to
make clear his ignominy for my flagrant disregard
of any respect, another more youthful figure stepped
past him and held out his arms. I have never been
so pleased to see my cousin Pedro.

"Catalina, do come take some punch, it is truly
wonderful. You might recall something of the taste
for the mixture is yet that of the summer drink we
were all so fond of in Aviles."

I felt as though I wanted to hug him, but simply inclined to receive the kisses to my cheeks. The cool
of the fruit-laden glass set in my hand restored
something of my sensibility, and I relaxed to the
group. Pedro took control.

"Do tell us all how you came by such a dashing escort. As I hear it, were it not for your healing hands
you might actually have come tonight unaccompa-
nied."

I chastised him for taunting me so, but in truth, I relished the opportunity to play again the word games that made up our childhood fun. Pedro, of all, took great delight in directing even the most formal event into a round of playful banter to instantly belittle any who might feel they were better than others around them. I had seen him reduce great generals to embarrassed social wrecks if necessary, but for the greater part the sport was regarded as such, few were rarely offended.

I playfully took a swipe at him and feigned embarrassment for my own self. In actuality what Pedro had done was to diffuse any sense of impropriety that might be levelled at me by any who felt a need to. Imbued as such with a gentle confidence I leant forward and kissed Gutierre in greeting. A smile returned to his face and he too saw the benefit in taking the opportunity to enjoy the lighter side of the situation.

"Indeed Pedro," he said, "I feel it is nought but the elegant comfort of the Governor's house that affords such easy recovery, is that not right Catalina?"

Always quick to impress upon people his generosity the comment elicited little in the way of assent from the group, but I was used to his immaturity.

"Perhaps you are right brother, however, I should keep a wary eye open for snakes lest you too should be in need of the healing charms no doubt encapsulated in your forsaken walls."

The gentle laughter and repartee retained the good nature of the exchange begun by Pedro. It was truly not right for any to deny the host his place at centre, but Gutierre was little match for Hernando in wit or conversation, and his love of the position he had gained overtook any sense of propriety he should have. The estate, in his hands, was comparatively lavish and unnecessary, yet it proved a fine venue for fiestas such as these.

Pedro took charge once more, his sensitivity matched in every way by his intelligence and instantly likeable character. There was much of my father in him, and his position as Governor at San Agustin, and therefore of all the Floridas, was well earned and truly rightful.

"I believe, Señor, your name is Ralph?"

"Indeed Sir, you speak the truth."

Ralph's deep, resounding English voice cut the air as much as a new melody from the musicians would. I could sense those around me warm to his natural eloquence immediately. There could be no doubting his breeding and good station in life, in fact he was already fulfilling the epitome of those fabled tales of the elegant, English Lord that had first set me in search of him.

"Well, Ralph," Pedro stepped to his side placing an arm around his shoulder.

"My experience of the English Courts is that they are renowned for the elegance of their step. I wager you could show us something of a dance from your country that would give us great entertainment."

I could not tell whether Pedro meant to take something away from Ralph's glowing stature, or perhaps he truly did think it would be fun to try an English dance. I felt an instant need to protect him.

"Pedro! Do not be so cruel. I feel sure that by entertainment in truth you would have us make fun at Señor Ellerker's expense. Take no notice of them Ralph. Pedro has always been the very worst tease."

"If you would excuse me one moment, my Lady, Gentlemen."

With no further word Ralph left us pondering on our inadequacies as hosts. I was disappointed that my escort had so easily been offended, further I felt some embarrassment in the present company. The talk turned to a polite, but more serious conversation and I was already unsure that I had been entirely wise to pursue my prize so publicly.

I felt a little angered, at whom I was unsure, but I was at a loss for sensible word and feigned interest in its stead. My thoughts were broken into as I noticed an unsure gaze from Pedro and others past me that I was unable to immediately comprehend. Their inquisitive look turned slowly to a knowing smile, but still with some question. I could not seem to catch Pedro's gaze to enquire after his thoughts, and before I could turn to ascertain for myself the source of this concern a gentle, soft voice spoke to me.

"Doña Catalina, I would deem it the greatest honour if you would accompany me to lead this dance."

I turned to face the bowed figure looking up at me with his wonderful smile and beautiful grey eyes. Around him the people stood in expectation, all waiting for me to respond to the elegant request. I proffered a hand which he took whilst standing, and I was led past rows of faces, all with their own questions, expressed through their whispers and nods. A ripple of polite applause accompanied us to the centre of the room where, already assembled and waiting, a number of men and women stood paired off and facing each other.

The musicians struck up a familiar tune, yet with an unusual rhythm. I was placed opposite Ralph and kept my eye fixed to his, aware that his intention was to instruct us as the music played. His words were firm and controlling, yet kind and direct. From the first bow little was needed for him to progress us through the mechanisms of the turn. Although our respective partners changed with each section, I, along with the others, had a legitimate reason to fix my gaze on our confident instructor. His elegance was a contrast to the others who faltered somewhat to begin with, but the simple repetition soon became learned enough for all to move up and down the floor with a consummate cohesiveness. Despite the lessening need to bark the moves I could not stop looking at Ralph. While this was true to an extent for the other revellers, I was constantly aware of our eyes connecting as he lorded over his captive audience. Eventually the revel came to its end, but not before each dancer was reunited with their original partner. Mine was, of course, Ralph.

The intensity of emotion which pervaded my body now seemed to cause time to hang still in the air. The consequent moment of silence therefore ran to an eternity which brought us to an uncomfortable stop. All eyes were now on me.

I came to my senses and clapped loudly, the natural response broke the silence as the dancers and those watching applauded and shouted words of congratulations to Ralph. Amidst the hubbub I called for a *cabaleira,* its jaunty reel eliciting more shouts and a general flurry to fill the floor as the music struck its jolly, strident first notes.

"Now it is my turn to instruct, Señor Ellerker. Follow me."

In contrast to the formal English dance we had all just enjoyed, we now could allow the exuberance of the evening to begin in earnest. As Ralph learned quickly the turns and quick movements, the dance took us into a night of such fun and energy that Santiago would surely have blessed us from marking his name with such expressions of joy.

The hours flew by in a whirl of dance, merriment, drinking and discourse. Ralph was every bit the guest of honour in contrast to his true position. For myself I became altogether enraptured by his constant and perfect companionship. There were no further remarks, nor conflicts to mar the enjoyment, indeed I retained the pride with which I commenced the evening and found excitement in all, surpassing anything I could recall from recent memory.

As the night drew to an end, and the guests departed, we two were loathed to make our farewells until such time as the musicians were exhausted. Our happy little group, Pedro, Alvaro, Thomas Bernaldo, even Gutierre, and their respective partners, all left, falling out into the courtyard still laughing and jesting as had been the tenor of the fiesta. The drink had loosened the boundaries of propriety and Ralph had become as one of their own.

The women ushered and chastised the carousing men in a vague attempt to steer them home whilst still intent on conversing more and sharing daring secrets and fantasies that would usually be best kept to the heart. At least I considered myself sensible enough to retain my inner desires, the wishes I could not share with any, especially he at the centre of these thoughts. Finally we bade farewell to all and I allowed Ralph to accompany me to my veranda.

In spite of the torment of emotions racing through my mind and body we remained true to the rules inherent in our relative positions, returning little more than a nod and a polite word of gratitude for the respective company we had offered each. Yet, as I turned to enter my door I became aware of a hesitation behind me. A swift turn and a single step echoed in the still, night air, but the expectant continuation of the stride hung tantalisingly, as if the progress of the hour had halted. I hesitated, but resisted the temptation to look over my shoulder. His voice eased gently into the quiet.

"My Lady, I wonder if you might consider a question from me of an incidental, but personal nature?"

The innocent words caused me to tighten inside at the myriad possibilities to which he might allude. Without a word, for fear of anticipating in error, I turned my face to him thereby consenting to the request. I had felt a need to gain more time with Ralph whilst still having regard for my position, this then at least lent something of that opportunity. A few words more would allow me an honourable extension to our hours. The intoxicating drink that had passed our lips already suppressed further any possibility that I might simply ignore his plea. I watched patiently as he formulated the structure of his impending question, the near dark affording him something of a veil across his furrowed brow.

"I trust you will forgive my intrusion, yet I beg of you that should your wish be to end any conversation, you might dismiss me without wait and with no fear of impropriety, as indeed any fault as such could only be mine."

I smiled at his excessive care. I saw the weakness of a boy standing in the frame of a man, and had no wish to belittle him through any conceit that might advantage me. Thus I called him to sit once more at my Solana, having first ventured inside to avail us of a decanter of wine. No word passed on the matter further, the only sounds a happy splash of the ruby liquid as I filled two crystal goblets, and the constant chirp of the cicadas about us. Once we were truly settled I led him to ask his question without fear of reprisal or vanquishment.

" My good lady. At the foremost part of the evening I could not help but be aware of the questioning, and sometime menacing looks that were directed toward you. Whilst I am much aware of the natural surprise at your attendance with a servant, I was also of the belief that my presence in the stead of your husband was of a greater concern to some. I wondered if perhaps you might enlighten me as to the story behind your present position, if it is not too impertinent a question?"

Having managed to ask the question he near emptied the filled glass, his lips and throat having dried considerably in the process. I leaned forward in some consideration whilst replenishing his drink. I sensed a concern that perhaps he had over-stepped the mark at which a question becomes an intrusion. However, I smiled and consequently watched him visibly relax. Taking my glass in hand I marked the lantern light through the dark liquid, contemplating on the point from which I might commence.

"My husband, Hernando de Miranda, was a most handsome man. I found his company very exciting, and we lived a busy life together. He was a fine sportsman, excelling at most outdoor pursuits, and as such was quite the life of many parties at home in Spain. Although I had never much considered marriage whilst my father was alive, in the years after his death I found myself much in the company of Hernando. He had served for some years alongside my father, and I would sit for hours attentive to the wonderful tales he would tell of their reckless exploits. His lively spirit helped me considerably to blow new life into my quieted bones, and the stories of their encounters with storms and pirates brought back delightful pictures of my father for which I was ever grateful.

"When I was younger my life had been full of adventure, if not with my father then with my brother Juan. Unfortunately, Juan was a spirited seaman who loved adventure more than I, adventure that eventually tore him from me. He was taken by a hurricane in the Bermudas which ended his life at a young age. With my father at my side my zest for excitement remained, but my happiness and playful spirit sank to the depths of the ocean together with my brother's soul.

"Hernando had much of the love of life I had enjoyed when young, and thus I felt at ease with him in my world, and something of my natural joy began to return. When he was offered the post of Governor at Santa Elena I could not believe my fortune. I immediately realised the opportunity to return to my father's land and to help build on his achievements. Marriage thus became a new and welcome adventure.

"That joy was tried much from the beginning of our union. I had not bargained on my new husband's love of gaming to prove so much of a draw. The day of his taking up the post arrived and passed, and we remained in Spain still. My impatience grew, and Hernando's persistent removal as he rode out hunting boar left me to ponder in solitude. Not being one to sit quietly at home I went amongst my many Aunts and Uncles to enquire after the state of things in our absence. My frustrations grew as little or no news was forthcoming. For two whole years I found other amusements to occupy my mind. As Hernando's sport took us to visit many of his fellow men, I set to building different companionships amongst the wives and families with whom we shared the diversions. Eventually some pressure was brought to bear on my husband to make preparation for his governorship and the responsibilities that rested upon his shoulders. Much was made of the departure, and I relished every minute of it. Not just because the many friends I had made were so very kind and generous in their farewells, but more so because I felt much as though I was returning home. The spirit of my father rested in the soil, and the air, the very fabric of the land we sailed toward; I felt a distinct return to his arms and heart.

"The reception in San Agustin, however, was far from the jubilant farewell. Chaos rang through the air, and there was little I could make sense of. Much was kept from me officially as all business was directed to my husband. However, I was not without friends remaining from my previous occupation here. It transpired that in the absence of Hernando taking up the post of Governor when he should have done, the task of over-seeing the well-being of Santa Elena fell to Don Diego de Velasco. I know that you already have some experience of this foul person. As you are aware, his is not the most pleasant of natures. His lack of knowledge and uncaring impatience for the indigenous peoples hereabout led to many incursions, resulting in loss of life and general unrest. Eventually the aggrieved natives attacked the settlement one too many times and the cowardly Velasco ordered the people back to the safety of San Agustin, abandoning the houses, crops and stock to be burned or stolen.

"Unfortunately, the responsibility fell, albeit in his absence, to the Governor. Unable to explain the loss of such an important outpost satisfactorily Hernando was sent back to Spain to be tried for a treasonable offence. My heart was broken, and yet I felt more anger than sorrow. I was angry at the cowardice and the consequence of this horrible little man who showed no remorse for his actions, and furthermore I was angry that purely for the sake of sport so much had been forsaken. If Hernando had shown a little respect for the position he had been afforded life would have been so very different. I swore revenge on the vile Diego de Velasco there and then, remaining in the land of my father to exact it.

"Worse yet was to come. I was much short of anything which might revenge my husband, and my settling in Santa Elena reduced the opportunity further still. How the news came to me I cannot truly recall, but I remember still the doubled pain upon learning that my half sister, Maria, had actually married Diego. I was never much warmed to this woman, and she neither to myself. I saw her as an unwanted blemish on my father's memory. I had never been a party to her introduction into our family, and I had no real wish to acknowledge her as such. My father had insisted that it was an unchristian act to reject her as she was the product of his seed, however, I could not believe she was ever conceived in love, but could only have been the result of some contrivance or circumstance that had left my father with a duty to which he honourably adhered. Maria was very much minded of my disgust at Diego's incompetence, and I truly believe her choice was fired as much by this as anything she might possibly see in him as a husband. His position gained her some social standing in her eyes, but moreover she delighted in my inability to ever come to terms with the union.

"Although I still mourn the loss of my Hernando and burn a torch of hate in my heart for this other man, my father taught me to construct from the bad, learn the lesson and build on it, not cause worse through blind vengeance or action directed by bad faith. He was very much a man of God. Indeed, his first action upon alighting on this shore was to instruct the priest to hold a mass upon the sands. His belief and faith in God gave him his strength and carried him through his whole life despite the very many perils he faced since he went to sea when only fourteen years of age. He died a happy man who achieved more than any other before him. As for me, my husband had wasted his opportunities and had allowed his life to amount to so little in exchange for nothing more than transient personal gain. I saw nothing of my father in his foolishness, and felt betrayed and even embarrassed. I could not face my sisters, but those friends I had still in this land were sympathetic to my plight without pity. They knew me well enough to respect that the choices which had led to this situation were not of my own making.

"Pedro Menendez Marques, whom you met tonight, is my cousin, the son of my father's brother. He was made Governor of San Agustin after my father's death and was quick to appoint Captain Thomas Bernaldo Quiros as acting Governor for Santa Elena. Peace was restored with the native population, and together with Hernando's brother, Gutierre, Santa Elena became the fine settlement it is today. Eventually Gutierre took on the official post as Governor. While he was not much in favour of Hernando's playful life, he was still taken aback to see me accompanied as I was tonight. Although, for myself, I consider my status to be that of a woman without attachment, and is thus of no consequence to any who might find objection to my actions. The circumstance of this night's festival was to celebrate the feast of Santiago, this is a time of dancing and happy exchange, and so it was. I must express my sincere gratitude to you as such for the part you played in ensuring it to be quite the success it was. You have brought me much happiness this night."

Although my lips had dried to a point of difficulty in expressing myself further, I sipped delicately at my wine, not wishing Ralph to perceive that the words had taken so much from me. His question perhaps might not be the subject of a conversation with that of a servant, however, I was finding it difficult to view Ralph as anything but a friend, or perhaps even more than that. I had taken the value of his life into my hands, and the action as such had fashioned a bond that I believed was beyond pure acquaintance. There was a belonging. I had his soul, he had my heart, but it was his heart that I wanted. The heart that had been locked away in some far flung English courtyard, the key held by a weak young girl unable to break the bonds of her kinsmen, even for the sake of love. I felt a need to know more about her, why should she hold the true love of this man, what could make her so desirable? And yet, if he were to tell me more it would so dilute the fervour of this night together. I was happy to believe my sense of connection was not so dissimilar in Ralph's heart. I had no care that it might be fired purely by the heady liquor and the excitement of the dance. The bond existed through his being there, and the thrill that was rising inside of me. I had to have him linger some more, his question now answered.

"So tell me, how did you find yourself acquainted so badly with my old friend Don Diego de Velasco?" I had snatched the question out of the air and happily he warmed to the request.

Drawing more on his remaining wine he pondered briefly before setting down the fine glass and relaxing back in his chair.

"Indeed, I am not much sensible of the entire story. I recall I was motivated by cowardice in my inability to face the wedding day betwixt Elenor and William. Worse still, I was supposed to be at William's side for the ceremony, as his chosen companion. I had pondered much on the day for some months, and made preparation to flee the place, telling none of my plan. I wonder still to this day of the disappointment or concern that may have befallen each at my absence. My notion was to travel to the Low-Lands, to do what I knew not, but I had made the one time acquaintance of a George Mainwareing who had bade me visit, should I so wish, into Amsterdam. As fortune would have it, my plan only took me to the place from were I was to sail. I remember little of my time there, but do recall waking in the dark hold of a ship where I was held captive for some time. It seems I was to voyage to the New World as a ship hand, despite my singular lack of seafaring skills. I was informed that the tales which had come back from that country of strange beasts and all manner of fearful things had caused a severe shortfall of any who would choose to undertake the journey. Thus the Crown had deemed it necessary to issue a decree allowing crews to be forced into service, as indeed I was. Having finally acclimatised myself to this strange adventure all was still not quite how it should have been.

"We were at the ocean some weeks when the alarm went up. A Spanish vessel had been sited off our port side which was steered toward us. Her intention was gauged to be anything but friendly and we were put to arms. I have never known the like before. The noise was unbelievable, and the sea of blood that washed over the heaving decks was sickening to behold. Some object connected with a previous hurt on my head, whereupon I instantly lost consciousness, only to become aware of myself on the deck of the Spanish ship as it was approaching the coast of this land. I was wet from a deluge of water cast over me in order to bring me to my senses, the shock of which did little to acquaint me much with my further changed circumstances. A muddle of information through my part-lucid state told me of my rough transport to the town and subsequent incarceration upon my arrival. There was a period of some questioning during which time some allusion was made to my Catholic family which consequently separated me from the remaining English men. I later learned that few survived from the boat at all, and those that did were mainly put to death by my captor. It seems my religion lent me some refuge, yet only enough to have me locked away in the space wherein you found me. In truth, I believe I did not begin living again until the moment the sound of your voice broke into the darkness wherein I rotted, and cast away my despair in an instant.

"In truth, I see not the darkness of this night that shrouds us even now, as the light of the life and the true happiness which has been my experience these past hours has dispelled the grief and injury that has been my mantle for so long a time. Those on the ship who bore me to this land spoke of the New World and its promises. Indeed it is a new world that has been shown to me, one that I had no thought of ever knowing. A captive man I may be, yet the bonds that tie me are those sweet manacles wrought from the love for life that it has been my good fortune to be a part of tonight."

As the words lingered still in the cooling air I became aware that the progress of the telling had brought him to lean closer, his arms now resting on the small table between us. I in turn, without conscious thought, had similarly moved toward him. The lanterns now burned low, little could be made of the detail, even at such a closeness. His voice had softened to a near whisper, and I felt such an overwhelming yearning inside of me. With the velvet touch of a mother's care he placed his hand upon my cheek. For a brief moment I fell to the gentle caress, floating in the warmth of the touch. My senses flew in every direction, yet I knew this to be so wrong. My hand rose to meet his. I fastened on, pressing it further to my glowing cheek, but then drew it away, not in admonishment, but in the shared knowledge that to venture further would be unthinkable. We sat in silence, still close, our hands remaining joined. In time the conversation resumed on a lighter note, sharing small likes and dislikes, happy and sad moments in our lives, but nothing of any real significance. The height of emotion we had exchanged briefly remained in our minds while the inconsequence of the words between us danced in and out like two butterflies at play in the light of a summer sun.

As the light of the morning drew golden outlines the pain of our separate lives forced us to a formal farewell. Ralph's beautiful eyes fixed on me for one final moment as he raised my hand to his lips. How I yearned for those lips to be pressed upon my own, and to feel the strength of his arms around me. My body was tearing inside and I knew I could make any selfish wish a reality, but to what consequence? As he turned and left me, watching his retreat, I shouted in silence, imploring him to come to me to dispel the pain I felt so deep. Whilst the words rang clear in my mind, the battle raged inside of me, and the songs of the birds chorused out undisturbed into the clear morning air. My eyes remained fixed on his back until such time as there lingered the ghost of his shape, apparent only in my now resigned mind. I touched my hand and brought it to my mouth to savour something of what might still reside there. The moment gone, I could not reconcile the anger at myself with the joys I felt in his presence, and the memory of the rapturous evening.

A dutiful application kept my mind trained to a familiar path, but my company was not sought out over the ensuing days due to my curt attitude to whomsoever I encountered. I made good effort to maintain my usual manner and yet I found myself less amiable to those friends who would address me, and even less approachable to those for whom I had little time. I felt the anger inside of me chewing at my guts, and the ache of my need to talk again with Ralph caused me to some considerable discomfort. I ate little, which added to my melancholic state. Through all of this time I still did nothing to further my plan. It seemed futile and churlish and yet so necessary. Remark was made by some close to me asking after my welfare, but I had no one to whom I could explain my feelings or reveal my secret yearnings. I felt something of my old sadness returning and a certain resignation that to continue would be a folly.

The weeks passed and I relied on occasional words from Juan and others to keep me informed of Ralph. There was little doubt that the moment had passed and surely now he could only believe that my short lapse of propriety had fleeted by and was of no significance. There came no message passed on that would indicate his need to speak to me. No question as to my well-being, indeed, I was certain that his mind would drift to thoughts of the beloved Elenor in his times of loneliness.

One afternoon in early August I sat quietly listening to the chit chat of the birds, and watching the insects in the air. A small greenish blue bird fought to hold its position over a perfect white flower as it fed from the sweetness within. I was minded of the line in the bible when Christ tells us to watch the birds of the air for they toil not. Yet here was this little creature working so hard in the heat, at a time when we deem it too hot, and took some sustenance as a consequence. His aim was true and his endeavour was well rewarded, and so he flew off to repeat the action until he should be requited. Here I was, so wrapped in my own pity that I had ceased to care for that which was in my own grasp. If one tiny bird could achieve so much then what could hold me from my true aim.

The twenty eighth of that month is a truly important day to us as it is the feast of San Agustin. I had already received my invitation to Pedro's festivities at his home. The celebrations would begin with a solemn mass in the church, this would take place in the early evening in order to enable journeys made from every quarter of the Floridas to be ended and well-settled. The night would then be made over to more worldly remembrance, a wonderful time of joyous thanksgiving for the foundation of our home.

When first word had come of this year's event my cousin had asked after Ralph, enquiring as to whether I would have him accompany me again. In my misery I had suggested it would be unlikely, not wishing to make more of the gossip that our first appearance together had been cause of. Now I was minded to alter my immediate decision. Perhaps I should muster up the strengths and determination of my little bird and have the courage to once more venture upon the dangerous currents that had caused me so much distraction.

Once I had set my mind to it I took on a whole new demeanour. I was forthright in my direction again, but now I was the soul of light. My humour so improved I probably lay ground for far more consideration and speculation than with my previous bad air. I thought much on the detail of the preparation. I determined that I should tell Ralph of his task at very much the last hour so as to give little time for deliberation. I wondered then, and so too now, if my hesitation was fuelled by contrivance or simply by fear. I felt a new excitement coursing through my body which I was at pains to control. The added ingredient to my pot of intrigue was that the attendance at the fiesta entailed a sea journey of some three days, more significantly a stay of at least the night in San Agustin, then the return journey.

The days passed until there were but two left before I was due to depart. The nearer the hour approached the more difficult I found it to steal myself to the asking. I was at a loss to bring myself to him as I had done before, added to which I had purposefully avoided him since Santiago. Eventually I recoursed to sending a messenger in the shape of Juan Ramirez to instruct Señor Ellerker that he would be accompanying me to San Agustin in order that I might celebrate the feast of our patron saint. He was to arrive at my door at daybreak on the morning of the twenty sixth in order to undertake the journey south. I breathed a breath of some relief at having enacted the order, yet I was still to wonder at Ralph's reaction and the reality of his wish to come or not.

In the dusk of the ending day I happened to espy Juan tracing a path to my door. I had not requested that he should return an affirmation so I was intrigued as to why he should call again at this hour. The news he brought with him caused me to vex at him and then apologise for my forthright manner.

"It seems, my Lady, that Martín de Yztueta, the chief carpenter, has enlisted him these past days to transport logged timber down to San Mateo where they are at present strengthening their fortification. I had not been aware of his absence as I myself have been for some time at San Agustin, only returning two days since."

All I could do was vent my anger at Poor Juan. Why had he not been aware of his being in San Mateo? It is only a short distance up the coast from San Agustin, he would have passed him by on his journey home. Why was Ralph about business other than our own? All these things I knew to be wrong in ascribing them so. In truth, had I been more diligent and less insular in my own activity then I should have known of each of these instances. I slowed somewhat and altered my tone. I saw something of the patient parent in Juan's face, and knew it was wrong to speak to him so, yet I was at a loss to explain why this was such an unholy grievance. Gathering myself I instructed him further, suggesting that some signal might be made to invite Ralph's recall to Santa Elena, a messenger or the like. I knew immediately from the tired lines on that familiar aged face that I was asking something which was in all honesty beyond what was sensible. Still with little regard for my dear old friend I dismissed him summarily, and once alone sank to the floor and wept. All the energy that had built within me those few weeks now spilled out onto the ground around me, leaving a limp, lifeless rag. My plans had been thwarted, and I was now conscious more than ever how much I wanted Ralph.

I lay for some time, feeling no strength within and much pity for myself. Why should he be absent now of all times? It was not that unusual for him to be away, but then I had taken so little notice of him of recent, truth be known I simply would not have noticed if he had caught a ship back to England.

Somewhere in the recesses of my mind a small noise sang quietly. Once sensible to its melodic turn I listened more intently, gaining some comfort from its melody as it grew louder and then softened again. The tune was familiar, but had an unusual lilt to it. It had me in mind of the dance at Gutierre's, and thought how cruel it was to remind me so of Ralph at this time. The whistled tune faded as the reality of its possibility shot into my head like a crack of lightning. I rushed to my feet and onto the veranda, peering toward the spot from where the fading tune still lingered. There was only one person who would turn the phrase in that manner, and although the physical evidence was not before me, I was confident that the logging task had reached an end at a most convenient point. I sought not confirmation of what I held to be so, nor yet did I press again for my original request to be restated, I drew a confident air and went about my business.

The early start gave me scarce time for conjecture. I had slept little through the night and was still some way from being fully prepared when a short knock at my door announced the arrival of my companion. I was sure that if it could be measured my relief was tangible at that moment.

"I am much pleased at your promptness Señor Ellerker. If you would be so good as to await my readiness, I am somewhat tardy this morn. Perhaps you might speak with the boy over at Stefan's, I have a vehicle prepared there of which I will require you to take charge."

"Indeed, my Lady."

I was now of a much muddled mind. I threw carefully laid out garments into a trunk with complete abandon. My need was to be patiently waiting for Ralph's return without sign of haste or fluster, thus the care of belongings became entirely secondary to my needs.

As the rig pulled to a halt in front of my house, the horse reined in by Ralph's strong hands, I was sat quietly reading, for all the world as though I had waited for an hour already. In truth I was fortunate the book even lay the right way up for all the attention it received. I rose without acknowledgement and took my place on the hard, wooden seat. Before I had requested of Ralph that he might fetch my trunk, he leapt down and loaded the small pile of articles to the rear of us.

"Thank you Ralph. And before you speak further I should be grateful if the tedious use of formality should be kept to a minimum throughout the duration of these next days. When we are without company I would ask that you address me as Catalina, I in turn shall call you Ralph."

Without further ado we set off on the uncomfortable journey to San Agustin. Much of it was by light sea craft, the fine weather availing us of a calm voyage, but the slow hours south provoked little exchange. I learned the detail of the work in San Mateo, Ralph some equally tedious nonsense about life in Santa Elena. Once we had arrived into the town I directed him as to where he should report and when I expected him at my side.

During Mass I sat at the head alongside Pedro and Doña Maria de Solis. Seated as we were, to the side of the chancel, it was possible to look down the church without any show of unseemly behaviour. On occasion throughout the service I glanced to see if I could spy Ralph's face amongst the congregation, but amongst such a great number the task was not easy. I was quite distracted and paid scant attention to the priest. Eventually, after much frustration, during the consecration when most people were kneeling, I caught a sight of him as he briefly lifted his bowed head. Whether it was a trick of the shadows that cast about the cool interior I was not sure, but for that instant he appeared to stare straight into my eyes. The shock at being caught so caused me to rapidly cast my eyes downward. When I was sure sufficient time had passed again I ventured a further look and enjoyed the solemnity of a man truly deep in prayer. The late evening sunlight struck a light across the group he was with, picking out his broad shoulders and his now much-lightened hair.

The tone of his skin had grown darker from the constant sun, but his English features remained unmistakable in the sea of Spanish faces.

I felt oddly uncomfortable at leaving the place without any contact with him. I talked idly with Pedro and Maria and other friends I had not seen for some time, but wondered who he was with now, and of what he might be discussing. However, at the appointed hour a quiet knock announced his polite await. My voice remained steady and in control as I informed him I should not be very much longer.

It may have been the same apparel he had worn at the previous event, but he appeared to me so much more handsome than ever I had seen before. I had spent time arranging my hair to stand high upon my head, but its sheer length and perfect straightness made the task nigh on impossible. I was so annoyed at my inability to present to him the picture I wished to portray. In the end I gave in and allowed it to flow naturally down the length of my back, running into the many folds of my dress. At least I could feel comfortable and not worry about pins or ties falling out through the evening. Certainly, when I stood before him he showed no disappointment, rathermore, I fancied I saw something of a short breath come to him which I could only hope indicated some pleasure. With his usual elegance he bowed deeply and proffered his arm, which I gladly placed my hand upon.

The dancing was commenced, and much of the drink had already been consumed if the passion with which people were jigging and wheeling was anything to judge by. The time I had taken in my preparation had perhaps left Ralph waiting for much longer than I had realised, but for all that he still remained the perfect gentleman. The reception this time was quite different to previous as Pedro and others greeted Ralph with hearty back slaps and much joy at their being joined by one of their own. There was nothing of the tension or questioning, and no discomfort from any of the assembled. Nothing that is until, with a grand entrance, Don Diego de Velasco entered the room with Maria on his arm.

She strutted about the room as if she were the hostess of the evening, making such a fuss, and talking so loudly to ensure everyone in the room was aware of her presence. Sadly, her over-coifed hair which sat in massive curls over her ridiculously layered dress seemed to attract the attention of every idiot man in the room, all virtually forming a line to request a dance during the evening. In response she would feign surprise with each plea and giggle like a schoolgirl, making a show of refusing for fear of upsetting someone, then explaining that all dances were reserved for her dear husband. Dear husband! I could not imagine anything more comical than the possibility of Velasco dancing with any sort of grace, that at least was some salvation.

I turned my back in the vain hope that she perhaps might not see me and I could avoid the falsities of a brief greeting, but her aim was true. She called my name from the far side of the floor giving me no chance to hide or give any pretext to avoid her.

"Catalina, my dear sister. Come tell me of any news from home that I may have missed through my busy little life."
Certainly there was nothing I would wish to pass on that I felt warranted her notice. How irksome that I was under so much witness that I was not able to reply as I should wish to.

"Maria. I trust you and your husband are both well. I am sure there is little I can tell you that would enrich your knowledge of my family and Aviles. However, my home here is much improved thanks to your good husband."

I was keen enough through my reply to see her noticeably falter. She could not help but stutter a number of times, her brow fallen somewhat as she obviously could not comprehend how for one instant I might have gained through some action of her husband's.

"How so dear sister? I was not made aware of such a matter."

I took the lead with a determination to have it remain so.

"I feel mayhap you have much need of recourse to your dear husband for he is found wanting then in his duties to you. Does he not tell you of his business? It would seem, perhaps, he does not consider it well to be discussed in the homeplace."

To my eyes her face changed colour three times, then with a toss of her myriad curls she turned and left, her final courtesy flung carelessly over her shoulder,

"I have many more important people I have to speak with. Enjoy your evening."

Her words disappeared into the general hubbub as she walked away with her false air of importance. I was sure that in no time she would browbeat her husband to extract what information he could be hiding from her, furthermore, I doubted that he would have any awareness to what she might allude.

As the evening progressed we crossed each other's paths once more, this time however, Diego was at her side. He had just begun a sickly smile and made to bow when his beady, black eyes came to rest upon Ralph, still stood beside me, my arm resting on his. He shot upright, looking around him, stumbling over the confusion, anger and disbelief painted on his face more lurid than the clownish cosmetic on his wife's cheeks. For a moment I sensed a fear for his own well-being, as he grappled to control the outrage at my parading his prize English Lord so, whilst trying to establish an absolute need to regain superiority in the situation.

His voice roared out: "What is this man doing here? I shall have him clapped back in irons this minute if he is not removed immediately."

I stood still and looked back at him, free from any expression other than pity. I had already noticed Pedro moving rapidly across to our place. He spoke firmly, but with a subdued voice as many were now alerted to the situation.

"Don Diego de Velasco! You will lower your voice and apologise to Catalina for your abject bad manner. This man is a guest at my feast, you have jurisdiction neither here nor over him. If I do not see a change in your demeanour I shall have no alternative but to ask that you leave."

My expression did not alter, yet Diego's face had turned a perfect white. Maria, standing at his side, displayed nothing but frustration as she could know nothing of what was happening before her. For certain, she never for one minute expected her husband to turn tail and apologise, as indeed he did.

"Catalina, I apologise for my impropriety. My impetuous reaction was borne purely from a lack of knowledge in these matters. Señor Menendez, forgive me for disturbing your celebration, it is unseemly for one of your officers to act so."

The apology was complete. Diego had realised the precarious position he had placed himself in and had turned it beautifully around with his usual flow of false platitudes. I knew the fire of hatred burning deep inside of him had been well stoked, and Maria was still bursting with all the questions she had for her demeaned husband, her own anger engendered from the sense that her status had been severely diminished as a result. Pedro, however, had watched the sport evolving and was not yet replete in his admonishment.

"Señor, I think you are forgetting some aspect of your apology. There is a third party whom you have failed to address in your fine speech."

The air of suspense was palpable to all that were witness to the exchange. It was as if everyone present were holding their breath, waiting for Velasco to burst. He knew he had little choice, but this really was too much to ask of him. He began with an inaudible mumble to which Pedro requested he speak a little louder. Clearing his throat the much-humbled Diego began his apology to Ralph. No sooner had he forced two words from his tight lips than Pedro interrupted again.

"Yes, yes, thank you. Come Ralph, I have a measure of exceedingly good wine I know you will enjoy. Catalina?"

His stride cut straight through Don Diego's words as he proffered his arm for my taking. The group of us swept away from the little man, his wife thundering at his ear, demanding explanations and redress. Now at least I felt I was gaining some ground in my quest for revenge. My second shot over Velasco's bows, due, yet again, entirely to Ralph.

The remainder of the evening flowed with great conviviality. I enjoyed my dances with my companion, and was much envied as a result. Though for the most part I spent time with friends whilst Pedro, Ralph and the other gentlemen enjoyed their own company. I was happy in the knowledge that the fiesta had been a great success. Toward the end of the night, as things quieted somewhat, I was talking with Maria de Solis of some nonsense to no particular end, when it came to my attention that the thinning numbers no longer showed signs of Ralph. The conversation wandered and followed no sensible pattern as my eyes were taken to the task of exploring the furthest reaches of the room. My mind similarly meandered aimlessly through the childish haunts of concern. I had not given much thought to his absence whilst all was merriment, yet in this quiet there existed some question that I felt needed answer.

Eventually I could resist no longer and made my apologies to those with whom I was engaged. The impropriety of the cut and the vagueness I displayed must have caused some curiosity amongst them, but I was not of a mind to care as I should have. There was no doubting that Ralph was not present within, so I headed to the door and the cooler night air. Small groups of late revellers, much quieted by earlier excesses and exhaustion, sat around here and there, talking some, drinks still in hand or laid carelessly on grassy knolls beside reclining, tired figures. Crickets now chirruped the single music of the night, and distant farewells too were being exchanged, but still I neither saw nor heard a sign of my companion.

I ventured further into the grounds about, catching the odd furtive giggle indicative of some playful assignation in dark corners, and I smiled at the innocence of those moments for they that played so. The air was heavy with the scent of the sweet night Jasmine, mixed still with the essence of the festive vapours. I drank it in and relaxed somewhat in my own satisfaction at a particularly successful fete. This small comfort only served to heighten the discomfort I felt as I stiffened upon spying the distinctive outline of Diego's Maria pressed up against some poor victim in the shadows, her secret meet kept discreet by the foliage around them. I wondered who might be her prey, and undoubtedly the subject of some future vengeful act should Diego happen upon them. Thus I made my way with some stealth over the ground so as not to elicit any discovery by them. The intrigue excited me, and I thought freely upon the sport it might afford me to catch her so.

When I was quite close enough I spoke, almost casually, as if in passing.

"Doña Maria, I trust you enjoyed the evening?"

Her sudden recoil was quite something to witness, but then, as quickly, her face gained a most satisfied smile, not a reaction I had expected from one so flagrantly dishonoured. Without word her hand pulled her conquest from the dark recess. My world fell away from beneath me.

"Devil's spawn!" I spat the words at her in the vain hope they might smite her between the eyes. An instant rage shot through my body throwing any sensibility quite to the wind. Dispensing with propriety, social grace or care for whosoever might witness me at that moment, I lunged forward, my hand raised high above my head in readiness to deal her an almighty blow.

Within inches of my making a contact with her painted face my arm came to a dead stop. At my wrist was a large, firm hand holding me in this fixed position, an equal force to my jealous rage, yet with a tenderness in its subjugation.

Before yet my eyes had loosed from the grip before me, the momentum of my manic lunge was diverted to a turn which took me full swing to my left, facing me away from my adversary. Now my eyes were levelled a breath's space from a familiar gaze. My anger evaporated as a cloud on the hottest of days. As I made to speak a finger came to rest upon my lips to hush me. A small movement drew my mouth slightly open allowing his lips to settle to the perfect kiss.

For a second time a fire rose from within me, yet this time it was not inspired by the voice of hatred, nor yet by any other reason but by passion. We kissed so full it was no small time ere the dewy bead that linked us broke as we finally drew apart. Ralph went to break the silence. Now it was my turn. I put my hand to his mouth.

"Hush! Not one word. Do not think I shall not chastise you still, I am yet your mistress and you must do as I say. Come quickly and follow me."

This whole time Maria had ceased to exist. I know not if she protested or just stood in mute astonishment. I paid no heed to her, but tore away with Ralph's hand in mine lest some precious minute should be lost through petty dalliance.

Once in my chamber I pushed the unresisting Ralph to the wall and kissed him with some force. He was in no doubt as to who was in charge. My mind span, and the blood coursed through my body driving me to a wild need to satisfy both he and I. With my one hand I held him tight by the hair at the back of his head, my other tore back the shirt he was

wearing, whilst our lips never left each other's indulgence. The heady party and the long day
smelled so well on him, and his body felt strong yet
unresisting. I stepped back, pinning him to the
place with an intense stare, and swiftly took my
blouse from my shoulders. My breasts, lit by the
moonlight through the open window, caused him to
take a step toward me. I pushed him back again,
asserting my authority once more, then placed my
body against his, kissing him again and again, our
hot, moist skin thrilling to each other's touch, my
nipples tracing across the rough hairs on his broad
chest as we moved. My lips left his and I kissed
him severally, first along his neck then on further,
making my way down across his heavenly body.
Once I was crouched low by his waist, I stopped
and looked up at him above me, still standing.
Slowly I untied his waistband. His gaze shot to the
ceiling as the pleasure of my touch caused him to
gasp. Whilst still holding him with one hand, I
reached back with the other and let my skirts fall to
the ground around me.

Standing once more I placed my hands around his
great shoulders and pulled our naked bodies together. I held his face, kissing him for all the world as if
it were the first and only kiss there had ever been.
His strong arms folded around me and pulled me up
as I wrapped my legs around his waist. Slowly I
moved upon him, still kissing him, we were wet and
hot and the intensity of my passion welled up deep
within me. My body tensed, lifting my senses to
such heights, the heat inside of me coursed through
every part of my being, every sense soared as our
movement quickened. I knew he would not last
much longer, but then I had no need of it as my

body arched and racked at the same time, the power between us cracking like sparks from a great fire, shooting bright flames resplendent into the dark shroud of the night. I felt we would never come down to earth as we floated high in the heavens, but was grateful for the air we both gulped in as we lay, now stretched out on the cold floor. His arms were still wrapped firmly around me, my head resting on his heaving chest, the silvery light picking out the beads of water that clung to him, maybe his sweat or perhaps mine, or even a sumptuous mix of the two, distilled and concocted from us both. For sure this lustful alchemy shone like true gold, yet the recipe was anything but pure, the ingredients so badly matched, how could this ever be? For now the moment was ours, whatever consequence lay before us. Our night continued in perfect joy, the fervour of our love undiminished by the returning day.

The homebound voyage could not have been more different to the previous one. We talked without cease during the day, and enjoyed our intimacy through each night. I was much aware of a pervading sense of unreality, particularly at our departure. A group from the previous night came to wish us safe passage, quite strong in number. Amongst them my dear Pedro who now, more than ever, seemed to have taken my care to his charge. The farewell was as fervent for Ralph as for myself. Much was re-stated of the friendships forged during the festive evening, promises made, and loose invitations to assure future exchanges at some not too distant date. There was no doubting Ralph's acceptance into our general society and even his popularity, but more than this there was an unspoken

sense of our being treated as though we were inseparable. I was not sure it was right to be treated so,
yet still the thrill was fresh and fed me well.

So what of the return to Santa Elena and the life I
had established so particularly there? I still had to
maintain propriety, I had to continue my position as
it had always been, I had to kneel at the altar of
good sense and correctness. The thought of it horrified me. The loss of this sense of belonging and
sharing would be so difficult, it was not something I
had truly experienced before, yet it was all wrong.
Ralph was still my servant and an Englishman too.
He may have engendered some form of acceptance
on one level, but that would be impossible to maintain under a normal circumstance.

The questions grew in my mind the closer we came
to Santa Elena, yet I could not bring myself to any
discussion on the matter with Ralph, I knew it
would only serve to break the spell and the illusion
would fade away before even it must.

Hell's teeth Captain, are we to perish yet within sight of our own land?"

My voice struggled to master the row of the incessant waves which rose to stare us in the face then as quickly dropped causing all to plunge after it as quick. To wake at such a clamour and chaos caused my previous state of mind to shift to a more pressing concern. Such a storm I had rarely seen before, and certainly never from the vantage of a vessel at the mercy of the sea. It was possible to discern something of the shoreline and we were assured that we were at the reef, although as yet unable to weigh anchor. How we were to make land was yet another matter. The wind tore the sails that remained still unfurled and dragged them to the foaming waters. As the deck heaved to impossible angles we held fast to whatever solid rail we might find. My safety was much improved by the provision of a mighty arm strongly wrapped around my waist. For this comfort I was grateful as I was fearful for my safety in such a grave situation. Miraculously, through the spray a dark shape drew near which in turn was discernible as a small landing craft which had marked our return, even from this misty shore. These heroic men bounced atop the curling waves cutting straight over them, and slowly made their way to us. The Captain of our small ship was keen to disembark us as quickly as he could, and thus ordered many to aid with securing our rescue party as soon as the little boat grew close enough. In all honesty I was not sure that perhaps remaining on board might be a safer course rather than risking the return journey in this vulnerable craft. However, I was given little choice, and so travelled the distance with as much fear as I have ever experienced in my life. To this day I cannot imagine how we were not dashed to pieces or thrown over, to be consumed by the fishes and a watery grave. But we did gain the shore without a single loss, and the ship took further out to ride the storm in deeper waters.

Wouldst that were the end of our struggle. This time of year we had learned to expect ferocious winds and rain, and yet this day seemed worse than any we had previously known. The howl of the wind made conversation nigh impossible, yet we communicated sufficient to co-ordinate a concentrated effort to return myself, my belongings and Ralph to my home. All was intact, the windows heavily shuttered, with just some loose objects outside journeying on the rushing winds. In getting to safety we were witness to many fallen trees and much damage to buildings. There were no citizens about, all sheltering where they felt most safe.

I felt so weary, and was grateful for Ralph's continued attendance in his furnishing us both with wine and some bread to regain our senses somewhat. No sooner were we settled to our small meal and comfort than a heavy hammering came upon the door. Immediately it swung open bringing with it leaves and debris ushered in by the relentless wind. At the entrance stood the panting figure of Anton the Tailor. Hurriedly he put his back to the door restoring a calm to the room, but not to his anxious self.

"Pardon me Doña Catalina, but there has been a tragic accident. One of the trees brought down by the wind has crashed upon a house breaking it to the ground and affording us no entrance. We are fearful that Señor Ramirez is yet inside and may indeed be lost."

Immediately I sprang to my feet, any fatigue cast off in a second.

"Show me, show me right now! Ralph, if Juan is trapped we must do what we can to save him. His life is so precious to me, come quickly."

I was annoyed by his pedantic good manner as he hesitated to allow me through first.

"Get on man!" I screamed, "Make haste!"

I followed with what speed I could against the might of the storm. The driven rain cut into the skin of my face, yet I felt nothing of it as I gained a position where a number had now gathered. All looked on helplessly at the pile of crushed walls and branches. A huge broken trunk meshed seamlessly with the remnants of shattered tabby and snapped frame. No sign of life, nor yet any sense of entry was visible.

For once I was at a loss. My mind span with the confusion of it all, it is my belief we would all have remained in that hopeless position were it not for Ralph. He took a sum of the situation in an instant and began giving orders to those who stood about. Some he sent to fetch branches of certain length and girth, others he directed to find rocks similarly of a specific measure. Whilst they were searching he surveyed the wreckage and took careful note of how things lay. On their return the enthused rescuers rushed to begin pulling parts of the wrecked home and so gain some vantage. At this Ralph became much annoyed and loosed the restraint he had exercised until now, yelling his commands there was no doubting his resolve and authority. No one was to do anything unless specifically directed to do so by him, each would have a precise time to exact their sole task, it was essential that every man listened and complied to the letter. Such was his intention that none dared question or disobey.

Strategically he directed the lengths of branch to be inserted at points around the site, behind each was placed one of the rocks. On a single shout all the might of the men was set to pulling down on the longer ends, levering the mess as a whole, thus the mass of wall and timber was slowly raised in one piece. Once a certain height was achieved they held on for dear life. With the plan executed as such it was possible to see in some way, Ralph took no time in crawling upon his belly into the depths of the rubble. Now it was my turn to yell at those whose strength lay between Ralph's life and certain death. The storm continued unabated. Occasionally airborne articles carried on the wind's back caused the men to dodge about allowing their grip to loosen resulting in some falling debris, and my screaming at their inattentiveness. Whilst I may have been a little unfair, for they were simply avoiding death or injury to themselves, my concerns were purely selfish and I was not afraid to admit it.

All braced themselves more, despite hurting at the great strain that was upon them. Two men, Domingo Benito and Anton de Olmos, held the front aspect with much of the heaviest weight balanced at the tip. I could see in their eyes a steadfastness and unerring duty, they were not about to deny me, Ralph or anyone. The log, however, did not possess the same loyalty as these two good souls. At a point close to the rock over which it was bent a loud crack was heard, even over the wail of the wind, and a piece lifted atop indicating its need to snap there. Horrified I tore off my waistband and ran to the place. The soaked material felt strong as I wound it tight around the fracture pulling as tightly as I could to try and bind it. Still I could see it push at the windings from within, showing no wish to be subdued by this feeble fetter.

I felt a madness surge inside of me built of anger that I would not let it happen, and a sense of desperation to preserve these devices at all cost. Just to hand was an unused bough, discarded as those that were employed were chosen for their greater stature. Rushing over I dragged it through the sopping mud, its rough bark and jagged edges cutting into the flesh on my hands. The weight under any other circumstance would have precluded my being able to move it, yet in this fury I found a strength beyond me. Slowly I lifted it into place aside the dying lever having first manoeuvred its end to the same point, all the time cursing aloud at the tempest which fought to take from me all that I hold dear. By putting my entire weight on the high end to try and effect some lift I gave opportunity for the two beside me to transfer themselves to the new support just as the old fell in two.

I fell to sitting in the swilling water at our feet and gazed into the black, empty space, now made smaller by this shifting. Weakly I called his name over and over, with no chance of it being heard above the tumult, yet I could not give up. By and by the time passed with still no sign of movement. Some of the men were crying with pain as their muscles burned from maintaining the hold. All seemed lost.

"Catalina! Take his hands and pull as I will push from here."

A frail old hand appeared at the opening followed by another. I grabbed both and dug my heels into the soft ground affording me a greater draw. Juan's lifeless body was less of the weight I expected and he came straight into the opening causing me to fall away. As I sat up and went back to him on my knees, Ralph came out at speed through the gap, rolling clear as the final strengths of the levers gave out and all came crashing back down. A quick gulp of fresh air as he lay on his back with the rain washing off the gained dust, and Ralph was back on his feet. Bending he scooped up the old man's body and carried him straightway to my house were he laid him on a bed.

"Is he dead Ralph?" I ventured, still full of the fear of the moment.

"He spoke to me, when I found him, of his love for you, and bade me promise to convey it to you as such, anymore than that I know not."

I grabbed some cloths and cleaned and dried him best I could. I felt no life in the beat of his heart yet proffered a small brandy to his cold lips. At its introduction it seemed to make no progress, yet its warmth caused an indiscernible movement, then a more marked cough. He was alive. I took from him any things of discomfort, but for the most part he was dry. Wrapping him in warm bed linens I smoothed back his hair, kissed his forehead and sat to the long wait that I knew would follow. Ralph thanked the small party of rescuers giving them each a measure of good brandy, and bade them take safety with their loved ones, any news would be passed to them on the morrow if all had settled then. Closing the door behind their retreat he returned to my side and sat in quiet reflection, watching in hope, joined in my silent prayers.

During the long night either one of us was attentive for the most whilst the other rested. There was a sense that if we were to sleep for any length of time we would lose his spirit, his link with the living world just a tenuous thread to hold onto. A low light kept us aware of any movement or need, and yet was dim enough to disturb him little. I lay my head on Ralph's lap as he gently stroked my hair, affording me some comfort. Thus my eyes fell level with Juan's and I stared ever-hopeful at the aged, sun-beaten, heavily lined, but familiar face. Each line led me down a journey to my past, at home in Aviles, adventuring out or listening to tales of suspense and excitement related by any who would indulge me.

Juan's presence usually meant my father was come home. So often his visits would cause great celebration throughout the town. Once the shout had gone up that his ships were heading in we would ride as fast as we could to the beach to catch the first sight. I recalled watching the white sails dotting the unbroken sea, the long pennants snaking from atop the masts, and the shouting children her-

·

alding a new return. We would gallop back at full tilt to join the people filling the narrow streets, all going down the steep pathways to line the estuary and greet the brave explorers as the ships entered the river. As I rode along the shore I would believe my father could see my long, black hair streaming out behind me in answer to his own flags, thus I would be the first thing he could see of his home as he entered through the familiar waters. Father's home-comings brought light to our lives, but especially to mine. I knew that there would be presents for me, strange and unusual objects that would always have a story attached to them. The stories would be told whilst many of the townsfolk sat around, enthralled by the excitement and fear that they consisted of. At the centre of it was my gift, and thus I was made to feel so special. Although my father would tease me with different ploys to deny it me, the huge smile that sat upon my lips from the moment his ship came into view never left my face for a minute. Whatsmore, I always knew the prize would eventually be mine.

Now, as my mind ran between the bright white buildings, I could see the faces of my friends, young and old, I could hear the music playing the familiar jigs that were common to our celebrations, and I realised that I was not alone in receiving, my father brought a gift for all, one of happiness. To grow up in that knowledge perhaps made me the luckiest child alive. My closeness to my father was without challenge, even my seafaring brother could not have boasted of a friendship quite so special as ours. Perhaps I was selfish, or maybe even deluded, but to this day I have no doubt of it. As the pictures trickled through my mind so the tears ran too. I missed my father so much, and now in front of me I was witnessing the life ebb away from my final link to him.

The morning light came quicker than I expected, clearly I had slept more than intended, no doubt due to the exhaustive day before. I could hear some business at my back, lifting my head and turning I saw a smiling Ralph carrying a breakfast across the room. Confused, I remembered the gravity of the situation and felt betrayed by his apparent lack of care.

"Morrow, Catalina. I thought you might like to join us in a little refreshment."

My head swung around at the significance of his light remark to be greeted by a smiling, familiar old face.

"Juan! Oh how it warms my heart to see you so. Surely I am both pleased yet surprised at how well you look."

Before Juan could answer, Ralph bade him rest and tempered my enthusiasm, reminding me that it was only hours since we thought him dead.

"You of all should know that there can be nothing better for him than absolute rest. There will be time for talking later when he is stronger."

I reached over Juan and kissed his cheek, nothing more than an exchange of smiles was necessary to impart what each had to say just then. Taking the proffered drink from Ralph's hand, in jest I muttered something of hiring him as my own nurse, to which he laughed and sat back to eat. I held the drink to Juan's mouth and reflected on my previous thoughts aboard ship. To this point at least nothing much had changed, I had been saved any further consideration, and for this moment I thanked God for everything.

The storm lessened over the day and next night, but remained enough to allow us an undisturbed refuge wherein we all partook of many hours sleep, much was it needed. As Juan regained his senses it had the consequence of alerting him more to the various hurts about his body which caused him to complain some. In time we realised the more he grumbled so the better was his recovery.

At the second day Ralph ventured forth to relate the news that Señor Ramirez was in repairing health entirely due to those who had fought so hard for his salvation. On his return he was much subdued and spoke little of what had occurred in the course of his visits. I questioned him not, but was no less curious. It was not until the following day that I felt secure enough in Juan's health to go out myself, it was then that I learned the reason for Ralph's quiet. The whole town was awash with talk of his heroic deed.

The first person I met was Francesca, wife of Anton the tailor, she had the detail of it all and had obviously delayed little in ensuring that as many of Santa Elena knew it by rote, so much so that it had already become folklore it seemed. I emphasised again the significant part her husband had played, and while she acknowledged this with some pride, the fact was that the Englishman's new found stature now appeared to constitute a notion of more importance than the actual recovery of Señor Ramirez de Contreras. I puzzled at the absurdity of this, but found satisfaction in listening to the wonder that sounded in their telling of it, more importantly, I sensed a turn of events that was possibly playing much in my favour. I was aware of the fickle nature of people that makes a hero one day a servant the next, yet I dared hope that perhaps somewhere amidst it all my prayers were being answered.

There was considerable damage from the storm, and many were busy at the repair of roofs, barns and chicken coops. Some others had received injury of various natures, but none had lost their lives. There were a handful of fatalities to the livestock, but that was to be expected through their inability to shelter, and some had been lost as stockades had broken, the cattle or pigs simply wandering off providing a healthy gift for the native populations. No matter the work that was to be done, each person I greeted returned a happy smile and left me with nothing but a good feeling inside.

I was much surprised to find Gutierre at work amongst the people, making repair to the church where a large branch had lodged itself through a side window. It was unusual to witness his solidarity with the workers, and I marvelled at it. I went to him not to gloat, but to earnestly praise him for his diligence and endeavour. I found a man ready to accept the meted praise, and not the usual sanguineous remark that so often was his ready wit in return.

"My dear Catalina, come sit with me awhile." He strode over and we sat upon the step at the entrance. He continued:

"I am already knowledgeable of Señor Ramirez mended health, and I must thank you for that. This has been a heady business and a deft reminder to us all of the sanctity of life and the frailty of our own. It seems we also have much to thank your English Lord for at this time too. The tales of his heroism have the place buzzing like bees at a hive learning of a new rich source for their honey-making. I have been humbled by the preceding days, both at nature's force by which our lives are steered, and by the resolve of the people of this land. I have seen with my own eyes the strengths and determination that have been brought here and with which we shall build a precious life. Now then have we also been witness to a baptism of sort. The water that has christened Ralph to our family was of a most intolerant sort and not offered gently, yet he has taken this place and its people to his heart, and has shown us a resolve that echoes much of the mettle we built our home upon. It has been suggested to me that some formality be offered to Señor Ellerker by way of reward and acceptance. I am in full agreement with this notion, and have already given orders to mark the occasion in a public fashion."

Rising to attend again to his work he displayed a kindly smile.

"In course I shall talk with you more on the matter, good day Catalina."

I was struck dumb. I had read of St. Paul's change of heart on the road to Damascus, to me this was just as much a revelation. Did I dare hope too much? If by this remark Gutierre meant that Ralph could now be seen as an equal amongst us what would be the consequence then? Would I have the propriety to be seen openly in my affection for him? I would be nervous of being acknowledged in this way, it would alter my authority, and yet I could be proud of him without fear of reproach. My mind was a jumble, but my feet scarcely touched the ground as I returned home with the news.

Thus one week to the day of our return to Santa Elena I found myself witness to our entire population gathered formally about the church steps where the most unusual ceremony took place. The walls were freshly painted and bedecked with coloured ribbons and flags, and a small group stood to the fore in order that all might see and marvel at the affair.

A short burst of trumpeted introduction announced the proclamation that Ralph Ellerker, a lost son of England, was, that day, and for all days hence, to become a full citizen of Santa Elena, with all its entitlement and freedoms. He was no longer in scrvitude, but was to reside alongside any other by choice and as an equal in every sense.

In concord with my earlier discussions, Gutierre and I had determined that a position of Estate Management be conferred upon him in order that he might be rightly employed with a fitting position. Juan Ramirez was never to be fit enough to resume his duties, and thus it was both sensible and fortuitous that his role should fall to his saviour. I was happy to see Juan at last rest his weary bones having served our family so fastidiously through the years, but the turn of events that lay before me this day I could not view as anything other than an absolute answer to my prayers.

To this end, upon the disassemblage of the crowd, I made my way reverently into our repaired church, crossing to the candlelit chapel wherein the beautiful image of our Blessed Virgin gazed down in benevolence. I knelt for a short time to thank her for her intercessions and to express my deepest reverence for the grace I had been shown at the hand of the Almighty. I rose and lit a candle to reside amongst the multitude of other lights there, in my mind placing the soul of my precious Ralph with those of my own dear friends. My worries softened and slid away as did the tallow of those melting prayers before me. My happiness overwhelmed me, and surged yet more as I turned to see a thoughtful, gently smiling figure waiting patiently at the door. I moved to him, placing my arm upon his, and walked proudly through the filled streets, accepting greetings and words of congratulation with small nods and smiles as we returned to the comfort of my house.

There was some detail yet to be worked upon, despite our outward ease, to this end I arranged a good house for Ralph which was befitting his station, and it was known by all that his residence was there, albeit that for the most time we were inextricable. We would talk for long hours into the evenings, and enjoy friends to dinner, and accompanied each other to various events and parties. Yet our relationship was treated with respect, and our separate lives noted by all. I was not sure of the propriety of my being entirely free of mourning yet, and Ralph too seemed to favour a less formal marking of our union. We remained discreet in our coupling, ensuring that on the many nights we remained together, the day still began with Ralph resident in his own place. On occasion when our fervour took us past the breaking dawn we were careful in how we appeared to any that might mark our movements, contriving elaborate ways that might fool them into thinking otherwise than the truth of our inseparability.

Whereas this might cause annoyance to others that would do the same, for us it retained a control that we both found essential to our being. The excesses of emotion we shared betwixt us ran beyond the norm of any match I had ever before been privy to. As such we were at pains to retain the intimacy of it, and the entirety of it for ourselves. This was not a love to be shared by anyone else, not something to be the meat of tavern tittle-tattle, or even to be supposed by young maidens imagining great tales of love upon which to dream and hope for themselves. This was our love, a love so deep that we transcended all human bonds when we made love, a love that joined us so well that our separate days were only spaced by the same air we each breathed, still existing in each other's mind the day through. I was happier than I had ever imagined possible.

As the months passed by our little heaven prospered and grew. The estate faired well under Ralph's hand, the respect he attained from those he directed and from those who came to him for help on all matters was complete and unbreakable. He gained no enemy and meted out praise and justice with equal care. His prodigious ability to master language caused him to extend our fruitful relationship with those natives who had come to trust us. Our trade increased somewhat, and there were no more incursions that had previously caused us to worry much.

I was pressed somewhat by Gutierre at times to cement my friendship with Señor Ellerker with some formal bond, perhaps even a marriage. This gave me some surprise at first, but Ralph's ability to turn serious conversation on this subject to a lighthearted banter amongst us tempered his enthusiasm to repeat the suggestion too often. I would laugh and play along with the absurdity of such a notion, but I oft noted a flutter that would skip within me at the thought. I did not allow myself to question whether I should pay heed to such feelings as it was clear that Ralph was steadfast in retaining our positions exact, for whatever reason, that was enough reason for me. I often think of how things might have changed had that discussion taken place betwixt us in a sensible moment, away from those who might sway us this way or that. Oft times did I lay gazing into the black of the night, my head resting on his gently lifting chest, my finger dancing slow circles in the wispy hairs there, daring myself to disturb his quiet slumber and venture the thought. But to risk losing anything, one single, minute portion of what we had together stayed my mind and sealed my lips lest I break the spell. Instead I would breathe in the heady scent of his body and re-live the moments before when we had loved each other so full, when our souls had remained locked in a marriage so much beyond the inadequacies of mortality.

The news came slowly and erringly. No one knew for sure what was true in the coming of it, but bit by bit the reality formed into a lucid and startling picture. It came first from the mouths of some of us who had chosen to fish far off beyond the reef. About the fifth of June in the year of Our Lord 1586 they had reported the passing of a large number of ships, various in size, which they swore to bear the St George, even though it were spied from so far off. It was noted how the flotilla lingered some while before making off to continue on by.

Their reports had been scoffed at, not for the inadequacy of their eyesight, but moreso because the reported northward direction would have likely had them travel some days hence before the might of Pedro's ships at San Agustin. We knew this to be a near impossibility as their vigilance was unmatched in these seas. One Ralph Ellerker himself had been testament to this some four years since. Yet the talk caused some concern and a great deal of supposition. When at last the detail came, it was two weeks later, at the hand of some very weary messengers. I was aware that a little discourse had unlawfully eased its way out to a few of those at hand before the full recount had been delivered to the intended recipient, Gutierre. The alarm on the faces of those who had this knowledge betrayed not the item of it, but certainly the tenor. These people were come not with news of anything good.

I made haste to seek the truth direct from Gutierre, yet I was unable to gain attention from him in all but a brief dismissal. Although I was much annoyed by this I was sensible to the fact that he was dealing with something beyond a simple courteous expression to his sister-in-law. He bellowed orders here and there and ordered a fragata to ensure him a swift passage to San Agustin immediately. Just as he made to leave the room, he halted and returned to me with much furtiveness.

"For God's sake lay low." he whispered, "Both you and Señor Ellerker. Remain so until I return. I ask this of you for your own sake and that of others for whom you care. At this time forgive my inattentiveness, but heed my words full well. God save our souls, God save our souls"

His words vanished with him as he swept through the open door, leaving me with a dread weight in the depth of my stomach. Not quite comprehending what he might mean by his dire warning.

The days passed with much conjecture, all aware that we were to await what news might be had from Pedro at Gutierre's return. It was of some concern that his fragata did not appear again for a three week, and the skiff that navigated his safe return across the reef made no hurry either. Upon reaching the shore I was comforted at least by his determined stride to meet me first, yet my comfort was fast dissipated by his countenance and subtle word:

"Come to me in one hour, I shall recount in full what has passed, but mark me, come alone, bring none but yourself. Your position as Adelantado and the place you still secure in the hearts of these people shall serve us well, your past or your future attendants have no place in this discourse."

I was numbed by his inference, but was in no uncertain mind as to the meaning of his instruction. I felt a strength in the playing of my duty passed to me by my father, but I was plagued by a sense of helplessness at the exclusion of Ralph. Never before had I experienced such a feeling. My life had always been well within my control, even when my father was the hand on my tiller I still plotted the course on the charts of my destiny. I fast became aware that I had nurtured a complete reliance on this one man that had become the centre of my world. Whilst I had gained by way of his strengths, I had similarly lost the singularity that commanded my life and any who were subject to it. Worse still, I was much in favour of this shift, and the thought of abandoning his guiding hand to return to that responsibility caused me to gain a growing fear, no doubt increased all the more by the unknown terrors of which I knew I would shortly learn.

The hour crawled by at a less than desirable pace. On one hand I was desirous to find out more quickly what it was that Gutierre wished me to know, on the other side I was at pains to avoid any sight of Ralph lest I should have to explain why he was not to be party to our meet.

By and by I came to the large house that had witnessed so much happiness through the fiestas and fine evenings we had all enjoyed at my brother-in-law's expense. It seemed somehow desolate and untidy in the burning sun of the noon on this strange day. The fences and trees, and even the timbers of the building appeared bleached into a oneness with the chalk white tabby of the walls. There was none of the colour that perhaps was usually apparent in the festive lanterns and other decorations that so oft hung about the place. It felt unwelcoming which only hastened the welling sense of foreboding that was turning any sensibility in me to that of an inexperienced child.

On entering I was escorted to a small office wherein I was to find our Governor, unusually inattentive to his guest, and visibly tired as he examined pages of written document.

"Lest I forget my manners, Catalina, please join me in a brandy, one I have kept for some time, but one of which I feel the need to restore my weary bones."

He passed the golden liquid, already poured, without waiting for my assent. The pleasant heat seeped slowly through my body wakening in me a considered approach to this encounter, gaining me a more solid composure that brought with it the Catalina I knew of old.

"Well brother, tell me what causes this furrowed brow, are we to understand what has passed these few weeks?"

He swallowed a very large measure of the brandy in his hand and stared at me hard. I wondered for some moments if I should somehow make a guess at his thoughts or how he might speak, but in truth he was at a loss as to how he should begin his recount.

"Mark me, Catalina, hear my story in full. Interrupt me at your peril for I shall not be stayed from the telling in its entirety."

I felt absolutely no wish to utter a single word. I clutched the vessel in my hand and fastened my eye to his.

"The information that was brought to me those weeks ago in this place was dark and told of some disaster by which I was most disturbed. The clutter in the informants mind seemed at times incoherent and thus difficult to follow, and moreso hard to believe. I took the journey south in order to ascertain for myself the extent of this man's ramblings, but I was not prepared for what did greet my eye.

"For some hours before we rounded the headland above the bar we could see rising grey smoke clouding the skies above. Just as many days had passed from the messenger's leaving as we had sailed in return, so this portent seemed an unlikely continuation and must surely signal some new occurrence we thought. However, the sight as we came through and into the port was beyond any comprehension. The smoke was still rising from the blackened remains of every building that was San Agustin. Not a single house remained, no store, office nor even the church.

"We were landed in no time, and the full extent of the devastation became yet more apparent. We stood in a complete wilderness. Worse than that, it was a living portrayal of Satan's hell. Forsure, one of Beelzebub's demons had flown over and put torch to every upright thing that had previously existed there. The crops were burned, the trees torched, the stockades gone, worse yet, the stench of burning flesh marked the fiery demise of all the livestock too. People sat about smeared with the charcoal that their world now consisted of. Some prodded the remains of their properties, sifting the embers for signs of anything they might salvage. Children wept for their inability to understand what had become of their homes and toys, and some cried for the loss of their pets.

"Never have I seen such desolation. In no time I found Pedro, his self marked by the foulness of the land. At every turn he gave orders to try and bring some sense to his world, and offered solace and comforting words to any he felt needed them, and there were many. As he spied us he stood looking at me with his arms outstretched and with an expression of desperate resignation on his tired face. Walking over I hugged him well and told him of the stores we had transported with us. At the first telling of it here I took allowance of the possibility the story had some truth in it. Now witnessing what I have already mentioned I wished I had been yet more diligent in my provision. Still, I had brought with me grain and fresh water, some canvas for making shelter, and much of some other things that would serve them well. In truth I believe I could have stocked just anything such was their destitution. Pedro led me to a tent wherein he had established something of a command post from whence he could direct affairs. Once inside he proceeded to the business of explaining how this had come to pass.

"It seems that reports had come to them for some months previous of the progress of a marauding army led by an Englishman, Francis Drake. His progress through the Hispaniola and around saw the demise of various places, in name: Santiago, Santa

Domingo, and Carthagena. Each sacked by this ruthless pirate. Those in San Agustin had learned of this action in time to prepare hurriedly for what must ultimately come their way. Over two weeks great trees were felled and set into the ground to fashion a fort that faced the beach on the far side of the river. It was felt at least that some obvious stronghold might cause the invaders to retreat if the going was not to be made easy.

"The ships did arrive, and the first of the enemy set themselves for two days to attempt an attack at the fort. At their failure to advance past this point a second retinue came abroad headed by the rogue Drake. His command brought up some artillery to the fore, which fired upon and broke the defences, Pedro being unfurnished with such a piece to return the same. Thus under cover of dark they abandoned the fort and crossed back across the river to guard the town. Full discussion led him to a belief that if they were to retain the women and children in that place they would be prey to the advancing enemy which no man was prepared to risk.

"So it was decided that the good citizens should be led out to the surrounding country and there laid in hiding to escape the wrath of this onslaught. Pedro and his men remained one day more at the town, the enemy not sure of the river and unable to make much headway. Yet again they moved up their ordnance and set about a bombardment. At this Pedro became sensible of the predicament he had now left the people of the town in. They lay hidden for now, but guarded only by a handful of men. It left them vulnerable and a weakness in his strategy. Thus it was decided that they should abandon the town in its entirety, the people in his charge the true priority. With great presence of mind they buried what little ordnance they had and decided to leave the King's chest at the fort by way of a prize that might be sufficient to satisfy the invaders. The wages had been paid and the remaining ducats numbered few and were so deemed to be of little importance.

"Once in the land they secreted themselves for the most with just a small group left to guard any entrance. When the English came to the town their number seemed immense, and Pedro was in no uncertain mind that his plan had been correct. Word came to him that two foreign members of the town had since gone missing, they being untrustworthy fellows. It was known that they were privy to the hidden ordnance and other things, and so it was clear it was like to be retrieved by those who had set about destroying the town. These same men also knew of the people's hiding thus it was no surprise when some of the others came to look in that place for the hidden townsfolk and soldiers. However, their attack consisted entirely of one foolhardy charge by a single officer coming upon them at full tilt presenting himself without care, an easy target to be slain immediately by those soldiers on guard. Once he was dispatched it seemed to melt the resolve of those others who might follow him, and so they abandoned any further assault, and went back to the ransack.

"In all they remained a further six days, diligent in their destruction, denying the people the means to recover anything of their existence. When finally they were gone, the ships were seen to be heading north to this place certainly, but whatever stayed them from the same course of action we can only thank God for. Indeed, it was Pedro's firm belief that we too would be facing the same devastation that they now contend with. We can thank God yet more, for although some of the English were killed not a single Spanish life was lost. Some have suffered since, both from the nature of their hiding so damp and so vulnerable for that time, and for the lack of provision. I have offered them comfort and a home in Santa Elena for any that might come, but their resolve is such that all have remained to rebuild or make good as they see fit.

"To this end I have given detailed instruction that as many ships as we can muster are to be laden with every imaginable item we can spare, and further that we cannot spare. We are now the only source of sincere supply to these good people, and we must do all that we can to ensure a speedy return to some ordinary living."

He halted in his discourse and looked to me with a softer gaze as he had noted something of myself of which I was as yet unaware, for a flow of tears had wet my breast, soaking the material there. He tenderly leaned forward and wiped a drop of it from my face whilst I sat yet unmoved by the knowledge of it.

"If I might now address you Señor? I ventured.

"But of course Catalina. Make bold to speak on any subject you wish to, I hold no objection."

I slowly rose from my seat and made for the small open window to the side of the room. I looked from it to the land and turned with a fresh resolve.

"Good brother. I would ask of you without any reserve that I be included in the cargo of one of those that now voyage to the home of my Father. I must make myself available to all who undoubtedly have need of me in this most unholy hour. The hurt that has been done to these, my Father's children, is without forgiveness, and for this my blood does boil. However, that will serve none at all. My hand is well trained at medicine and other cure, and I can at least be of use in a more structured manner through this skill. My place is where my father stood those years ago, I must stand in his stead and provide what succour I can to these poor souls in their present misery. I shall instil in them that which was given to me by my great Captain, and draw upon the strengths that he set down those years ago, the foundations that yet remain in our land. Please do not attempt to hinder my progress nor remind me of my duties to Santa Elena, my Father shall always come first and his legacy is both here and in San Agustin. I shall not be swayed from this course."

He came across to me taking my small hands in his and placed a kindly kiss upon my forehead.

"I would not consider for a minute to hinder your path in any way dear sister. Please go pack what things you need and I will make preparation for your voyage. I will be glad of such representation that I can rely on, for your sincerity and ability are beyond redress. If I might be so bold, I would ask that you carry with you some papers and other details of office for your cousin, you would serve me well, and I would be ensured of their safety and complete delivery."

I returned a short smile of assent and strode from his house to gather whatever I could think might be necessary for this difficult time I now faced. I felt sure that most in Santa Elena would already have a general knowledge of the situation in their sister town, more detail would undoubtedly be learned within a few more hours. I hurried to my house and made lists to enable me to stay fixed upon my task. It was essential that I remembered everything I would normally have had to hand in my little hospital. My little hospital that would no longer exist! I wept some more for the loss as I packed whatever receptacles I could find. I was minded to take a minimum of my clothing sensing that any unnecessary items would only serve to lessen the space available for more essential items. Then I reflected that perhaps clothing would be one of those very things most needed. So I included as much of this too. Once I was set to go I called for hands to contain and transport my wares to the boats that would enable them on board whichever ship Gutierre had organised. I was vaguely amused at the faces of those who came as I was immensely overloaded, yet I considered it all to be of the essence. They did not question my authority of course and the bags and boxes made their way across the shoals by small boats to join the rest of the stores bound southward. Gutierre, good to his promise, had made my passage a priority on the largest of our ships, and I left within the day.

As the coast slipped by, I thought on the plight of those whose fate I was about to be a party to. How must they have feared the coming of the barbarous English who had razed their homes so callously, what terrors would await them in their dreams as they slumbered? A huge shock gripped my stomach in an instant shaking my whole body and causing me to utter a small cry that I was at pains to subdue. What of my English man? For God's sake, I had not only forsaken him in my ambition, but worse I had not equated his origin to that of these hurtful creatures. I was at once torn into a thousand pieces by the many aspects of this predicament. I had failed to signal my departure to him or give him farewell of any sort. He would not know of my leaving until someone might mention to him that it is so. Worse still the news of what occurred in San Agustin will no doubt reach his ears and cause him much fear and dread at the recrimination that could be in store for him. I could not protect him, perhaps neither would I want to. He is an Englishman. It was his own countrymen who wrought such hurt upon my own people, destroying my father's work, how could I forgive him? I wanted him there, I needed to speak to him, yet would I fly at him, or strike him? How could this become so, we had no future now surely. I hated him in his birthright. What manner of man had crept into my life to suck the very goodness out of it, and gnaw away at the golden core of my life?

I flew below decks to my quarters and buried my head in my hands. There I remained through the night until daybreak, unable to sleep, but weeping unceasing, needing to feel the caress of his strong hands. I wanted him so badly to take the pain away, and yet at the centre of the pain he was there. My insides pulled at every sinew, a deep set feeling that could never leave me or yet be resolved.

I must have slept at some early hour as I was awakened by the roll of the waves as we had made good progress against the tides. The feeling had subsided somewhat and I felt it necessary to go take the air and partake of some sustenance to keep me well for the ensuing months. I sensed that my sleeping mind had made some order of the chaos and I had chosen to stay fixed to my course. I could not allow games of the heart to deter me from my set duty, and although my stomach plunged occasionally as the picture of his soft grey eyes came into my head, I was able to fix upon my goal and return to a sensible determination.

The work was gruelling in the extreme. Despite Gutierre's detail the reality was beyond any match to my imagination. No simple narrative could begin to describe the desolation and destruction I was witness to. I felt and bore the pain of each and every individual in that wasteland. The filth made it nigh impossible to tend with any cleanliness to those who needed my attention. I did take some heart at the people's resolve to work a seamless shift through, they laboured night and day to bring some order to the place, and this basic need was achieved within a few days of our arrival. Once the boats had been unloaded it brought a hope to their hearts and a lighter foot with which to set to building and cleaning, organising fair rations, and establishing new clean waterholes. This was the essential matter from which sprang the roots of a new town. I was minded of the fact that some good few men had been with my father those years back when this land had to be taken from the bare earth, unbroken and hostile in its reception. That same ambition upon which my Father established San Agustin I saw return in the presence of his spirit.

As the smoke cleared and the buildings began to rise, so did the voices of the diligent workers. On occasion a tune would start up and some group would work to the tempo of it. Meal times out of necessity were large communal affairs which increased still more the conviviality and comradeship so essential to the effort. My hands remained as muddied as any, for my work ran well beyond the mere tending to the sick and broken, I too carried materials, hammered pieces together, and patted tabby to new walls. This experience brought me to a level of understanding and closeness that I had never before had the good fortune to experience. I learned much of the people's ways and their minds, and enjoyed so much of the life that they built for themselves. Where I had previously given instruction I now became the student, and I marvelled at what it was possible to achieve. Had either of my sisters come by through those days I doubt they would have recognised me, they most certainly would have denied me. My clothes were for the most tattered and torn and dirtied from all manner of things. My hair too was tied back in an unkempt manner that owed nothing to fashion and all to function. Pedro, who was as actively involved himself, had much fun at my expense, but in return I would simply cast some wet plaster or charred wood in his direction and we would laugh not unlike we had when we played as children. In truth I had found a blessed freedom in the tragedy that I did not know I missed. That same freedom that had taken me out from the house in Aviles on so many long summer adventures when my responsibilities could be numbered on one very small hand.

It was in excess of three months before we slowed to a pace when something of our formalities began to return. There was much order to the place and the majority of buildings were near finished, crops had been sown and the stockades were filled with half of Santa Elena's livestock. It would be some time before we would see a returning yield from the newly planted fruit trees, and the food supplies were carefully measured to ensure they lasted until the next harvests were due. There was still something of a preoccupation in conversation with the ever-present threat of a further invasion. To this end even Diego de Velasco had played a diligent part.

Together with the strategists under Pedro's guide a plan was devised to build a substantial fort to guard the town in case of future incursion. This was a priority for many so the first drawings were of a substantial stronghold reliant in the main on the timbers from the surrounding forest. They would be fashioned and erected in a well-conceived order to be most effective, but plans of a greater stature were also drawn up to replace this first structure with a much bigger and more permanent stone fort. This would offer protection from every vantage point and would ensure a complete refuge for the entire town should it ever be needed. I believe that for Diego it was like building his own palace, but for the inhabitants of San Agustin it was to represent a truly established town, one that would last forever, a fitting tribute to its founder's tenacity and bravery.

My work there was near done, and although I felt I was much a part of that town, my thoughts began to run to my home in Santa Elena. Naturally this included Ralph Ellerker, yet I still kept my mind shut to thoughts of him as much as I could for fear of the madness that would once again course through my veins. However, the less recourse I had to my manual duties the more my mind wandered in that direction. I felt I had to return and face whatever there was to face. I was aware in that space that no word had come from home during my absence, nothing of my estate nor its workings, no mention of how the people there faired, and certainly not an utterance from one in particular. The ships came regularly with stores and materials giving ample opportunity for any who might wish to send word to me, yet any correspondence was limited to the perfunctory cataloguing and accounting of the content between myself and Gutierre.

My choice was made for me in the end. A convoy of ships arrived in port from Spain, the first supplies to come not from Santa Elena. The king had been generous and the provisions were plentiful and rich. Once the ships were unladen and the bounty variously placed where it should, the town fell to a great celebration. We had reached a day that truly marked a re-birth, San Agustin lived again. We partied through the night and much into the next day. I felt some sadness as I retreated to my formal role for I no longer really belonged amongst the ordinary folk, not through my choosing but purely by their manner toward me, my Father was Pedro Menéndez de Avilés y Alonso de la Campa, none would forget that, and it was not a role I could or ever would deny or relinquish.

During that next afternoon as the town lay quiet, Pedro called me to his office with some formality to hand he wished to discuss. He had a directive brought to him from Spain the content of which he would have me learn. His manner was light as ever it had been to me, and we sat partaking of a cool fruit punch, a welcome relief to the excesses of the previous night.

"My dear Catalina, I have been given an order from the authorities that will have to be taken to all our outposts, including Santa Elena. I should like to ask that you be the courier for this content to your town. It will mean you leaving us for now, but this is a loss I can accept as I know you have a need to return."

I went to protest but thought again of the necessity he had spoken of, instead I enquired further:

"Tell me dear cousin, what is the instruction that I must carry on this voyage, for I fear it might not be enough to remove me from this happy crowd."

"I feel you may not embrace it so lightly, for it is a dictate from Spain to remove the entirety of our other sites to just one, and that place is here in San Agustin. There can be no question, and no exception."

Pedro was entirely right, the lightness of the mood crashed to the floor as the significance of the request became apparent.

"What then will become of Santa Elena? Surely it is not simply to be abandoned after all this time?"

My mind ran to the futility of my husband's supposed failure, I saw pictures in my mind of that happy land wherein I had found so much joy. It was my town, my piece of land, and now I felt I had betrayed it. Here was I celebrating the resurrection of the usurper, that which was to take my people from their homes and deny them the years through which they had endeavoured to build their lives. Whatsmore I had played a part in this plan, unknowingly paving the way for the very destruction of Santa Elena.

"I sense a tear in your eye, sweet Catalina, but see it for what it is intended. You will once again reside here, with us, all safe in one place, hardened in our resolve to retain this land for ourselves and for Spain and for the memory of your father.

"Take this charge and explain it well to your kinfolk for they respect you and look to you for their own strength and belief. Thus show them the spirit of Aviles and the fortitude that comes from this union, dwell not on the loss for they should not see it as such. Go now, and take my blessing with you for this is your duty."

I took my ease in the comfort of a large caravela for the return voyage to my doomed homestead. The will to go there lay around my ankles like lead weights. I could not have wished for any task more onerous. Still worse, I was to deliver this edict with a smile and enthusiasm that would betray me as naught but a liar. As the strong current ushered us to the task I grew a resolve to mourn the loss of Santa Elena alongside my people, I could neither continue a happy heart that would be believed, nor could I bear it. Beside, I had more to contend with than most. My heart already lay shattered on that soil. I could still not really know my mind on the matter, but I was at least aware that his cold heart had steered him not to write or send word of mouth by even the lowliest sailor that had ferried goods southward during my tenure abroad. He cared naught for me for sure, no matter it had been my inattentiveness on departing that had laid the ground for such an unfounded action. I determined I should not seek him out at my arrival, but should go about my business and perhaps learn something of his whereabouts and habit through passing comment. There would be those whose mention would lead me to ascertain mind and mood, I should learn fairly quickly whether he was wont to see me without appearing keen myself. Thus would I save myself from any foolhardiness.

For all this resolve the approaching familiar coast-line caused in me a perceptible tremble that I could not cease nor control, although I was of a mind that too much time stood on deck in the cool sea air at such an early hour may have lent me a chill. The growing sun's warmth helped quell it to a degree, but now I could not wait to regain the earth and set about my task.

Gutierre was insistent upon my joining him for a small breakfast before he would allow me to any business. The day was young and the hour was not yet come to indulge in matters of state. In this he was most like his brother, my dear husband, whose days were punctuated most emphatically with a right time and a wrong time for any formality. I believe Hernando had considered this his right hav-ing adventured fully with my father when there was never a time for anything but the task at hand. A measured, ordered life had been his reward for the hectic and unplanned pace, even if his own plans only ran from one hunting trip to the next.

The surroundings were pleasantly dappled with the low sun lighting through the small windows mark-ing the new day on the bright, white walls, and the fruits were most welcome and refreshing, yet I could not settle to any comfort. Eventually I could bear it no longer and reached down to retrieve the folded parchment placing it on the table between us, the seal still intact, staining the skin like spilt blood.

"What is this my little messenger?"

Gutierre's playful face comprehended not the drama I was bringing to the stage as he reached for it without hurry or much care. I did not move my hand from off it despite his attempt to take it. He looked up at me and realised that something was truly amiss.

"A warrant." I stated plainly. "A death warrant."

Still we remained in that self-same position.

"For whom?" he guardedly asked.

"For Santa Elena."

I sat back and watched him snap the seal as he picked it up, casting his eye over the content. I waited silently as he read the detail again and again, perhaps expecting the words to shift and a different meaning evolve before him. He sat back and appeared relaxed, screwing up the papers and placing them discarded at the side of the table he picked up a fig and nonchalantly peeled it. Through a mouthful of juicy fruit he spoke calmly.

"This is nonsense, just complete nonsense. They have it wrong, I know they do. They do not mean this place too. I mean, Tequesta, Tocobago and San Anton I can understand, and also Santa Lucia, even San Mateo, but not Santa Elena. Of course not."

Imperceptibly his voice grew in crescendo until he spat the words out forcing him to wipe his mouth with the back of his hand. Rising he paced as he railed some more.

"This is our Capital, this is our centre, not San Agustin. We have a population of nigh on five hundred citizens now, our lives are fulfilled, and we work and live in peace. Did *we* get attacked? Do *we* make any demands on others? What lunatic in Spain looked at a map and made decisions without sensible exploration? No doubt some old fool who should have been retired long ago. This is complete nonsense."

He sat once more and ran his fingers through his hair, I remained unspoken, I had no need of it, I too had paced out the same questions and suppositions, and argued against the insanity and unfairness of the decision, but there it was.

"How must we tell the town of this Catalina? The paper says we have just a six month to be gone from here in our entirety, we must start now then. Oh Lord, why this?"

I cannot say how long we sat in discussion for there seemed no easy answer to his question, and both of us were at a loss as to how we should present this proclamation. The day was yet past and my body was wearied from the journey and the discourse through the hours. Gutierre called for a bed to be made up to save me any more concern. I welcomed the invite and soon laid my head down to reach a deep slumber before even my eyes were shut.

Our resolve was settled upon a formal event. There could be little room for a demonstration of the emotions we ourselves had struggled to contain. Our removal from this land was a fact, a command that did not warrant discourse nor debate. The honest folk of Santa Elena did not deserve the agony of protracted argument that might consider some other end when in fact there could be none.

Notices were pinned around the town announcing a meeting, all were instructed to attend. The summons in itself caused a sense of foreboding without its purpose yet known. It did not take much more to ensure that our entire population was assembled before us in the space at the front of the church we had restored those months since. I stood aside from Gutierre who had attired himself most extravagantly, mustering all the formality he could in order to lend the moment the utmost sincerity. His aim was to ensure that none were in any doubt about what they must do, although I felt he did not have the strength to face questions, or to significantly justify what he was to say, by this means at least he could hide behind the façade of his office.

"Good people of Santa Elena. I have called you to this place today to relay a certain order that has come to us from our Sovereign in Spain. I believe you are all aware of the distress that has been the lot of our dear friends in San Agustin, and the valiant effort that has gone into restoring it to the fine place it was before.

"We have already given thanks to God that we were spared the same fate or worse at that time, for what reason only the saints know. I have in my hand a royal edict that sets out to preserve our great nation in this land. The content is such that some measures are to be taken to ensure that no such loss of Spain's sovereignty here shall be entertained again. There is to be a pooling of our resources, and to that end our people too.

"Thus, within a six month, without question or hesitation, we are to remove ourselves, our belongings, indeed our very lives from Santa Elena to re-plant them in San Agustin.

"I am very aware that this will gain little favour amongst you, nor perhaps will it be perceived as being of any great sense. However, we came to this country with a great fervour and have planted the seeds of our history in its ground. In truth, those seeds have grown into the fine town we now have. Yet I tell you, the manner of it is not in the soil, nor in the foundations of our houses, not in the crops that grow around us, nor yet in any other thing we consider to be of material worth. It is within our hearts, that is where Santa Elena resides. No matter where the winds of fortune take us, that is where it will always be. Let us take that strength and carry it to another shore, to build our lives as the Spanish of a new world that none shall ever take from us."

The silence was remarkable. Gutierre had spoken the words of a true Governor which at any other time would have raised the spirit to great cries of assent, yet now all was quiet. Although he was caught quite off his guard by the mute reaction, Gutierre was in no mood to delay lest it should lead to dissertation or debate, thus he continued.

"I shall be drawing up a considered approach to our removal which each shall follow accordingly. Our journey to San Agustin shall be orderly and dignified. Groups of men will be formed to oversee the various aspects, as such any questions should be addressed to those who are most concerned with the specific matter. These orders will take effect over the next few days, and the noting of them shall be seen by way of postings about the place, together with tables indicating dates by which each task shall be finished, and by which day we shall finally depart these shores.

"May God support us in our endeavour."

I sensed an unease in his voice through the last part of his address, indeed no sooner had he finished speaking than he made a hasty exit, no doubt praying that none should interrupt his strident march back to the seclusion of his estate.

The voices slowly grew like the gentle incursion of the myriad cicadas that entertain the night air, from a single note eventually to a grand chorus. I had not the escape Gutierre had contrived and was soon accosted by a tumult of insistent questioning from every side. I could do little but answer each with no more than repetition of Gutierre's own dictates. I could not possibly consider a reply to each and every one, and yet I could understand the sense of despair and bewilderment present in their voices. These people were my friends, my neighbours, my charges consequent of my inherent position. Thus, much as they were coming to me with their impossible pleas and requests, I was at pains to at the very

least give them some reply albeit of no consequence.

As the crowds lessened, smaller groups moved to
discussion at home, debates already being raised as
to who should take responsibility for the various
tasks at hand, I found my mind take an unusual turn.
There was one whose organisation had brought so
much to Santa Elena previously, one whose presence was distinctly lacking. I had given him little
thought for some days, but with the whole township
congregated before me I had seen nothing of the
Englishman. No mention had been made of him,
which could be seen as curious but for the circumstances. There was no excuse I could conjure that
would make it easy for me to ascertain from anyone
if he had been seen, or if indeed he was still in Santa
Elena.

I could not think that he had travelled out of this
place, yet surely his tenure here would be poorly
tolerated. The fact that none spoke of him nor suggested him for any of the tasks before us gave me
no clue. I was still not sure that I could address him
civilly or want him near me. It had suited me for
the period of our estrangement that I had not made
sight of him, but this absence of any reference to
him was starting to unsettle me. Somewhere deep
within me lay a need to know what had befallen
him. If he had made good his departure, then by
what means did he make his escape, and to what
place? It would not affect my sensibility nor en-
courage me to renew our acquaintance, but I could
at least put to rest something of an unfinished business, an untidy business.

The people had thinned sufficiently for me to move about them. I responded to those who would ask of me, but my eyes searched, and my thoughts ran to this other irritating matter. I enquired not of anyone, and felt fatigue take me to the quiet of my home. This was going to be a busy time and useful people were of a premium. I felt a need for the wisdom of my father, and the safety of his care. There was little doubt in my mind that we would not hesitate nor question under his guidance. Advice from others was what I craved at this moment. I had spoken without much direction throughout the day, now the evening was drawing in around me and I needed the comfort of another's surety. I was weak, and ineffectual, and alone.

After a fortifying sup of wine and some light food, I settled on visiting my dear father's aide, Juan. I knew he was to need help in his removal, the accident in the storm had caused him sufficient damage to leave him with much difficulty in physical work. Whilst he would likely ask me of that which had already been the content of so much discussion through the day, I felt he at least was still of a mind enough to offer me some good words and inspired direction. Thus I could draw some strength from him with which to renew my spirit.

I walked the quiet paths, closed doors guarding debate between families and friends, set to go late into the night. A half moon lit the way sufficiently for me to wonder at the silhouetted beauty that was to be forsaken so readily and so cruelly. As I approached the little house at the end of the town a warm light within informed me of Juan's presence, I entered with a gentle knock. His old face turned slowly at the sound of my entrance, and I was startled by how much age he had gained through the previous months. I looked upon an old man whose years were surely numbered. The able fellow who had been my rock after my father's death was now but a shadow before me.

I knelt at his still seated side and hugged him as one would embrace a grandfather. Kissing him on the forehead I set back across from him, but could not discern much of his greeting. He smiled and spoke my name, but there was a distance in his eyes that I could not quite understand. Through the years we had spent long evenings in deep conversation, laughing and drinking, yet my dear friend seemed listless, and was decidedly short of words.

"Shall we have some good wine between us Señor?" I ventured.
"Surely the news of the day has knocked you senseless, and quite rightly so. It seems I have come just at the right time to take your care into my hands. I cannot think that you should have been left thus to maintain yourself."

He looked about him and smiled weakly, grunting something of an incoherent reply. I felt saddened by his sorry state, but quite disconcerted too, and wondered how he was managing to care for himself. As I fetched the bottle I could see there was an order to the place, and indeed the wine was well stocked, perhaps I was only concerned at his inability to relate to me in the way I felt he should, my sudden appearance had caught him somewhat off-guard.

Sitting again with two large measures of wine heaped with sugar to brighten our minds, I thought we could now settle to something of the familiar evenings that had marked our old friendship. Juan's kindly face drew no expression from which I could draw some comfort however, and sensing little of any conversation forthcoming I chose to speak some more. The content of my discourse was of little significance for sure, but I was now of the opinion I was attempting to hold a conversation with a stranger. I grew quiet, content with the provision that this old man had suffered considerably and was now no more than a hollow representation of the gentleman who had meant so much to me. In the silence between us I reflected on the times we had spent together, and a sense of overwhelming sadness came to me.

I swallowed the last of my drink, rather in haste as I was gaining little enjoyment from my visit, rathermore I felt I was perhaps an intruder and should take my leave. This had been a difficult day, but now more than at any other time I felt vulnerable to the injustices that seemed to be taking my life in hand.

"I shall leave you in peace dear Juan. Forgive me if I intruded on your evening, coming as I did unannounced. I wish you a restful night, and will visit you at a more proper time when next I may."

I kissed him again and was sure I saw more enthusiasm for my preparation to leave than for my arrival, which distressed me some more. Indeed, the sadness welling up deep within me was causing my eyes to tears of self pity which I endeavoured to hold back lest I in turn caused some distress. I moved swiftly to the door and reached for the catch.

"Hey old man, I ..."

I froze as the voice trailed to a stop. The entrance from upstairs had been hasty and unaware of any that might be visiting, but the suddenness of the halted sentence hid nothing and spoke all. In that moment before turning around I realised why I had been greeted with what I now discerned as fear, not just discomfort, but fear at my learning that this was were the Englishman was hiding. My dear friend was harbouring an enemy of the people.

What I could not settle to was whether I should just continue out through the door, or if I could turn and look upon the face of someone who no longer existed to me. Angry at my weakness I slapped my fist to my side, drawing it away from the cold, metal latch. I waited for some further words from behind me, but nothing else came. Frustrated I turned, but spoke as I did so.

"Well? Must I enquire of you then?"

The anger must have showed well in my face. An anger borne not just out of a general hatred, but also for having my precious friendship with Juan tainted as it had just been. From out of the shadows the voice came back quietly:

"Forgive my intrusion good lady, I was unaware of your presence and would not have marred your visit by choice."

The elegant line was familiar, but the voice was not so. There was a faltering, and a distinct lack of quality to the speaking of it. Spurred by an insatiable curiosity I asked him to step forward into the light.

"I think it not wise, Señora, if you will excuse me, I ask that you forgive my poor manner."

Without waiting for my permission he was gone as quickly as he had appeared.

"Forgive me Catalina, I had no wish to deceive you. There is much I should like to tell you, yet I sense there is little you would wish to know." The old man's voice now ran with the warmth of its familiar tenor.

"Juan, Juan. I thought I had lost you somehow, now I see the light back in your eyes, and yet I cannot understand how this has all come about."

The old man drew the drink that remained in his hand to his lips and spoke again.

"Please Catalina, do not ask after this of me. I cannot explain nor tell you of the circumstance, please leave this matter well alone."

The intrigue had me kneel back beside Juan and press him further for an explanation, but he was determined in his resolve to keep any detail from me. This only seemed to re-kindle something of the anger I had just felt and drove me all the more to understand what had happened. I could not even be sure that the person who had just left was in fact the man I had believed it to be.

"Please don't do this Catalina."

Juan's plea only served to propel me to my instinct and thus, ignoring the respect I still had for my friend I strode the room to take the steps to the upper floor where I knew the answer to my vexation lay. On my way I picked up a lantern to ensure that I was not to be denied a face to face audience with my quarry, undoubtedly lurking in the shadows again. As it happened he was not hid away, but quite still, his back turned toward me. He was sensible of me and spoke further,

"I ask of you again to forgive me, but if you cannot, at least do not deny good Juan your friendship if it has been at all harmed by my presence here this night."

I was incensed.

"Do not begin to presume I have a wish to grant favours to any person who does not have the decency to turn and face me. I demand you show me no more your rude back."

He sighed heavily, hesitated and eventually, slowly turned around. I could still see little of him and was in no mind to spare him any humility. I sprang forward and thrust the light toward him.

"God have mercy on you!"

I was not prepared for what I could now see so clearly before me. That beautiful, kind face was torn and bruised, swollen so badly that if it were not for those familiar grey eyes I would have believed it to be someone else.

"Ralph, what have they done?"

I knew now why none had spoken of this broken man. Touching my fingers to his misshapen mouth I discerned why I had found difficulty in recognising his words. He barely disguised a wince as the faintest touch had caused him pain. My heart did soften in that instance, and my resolve and hatred flowed out of me like a melting wave on the sand.

"My precious Ralph, what have they done to you? Tell me it was come about by some terrible accident, surely not through anger?"

He answered not but turned again as if ashamed, or perhaps to save me the pain of association with the barbaric act that had been visited upon him.

"Let it not be your worry fine lady. Our worlds have flown in different directions, do not concern yourself with things that have no place in your life now. Your people need you, of mine I bear an unforgivable guilt, the pain of which I cannot press upon you anymore than you have known already."

"No Ralph, no. This is not your doing."

With a touch of his shoulder I had him turn back and face me. The pain was written deep in his countenance, both marked by the cuts and bruises about him, and deeper still, within his heart.

"I have known you more than I have known any other living person, and my heart tells me the truth, the truth that could never cause you to make hurt to me or any other. This wrong that has been done to you is no less than that which has afflicted my people here and in San Agustin. It is unfair, unjust and wished for only by a few who know no better. In truth I count myself amongst that number, for I placed you amongst those who sacked our lands and caused us so much misery. Now I regard the outcome of my selfish action in the damage that has so vilely hurt this beautiful face. I do not expect forgiveness, but I do beg that you allow me to bathe each and every wound, soothe every bruise, and ease the pain that tortures you still."

"Catalina." Just hearing him speak my name once more caused my heart to ache again. He spoke softly and with the gentility that only he could.

"To look upon you and hear your voice close to me once more is all the care that I require. In faith dear Juan has kept me from death these past weeks and restored me sufficiently that I have this time with you now. I learned of the news you brought with you this day, in truth it is the final seal upon our farewell. I cannot remain in this land, yet my heart will always be in this place and the people I have loved here, but most of all with my dear Catalina."

I fell to his open arms and wept for all the uncertainty and despair of our separation, more still for the certain end to our days together as he had spoken a truth I already knew. His breath caught once or twice as my hands touched on further damage about his body, the extent of which I learned more over the next few days, but he would not relinquish his embrace for the remainder of the night.

I spoke to no one of his whereabouts, but tended his broken body diligently every day. None ever suspected his presence in this place, few cared. As his body regained its strength we spent more loving times together, existing in a world aside from the turmoil of the evacuation around us. I kept my duties to a minimum, indeed Gutierre's administration left little to be guessed or asked of. The days passed swiftly, and with the hours not holding enough time for us they flew by too quickly.

Oft times the three of us would talk late into the night, filling the air with tales that drew our imagination away from the cruel reality within which we lived. Little was discussed of Ralph's departure, or even what he might do once we had left. It was the moment we respected and we succumbed to the seduction of that ignorance, happy in each other's arms through the night, and caring for each during the day.

By the middle of July most of our town was already departed, the official date having passed. Through my position I had remained until last and Juan also due to his age and infirmity. However, the day was come upon us when we should leave, and the consequence for Ralph was now a real concern. On the twentieth a shout went up as a small boat came into shore. It was not recognised immediately, but was considered one of the many transports travelling back and forth to San Agustin. With some alarm it had been ascertained that it did in fact contain a number of Englishmen who expressed in all innocence that they were lost and needed to know where they were at. The Captain, a man called Edward Spicer, professed they were bound for Roanoke, a place in Virginia. This was something of an odd notion when it was considered they were travelling in nought but a small flyboat. The few workers who remained with us were suspicious and naturally considered their arrest and transport to San Agustin was simply a matter of course, no matter their uncertain fate there. I instead looked to the heavens and thanked God for the gift that had been bestowed upon us.

I persuaded those few that it was much in our interests to show mercy and benevolence, the mark of a truly civilised nation, and help them to their journey. Although this caused some surprise all were finally of the opinion that it would serve us well, we were tired of conflict. The chance had come quickly and with no warning, and although happy for the opportunity that this was, I shook for the desolation it signalled within me. I arranged for some of the men including Captain Spicer to be escorted to Juan's house. Señor Ramirez still had old charts and a fine knowledge of the coasts about us to ensure the safe passage of these lost souls. On departing none of our company had noticed that their number had increased by one.

Standing alone, the wind creaked the tall trees behind me, the bright white of the shore upon which I stood caused my eyes to narrow, yet still I watched until the faintest sign of the small craft disappeared from my view. My gaze remained fixed upon the line betwixt the sea and sky for some time, unable to make the release that in reality had already passed. The little prayer that whispered past my lips faltered as two noisy birds swooped and called to each other in the blue above me. I sat down quietly and watched them in their playful attention, almost jealous at their complete freedom, unfettered by politics or human conflict.

I dug my hand into the warm, soft, white sand and watched the silvery grains glitter as the light caught their waterfall flow through my fingers. They marked the passing of the days that had been our time in this place, and more, my inability to contain them and have them in my keep. Thus was he gone. Yet for my life on, the richer for his having visited, I can recall his kindly grey eyes, and the strength of his love, just as I remember those shores which contained us in that moment. I can never love like that again, and yet the memory will serve me well for the remainder of my days.

Book 5

Log Book of
John White

Roanoke Island, Virginia, 1587

25th July, 1587

The early morn brought with it the most favourable
sunrise that quite lifted my soul. As I stood in quiet
contemplation upon the sands, the sun lit the trunks
of the trees behind me with the most exquisite glow,
and as such the land was lent a warmth that served
entirely to familiarise that stark place. Looking
back to the ocean even the ever-present dark shapes
of the moored boats beyond the bar lost their aura of
menace, the light playing prettily around them in the
myriad small waves. For that moment I was given
the pleasure of a brief respite from the depressing
truth of Fernandez' stance, determining our enforced
encampment.

I can still not yet conceive that his contrary actions
through our voyage were consequent of a simple
whim on his behalf. To my mind there must be a
greater force directing his malevolence causing him
to such unnecessary obstruction, even so, I am determined it shall not equate to a mutiny as such. In
truth there are those amongst us who would entreat

me so, some who are of the mind that a stronger reproach would elicit some more favourable response. Yet I am sensitive to those whose greatest fear would be to witness the departure from these shores of our only means to survive what fate we have now determined to have been that of Master Coffin and his men. Moreover I am of a mind that this stand-off will prove naught but a short lived show of strength, a childish declaration of bravado, something to which I dare not display any weakness. I am firmly of the opinion that we shall continue our voyage to the Chesapeake, and achieve our set purpose.

I am determined though that any report of these misdeeds shall reach the full cognisance of those who have secured this voyage, including Raleigh himself. I shall continue to exemplify an unshaken mastery over my command lest any should try and propose it be anything less than a success. I have learned much from those whose authority I witnessed in our previous two expeditions, I could want nothing more than to be deemed an equal to their undoubted skills.

I have variously noted that I am more inclined to the sensitivity of those natural inhabitants around us whose mannersome co-operation we shall undoubtedly have to rely on if we are to succeed here. I have marked with some careful observation those mistakes which previously marred progress, and am determined that we shall make good in avoiding the same this time. I shall instigate what discourse we can achieve to successfully build relations with the Indian population. This shall be aided in the most by our party containing the former native, Manteo.

His language and the respect he maintains as the son of a chief shall undoubtedly allow us to make gains in this manner more quickly and with much purpose. Despite his appearance, which still bears an essence of fear through his tattoos and sundry markings, I find him to be the most convivial person. I sketch him often, and in my portrayal my purpose is to express his gentle and intelligent manner whilst still maintaining his nobility. My record as such will stand as a monument for our country to hold sacred in its truth, expression, and perspicacity.

*

I did not think to be writing more of my journal this day, yet I have just been witness to what I can only consider to be something of a miracle. Upon our departure from the Portuguese coast those months ago the contrivings of Fernandez played out the first of his many deceits. We had gone but a few hours when it was brought to my attention that we had sailed without the flyboat, which we could only conjecture had been left at the port still, in its preparation. I was aware that Captain Spicer, whose charge it was, had the least experience of any of us, and certainly nothing of the exacting knowledge of our pilot, Fernandez, upon whom we all relied for his ability in taking us on to our place safely and well supplied.

I had been saddened by the loss, but comforted by the belief that the inexperienced crew would not attempt to follow us on such a long and treacherous voyage. Yet today, without warning, the small craft came upon our shores seemingly quite undaunted by the experience. I cannot be truthful if I deny a deep feeling of satisfaction at the undoubted displeasure that this has given to Fernandez and his men. He was firmly of the opinion we had seen the last of this boat and its crew, and yet here they are. Not only has their appearance re-kindled a sense of hope and joy in our party, but it has also served to severally undermine the importance of our pilot. We no longer feel the absolute reliance on his skills that has proved his great power over us. I believe in this moment I have regained much of the respect that has been diminished since our landing.

A great celebration was arranged for this afternoon in order that we might all enjoy the wonderful event. There was much to talk about on both sides, we were to enjoy the tale of their lone adventure, and some explanation for our own predicament was needed for them too. In the process of their telling we were astonished to learn that they had actually landed in Spanish territory, and had not only survived to continue their journey, but more surprisingly had gained some help in their progress. In truth were it not for the provision of maps and guidance it is possible they would not have reached us at all, despite their proximity. Although alarmed upon hearing of our having found but the skeletal remains of Master Coffin when we had first arrived, and the settlement gone to ruin, in no way did it diminish their joy at finding us still in this place. Edward Spicer has always been a likeable fellow, and now he is acclaimed a hero, as such the attention of all is very much his prize. However, as the evening drew in and the ale stocks diminished, I was less inclined to believe the extravagant embellishment of his seafaring adventures, yet I thank God for the smiling faces that I see before me.

There was one more oddity that has befallen us this day. Along with Captain Spicer and the flyboat came another fascination in the form of an English gentleman that had not begun the voyage with us. He has remained quiet for now, and I feel there is much I should like to know from him. However, I am happy to leave such interrogation to another time when the spirit is not likely to be dampened by anything that might mar it. What a joyful day.

**

Two days have passed since our supplies came with Captain Spicer, and my time has been taken up with the administration that is the burden of charge which my position affords. Good organisation is the mark of a civilised people, and I am keen to ensure that this is how we shall be perceived by the various native populations and by the world at large. It is more of a responsibility to plant a colony that includes such a number of women and children, than when in my previous expedition with Sir Richard Grenville and Governor Lane. Then we knew our places as a purely scientific and military contingent, each only to care for their self. Now I am not just a Governor to all, but still a father to Elenor and a prospective grandfather, and yet I am also considerate of my continued duties to science in my drawings, paintings and other painstaking observations that are an essential part of our exploration.

The southern island of the sand bar contains a people called Croatoan who are sensible to our good intentions, due in no small measure to Manteo's return with us, now as much the dashing Englishman, displaying little of the savage dress he represented just a three year since. In truth, my confident air would be greatly lessened had it not been for his speaking out in his own tongue to re-acquaint ourselves with the inhabitants of this hostile land. My earlier visit to the place with Governor Lane would have undoubted gained greatly had we then the ease of communication that serves us so well at this time. Indeed, I am very much of the opinion that under my guidance we shall create a peaceful and harmonious life integrated with the people here. I hold little credence in the heavy-handed methods that marked those former incursions as they seemed to engender naught but disharmony and anger at our presence. We gained many enemies through that time, a practice I wish to avoid in my charge.

Although I have had no time to interview the newest member of our population, it would seem he has already an unusual ability to exchange with Manteo, learning quickly of his language. Some have reported that he has a knowledge of similar dialects, albeit quite different. I am keen to hear his story, and have determined a time to speak fully with him tomorrow. The weather is still favourably warm, and our people much fortified in spirit. The buzz of dissent has been replaced by a faint hum of contentment, and a greater air of hope has settled upon us at last.

**

We are now at the 28th of the month and I am much pleased at our progress. When I was previous in this place together with Governor Lane and Captain Stafford we remarked on just how much the island provided a sound settlement. So, albeit that this is not the landing of choice, it has in fact previously been referred to as 'God's place on Earth', and its rich lands and plentiful shelter provide much comfort, guarding us from inclement weather and other things that might trouble us from the sea. The country is not only pleasant upon the eye, but its soil also does support all manner of food we can grow; melons, pumpkins, corn, and more. The channels about us are of a generous nature and thus afford us a good protection from any tribesmen who might wish us harm.

I have no doubt that there will be many abroad who will remember with little favour the unkindly behaviour of both Grenville and Lane, thus whilst I have plans to turn such vehemence into a successful exchange which can only serve to promote a mutually beneficial relationship, I am for the moment grateful of any defence that is within the structure of our new home. I am responsible for over one hundred men, women and children, and it is not my wish to endanger their safety through any ambition of mine, no matter the good intention of it. Even though fate has kept us from our intended landing north of here at Chesapeake, I am determined that Raleigh will be best pleased with Roanoke as though it had always been his intention.

I have spoken at last to our newcomer. His name is Ralph Ellerker of Risby in Yorkshire. He has told me of a quite extraordinary tale as to his being here, yet I have some way to go before I fully believe him. It seems he has spent some few years in the company of the Spanish, which in itself is a matter of some concern, and may lend question to his intention, but further he even doubts the wisdom of the great Sea Captain, Sir Francis Drake, whereupon I have had to remind him of his duties as an Englishman. Yet for all his strange manner I find him uncommonly good company, and an amiable fellow. I am motivated by the young man's story to paint and draw some more of our own adventure in order that many more may marvel at the wonder of it, moreso than at the mere re-telling of it. Ellerker has spent some time with Manteo and is of the opinion that there is much to be gained from understanding his countrymen. I believe that they too shall gain much from what we have to bring and teach them.

The day has ended with a most unsavoury event and has stalled me from exploring further the potential of interaction with the natives. We have suffered our first loss, and such a loss. One gentleman of my council, George Howe, has been set upon by a brigand group of savages whilst out on the sand banks crabbing for us. I have instructed that we should not venture out alone, and indeed I believe that was not George's intent. However, his earnest endeavour took him well away from us, and whilst in his solitude, armed with naught but a small crabbing spear, he has become prey to a vicious group of tribespeople who have shot him with their arrows and beaten him brutally to his death.

The report came to me by Tom Steevens, who even now has taken it upon himself to explain the unhappy event to George Jr., a task I would not relish. We are once more in fear of our lives, and a return to our earlier dissatisfaction is much apparent. I cannot honestly persuade each that this incident is isolated or avoidable, but I have asked of the remaining eleven councillors that they do what they must in order to reassure our population. I set out on this journey with the intention of leaving behind the over-zealous mistakes of Lane et al, yet now I feel a great urge to exact a punishing revenge on those unholy animals. I am exhorted to that exact course by Captain Stafford, and I would be truly justified so to do. The fact is, his command of the regimental aspect of our colony is decidedly difficult to overrule giving me little choice in the matter. However, Manteo has pleaded that restraint be shown in the first, thus allowing a space for our blood to cool.

Likewise the newcomer, Ralph Ellerker, has sided with him, and his great eloquence has swayed me much to a more guarded approach. Indeed, I am persuaded to talk more with our close neighbours the Croatoans, both because of the ease with which we are afforded such an exchange through Manteo, but also because I believe them to be true to their profession that they are a peaceful people. In the first I have agreed that Stafford should make a peaceful foray into the island of Croatoa that some discourse should be initiated. Perhaps Ellerker should join them as he has experience with other tribes in the south. He at least will have less of the uncertainty that is borne of the shock from the event witnessed by George Howe's fellow settlers.

**

Stafford has reported to me successfully on his journey. I sent him with twenty of his men this thirtieth day of July in order to ascertain both knowledge of the tragedy, and perhaps broker a

330

treaty of sorts between ourselves and the native population. It seems that at their spying the advancement of such a fearful set of men on their shores, the people of the island fled, albeit that their initial intention had been to show a certain hostility. Manteo was quick to halt their flight by hailing them in their own language. Once perceived as a friendly party the group of Croatoans were quick to turn about and welcomed them with open arms. It is clear they possess a deep fear for anything foreign, perhaps not altogether unduly so, as of our previous year's incursions they still bear the scars.

They talked at some length and were quick to assign the killing of George Howe to those of Wingina's men who remained angry at the killing of their own by Grenville and Lane. The fear of retaliation by the white man, that is to say us, was of rather more importance to these peaceful sorts though, and they felt there was a great necessity to mark some differentiation between their selves and those who would relish further conflict. Stafford agreed that some pertinent measure should be taken, and suggested a conference with myself included as a good way forward. It was arranged then that we should meet on the morrow, with all of those who should wish to progress anew.

I was thankful that Stafford and the men were treated so well by these people. Once it was established that we are not here to take from them what little they have by way of provision, as had happened with previous expeditions when we had indeed relied on them for food, they then took the group and feasted them well. Whilst in their settlement Stafford was shown a man who still lay injured from when he had previously been mistaken for one of Wingina's men by Lane and had been shot in the leg, a wound to this day that had not mended. This makes for a very valid reason to arrive at a satisfactory method by which we can distinguish them.

On his return I found Captain Stafford much less inclined to action directly, but indeed he has a more content attitude about him now. I feel that perhaps the trust I placed in him to perform this task has strengthened our working bond. I shall sleep little tonight as I have much to think over in preparation for our meet tomorrow.

**

The first of August and I feel a propitious start to a new month. We did this day sail to the south island. It being part of the bar of islands we can keep to the inland aspect and so the distance is passed with ease in our small boats. There is a mix of feelings aboard, all borne of uncertainty, but not so much as amongst the majority of those we leave behind on Roanoke Island. I find it somewhat at odds that the women folk have much the most calming effect. I would have thought their fear would be uppermost and in need of some protection from the men, yet they do seem to find a strength from within that has halted any rash thinking or reaction. This at least has stayed the hand of instant retribution from amongst the angry menfolk, allowing me such time as I think necessary to explore more peaceful means to vouchsafe our well-being.

For the main part we have contrived that we should convey an invitation to meet with all the peoples around. This shall at the least encompass the people of Secota, Aquascogoc, and Pomiok. It is my intention that we shall secure an agreed peace amongst all of those, and to this end I have high hopes in regard to our meet today with the Croatoans. They are a most amiable sort, I am quite taken with their intellect. Indeed, albeit that there is a faltering dialogue due to our differing tongues, their eloquence is still apparent, and their ability to plan belays any sense of their savage living. With the help of Manteo to translate, our intention should be clear and unambiguous.

*

Our landing upon the Croatoan shore was without ceremony, but we met with smiling faces, and a genial greeting. Our friends led us some way up the shore into the land wherein their settlement lies. We sat quite comfortable and all were much at ease. We were offered vessels filled with a sweet liquid, a most welcome refreshment. Upon our first exchange I was somewhat disturbed at Captain Stafford's immediate allusion to the killing of George Howe, and his oft-repeated reminder to the natives that we reserve the right to retaliate in whatever way we think fit should we be provoked again. I could not see the reason for admonishing these peaceful folk with such an unnecessary warning, yet he bade me adhere to the stance as we were best not to show weakness, even amongst these people. I am of a mind that he is merely trying to affirm his position of seniority to those with whom he met yesterday. I personally find his manner a tad disagreeable, and would prefer to relate to them in a more civilised manner as their hospitality has made quite possible.

I have such a belief in my thinking, and wish for nothing more than a cordial existence in this land, yet I sometimes sense that Stafford's intention is quite contrary to this. Certainly I feel very little support from him at this juncture, instead I sense the uncertainty that was bred from our previous expeditions when any friendships we may have gained were lost to ignorance and barbarism.

I pressed on with my saying through our interpreter, "I wish only for the old love that was between us and the Secotan to be renewed." hoping that the Croatoan would find some comfort from the peaceful intent. I had also with me James Lasie and John Wright, both of whom had seen each side of the duplicitous nature of Wingina's people in previous years. They knew this was a vain hope, but I truly believed, with the help of the Croatoan, it was indeed a possibility. I could sense the uneasiness around me, and I feared my well-laid plans were slipping from my grasp already.

I thank God for my decision to include our new friend Ellerker with our party. He had remained quiet at the rear of the group throughout our exchange thus far, but now, sensing the discord he leaned forward and proffered a suggestion. His voice brought a certain calm, and his use of some few words in the native tongue leant a gentile order to the place. His suggestion was simple, but proved to be an immediately healing notion. It was agreed upon that the Croatoan people should wear a token around their necks, fashioned in such a way as should be instantly recognisable by us and thus avoid any possibility that they might be mistaken for those tribes whose intent was to cause us harm.

In this way they were much calmed and our discussion continued in good fashion. They agreed to act as messengers to all from us. I asked that they might speak to the leaders of each tribe and have them meet with us in this place on a day some seven days hence. Whereupon we would forge an alliance, each receiving further distinguishing tokens to aid recognition, and mark their allegiance and belief in a single, peaceful existence.

The Croatoans appeared to enjoy the prospect of their role, and they certainly seemed to understand the arrangement. I felt distinctly confident that our mission was successful, and after some further brief, but happy exchanges, we set off to return to the boats. The sense of surety that we were about to achieve a peaceful settlement in this wondrous land was the majority of the discussion as we began our return journey. After a while we fell quiet. Some few of us took the time to sit and watch the fascination of the tree-lined land slipping past, lost in our thought as to how our lives would now be shaped. This was not the land we came to settle, yet fate it would seem had steered us to great possibilities, and it was up to us to make those chances a reality. The myriad noises of indistinct animals upon the land echoed amongst the trees, accompanied only by the gentle dipping of the oars through the steady waters. An enormous contrast to the barrage of questioning and further planning that was to greet us on our arrival back at Roanoke. At last I felt I had regained my true command, I was the Governor of a new land, and a happy people looking to a great future. Stepping from the craft I took notice of a glance that passed between Ellerker and Stafford that to my eye conveyed something rathermore disquieting. I am keen to avoid any unrest between ourselves. Truth be told, if we cannot keep the peace within our own ranks, then surely we shall struggle to do so with strangers. I have determined that I shall speak with the newcomer and ascertain his intentions, I cannot allow dissension, no matter his usefulness and perspicacity today.

*

There has been a great deal of activity around the island since our journey to the Croatoan, the house-building carries on apace, more food planting is achieved, and the planning for further incursions to secure peaceful coexistence has resulted in many conversations and ideas to be discussed and mulled over. However, the wait is long, and the closer we get to the appointed day there seems a growing sense of uneasiness, even fear hanging sullenly over us. My own greatest fear is that we shall suffer yet another attack before the meet, such an event would surely spell disaster for us. The journey has been long and hard, surely we deserve nothing but good fortune now.

*

I sat for some hours today with young Ralph Ellerker, and yet learned little more of his journey here. It is clear that he has been gone from England's shore for some good few years, and his leaving was not entirely by choice. Respecting his privacy I questioned him only lightly on it, preferring instead to listen more to his appraisal of our situation. I told him of our own woeful journey; of the bad landings we had made for food and water, the poisonous pools that burned those who drank from them, the barren lands devoid of any animal, and the constant disappointment at not finding the supplies as had been promised by our pilot Fernandez. Together with our abandonment the reflection had me consider our pilot's honesty and intent somewhat, but I know him to be a trustworthy fellow. That being so, I am beginning to understand why some of our settlers had felt so aggrieved and had called for action against him at the time. Just as I was questioning my judgement on this matter, Ellerker was quick to point the finger elsewhere. I was taken aback when he suggested perhaps I should keep a watchful eye on Captain Stafford. It seems I was right about the tension between them. However, Stafford's rank and good company in London would have him ensure a place of complete trust in my estimation. His over-zealous nature is nought but a reflection of the time he has spent in the company of both Grenville and Lane. His office is such that his intention can only be for the greater good, his authority is absolute in military matters, therefore his consideration will always be made from a position of strategic competence.

Perhaps I have put too much faith in my appraisal of Ellerker. Is it that good breeding and intellectual ability does not reflect so well in common intelligence? I do enjoy his conversation though, indeed he is much appreciative of my drawings and my watercolour paintings, and for this alone I have savoured his company and undoubtedly shall spend many more hours just so. Yet I am wary of his judgement, and shall continue to rely on my own senses. I now have one hundred and seventeen

337

men, women and children who shall continue to trust in me, and I shall not be swayed from my course.

**

We have marked off the days and counted the hours 'til now our day is come, and yet it should be noted that little was spoken of an appointed hour. The patience of civility affords us the space to wait until such time as the people of this land are ready and see fit to join us in the great task of unification that we dare now speak of. I did find a sadness in that some few have little regard of propriety and manners, instead they have griped since the early light as if willing the tribesmen to stay away. I have a strong faith in the native people, and am of the opinion our forbearance will find its reward in their coming.

Even so, the day is now already nearing its end and I cannot help but feel a little uneasiness creeping upon me. To occupy my mind I have practised what I am to say, and have perfected even some of the common language in order that I might greet them at least in their own tongue, and thereby set them at their ease. Stafford is quiet and appears much at rest himself. He seems to have a masterful control over the men at arms, and displays nought but a picture of duty. His commanding figure shall prove undoubtedly useful when persuading the various tribes to accept our dictates and our peaceful proposition.

*

I had determined that a second visit to my journal this day was inevitable and would summarise the exchanges, the joy and the new found security in our carefully crafted treaty. Yet I am in need of a strong draft to keep my hand steadfast to the task. I am sat quite alone, whilst around me a great hubbub has matched the crescendo of the evening insects whose noise has heralded already the coming of the night. My heart is heavy with just the faintest glimmer of hope, which in truth I know is past re-demption. I had dreamed that this time would echo to the sound of festive and lively discourse, to ex-changes consisting of gestures and trading of trin-kets and laughter. Our guests came not, and the desolation I feel is beyond anything of previous despairing. Indeed, when last I departed this shore it was in some haste, and the safe keep of my paint-ings, drawings, and writings was given over to the dubious care of Grenville's men. They had not the mettle of their master though, and fearing the loss of their own lives through a little roughness of the sea as they manoeuvred the small crafts toward the boats of our homeward passage, they chose to heave my precious cargo overboard to the salty depths ra-ther than risk a little swim. Months of detailed ob-servation recorded in order that the rest of the world might learn from our experiences. Fine watercol-ours portraying the extraordinary faces and figures of the chieftains and their women, a record of their habits, dwellings, livestock, flora, animal and insect life that is Roanoke. The most comprehensive cata-logue of a new place ever recorded by one man was what I had hoped to present to the people of London on our return. Instead I listened to the careless ex-cuses of the illiterate crew who saw little of any value, and had cast it so freely. I thought it not possible that such a low I should ever encounter again, yet this betrayal I bear more deeply. There can be no opportunity to put right this failure, I cannot fix that which is beyond my control. I am betrayed. Betrayed by the Croatoan and the others, betrayed by my inability to bring this event to its right conclusion, and further, betrayed by the title that was conferred upon me to take charge of these good people.

There is in this moment a tangible futility for us having come here. I am vexed that for so long I have protected the scurrilous actions of Simon Fernandez in his persistent attempts to hinder our progression, that I have watched with a head held so high that any plea for abandonment, or notion of regret has passed me by unheeded and unnoticed. My swollen pride has led me to notions of such greatness that any sensibility or jurisprudence has not been my concern, indeed has been ignored. I have been so inconsiderate in my duty I now sense the discontent around me with an acute pain that shall have me listen as never before.

I will consult with Stafford and rely on his experience, and I shall listen more than I shall command. The people in my charge shall see a new, stronger leader, not the stubborn visionary of before, but a pragmatic governor. I shall be man of determination. One who is driven to see this colony succeed in all its aspirations. We came to this place to build a successful future for ourselves, and by God we shall. This ninth day of August shall not be forgotten quickly, and yet I could wish for nothing more.

**

Stafford was immediate in his response. His newly attained position of respect had him prepare us with haste and determination. His training told him that the only response to the killing of George Howe should be a swift retaliating action against the remains of Wingina's tribe, the perpetrators of the slaying. He hand-picked twenty-four of the most able men, and detailed their venture. They were to take Manteo in that they should not be mistaken as to the place. The Captain reminded them of the ferocity of the attack during which George was butchered, and even though I was minded of Ralph Lane's appearance at the previous year's incursion when he had held aloft the severed head of Wingina, their chief, which I felt might give some reason to the attack, I was mindful of my earlier pledge and accepted the leadership of Stafford at this time.

Thus we crept with much stealth to the place wherein we knew the Secotoa to inhabit, and being completely under cover of the early morning dark we gained a close vantage to espy a group of them sat about a fire, completely unaware of our presence. This at least would afford us the upper-hand, thereby reducing any injury, and inflicting as much on them as possible before they were fully cognisant of us. Our surprise was that they took flight immediately we fired upon them. Taking some cover amongst a reed bed we followed with much haste firing as we went, not wishing to lose the advantage. Still no fire was returned despite some of their number falling before our attack.

The panic we heard in the distinct cry from Manteo brought us to a very abrupt halt. The silence after the shouts and screams of the previous moments had us detached as every animal had fled that place, there were just the faint sounds of the wounded groaning at the pain from their injuries. I came to Manteo as quickly as the reeds would allow my aching legs. The truth of our folly lay directly before me, these were not the people of Wingina's tribe, but indeed were the very Croatoans we had met with in peaceful discourse just days earlier. Now as the creeping light afforded us a greater clarity we saw those same tokens about their necks designed to avoid this very dreadful mistake.

There was some good news in that none of them were killed, and but for a child borne upon her back, a woman amongst them might also have been hurt as she too was mistaken for a warrior in that dull light. Manteo surprised me somewhat, and heartened me too as he was quick to deny them for their lack of care in being at that place instead of at the arranged meeting. I had thought he would show again the nature of his birthplace, yet he chose the position of the true Englishman he now represented. As the wounded were treated and the frightened comforted, Manteo outlined to me how they had come to be there. They had known the village to have been empty, the tribesmen having fled for fear of reprisal for their cowardly act. Their was yet a good stock of grain and other foodstuffs, thus the Croatoans had afforded themselves the taking of it for their own people before the animals should take it in their stead.

Whatever the reasons, and despite there having been no loss of life, the fact remains that my dream of concord and friendship has turned into increased hostility from even those who have professed to harbour a friendship with us. We have done what we can to calm them having brought some of them back with us into our settlement, together with the food so unceremoniously abandoned. Yet for all our good intention I am bereft of any thought other than utter desolation. How could so much have gone so wrong? I feel that even the Lord our God has forsaken us in this moment. I have tried to sleep, the hour now late and the majority now settled, yet in my mind I hear the terror in their screams, and see the fear deep in their eyes as they looked at us, incredulous that such a hurt should have been vested upon them by ourselves. I wonder should I question my role as Governor, certainly it is proving to be an unnatural mantle, and yet I still believe I have so much to give, both to this country and to England. I am heartened somewhat by our achievement in transforming the native Manteo into as good an Englishman as any. Perhaps if we can turn our focus to this good aspect of our making, with a sight set to repeating the same with others of this land, then the tragedy that has become this day may be forgotten. I can but hope so.

**

We are at our third day now of quiet. The weight of our sorrow has lightened a little, and we have talked much in respect of our mistaken incursion. I have continued to catalogue in my drawing and painting those we brought with us to here, and it has pleased them much. I began this day a detailed and faithful study of Manteo. His many tattoos about his face and head present a formidable challenge. Now the day approaches when he shall be baptised to our true faith, in order that he can live a full and blameless life in the knowledge that not only is his outward self of our nation, but also shall his soul be saved for all eternity. This shall mark the full achievement of his journey, and shall afford us the opportunity to lift all our spirits with a fitting celebration.

**

The day of Manteo's christening is arrived. It is determined by decree that not only shall he be led to the path of righteousness to safeguard his soul in the next life, but that he shall also be honoured in this life. He is to be named Lord of Roanoke and of Dasamonquepec in reward for his faithful service to England. The title shall bestow much on him in respect of rights to the lands hereabouts. He has proved himself to be a fullworthy Englishman, and his representation in these parts shall carry a weight in all quarters.

*

What a festive day this proved to be. It is with a deep joy that I thank God for the celebration that has brought with it so much happiness to us. The shore's edge was chosen for the place of Manteo's christening. The air was still and the sun shone from a perfect blue sky. For once the silhouetted ships upon the horizon proved no rude taunt, but a comforting link with England, a window to the memory of our own chapels and churches wherein this day might well have seen the same ceremony too. The difference being our holy font was decidedly larger, and the water somewhat briny.

The baptism was led with such a solemnity that all felt a peace descend upon us together with an intense perspicacity, an understanding of our precious place in the world, that we should have prayed all day had we the chance. However, the pronouncement of Manteo's full acceptance into the holy church drew such a rapturous shout that we hesitated not in moving up the sands to where the food was already prepared and cooking, and a great celebration ensued. That same number of Croatoans that had come to our settlement were still present through this day, they bringing their own dances and songs to bear. All be they not what we would term musical, it cannot be argued against that they do stir the spirit with the tempo of it. Indeed many felt impelled to join with them in their vaulting and calling, and much entertainment was had by it. None of us looked as though we were made to perform the turns, each lacking the rhythm and natural gate of the natives. There was something odd about seeing Manteo in his natural revelry, yet still retaining his figure as an Englishman. For ourselves, I had not appreciated the talent in the abilities some had with the few instruments we brought with us, and some more where magnificent in their singing.

At the fall of the evening the full bellies and the headiness had most sat in groups telling of adventure, love, and tales of great beasts. There were some, like Roger Baylye, who were much the worse for a surfeit of ale. He was unable to speak with any intelligence, his laughter taking over his every other word until all about him were likewise gripped with uncontrollable mirth, the like of which I have never known before, quite exhausting us.

Our new man was exhorted to tell us something, and he did talk at length about a wondrous festival that he did attend amongst the Spanish people in the south. Although it drew some fascination, thère was an air of incredulity that dulled the flow of the evening a little. He, to his favour, was cognisant of this and chose to tell us else of a drinking party he attended in London when he was young, wherein a portly priest of a most pious nature lectured them for their rowdy behaviour and then proceeded to drink them all into a stupor. He then remained still at his pulpit in that he ended by preaching to a heap of snoring bodies littering the floor, but he was too insensible to be aware of their unconscious states. He has a good ability for the telling of such tales. I cannot re-tell the story with the same wit and feigned candour with which he imported it to us, but I remember the night rolled on well with the jollity of the tale and others. For a complete stranger he has fitted to us well, but I fear he is still something of a fish out of its pond.

I presented to Manteo one of my drawings of him-self by way of a gift to mark this day. At the for-mality of the ceremony earlier I, as Governor, presented to him an official document determining his newly appointed title, and witnessed by the hand of Sir Walter Raleigh himself. Despite our odd dis-embarkation I had still secured the scroll together with my belongings, and thus it had remained intact with the great, red seal upon it. These two things he now considers his most precious belongings, and the picture of pride and happiness that shone upon his face I must now consider my own most precious possession.

**

It is now the 18th of the month, and such a clamour came to us in the night. I was already to my feet when Ananais, my son-in-law brought the most fearful face to my quarters. I was quick to reassure him that all will be well as I was fully cognisant of the situation even though it was the first news I had of it. I strolled to where the cries of my child echoed around, Ananais skipping back and forth in an attempt to hurry my progress. My years have lent me the benefit of experience in these matters, I knew that this was but a prelude to the main event. I enquired of the women with Elenor as to her progress, and thus satisfied I took the young man off to where we spent the next hours imbibing and talking of sundry items of no consequence to while the time away.

*

Just as the day had crowned the edge of the sea and spread its fingers to first touch the land about us, Margery Harvie came over and bade us follow her. This day was born to my dear daughter, Elenor, a beautiful baby daughter. The sight of my little girl holding that infant was quite the most uplifting and joyous experience. Ananais bent and cradled both in his arms, and we all set to weeping tears of great happiness. Not only is the health of my daughter good, yet so is that of my new granddaughter. I have never seen a baby in such rude health before. She has a good appetite and her constitution seems meet to cope with anything that this place might throw at her. I believe that consequent to her having been carried through the journey here and all of our subsequent trials surely she must be fit to endure anything else in life. She has a mop of dark hair already, and her eyes have something of my daughter in them.

The word soon spread to all, not that there were many who did not know what was occurring through the night. The settlers each came to pay their respects and to thank God for her safe deliverance to us. We very quickly came to the notion that there could be no other name for her but Virginia. I cannot contain myself at the thought of relating to those back in England how my granddaughter now bears the name of our Sovereign's land. This has made me quite the happiest man. I feel we now have a real foothold in this vast country, and that truly anything is possible. My mind continues to run, as it has throughout the day, on the many possibilities for us. Perhaps it was fate that brought us to this spot instead of to Chesapeake. This land is so fine and bountiful, and there is a sense of good about the place that shall serve us well for many years to come. God bless my beautiful Virginia, and may the Lord guard her mother and father that she might have a wonderful life with them in their guardianship.

**

It is now Sunday, and young Virginia Dare has been christened this 20th day of August, 1587, bringing her into the fullness of the holy Church of England. The first English soul to be born in this land, yet still a complete citizen of our home, and now a child of God too. We have celebrated much these past few days, yet I consider this occasion to be the most special and most significant of any. I must admit to the soreness of my head bearing some testimony to that, I more than any have felt the need to drink the infant's health for too many hours. I cannot help but wonder how often I shall be inspired to paint and draw that little angelic face as she grows over the years into a beautiful woman. I shall sleep soundly tonight and dream of the days to come with me and my little grandchild, Virginia.

*

Good news in that the ships are nearly finished with their caulking and general readiness, the entirety of the goods on board are finally unladen, and Fernandez is determined to return for the replenishment of our stocks and to carry with him the tale of our journey thus far. The news of the birth of Virginia Dare shall undoubtedly cause much excitement when it is learned of, and the future of the settlement here will be in no doubt.

**

How this land does play with us poor specks of inconsequence. We awoke this morn to a powerful wind and dark skies, in great contrast to the fine and bounteous air of recent days. It had been planned that today should have seen the departure of the ships back to England laden with our instructions and needs. In the stead of which it was clear that no vessel was able to cross the shoals, indeed there was little choice but for the ships to head off to deeper waters to ride out the storm. As the morning passed the seas rose still higher and the Lion and the fly-boat did go from our sight.

Despite the necessity, and the assurances of my assistants, there were many who were most disconcerted by the removal of the ships from sight, they feeling some sense of abandonment. What, with the noise of the winds and the ever heavier rain now, some confusion has arisen and it is much our task at present to contain any panic. My experience is that these parts at certain times of the year do suffer much from storms of great magnitude. It is the destructive power of these winds that we should guard against rather than worry for the departure of the ships. I know Fernandez is a keen captain of his crafts, and the deeper water will allow him more governance over their handling. For myself I cannot conceive of a worse place to be in such inclemency than at sea. The land at least does not move from under us. I have instructed that we should make the most of the larger buildings wherein we can gather in groups, reassuring each and finding some safety in our sharing. The trees are bent till their heads touch the ground, there is much debris that travels with the rain, and the voice of the wind dominates our conversation.

Some have risen well to the task and many tales have been told of lives, and heroes, and sundry living. It is want to cause a sense of longing for home, but it is well that our minds are taken up with this diversion. I am sat with a group together with young Ellerker who had us enthralled with his stories of pirates and battles at sea. Through it though, at last, he has told us of how he came to these shores, not by any design, but by the vagaries of fate who has dealt him a most strange hand. It seems his original destination was in fact the Hollands, yet he found himself press-ganged and bound for the Americas, on one of our earlier expeditions no doubt. I was much against this form of acquiring men for those voyages. Truth told, the tales of great beasts and man-eating natives that supposedly inhabit the New Lands made it a necessity for the Queen to allow the enforcement of crews as those who were naturally keen to travel were proving few and far between. The drawn breath of those listening to the story grew in intensity as he reached to the part when the ship was set upon by a Spanish counterpart, whose greater size and firepower made its taking a simple task. The ferocity of the attack left many dead before the Spanish did board. Once they had possession they began to empty the holds and took each remaining man to ascertain his allegiance. Most were put to the sword as the Queen's faith proved too great a provocation for the zealous Spanish, but Ellerker's obvious breeding led them to question him further. In fact, although he has obfuscated the fact somewhat, it is clear he has some allegiance to the old Roman church, certainly sufficient for his life to remain intact, albeit that his status was reduced to that of a slave no less.

The story carried on in some detail explaining how his miserable captivity which ensued was cut short by rescue at the hands of a beautiful woman who took him to another Spanish town where he grew to be a part of the people who lived there. At this point all were clearly intrigued and thought the story very romantic, however, for the most this was when the sense of reality started to fade away, yet we stayed listening for the sheer storytelling of it. There was some correlation with Captain Spicer that indeed it was a woman with long, raven hair who came to their rescue when they were landed there by mistake. It was she who added Ellerker to their crew, and thus he came to join us, but for the rest, it was too tall a tale. Perhaps we shall never know the truth, but his story filled the air for hours and kept our minds full. I feel sure that some parts of it will be told by the women folk for many years to come.

**

It is the second day of the storm and still it seems there is to be no lessening of it. The discomfort continues to grow as few people trust Fernandez many believing that we shall never see the ships again. I pray that this weather will break in order to allow him safe passage back into the bay and settle those distracted minds. One of the women was relating a tale told to her by her brother just before we left England, and it served to make Ellerker most unsettled and he questioned her much afterward. Elizabeth Mainwareing has a brother George who has lived some time in the Hollands, but on his last visit home to see her before her departure he related something of which he had been told on his travels. Indeed it was an heroic tale which we all enjoyed, that of Sir Phillip Sydney who was at battle alongside Lord Leicester against Philip of Spain, aiding the Dutch rebels. All the ingredients of a wonderful story. However, he met with a tragic end on the battlefields of a place called Zutphen where he had inflicted upon him a mortal wound to his leg. It bled enormously and he was sure of his death as he rode with his attendants from the place. As they were leaving the battlefield Sir Philip espied a fallen soldier at the side of the path and insisted that he should be given Sydney's own precious water, he no longer having any use for it. One of the attendants carried the water sack to the man who himself was grievously wounded, and held it for him to drink. As he did so the brave poet and Lord called to them to ask after the soldier's name. 'William', came the answer, 'William Ferrers'. He was described as most handsome, and was gracious in his receiving such a gift from someone so noble. What became of him they did not know, but the tale of unfettered generosity passed through the ranks and lifted the spirits of the troops more than any General could.

I could tell that Ellerker was agitated and wished to question her at the mention of the name, but he was generous in his allowing her to finish so as not to spoil it for all. I questioned him later, but he was not forthcoming with any explanation for his interest nor his change of demeanour. I can only guess that the name meant something to him, but for the life of me I could not understand why he was so unwilling to divulge anything of it. He and Elizabeth have talked between their selves since that time for long hours, but I sense she at least is tiring of his enquiries. There were more stories tonight, but the mood of the people is changing, and they are losing interest in the diversions now. I worry much that this storm will last longer than I would hope.

*

The later hours have brought with them a most discomforting turn of events. Just yesterday there was some discourse as to which two men should return to England in order that we might ensure the safety of our letters to home, and request provision to aid our continuance here. Rightly, there is no sense in our relying on our Admiral, Fernandez, and so it is only sensible to send a representation from my council. All but Christopher Cooper of the twelve refused to go much to my surprise, and yet I thought perhaps that he alone might prove sufficient. However, this night they have entreated me again. I was of a mind to believe my persuasion of Mr Cooper had been quite sufficient, yet it would seem that even he has been coerced into a change of heart. Whilst I can conceive of no earthly reason why he should wish to go back on his word, the general mood is quite apparent. For some reason, and from whose suggestion I cannot fathom, it would seem they are of one voice in that it should be I that takes the voyage.

Their arguments are valid and have some strength in their confidence in me, yet I have spoken long on the subject in that I cannot possibly leave my duties here. I would be failing my post as Governor, I would be deserting my family in my daughter and new granddaughter, I could be considered negligent and uncaring. No doubt were I to return alone to England there are those who would see my abandonment of the colony as by complete design, it might appear that I did never intend to remain in this country. Still they exhorted me with promises that they would write some to the contrary that none might say these things of me.

I have no reason to return, and I argued still more with a real and true belief for the safety of my belongings. It has already been discussed at length that for our safe-keeping in the course of our settlement we should journey some fifty miles up into the land. I am fearful for the containment of my belongings, especially if this move should be made whilst I am gone. The loss of my previous fine records was a sore grievance, and I cannot bear the like to happen again. What if when I return I find I am divested of any or all of my things? How should I replenish them? In this argument they could not assuage me with promises and good words. There is a deal of discontent now, but I shall not relinquish my position, I have too great a care for that.

**

For three days now the storm has persisted, but its insistence is now belittled by those who would have me sail to England. They continue to entreat me hour after hour, and I feel a sense of loss. It would seem that the greater weight is against me remaining, and my authority is waning much. There has been talk of a written contract contrived to ensure the safety of all of my belongings, but I am yet to see such a thing. I have spoken to Ananais and Elenor, both do not wish me to leave, yet I cannot expect the father of my grandchild to go in my stead, in spite of he being the only one of my assistants who has shown me any support. Ellerker, with no surprise to myself, has volunteered in my place, his anxious desire to return to England no doubt fired by the discourse he has had with Elizabeth Mainwareing, but he is neither one of my council, nor is he, in fact, one of the colony. No doubt his clear mind and erudite manner would prove sufficient and serve us well, but my assistants will not hear of it.

**

I believe this day to be the 25th, yet the black skies and incessant rain do blend in day to night confusing us all, each not knowing to sleep or wake. The group have delivered to me, as promised, a considerable document to satisfy my material concerns. The pressure of the general people has increased through the days and now they have presented me this promise set with their seals and signed by their own true hands, each willing to swear by its content which is set down here:

May it please you, her Majesty's subjects of England, we your friends and country men, the planters in Virginia do by this presentation let you and any other understand that, for the present and speedy supply of certain known and apparent shortcomings and needs, most required for the good and bountiful planting of this or any other land in Virginia, we all being of one mind and agreement, have most earnestly entreated without ceasing to request John White Governor, of the planters in Virginia, to take passage to England for the better and more assured help and procurement of the aforesaid supplies, knowing that he is best to work hard and take pains to represent fully on behalf of us all. He has not once but often refused this for our sakes, and for the honour and maintenance of the colony, yet he has at last, though much against his will, through

356

our importuning him, acquiesced to leave his gov-
ernment, and all his goods among us, and on behalf
of us all will take passage into England, as his
knowledge and faithfulness we are all assured of as
witnessed through this paper, and do trust you en-
tirely by it. Given this 25th day of August 1587.

The content of it is most detailed and leaves little
room for any disbelief, indeed I am pressed to take
them by their word for this oath. My will though is
still not set to it, but I am moved to consider it fully,
and shall take some time to examine the detail
more.

*

I have sat in some quiet the day, my solitude at least
allowing my mind a space to ponder upon the possible outcomes of this strange turn of events. There
is a lessening in the wind too as this sixth day of the
storm I feel has taken a heavy toll on any reasoned
thinking, and may indeed be somewhat responsible
for the many who have come to implore me in these
past days. I am truly touched by their belief that I
am the only one of them capable of delivering our
lists and letters, and I would perhaps concur that
there are many for whom the task would prove too
arduous. My only visitor for any length of time today has been Ellerker. I am of a mind that my being
left at peace with their written promise to hand was
quite possibly at his behest, he being the most like
to realise that I will not make a decision whilst I
have dogs baying at my door. He has re-stated an
absolute need to return himself into England, although he is not forthcoming with a reason, yet at
least I feel I can discuss the matter with him, and

enjoy sensible and balanced opinion in return. His own needs aside, he believes that the decision to assent to the colonists' requests is essential in that there would be no peace again, nor respect should I continue to refuse. That loss I could not bear. My children I would miss for but a few months before my return, but the respect of the citizens of Virginia is of the utmost importance to me, and would be most difficult to return once lost.

He has said he will accompany me, and while I am still unsure as to his intentions, it does provide me with certain safeguards. He has suggested that we travel in each ship and carry a copy of the replenishments needed so that should harm befall either, the other may still continue with the task at hand. Whilst I can see merit in his suggestion, I yet lack the trust to allow him such a responsibility, besides, others might confuse the issue should I return after he, seeing my journey unnecessary after all. I have told to him a notion of what is required, but the detail of it I shall reserve for my own safe hands.

*

As I move to sleep and listen to the storm abating at last, a sense of calm has descended upon me, and I have decided to acquiesce to their wishes. I shall tell it to them as the day breaks.

**

There was little time for me this bright clear morning. The land looks clean and still, if a little broken in places, but there is a tangible sense of freshness and renewal. The day is as it had been before the storm, and I have wasted no time in telling all that I shall leave for England straight away. The ships can already be seen in the distance, and it was barely gone morning when I clambered on board the boat to cross the shoals and go out to sea. I was glad of the hurry as a more lengthened parting from my little family I could not have borne with ease. I watched the silhouette of Ananais, and Elenor, she cradling the tiny Virginia in her arms. Most were on the shore to wave me off for a fair voyage, and I felt a deep sadness but beset with a great pride as I watched them grow smaller the further we went. They remained for some time, but turned and set about their business whilst yet I could see them. I felt the loss distinctly, and was forced to wipe a tear from my face already. It was near midnight by the time we joined the Flyboat, and we are now sailing about the bar waiting for the Lion to assemble. The journey ahead seems long in its beholding, yet we are all safe aboard with our few belongings.

Young Ralph Ellerker I have sent in the other boat to travel in the Lion with Fernandez. Whilst I would have preferred the comfort of the larger vessel, I am keen to travel with Captain Spicer rather than face the surly tongue of the Portuguese pilot. I doubt I will have regained any command over his wayward actions, and I find Edward Spicer a most amiable sort, and good company.

The Lion did not join us much before the morning, and we are anchored beside it now to wait until all are readied for the voyage.

*

It is now later in the day and it would seem Fernandez is content that all is favourable and has weighed his anchor signalling our departure. At this moment I cannot think of any other thing than the moment when I shall see again those sun-drenched shores and the wonder of my beautiful Virginia Dare, that day cannot come soon enough.

Book 6

Ralph Ellerker
Baddesley Clinton, Warwickshire, 1632

The cool air of the house with its dark panelled walls, and stained glass windows, has the small, hunched figure in front of me wrapped in layers that would seem to make his task somewhat difficult. Indeed I would have thought a free arm and a nimble approach would be a necessity to his progress, yet he assures me he is most in need of the warmth he is afforded by his attire. Were we outside, by contrast, there is a gentle heat and an air of expectancy heralding the beginning of a day that will probably meet with the same blue skies and the same slight breeze of yesterday that had the world humming with summer's promises. For all that potential I am content to remain within this familiar room, sat for this gentleman of the Arts whose task he knows well, and who shall mark the memory of my being for some years yet.

His hand moves with a surety and determination despite his fragile semblance, pushing the stone pestle deep into its partner, grinding a genesis out of the destruction of the minerals, allowing them to draw up the gentle trickle of the heady-scented oil poured from the small glass phials, transforming them into his creative paste. I have never before witnessed the extraordinary endeavour that is necessary in the artist's preparation. This does seem to add substance to the very creation of his work, and yet such a moment could never be a part of the experience for those who would criticise the finished painting, nor probably would any aspect of its coming to life be theirs to behold as it is for me now. The privilege is perhaps a singular act that only one of such an age as I would even take the time to muse on. In truth, the concept of gaining in years is all too strange. My body tells me that it has not the suppleness of my youth, but my mind tells me otherwise. I am still the Ralph I was when I first came to this house full of adventure and dreams, now my head is full to the brim with memories, but then they are but a mark of my travels and the people I have known and met. I laughed at an old man once for his slow mind, and his dogged continuance to talk without an audience, yet now it would seem I possess a body that resembles something of the old cart that he then drove, creaking and groaning under the steady movement still. That day is now fifty years gone by since my journey began, I but twenty three years of age then, and yet the blue skies, and the dappled shadows of the trees as we lurched forward still drift across the face of my thoughts as though it were but a few weeks.

This artist has a most serious nature, I am glad of my learned years for were I still that young man I would not have kept a face so straight, nor would I have been able to stay myself from some mischief which would have had him cast an item at me, or forsake his task in disgust. Thus he must find me a good and easy subject for his skill to train upon, when in fact my mind is elsewhere.

I can hear the laughter of my grandchildren now, running out in the early sun, teasing and shouting, and most probably entertaining themselves in much the same way as we too did all those years since. The same carp pool remains to this day, a place of small parties and pranks, the same archery targets thud to the sound of the arrows as they hit home. The thought of those days fills me with such a warmth, I could not have known just how happy we were then. I miss William and James, but perhaps William most in the heat of the summers that were our unhindered playground. His golden hair was much of the Greek Gods we learned of, although I would not have hinted as much to him then. I remember I was oft in awe of his ability to charm those around him, no doubt it could be termed a jealousy, yet I felt perhaps rather a sense of pride at our closeness and my association thereby.

It was a strange mix of grief and elation that gripped me on the day I discovered he had been a victim of a grim and desperate war. The day that Elizabeth Mainwareing told her tale was a whirlwind to me. There was so much that fell upon my dulled sensibility the moment she mentioned William's name. In that instance I became aware that not only was she the sister of the man I had met in the inn those five years previous, but she was also telling me that my dear friend was dead. Yet through it all the message rang clear, my precious Elenor was now a free woman. I cannot tell you of the tumult that went on in my head from then on. I believe up until this point I had resigned myself to an existence in that distant land for the rest of my days. I saw no shame, nor desperation in it, but had gained a certain respect for my life lived as such. I knew that my relationship with Elenor could never have a future, I believed that I had found the greatest love of my life in Catalina, and I believed I would make my home in that strange land and amongst those kind people. With this settled understanding of my place I believed I was content. How wrong I was. The very instant William's death was known to me I felt something so strong I was quite overtaken by it, and that steadfast faith was redundant. The mere thought of returning to England and holding Elenor in my arms once more made me so heady I could not put my mind to sensible thought, I was dizzy with the overwhelming realisation that I now had the power to change my life right there in my hands.

I feel sure that I became a thorn in the side of John White in my pleas to him for an instant passage back to England. I had a true belief that God must be on my side as I found myself in the midst of those who refused to leave themselves, but insisted that he should take the journey home in their stead. Therefore, as one who wished to go, it was no difficulty for myself to gain a place on the voyage with certain ease. I was much relieved to sail in the other ship though as I had not of any great trust in White's abilities to organise anything with too great a skill. Despite this, I did have some sympathy for him in his desperate attempts to govern his settlement with any degree of success. I am sure I have never known a man who would try as hard to achieve so little. He had the surest ability to disregard the sensible in favour of that which he considered right, but which was invariably wrong.

It came to me by chance during some social exchange some years after my return to England his poor luck had followed him still on that same voyage. It seems that on setting off, the anchor of the Flyboat became ensnared and would not lift easily, in the operation of the capstan the strain proved too great, one of the spindles snapped and the thing span without control. In so doing the remaining spars smashed the legs and arms of those sailors in its working reducing the crew to those few who did not suffer from the mishap. Their journey took a month longer than ours due to sickness and bad winds, our route being with the more experienced Fernandez. Most died of their wounds, starvation or illness, but John White himself made it home through Ireland. His late arrival did nothing to enamour him to Raleigh and others, the story already having been told to disfavour him in his absence. In addition, the imminent arrival of the Spanish Armada had all shipping stayed at port, thus he was not able to return to Virginia for a number of years by which time there were no signs of the people we had left there. I believe to this day that remains so. (6)

For all his shortcomings I would never have wished any such disaster to have befallen him. He was a very proud man, and he achieved a great deal, his prowess in painting and drawing was a wonder to behold, and I found his company to be of sincere interest. I never heard from him again nor knew anything more of him, but I often wonder how the baby, Virginia, and her mother, father and others faired.

Although the mystery of their well-being caused much questioning in my mind, I was never much inclined to a need to know what became of Catalina and the people I had learned to love and care for. It may seem much of a strange thing, yet that has had to remain another life, not a part of this world, an existence that belongs far from my reality.

The strength of that woman was unequalled. Catalina's belief in herself and her destiny will have forged a certain future I have no doubt. I cannot believe that she has not remembered me and our time together for it has undoubtedly left its mark on me, but I cannot think of that time. Although I owe most of my strengths and so much else to her and those wonderful people, I still have it kept hidden away in a sunny corner of my mind. I believe my heart was broken through that time, but not in a way that would make sense to any I know. My heart was broken when I turned my back on my Elenor for the love of another, my heart was broken by my own countrymen who contrived to destroy my little world safe in Santa Elena, my heart was broken by a woman whose love for her people and her Father was stronger than any mortal bond that might have kept us together otherwise.

I have spoken little of my years there to any. I cannot believe there are many who would comprehend nor appreciate the turns that my life took, indeed I was nearer death when I arrived than at any other time in my life. Not in the manner of the snake bite or any other mishap, but close to death when you have no other choice other than to believe that you shall meet your creator at any moment. That is a strange feeling like no other. The sense of incredulity when I was taken from that abysmal hole by what could only be an angel then left me with a sense of unreality that I never in truth lost. I had never before seen any woman so striking. Her hair was a black that even a moonless night is unable to match, it hung flawlessly straight, almost to the back of her knees, and the tint of her skin gave her face a line that was unmatched by any. Most of all, her certainty and manner was such that she commanded obedience from all and everyone. Through our closeness she took me to heights of sensation that no mortal man should ever attain.

I do remember feeling something of a fear at first whenever she was about, but once we grew together that was also when I saw her vulnerability. It was that weakness which no other knew of that took her from me. When she was most fearful she would turn to the spirit of her father. His legacy was strong and deeply ingrained into her being, thus it would override any emotion that would steer her from the correct course. She did not have to fear that she would make a wrong decision, for her Father would have had a set way, and she would always know what it was. Thus, although I knew her heart was torn in half at our parting, she knew her decision was the right one, and of course, it was. I often suspected that she was much of a mind that she was to try and stand in the stead of Elenor, yet I was not able to impress upon her that there was a difference between them that made it not a contest, but two faces of a single coin. In truth hers was a raging fire that was impossible to quench, exciting and dangerous, with Elly it was a golden ray of sunshine destined to remain lighting the corner of an English garden forever. The difficulty lay in the unavoidable consequence that a fire will eventually run short of fuel, and I always knew this to be so. Ours was not intended to be a life together, but was meant to be a collision of two stars, brilliant and transient. Just the recall of it though makes my heart heavy. I experienced a belonging in that place the likes of which perhaps we are not meant to keep or own. It was a sense of place that did not rightfully belong to me. My soul danced those Spanish dances through the nights, and my life was filled with adventure, yet a man cannot live his whole life at that pace, for it was such a hurricane of emotion that I am truly satisfied with my peaceful life, now returned to Baddesley.

My time since my return has ranged about, mainly to my old house at Risby. Risby was home to my growing family yet not one of my children remained within its dower walls. Each of them found their joy as I had done in the leafy escapes of Warwickshire. Now my final days I have chosen to spend at Baddesley Clinton, that warm caring old house full of memories and fine people still. However, my return to this place after Virginia was anything but a peaceful event, it perturbs me to think of that time.

My journey across the ocean was uneventful, but seemed interminable. The weeks dragged by with nothing but the roll of the sea, dull and frighteningly reminiscent of the sound that had greeted me when I was dragged from this country in confusion and discomfort. I spoke little to those with whom I travelled, but I learned something of the craftsmanship required to make such a voyage. This at least kept me busy with something, but most often my mind was occupied with thoughts of my joyful reunion. As the days passed I was given to doubt my return as I was not to know what would be Elenor's reaction. She may have had such an overwhelming love for William after her years of marriage that her feelings might in no way turn back to me again. This notion I could not bear, and I tried to push it to the back of my mind, yet still the fear oft pushed its way to the front.

I kept my head full of the many times I could remember when we had spent days together, the games we played even from very young, anything to dispel notions of rejection. Most often I remembered that last afternoon we had together. It was something of a dream, perhaps moreso because we said so little to each other. I had lain her down in the long grass beside one of the two top pools. This place had always been special to us as it afforded us secrecy yet was tantalisingly close to the house and all those who could not know of our tryst. Ofttimes someone would walk the path by us, completely unaware of our presence as we kept low, although on occasion I was moved to cup my hand over Elly's mouth to stifle the giggles she could never quite contain. This time there was no hint of mirth or playfulness, in this moment there was the love and care of all our years together wrapped up in a single expression. Our loving was as the first time we had dared step into that wonder, a prayer, a solemn promise to each other that we were destined to remain as one for all time. I remember still this day the intensity and yearning in her beautiful green eyes, meaning every second of our sharing as a precious gift beyond gifts. That moment is still my most prized possession, and will light my way into the next world with a belief in the purity of our emotions.

There was some frustration in that Fernandez took a course toward his homeland of Portugal, which is when we departed our ways from the Flyboat and John White. I sensed something of a perverse pleasure in the Captain's so doing, and I pondered somewhat on how much a part this man may have played in the poor Governor's downfall. As it turned out, we only went so far as to meet another ship in that direction with whom we exchanged a few items before making good our voyage. Thus I found myself with the odd sense of being a stranger on our own shores. I think it might be true to say that at the moment of my disembarking from the Lion, I felt an acute loss. A loss of all the friends I had made, the loss of the characters I had enjoyed, even the enemies with whom I had sparred. I had fond thoughts of the lands that had been my home for all those years, and here I was, unknown by any at our port, five years older than when I last stood on English soil, and still uncertain as to how my life would turn.

Before we left the shores of Virginia I had kindly been given sufficient coinage to see me safe to my home, and thus I furnished myself with a solid horse in order that I could at last take charge of my destiny. I was no longer blown by the winds of fate, nor was I subject to the politics of our world, the whims of those with power, or the nonsense of the sea. I suppose I had been a prisoner for those years without really recognising it for the most. I was certainly a captive at the hands of the vile Don Diego de Velasco, I was for some short time similarly a servant to Catalina, after which my enslavement was in the hands of the land that bound us and kept us from where we should most want to be. Now I tasted freedom. As I rode through the countryside at speed I savoured the lash of the soft rain upon my face, I was embalmed by the sweet scents that filled the air. Even to this day I still notice those English smells that make this place home. I do not think that it is possible to appreciate such a thing unless you have been denied it for so long.

As my path took me closer to Baddesley I slowed my pace, and all the uncertainties that I had toiled with whilst on the ship washed over me again. Now they were even more keen, as my goal was no longer a dream, but a certain reality. I felt the years stretch into a lifetime, removing me from people's minds, and from their thoughts. I must be forgotten surely, and if so what a stir would I cause on my reappearance. Could I even be sure of whether the courtesy I might be shown were intended or feigned? I could be an embarrassment, or a problem to solve, or just a person who turns up when they have been absent without reason and without favour. The possibilities became endless, and served only to doubt my very existence. Then early on the twentieth of October 1587, Ralph Ellerker stood in front of the bridge that spans the moat before the house where Elenor Lovaine, no, Elenor Ferrers resided.

I left my horse in the field before, and headed across the span with the least noise, not wanting to attract any kind of notice from those within. The ducks that always sun themselves on the grassy slopes quacked noisily and waddled off, and I made a futile effort to shush them. The great wooden door with its iron studs yielded easily to my push and I walked, still unmet, into the courtyard. The ornamental gardens looked the picture of perfection they always had done, and yet I felt nothing of anyone. As I stood at the door wondering how I should make my entrance a voice spoke to me from some distance behind.

"Can I 'elps you sir?"

I turned to see in the far corner an elderly gardener who was responsible for the order around. I was relieved to find someone of whom I could enquire.

"Tell me good man." I started, "where might I find the household?

"They're all up in London now sir." as if I might know that to be.

"So what of the Lady Elenor?"

"Well," he hesitated, "You know she went back to Packwood?"

Of course, I thought, she wouldn't have stayed there once William was gone, her father and her home would be her natural retreat.

"Thank you, of course, how foolish of me."

The man looked quite quizzically at me, but I did not wish to stay a moment longer that he might question me and have me discovered by any who should want to divert me from my task. He went to speak some more, but I was quick to make my exit and did not allow him any further conversation. I felt sure he was most keen to carry on with his precise work, and did not wish to be distracted by unnecessary prattle from a stranger.

This news came as a spur to my quest, I felt elated that she was back in the safe haven that had always been our home in those childhood days. I kicked my horse off at great speed, crashing through the trees of the Kings Wood, past the great barn that heads the straight path between those two pools bringing into view that most beautiful house wherein was held my pearl. My heart beat more rapidly and with more noise than a drum band might, surely heralding my arrival so. I leapt from my mount, letting it lose without a care, and threw the door wide making much of my entrance in complete contrast to that of my previous approach at Baddesley. The house was quiet, but I could feel life in it and knew a quick search of those familiar rooms would yield me my prize.

There were none of the usual signs I associated with that busy house, yet there were smells and small sounds that indicated I was not alone. Surely, I thought, this place is not similarly abandoned to the city. I could think of no reason that would have everyone off at the same event, but the possibility did occur to me. What an absurdity that would be to have ridden away from the very people I wished to see. My search took me up the stairway, across the gallery that looked back out over the entrance with its polished stone floor, the wooden floor creaking for all it was worth announcing my every step. The upper storey contained smaller, less frequented rooms, thus my search was more broken and increasingly distracted. Eventually I felt a warmth emanate from the little corner chamber the moment I pushed the door. Peering around into the cluttered room I saw a changed, but familiar face sat by the glowing ashes of a dying fire in the little hearth.

"Nanny Walker", I spoke out.

"What? Who is there? Come closer I cannot see you."

She had not been cognisant of my arrival, and there was some irritation in her voice at having been disturbed. It was clear she did not recognise me, but her failing senses were undoubtedly causing her some frustration. I stepped right into the room and walked over to her smiling with a genuine relief and joy at seeing her there. As I bent to kiss her forehead she pushed me off and showed alarm at the approach of a stranger.

"Nanny, it is I."

"Wait, wait!" now clearly quite flustered, "turn into the light. I'm blowed if I know who you are, and yet you presume as much as p'raps I should!"

As I faced toward the small latticed window, the morning sun not yet quite filling the room, I heard her breath come short, announcing her recognition of me.

"Bless my soul! Master Ralph! Is it really you?"

She dropped the small sampler she had been picking at on her lap and pushed against the arms of the old chair she was in. I turned and knelt quickly by her to save her struggle and clasped her hands whilst looking into her aged face. The tears fell in an instant, I was warmed by the emotion and moved to wipe them from her with little chance of success. Instead she mopped her face with the edge of her apron. I knew her too well, and before I could utter a further word she berated me for my absence, asking where I might have been for all this time. Then, just as quickly, she melted again, her soft smile full of sympathy, welcoming me home after my travels.

"Where is everyone? I enquired. "I went at first to the other house, but they told me she was here, and I know already what mishap has befallen William."

"Oh my dear Ralph. I am sure you have much to tell, but there is more you must needs learn of first."

So she began her lengthy telling of it. She first bade me pull up a comfortable chair, and I added some wood to the fire for the air was still a-chill. Her immediate concern was to tell me of William. Sadly, it seemed she grew to disfavour him in their marriage as his attentions were not what they should have been to Elenor. I was reminded also of a malignant character, Francis Throckmorton. I had warned William of his ill-advised acquaintance with this man, I certainly had never counted him amongst my own friends despite his frequent visits to the house. In the outcome it seems my unheeded entreaties to him to break the association had led to some dire consequence for all the family. Whilst I had never found favour with William's pompous and stuffy brother, Henry, it was he who had saved him from a sure death at the gallows or worse. To hear of Charles' part in the events, I was much moved to believe he was probably more to thank than any. His house at Raynham in Norfolk lay close to one of Leicester's seats, and as such their families had always been very close. Without the intervention of the Townsends I cannot perceive of even Henry being much able to cause such a turn of events. I already knew that Walsingham was not a man to be trifled with, but Charles was a gifted emissary, and his allegiance and friendship with Robert Dudley would have contrived to turn the outcome about. I saw in my mind William's acceptance of his fate, a childish *tut*, and an altogether blasé attitude to the whole event. I felt that had it not gone in his favour he would have charmed the hangman yet and maybe escaped by that route, or at least he would have thought he could.

In his usual run of good fortune he found a renewed vigour in his life within the army, and I have no difficulty in imagining him in an heroic pose upon the battlefield. My memory of him as such is now very much the hero of our day, and his death upon the field a circumstance befitting his stature, albeit a great and sad loss. The distressing aspect for me was the sad loneliness that Elenor had experienced within her marriage. I could never have foreseen that would be so when I reflected upon the fun and excitement we all knew as children. It hurt to hear it, and I berated myself for any weakness in my flight, believing that perhaps had I remained I could have brought some light into her life then. Of course the reality would have been an involvement way beyond the deceit of our earlier dalliance. To risk the hurt that might be caused to a marriage, the consequent loss of dignity, the shame, is not something to be conceived of by a true friend. Still, I felt her pain and wished it hadn't been so.

"So what of children, Nanny?" I enquired. "Are there any?"

My mind was running with questions. A child surely is the most vulnerable to any detachment within a family. That would have been a stronger reason than any for me to deny myself any intervention, for whatever reason. Elly had talked much of her need for a large family. I imagined she must have a number of children who would be running about the place, finding the dangers we had discovered, and causing much mirth and mischief.

Nanny Walker sat back and looked to the ceiling disconcerting me somewhat. I sensed that perhaps she had not had so much of the joy she had expected from such an experience. There was a tinge of excitement that there was still time to put that right, to turn Elenor's dreams to reality. For a fleeting moment my mind ran to a family together. I had always imagined myself in that place as Elly detailed the number of children and whether they would be boys or girls, but then I had resigned myself to the fact that it could not be so with me. I knew I was jumping ahead and listened again, although I did not hear that which I had assumed, for indeed there was a child.

"My little Elenor bore a son in the first year of her marriage. They named him Henry, after William's brother of course."

I could feel that Nanny was ill at ease in the telling of it, but for the life of me I could not fathom the reason for her discomfort. I sat patiently and listened intently to her words. He was a playful child, but again I sensed her reproval of William for the boy knew little of his father. I found no real surprise in that, I had never known Will' have any predisposition toward young children, and babies had always positively reviled him. I remember him getting a beating one day when, upon a visit from an aunt who herself had a new child, it was decided, without invite, that the infant should be placed, with various noises of encouragement, onto William's lap for the entertainment of the women in the room. Will' made no disguise of his disgust and simply stood up and walked away leaving the baby to fall to the ground. Of course there was such a commotion, but he was not to be persuaded away from his opinion and took the punishment with pride.

So the marriage had foundered on all sides it seemed. However, the introduction of young Henry into Elenor's life brought with it an energy, and a centre for her to grow again and enjoy her life. He was everything to her, and his care was her only want. The two of them had removed back into Packwood in the October, the month following William's death, she having no wish to remain as the lady of a house where she did not feel she belonged, and were her memories were of little happiness. The two of them played together the days through, and she read him stories and made him clothes, they went on picnics together and visited the secret places that we had known through our time. Nanny made it quite clear that her happiness was somehow linked to the joy that we two had found in each other's presence. Her telling of it brought an intense warmth into my soul, and I could feel the link renewing in strength, I dared think that perhaps I hadn't lost her at all.

Taking great care with her words Nanny Walker tried as best she could to describe young Henry that I might know his every detail, in his eye colour, and his hair, but I was not able to gather what it was that she was trying to impress upon me. I just smiled more intensely and asked her for further detail of their playing together, and the places they visited. After some length, and frustrated by my lack of comprehension, she finally brought me to the realisation that she was telling me something I should know. He did not have the familiarity of his father's blonde hair and blue eyes, she was describing me.

"He was yours and Elenor's Master Ralph. Made that last day of your farewells."

My heart leapt from my body and I knelt once more at her feet imploring her to tell me more whilst interrupting her every word as I continued to ask questions. When did she know of our secret? Who else knew? Had William found out? Did he know of our hidden life ever? Nanny had me sit back down and set to the telling again. She told me how she had known about us for some years before the day I left, and of the shock on Elenor discovering so on her wedding night. She even divulged to me that there was something of an unspoken knowledge of certain conceits that were worked to conceal any doubts that might have arisen out of it all.

I found myself actually excited by Elenor's nanny being a part of it all, and I now felt that she understood just why I was so keen to know what had occurred these past five years. We had a child. We had a boy. None but the three of us knew the truth, but God and the angels knew, and the truth was that the world had not conspired against us.

"Where is the boy now Nanny? Where is my son? Does he look like me still?"

Nanny Walker's face was always of a serious nature, but this expression was not her usual, there was a softness, perhaps even a sorrow in it. Henry did not look like me then I said. She assured me nothing could be further from the truth. He was a mirror image of me, and Elly watched him closely as he played and remembered me through him. If any had put their mind to it, she said, they would have seen something and spoken of it, but none did, for whatever reason. However, for all his happy and joyous vigour he took to a fever that had visited many others at the time, and at three and a half years of age, two days before this last Christmas, his little soul gave up and took its place with the angels.

Such grief they had never seen before. Elenor had stayed with him through every hour of every day. She had told him stories of heroes, and they played with his little wooden soldiers on his bed covers until he could no longer hold them. Nanny was busy carrying hot broth and soft meats for them both, but more often than not they went unheeded. He had fought with such bravery, the sickness causing his slight body to fade away, and eventually the last breath from his thin, white lips passed as he lay in his mother's arms. I felt such a deep sadness in her voice as she told the story, and I could not help the tears from falling for the son I never knew.

"We were heartbroken my boy." She spoke, unsteady, and full of weeping.

I said nothing in reply. I rose from my seat and strode over to the window. The day was quite alive by now, the sky was full of lazy clouds and I could sense nothing of that bitter sorrow which must have engulfed every living thing then. I was torn in so many different directions. To know that I had fathered a son, a beautiful son, mine and Elenor's. Yet my own selfish actions had barred me from being the father that could have loved and cared for him, yet would I have been told the truth even then? Did that matter? I felt moreso that whatever the circumstance it was Elenor that needed the love and care. It was now ten months since that unhappy time and she had been alone in her grief.

"How does she cope with it all Nanny?"

"How do any mother deal with such a thing? It was terrible to watch."

The whole neighbourhood had come to learn of the afflicted boy and the devotion of his mother. Prayers had been said in every chapel from Lapworth to Rowington, and even in Warwick itself. Those who knew the little boy, and even those who had only heard of the unbroken attention of Elenor in her profound dedication to his care, were moved to ask God to show them both his mercy and love. Thus it was that a hushed cloud of mourning settled over every man and woman for miles around when they learned of that sad day.

Elenor would not leave him, and those in the household found great difficulty in persuading her away from his lifeless body, and all had a true fear for her own well being. She attended the funeral, held at Baddesley, on a severely cold morning in the last days of that year. She was pale and thin and took support from those who would help her to the place where he was to be put to rest. Although the church was but a few hundred yards from the house up a small grassed lane, her weakness slowed the procession, even to her pausing to regain some strength before they reached the little churchyard at St Michael's. His precious body was lain beneath a newly placed oak tree. It was said to represent his father in its strength and character, and I was of no doubt that she had meant William, and I was glad of it. The cold of the day made her shake, and the tears fell like raindrops all around. Despite the bitter winds none left the graveside until she felt the need to return home, although it was much at the behest of those who wished to save her health from further damage that she did turn from that sad spot. There was hardly a celebration of the New Year, none felt much inclined to make merry, the day staying raw in their minds until past then.

"So how is she now Nanny? Does she still suffer from his loss, and also the loss of William too I would think?"

"There was more loss than any soul should contain in those months, but you has to be mindful of another loss too, one she felt most distinctly."

She meant me, and my guilt now was as keen as at any time. I had forsaken her. If I had cared then surely I would have stayed. I had supposed that she would never be of a mind to think past her family life once she was married. I even felt that it was sufficient she would know I was still thinking of her, and maybe that I would return when I had enough courage to accept the turn of the world. On reflection, my decision to flee the wedding seemed foolish and childish, certainly not a well-thought plan or something a true friend would contemplate. Yet I still felt the pain of relinquishing her from that heaven we had shared, the delights of our love that had been for us and no one else. Now I had experienced a pinch of the love she had shared with our little boy, and I felt the loss of that day again. I knew the power of her deep care and affection, and the unconditional way in which she gave it. Although I had no right to it, none could take what I had had away from me.

I needed to know where she was now. Had she taken refuge in some convent or other such retreat? Could I still speak to her, or more importantly would she now accept me in my return? I knew Nanny Walker was hiding yet another secret, but I felt sure that her understanding of how important we were to each other would break any bond or vow of silence. I leaned forward to insist upon a response. She reached into that ever-resourceful large pocket at the front of her apron, and fingered something without removing it.

"Do you remember Little Fishy Corner?"

The furrow from my brow disappeared and a smile returned to my face. Of course I did. There were few who knew it as such, but I was certain that little Henry had known it, and the song. At the far side of the big lake there was a grassy slope that led up to the bank. Its tufty rim hung over the edge and it was possible to lie upon one's front and peer down into the still water below. Although the sunlight would hit the water well from an angle late in the afternoon, the slope upon which we would lie shaded the spot below, thus it was possible to see right to the bottom. With the sun coming in so, and no reflection above, the fish would swim around layer upon layer for the water was most deep here, and yet the swaying green weeds that sat upon the bottom were just as clear. The fish would swim in and out of the green fingers and then up to the surface where insects had stopped for a drink unsuspecting that they were then a tasty snack. To see them snap and shoot to the bottom again was a pastime that had wasted many hours, but it had been a very favourite place to be.

We were there one very hot and lazy summer afternoon and had been talking about things that were of little consequence. I was lying on my back gazing at the clouds as I went on about how some horse had caught out the blacksmith by kicking him when he was least expecting it and I had thought it very funny. Whilst I was talking away giving the story in much detail, I became aware of Elly's complete boredom and inattention as she was now singing, apparently to the fish. I stopped and listened some until I could contain myself no longer. My laughter caused her to turn and hit me on the side of my head, but I still couldn't stop laughing. Then I had become serious, and feigning interest in the song asked her to sing it again. Of course she was not about to make a fool of herself and refused, lying on her back herself now, looking up at the floating, white clouds. I rolled over and touched her nose lightly encouraging her to teach me, then kissed her, promising more if I could learn the meter of it. That was sufficient enticement, and we rolled over and peered into the pool below.

She indicated specific fish giving them names such as Jeremiah and Jed, then started on her song whilst pointing each out as it went, my grin still as big as ever.

"One little fishy,
Two little fishies,
Three little fishies,
Four,
Five little fishies,
Six little fishies,
When will you love me more?"

At which point she turned and kissed me. Now I felt perhaps there was a point to the song and as she encouraged me I took a turn. I had to name my own fish first of course, but began,

"One little fishy," and so on.

We soon were singing it together, and after each time through our kisses grew even longer. Then we were up on our feet, holding hands and spinning around, singing at the tops of our voices. There were no fish now for sure, all of them hid from the noise.

"One little fishy,
Two little fishies,
Three little fishies,
Four,
Five little fishies,
Six little fishies,
When will you love me more?"

As we kissed again, a large drop of rain came heavy upon my shoulder. We both looked up at the great black clouds that had rolled in over us, and by the time we had looked back again with that smile of expectation at being caught out, the heavens opened. We ran back around the lake to the house just as fast as we could. As we ran, despite the torrent, we sang as loud as we could to try and overcome the sound of the crashing rain. The large droplets were warm, and nothing would stop our song nor our laughter. That is until Elly's small shoe stuck in the increasing mud and came right off her foot. She screamed and we laughed at our soaked state, her foot now bare and covered in the mire. As she picked up the shoe I swept her into my arms, and carried her into the house, placing her onto a long bench by the fireplace. I told her I would light a fire to dry us out, but she grabbed my arm, pulling me back and we kissed again. I looked at her rain-streaked face, our clothes dripping great rivers of water and clinging to us, and on the tip of an eyelash stood a single droplet of crystal water. I gently removed it with a brush of my lips and gazed deep into her soul, she loving me back just so.

"My little fish." I said quietly. She smiled and then sitting up shook her hair over me, laughing again. We sat for the rest of the afternoon by a roaring fire, the house empty we could stay quietly in each others arms until we were quite dry again. Of course, as Nanny had said, from that day on it was called Little Fishy Corner, and the memory of it had brought back all of the power of our love to me.

My mind regained the room I was in and our conversation for I had quite forgotten myself as I recalled the adventure.

"Why do you ask me about Little Fishy Corner?"

"It was much her favourite place to go sit and while away her hours when thinking about the child after that. I knew as why she should choose it, but there was them who wondered if she were losing her mind staying out there in the bitter chill."

She continued to tell me of the continuance of that year with little change in Elenor's demeanour. The smile did not return to her face, and she was not minded to enter into any idle conversation. When she was not outside on her own then she was with Nanny Walker. As the year progressed she began to talk of things again. Little moments, days she remembered that were full of hope and happiness, but remembered as though they were lost forever. The summer went by, and her stories were more and more those of our times together. She told Nanny of adventures that she had no knowledge of before, and she was much surprised at them too. Then one day, at the end of August, she came into Nanny's chamber as was usual, but she came with a request. It was now that Nanny pulled her closed hand gently from within her pocket.

"She gave me this and told me something that I found most at odds, I was not made privy to it afore, and I was not so sure of its significance then. She told me that I had to promise her something. Of course I said yes. She said if ever Ralph should be alive and come home again I must give him this back and tell him it were true. I can tell you, I am still not sure of its message, but I made my promise and so here it is."

She opened her large, lined hand, and sitting in the middle of it was a small ring with a blue stone. Before I took it, she continued with her story.

After making Nanny promise again that she would perform her simple task she left the chamber as usual and went off to Little Fishy. Nanny was oft prompted to send out one of the men to fetch her back inside as the night air descended. This night it was Eddy the boy from the kitchen. Nanny heard a noise downstairs and a number of raised voices. Sensing something was wrong she called down and asked what was amiss, but getting no reply she made her way down and into the hallway just as a number of people were coming in through the door together. When she saw they were carrying something it did not take her a second to realise what it was. They laid Elenor's drowned body upon the table there, white and lifeless, but with a look of peace upon it at last. Eddy explained how she must have stepped too close to the bank on the deep side and it had given way, taking her into the murky depths. Nanny had walked the place in the following days and saw no broken bank, but she looked to the fish and told them she knew.

Now I sit for my portrait, an old man, but my memories intact. I have had a good life since. I married a faithful wife, Jane who was from Everingham, near Risby, and we had six children. They too have produced grandchildren aplenty, and have brought me much joy. Henry moved into Kingswood Manor some thirty years back, he then letting the house to various ardent Catholics who have taken up their home here since. Once my children were left, and my wife had departed this life, I moved permanently to join the odd collection of transient residents in Baddesley Clinton, happy here with my beloved Warwickshire countryside, and my sunny recollections.

Since that day, and to this day still, on the little finger of my right hand is her ring. I have given the artist strict instructions to ensure that it is portrayed as detailed as is my face, for here in my painting is my Elenor. She has never left my heart, and, as it was then, inside of the small band of gold, warm against my skin I can sense the writing struck into the soft metal, 'Always With You', and so it shall be, forever more.

Notes:

1. The practice of drinking a measure of mead during the preceding month of marriage was the root of the term 'honeymoon'. It was meant to increase fertility.

2. It was customary for guests to bring cakes to a wedding feast, the tradition of their being piled up for the bride and groom to kiss over became more and more contrived. A French chef conceived of the idea that pouring icing over them would keep them from falling, thus introducing the modern custom of a many-tiered iced wedding cake.

3. Lettice Knollys was Elizabeth I first cousin once removed. She married Robert Devereux, Earl of Essex, a close favourite of the Queen, gaining her no favour by doing so. When he died in Ireland she secretly married Robert Dudley, Earl of Leicester, who was even closer to the Queen. This caused her to be banished from court as she was hated so much by Elizabeth for having taken him from her.

4. William Davison was actually a double agent working for Walsingham. There is no certainty as to whether his errors were purposeful or not.

5. It was believed that William Shakespeare was often a visitor to battles of the day in order that he might accurately describe the practices on the field.

6. The story of the Lost Colony has puzzled many since that time. There have been reports of blue-eyed, fair-haired natives around the area, and there is much supposition that they did indeed move up into the country as planned, and rather than meet their end actually became a part of the indigenous inhabitants. Effectively proving White's belief that the 'friendly approach'

Appendix
Names & Places

Assistants to the Governor of Roanoke: Ananais Dare, Roger Baylye, Christopher Cooper, John Sampson, Thomas Steevens, William Fullwood, Roger Pratt, Dyonise Harvey, John Nicholls, George Howe, James Plat, and Simon Fernandez.

Aquascogoc: a native village in Virginia between Secota and Pomiok.

Baddesley Clinton: a large, moated house, built sometime in the 13th century, located in Warwick-shire some two miles south east of Packwood House. It was the home to the Ferrers for a greater part of the time, they remained Catholic recusants and as such the house contains a number of priest holes.

Bassett, James: a name associated to the Bassett family, a contemporary of that name is undoubtedly a descendant of Sir Arthur.

Bassett, Sir Arthur: of Umberleigh, Devon, a West Country Puritan and associate of the Earl of Bedford. Served under Leicester in Holland.

Coffin, Master: a member of Grenville and Lane's last expedition to Roanoke, left behind to establish a settlement, but killed by natives before the arrival of John White.

Croatoan: a native village in Virginia at the far end of a bar of land to the south of Roanoke. The original home of Manteo. The place where the lost colony last indicated they headed to.

Dare, Ananais: the husband of Elenor Dare, the daughter of John White.

Dare, Elenor: the daughter of John White, and wife to Ananais.

Dare, Virginia: the first born white American and feted as much for that fact. Daughter of Ananais and Elenor, grandchild of John White.

Dasamonquepec: a native village in Virginia closest to Roanoke, just across the water on the mainland.

Davidson, William: eventually became Queen Elizabeth's private secretary, and was nearly hanged for his part in the sentencing and execution of Mary Queen of Scots. He was a spy for Walsingham for most of his court life, and worked his way through various offices by working with Walsingham.

Drake, Sir Francis: the Queen's pirate. A privateer who made his name by gaining great treasures for Queen Elizabeth. He was vice Admiral to the fleet, and a hero to the people of England. To the Spanish he was just a pirate, and was known as El Draque (the dragon).

Dudley, Sir Robert, Lord Leicester: Sir Robert was a sweetheart to Elizabeth I, and a very powerful man because of this. He was very wealthy, but much of his wealth was spent on lavish events to entertain the Queen, most famously at his home in Kenilworth. His greatest disaster was when he was sent to Holland to aid the Dutch rebels with 6000 men. He never really recovered his position, his life style, or his friendship with the Queen from that point on.

Ellerker, Ralph: b. 1559, was the son of Sir Ralph Ellerker. He was the eldest of nine children. Mother's name Anne Gower. He, his father and two brothers, William, and Robert, were made knights on the field of battle for their gallant behaviour at Flodden. Family home was Risby, Yorkshire. Married Jane Constable, from Everingham, near Risby.

Everingham: a village close to Beverley in Yorkshire, and also near to the site of Risby Hall.

Farnesse, Alexander, Duke of Parma: Philip of Spain's right hand man in Holland.

Fernandez, Simon: a skilled Portuguese pilot who contrived under the control of unknown direction to sabotage John White's expedition to Chesapeake.

Ferrers, Henry Sr: known as 'The Antiquary', he was a scholar and was responsible for much of the updating of Baddesley Clinton. He instigated the addition of stained glass windows into various parts of the house to record the various members of the family.

Ferrers, William 7th Earl of Derby: younger son of the 5th Earl of Derby and Margaret de Quincy.

Lived at Baddesley, has his own stained glass window.

Flyboat: a ship of Dutch origin, having a high stern, broad beam, shallow draft, this one was only 20 tuns..

Grenville, Sir Richard: a fearsome soldier who commanded much respect from those who knew him. He was also vice-admiral of the fleet during the Armada. He had planned to circumnavigate the world, but Elizabeth gave that task to Sir Francis Drake. He was a cousin of Sir Walter Raleigh. He was said to show his fearsome nature by crashing a glass to pieces between his teeth.

Heneage, Sir Thomas: notably treasurer at the court of Elizabeth I. Great friend of Leicester, and also Sir Philip Sydney and Hatton.

Hohenlohe, Count Ludwig: one of the famous German princely family of that name

Howe, George: one of John white's assistants, killed whilst crabbing alone in the shallows off Roanoke.

Kingswood: an area half way between Baddesley Clinton and Packwood House.

Kingswood Manor: is now called Lapworth Manor House and lies in the North West corner of Rowington, Warwickshire, between Packwood and Baddesley Clinton.

Knollys, Lettice: wife to Sir Robert Dudley. She had been married to the Earl of Essex, but whilst she was at court with Elizabeth she had an affair with Sir Robert. This eventually led to their marriage, and she was banished from court.

Lane, Ralph: an explorer who together with Grenville caused much of the discord between the English and the native Americans. He was the first Governor to reside on the Island of Roanoke, before being taken back to England after Grenville's second expedition.

Lapworth: a village which encompasses Packwood House, although Packwood is a separate area.

Lion, The: the flagship of the John White expedition. It was about 100 tuns.

Lovaine, Elenor (Eleanor de Louvain): was the daughter of Matthew de Louvain, Lord of Little Easton. Married firstly William de Ferrers. Mentioned in William's stained glass in Baddesley.

Mainwareing, Elizabeth: one of the names on the ships list of passengers bound for Virginia with John White. Her brother George maybe fictitious, but he was constructed before her name was discovered on the ship's manifest.

Manteo: a native of Croatoan. He was the son of a tribal chief, but was taken back to England to become a much respected English man. He was originally brought to court with another, Wanchese, but only he managed to last the course. He was honoured for his achievements as such and became

Lord Dasamonquepec, the name of a large village in Virginia.

Mendoza, Don Bernadino: was a Spanish military commander, a diplomat and a writer on military history and politics. He became the ambassador for Spain in London, and plotted with Francis Throckmorton. It was his correspondence with Phillip of Spain in a code that had been broken some years earlier that uncovered the plot and had him expelled.

Marques, Pedro Menendez: nephew of Pedro Menendez de Aviles, Catalina's cousin. Governed San Augustine after his uncle died.

Menendez, Catalina: 3rd daughter of Pedro Menendez de Aviles, 1st Governor of Florida. Named after Pedro's sister. She was famed for her abilities to tend to sick and wounded soldiers. As such she would convert her homes into working hospitals. She retained the title of 'Adelantado', Governor, from her father when he died, although as a woman she was not entitled to govern as such, but still retained the respect the title inferred.

Menendez de Aviles, Juan: Catalina's brother. He was an adventurer at sea much like his father, but was shipwrecked in Bermuda during a hurricane and was lost.

Menendez, Maria: Catalina's sister who joined a convent.

Menendez de Aviles y Alonso de la Campa, Pedro: the first governor of Florida, the first real settlement in America. He was a great seafaring adventurer, with a sense of what was fair and right, but a strong leader. Although he killed many Frenchmen in his resolve to take Florida he was of such a pious nature that he considered them murderers and Barbarians thus excusing the act. He named St Augustine, and established a number of other Spanish outposts along the coast. He had 19 brothers and sisters and was at sea from the age of 14.

Miranda, Gutierre de: was the brother in law of Catalina and brother of Hernando. He took over the responsibility of governing Santa Helena after his brother was accused of treason.

Miranda, Hernando de: husband to Catalina. He cared more for his sporting life than for his position. Thus he was slow to take up his office in Santa Helena, two years late in fact. In his absence the place was lost to the native population and as a consequence he was sent back to Spain and tried for treason.

Morgan, Colonel: was something of a Special Forces operative. It was his guerrilla tactics that led to most of the successes that were achieved in the Dutch war.

Olmos, Anton de (the tailor): Anton was the tailor in Santa Helena. He was also a taverner and a soldier with a four-generation family and an Indian servant who was treated as family.

Onslow, Sophia: is a name that has always had links to the Ellerkers, it was my great grandmother's name and has some fascinating associations with the family history in that line. She recalled living at Risby Hall when she was very young.

Packwood house: the house is a much-loved Elizabethan house famous for its yew tree garden, purportedly depicting the Sermon on the Mount. It is located two miles from Baddesley Clinton, half way between Warwick and Birmingham. It has always been a favourite haunt of my family and countless others.

Philip II of Spain: he ruled the largest global empire the world had ever seen which included territories in every continent except Antarctica.

Pomiok: a village on the mainland near Roanoke.

Quiros, Captain Thomas Benaldo: acted as interim governor of Santa Helena before Gutierre, he left in 1580.

Raleigh, Sir Walter: a man who came from Devon and charmed his way into the Queens court. He gained much favour with Elizabeth and set about claiming America for her. He was much disliked by most of the other men at court for his boorish and uncouth country ways. This was exacerbated by the riches and consideration Elizabeth lavished upon him. Thus he made many enemies at court, not the least Walsingham. He was eventually beheaded once the Queen was no more it was easy to indict him with some act of treason, true or not.

Ramirez de Contreras, Juan: was a soldier, hunter, and interpreter. He was a faithful companion to Pedro Menendez de Aviles for years. His abilities with language made him very useful.

Raynham House: is in north Norfolk and has been the family home of the Townsend family for years.

Risby Hall: the home of the Ellerker family. Sited in Yorkshire just north of the town of Beverley it is no longer in existence it having been burnt down over 100 years ago.

Roanoke: an island off the coast of Virginia, just south of Chesapeake Bay. It was protected by a sand bar that made it very safe from attack.

S. Will': it is known that William Shakespeare witnessed a number of wars in order that he should gain a knowledge of it for his plays, it has been suggested that this particular Will' was in fact Shakespeare.

San Agustin: St Augustine was the first outpost in Florida containing the main garrison of soldiers. Different levels of fortification were constructed there over time. Its strategic importance led the Spanish to believe it to be the better stronghold to restructure the colony after Drake's attacks. The stone fortress finally constructed there in 1672, Castillo de San Marcos, is still in existence today.

San Mateo: an outpost north of St Augustine with a fort, and used as a missionary outpost too.

Santa Elena: it is now called Pariss Island and is a Marine Corp recruit depot. It is actually in South Carolina, rather than Florida. Although St Augustine was the main garrison, St Helena was considered to be the capital of the new Spanish world.

Secota: a native village in Virginia to the south of Roanoke.

Sherley, Sir Thomas: a Member of Parliament, and war treasurer who ended up bankrupt.

Solis, Maria de: the wife of Pedro Menendez Marquez

Spicer, Captain Edward: faithful friend of John White who helped him get back to England through Ireland. He returned with White to search for the colony some years after, but was disastrously drowned as his boat capsized in rough water in Roanoke sound.

St Michael's, Baddesley Clinton: the church situated just a few hundred yards from the house.

Stafford, Captain Edward: Captain at arms for the Roanoke colony voyage. He was Ralph Lane's former officer, and commander of the third boat, the pinnace. He travelled back with Fernandez and reported much of how he had seen events in Roanoke.

Sydney, Sir Philip: became one of the Elizabethan Age's most prominent figures. Famous in his day in England as a poet, courtier and soldier, he remains known as the author of *Astrophel and Stella, The Defence of Poetry* (or *An Apology for Poetry*), and *The Countess of Pembroke's Arcadia.*

Throckmorton, Sir Francis: one of the ancestors of the Throckmorton family still in residence at Coughton Court, Alcester. He was caught with an incriminating letter in his possession by Walsingham wherein was listed ten names of co-conspirators. Although he retracted his confession he was executed along with the others.

Townsend, Charles: the Townsends have often been intrinsically linked to the Ferrers through marriage. The family seat is in Norfolk at Raynham Hall.

Valdes, Captain Alvaro Flores de: was an inspector of Florida on behalf of the Spanish monarchy.

Valdes, Pedro & Ana (nee Menendez): Ana was Catalina's sister, a great socialite and married Pedro to enhance her status at court.

Velasco, Diego de: he was placed in charge of Santa Helena during the absence of Catalina's husband, Hernando de Miranda. He antagonised the local population and eventually succumbed to a major attack from the natives. Rather than standing his ground he ordered the town to be abandoned thus causing the charge of treason to be brought against Hernando.

Velasco, Maria de: Diego de Velasco's vain wife, and the bastard child of Pedro Menendez de Aviles, and Catalina's half-sister.

Walsingham, Sir Francis: the ruthless spymaster of Elizabeth's court. He was most often in charge of everything that went on within the politics of the country earning both reliance on him and disfavour from the Queen. However, he was an innovator in exploration, colonization and the use of England's potential maritime power.

White, John: the leader and governor of the third expedition to colonize Virginia. He went to relieve those last left on Roanoke and ended up colonizing the island instead of the intended destination of Chesapeake. He was a great artist, able to record all in detail, with the eye of both a botanist and an observer of civilization. Engravings were made of his paintings and drawings by Theodor de Bry in 1590, and can still be seen today.

William of Orange: also known as William the Silent. He was the main leader of the Dutch revolt against the Spanish that set off the Eighty Years' War and resulted in the formal independence of the United Provinces in 1648.

Willoughby, Peregrine Bertie, 13th Baron Willoughby de Eresby: Lord Willoughby. In the Netherlands, after the Battle of Zutphen, in 1586, he was made General of the English forces in the United Provinces

Wingina: was the chief of the Roanoke tribe. Their principal place was Dasamonquepec. His head was cut off in a vicious attack by Ralph Lane.

Maps

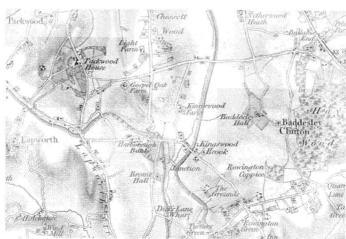

Packwood and Baddesley in 1831

William's Holland

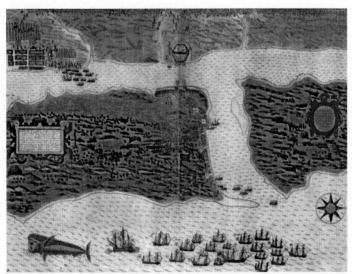

St Augustine

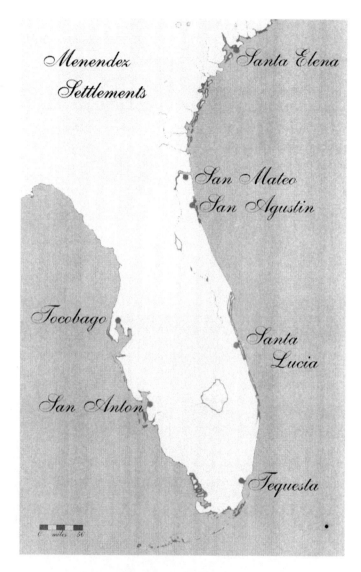

Menendez
Settlements

Santa Elena

San Mateo
San Agustin

Tocobago

Santa
Lucia

San Anton

Tequesta

The Menendez Towns

412

Roanoke Island

The Pew

For more information about the author:

www.mailer-yates.co.uk